I0666731

Praise for the Artesans of Albia series:

"Cas Peace's *Artesans of Albia* trilogy immediately sweeps you away. The series propels you into a world so deftly written that you see, feel, touch, and even smell each twist and turn. These nesting novels are evocative, hauntingly real. Smart. Powerful. Compelling. The trilogy teems with finely drawn characters, heroes and villains and societies worth knowing; with stories so organic and yet iconic you know you've found another home—in Albia. So start reading now. I, for one, can't wait to find out what will happen next.

~Janet E. Morris: author of *The Sacred Band of Stepsons* series; the *Dream Dancer* series; *I, the Sun*.

✣ ✣ ✣ ✣ ✣

"Cas Peace has really done it up right this time. The Circle of Conspiracy Trilogy is a real barnburner. In past books Ms Peace has demonstrated the ability to create fast-paced action and unremitting tension. In this novel she shows a maturing ability to handle conflict, orchestrating the suspense beautifully."

~Gordon A Long: *A Sword Called Kitten; Why Are People So Stupid?; Out of Mischief.*

✣ ✣ ✣ ✣ ✣

"A superb read. Non-stop intrigue and action. I literally could not put it down. Anyone needing a good series to read should take up Book 1 and get started. Cas Peace has created an unforgettable hero(ine) in Sullyan, and a world that ranks alongside Middle Earth and Westeros."

~David C Snell: Amazon reviewer.

"This book is an epic (and heroic) fantasy, a genre I like very much. Though I won't try to compare this book to the masters, it has a depth of history and a magic system that is really strong. The conflict in the book between characters is also powerful, because of the relationships between them. Honor and Duty are difficult values to adhere to when they come into conflict with love and affection. I think that the characters are very much the strong point of the novel. I was very impressed.

~J P Wilder: *Schade of Night; The Crusader; Blue Eyes at Night.*

✣ ✣ ✣ ✣ ✣

The author does a great job developing very complex characters. There is a great deal of suspense in this book, and it really held my interest. Cas Peace is a master storyteller, providing a depth and breadth of information about her worlds and their people that is just staggering. I heartily recommend this series to anyone who enjoys epic fantasy, strong world-building, and beautiful storytelling. Highly recommended!

~Katy Sozaeva: *Amazon Vine Voice*

Published by Albia Publishing 2015

First American Paperback Edition

This is a work of fiction. Names, characters, places, and incidents either are the product of the author's imagination or are used fictitiously. Any resemblance to actual events, locales, or persons, living or dead, is entirely coincidental. The publisher does not have any control and does not assume responsibility for author or third party websites or their content.

Visit Cas Peace at her author website: www.caspeace.com

ISBN-10: 1939993636
ISBN-13: 978-1-939993-63-2

Dedication

To Bob Watson,
with grateful thanks for website advice and maintenance

Acknowledgements

As always, my very grateful thanks to everyone who has helped me with, or who has read (and especially left a nice review of) my Artesans of Albia series. I could not have done it without you.

To Dave; to my parents, Barbara and Dennis; to my brother David: I love you all!

To Milly and Milo: thanks for all the cuddles and walks.

To my editor Diane Dalton: special thanks for your expertise and for saving me from potential embarrassment.

To Mikey Brooks: for yet another stunning cover.

To NTN (David Snell, David Shepherd) and to Susan Mallett: many grateful thanks for the music and the fun.

To Bob Watson: for website advice and maintenance.

To Janet Morris: special thanks for that wonderful endorsement.

To anyone who has reTweeted, posted to Facebook, or otherwise helped spread the word through social media, and to anyone who has taken the trouble to write and post a review.

I hope you enjoy this book!

Other titles in the Artesans of Albia series:

Trilogy One: Artesans of Albia

Book One: King's Envoy

Book Two: King's Champion

Book Three: King's Artesan

Trilogy Two: Circle of Conspiracy

Book One: The Challenge

Book Two: The Circle

Book Three: Full Circle

Full Circle

Circle of Conspiracy

Book Three

Cas Peace

Albia Publishing

The Kingdom of Albia in the Realm of Albia, (not to scale)

Realm of Andaryon, (not to scale,)

Chapter One

As entrances went, Taran had to admit he had never seen better. The bolt of lightning Sullyan had called forth seemed to pierce the hilltop like a spear of the gods. The brilliance hurt his eyes and his skin crawled with static. He was nearly deafened by the colossal noise and his pounding heart raced. The two armies clashing below had ceased hostilities to turn disbelieving stares upon the spectacular tableau. She couldn't have found a more impressive or commanding way to announce their arrival.

Satisfied she had captured every eye with her display, Sullyan released the lightning. It snapped up into the clouds with a titanic crack, bringing most of those gathered, both Albian and Andaryan, to their knees. It was appropriate, thought Taran, that they should kneel before the Crown Princes of two realms.

He followed Sullyan as she guided Drum down the hill. He could now make out Anjer and Elias, only fifty yards apart, with their respective forces gathered round them. An avenue opened through the press of men, seemingly of its own accord. Every Andaryan recognized Aeyron, even in his sorry state, and every Albian recognized Sullyan.

Taran saw many of the humans grinning as she rode serenely through their ranks, and a chant rose from the gathered men. Those on the Albian side sang Sullyan's name, while those on the Andaryan sang Aeyron's.

The noise increased until it swelled about their ears. It

1

accompanied the two Princes as they were carried to the center of the field.

Sullyan took no outward notice of the acclaim. She appeared unmoved, completely serene. Yet Taran was close enough to see it was the calm of exhaustion—she simply didn't have the energy after that spectacular entrance to do anything but keep her seat and hold Aeyron erect.

General Blaine couldn't keep a smile of pride and relief from his face, though it was tinged with concern when she came close enough for him to see her bruises and swollen mouth. His expression was mirrored by Anjer. Taran saw the generals share a look of understanding.

King Elias sat transfixed on his roan stallion, staring hungrily, almost fearfully, at the small wrapped bundle Taran bore. Robin was beside the King, his back rigid. Many emotions crossed his face, but the foremost seemed to be anger. Maybe it was because Sullyan was still with Taran, or maybe there was another reason entirely.

Sullyan herself looked neither left nor right. Taran knew she was struggling to hold Aeyron upright. She would not let him lose any more dignity than he already had. She halted Drum and with a wave of her hand sent Taran toward Elias.

Taran rode close to the mesmerized King. The baby was closely wrapped within Taran's cloak, both to shield him from the rain and to muffle his ears against the thunder. He hadn't made a murmur at the tumult around him, and yet it seemed he also knew something about entrances. As soon as Taran uncovered his chubby face and held him out to the King, Eadan gave a happy, gurgling cry and reached for his father's face.

Taran had never seen a grown man break down so thoroughly, nor cry so pitifully. He turned away as Elias took his son, hugging him and sobbing, his head bent to his breast. Many of the men dashed their tears away, shamed by their reaction. Elias had no thought or care for appearances. He had thought the boy lost forever. Now he had his precious son back, and his emotions overflowed.

Ignoring the overwrought King, Sullyan nudged Drum toward Anjer. The Lord General frowned with concern when he saw the state of Aeyron. He bent his head to his Prince, who was barely conscious and didn't acknowledge his salute.

"So," breathed Anjer, "you did it. We've all been praying you would. My Lord Marik will be very pleased and relieved to see the two of you, and the Princess will be overjoyed. She has suffered much over her father and her brother."

Sullyan regarded him from bruised, red-veined eyes. "I must get Aeyron back to his father," she said, her weak voice and lack of formality betraying her highly emotional state and profound exhaustion. "Will you inform General Ephan of our imminent arrival? Ask him to have Deshan standing by. The Prince is gravely wounded."

Anjer called over his shoulder and a group of men came forward. "You look like you need some attention yourself," he growled. "These men will go with you, both as protection and as honor guard for his Highness. I will see you later. Go swiftly. I will tell Ephan to open the gates for you."

Sullyan accorded him an Andaryan-style salute, which caused raised brows among many of the Albians, not least when Anjer returned it, love and respect shining in his eyes. She did not acknowledge King Elias as she turned, sending Drum cantering toward the Citadel with Anjer's honor guard ranged around her.

Only then did Taran notice Robin had vanished, and profound unhappiness flooded his heart. There was much hurt there that needed healing.

He reined Morlech around to follow Sullyan, but Blaine

stayed him. "Adept Elijah, might I ask that you wait with us awhile? The King will require the tale of his son's return when he has recovered, and you are the only one able to give it."

Taran couldn't refuse, no matter how much he wanted to follow Sullyan. He felt bound to her, more than ever, and she needed care and rest. Yet Elias also needed to learn of Baron Reen's treachery and the Queen's possible involvement, so Taran acquiesced with a reluctant nod.

Blaine then formally approached Anjer to end the hostilities. It was up to Blaine to salvage some shred of dignity for Elias from this debacle, although the King was clearly in no state to worry about trivial things like embarrassment over his wrongful invasion.

He drew a breath, his expression apologetic. "My Lord General—"

Anjer cut across him. "General Blaine, you need make no apologies. I am relatively new to fatherhood myself. Had it been my child abducted, I might have reacted the same way. This is awkward for us all. I suggest both sides withdraw to a discreet distance and make camp. We are all wet, tired, and hungry, and I believe King Elias is in no condition to deal with matters of state. After a few hours' rest, those responsible for sorting out this mess can meet again. Shall we say sunset? I will have a pavilion set up between our two camps. Does that meet with your approval?"

Blaine bowed his head. "You are generous in your compassion, my Lord. None of us wanted this war and did all we could to dissuade the King. I make no excuses, you understand; we are all to blame. I thank you for your magnanimous gesture and I assure you, when Elias has recovered his … strength, he will make whatever reparations are necessary."

Anjer gave a curt nod. "One thing I'll ask of you, General. Send runners to the towns of Andeno and Sharrett, ordering your men to withdraw at once. I take it none of the inhabitants was injured, nor buildings destroyed?"

"Only minor injuries to a few townsfolk who resisted our entrance," Blaine said. "It shall be done at once. If you are in agreement, I will instruct the men who currently occupy those towns to join us here. I would also request permission to bring up our healers. We have wounded who need treatment before they can return to Albia."

Anjer nodded. "By all means. But they are to place themselves under the command of my men. You may send an officer to convey the order, and I will provide him with an escort."

"Very well, my Lord, I will see to it right away. Until sunset."

The warleaders parted and went back to their men. The two sides withdrew a safe distance and settled down with no demur. Sullyan's spectacular entrance and the King's reaction to the return of his son had subdued them all. Both races recognized a momentous event when they saw one.

General Blaine approached the King, who had now dismounted from his warhorse and was walking about, talking softly to his baby son. He seemed oblivious to the comings and goings of the men around him. Only Taran remained nearby. Robin and Valustin were off about the camp, seeing to the comfort of the men and tending the wounded. Midday had come and gone. Everyone was tired and hungry.

The rain had mercifully stopped. The thunderclouds called by Sullyan had dissipated without her touch to hold them. The General approached Elias and beckoned to Taran, who reluctantly joined them.

Blaine laid a hand on his monarch's shoulder. "Your Majesty."

Elias started. He was so wrapped up in his son he seemed to have forgotten everything else. Taran was concerned that the King's mind might have been permanently damaged by his desperate ordeal, but the look Elias turned on his old friend was sane, if overwrought.

"It seems you were right all along, Mathias." The King's voice was hoarse with emotion and shame. "Sullyan was right. I should have listened to you both. I don't know what I was thinking. I was wrong and I'm sorry. I must apologize to Sullyan at once. Where is she?"

Blaine cast a glance at Taran before replying. "I believe she has gone to the Citadel. She managed to rescue the Hierarch's Heir as well as Prince Eadan, and she has taken Aeyron back to his father. I'm sure Pharikian is as desperate to see his son as you were to see yours."

Taran heard the implied rebuke in the General's tone, and Elias winced. "Yes, you have the right," the King whispered, hugging Eadan closer. The little boy seemed not to mind his father's tight embrace and continued to suck on a corner of his expensive cloak. Elias sighed deeply. "It will have to wait till she returns."

The General squared his shoulders. "If you're ready, Elias, I've asked Adept Elijah here to tell you the details of your son's rescue. Will you sit and hear him?"

Someone had lit a fire and put water to heat for fellan. Stools had been set out in the center of the encampment, and a large square of oiled leather had been stretched on poles to provide a makeshift shelter. Elias allowed Blaine to steer him toward it and sat, his son cradled in his lap. The welcome aromas of fellan and hot food filled the air, and Taran waited until the King had been served before beginning his tale.

Elias and Blaine sat in attentive silence as Taran spoke, starting with Sullyan's suspicions concerning Reen when they had first set out from the Manor, and then relating the entire catalog of events to the present.

The King raised his brows at Ardoch's involvement, and scowled when he heard of the Baron's cavalier treatment of Lady Jinella. His expression turned thunderous as he listened to what the First Minister had discovered in the treasury records, and what he and the Torlander had seen in the castle dungeons. But when Taran recounted the actual rescue of the Prince, his freeing of Sullyan and Aeyron from the burning circle, and their subsequent fight with the Baron's men, Elias's face wore the threat of murder.

"Where is the traitor Reen now?" he demanded.

"The First Minister used his authority to raise the garrison and ordered Lieutenant Major Denny to confine the Baron to his mansion," said Taran. "But he was concerned about how the Queen would react and what she might try to do. No one can prevent her seeing Reen."

The King growled low in his throat. He was plainly in no fit state to fully comprehend, let alone deal with, the implications of the Queen's involvement. He steered Taran away from the topic.

"You say that poor backward boy, Huw, was somehow Reen's tool in all this? Some kind of … natural Artesan? And the Baron killed him?"

"Yes, your Majesty. Sullyan said he was a sport. No one knew about his abilities, and even she failed to sense him. They're difficult to spot, apparently. I don't really understand it. You'd have to ask her. But that's not all he was."

Elias raised his brows, arrested by Taran's tone of regret. He sounded almost fearful as he said, "What do you mean? What else was he?"

Taran lowered his eyes, not entirely sure he was doing the right thing. Yet he thought Elias ought to know, and Blaine too. Sullyan had suffered enough. Some was at the King's hands, and he needed to hear why she was reacting this way. Maybe he would understand her better.

He raised his head and looked Elias in the eye. "It appears he was also Sullyan's cousin."

✤ ✤ ✤ ✤ ✤

Sullyan only just held on to Aeyron long enough to reach the Citadel. The honor guard around her would have helped, but Aeyron was moaning again, almost delirious with exhaustion. Drained though she was, she would not abandon him again. She was supporting both of them almost completely now with the strength of her psyche alone, and was thankful to see the Citadel's western gate open to her escort's horn. General Ephan was waiting to usher them into the palace.

One look at Aeyron's condition and the General gave the order to clear the streets. He wasted no time on greetings or congratulations, but conveyed her to the palace courtyard with efficiency and speed.

They lowered Aeyron gently to the ground and laid him in a litter. He clung desperately to Sullyan's hand. They were linked through the contact and she knew it was his lifeline. There was only one circumstance under which he would relinquish it, and for that reason she requested they be taken immediately to Pharikian's chambers.

They were halfway there when Marik and Deshan arrived. Marik put an arm about Sullyan's waist and tried to support her with what little power he possessed. His love and care flowed into her and she nearly fell into his arms for weariness.

Deshan moved to Aeyron's side, his hand on the Prince's forehead. The Master Physician's brows quirked upward as he found no sign of infection, and the look he gave Sullyan was close to awe.

"I don't know how you did this, my dear, but you will be the most revered person in the entire realm for what you have done today."

"How is Timar?" she asked, exhaustion marring her tone.

Deshan gave a small smile. "His body's recovering well. His mind will heal when he beholds the face of his son. He is physically stronger at the moment than either of you."

She smiled back, but had no strength for further speech. As they continued to the Hierarch's quarters, she noticed Marik giving Deshan pointed looks over her head. He must have seen the wound on the back of her head. She had almost forgotten it. The wound in her thigh was invisible beneath her combat leathers.

At the door to Pharikian's chambers they were met by Princess Idrimar, whose belly was already swelling with the growth of her twins. Her hands twisted nervously, her expression swinging between worry and desperate hope. As she saw them she gave a squeal of shock and excitement, and sprang toward her brother. The sight of his ravaged frame brought her up short.

"Will he be all right?" she pleaded, taking Sullyan's free hand. "Please tell me he'll be all right!"

Sullyan squeezed her hand. "He should be, Highness, once he gets some treatment and rest."

Marik took his wife's shoulders, gently pulling her back. "Don't worry so, my dear. All will be well. They're going to awaken Timar and then you'll see. Stay back and let them work."

Idrimar let herself be steered away, tears sliding down her cheeks. Aeyron was so pale, so gaunt, the bandages on his arm and hand dark with blood. He didn't look like he could possibly survive.

With Deshan pouring strength into the Prince, they brought him into Pharikian's chamber, laying the litter alongside the prostrate man. Aeyron opened his eyes. He immediately sought Sullyan, reaching for her despite his hand still being clamped around hers. She came even closer and stroked his cheek.

"You are home now, my Prince. Be strong a little longer, and then you can rest."

Persuading him to release her by placing Pharikian's limp hand in his, Sullyan moved around to the other side of the bed. She sat and tried to marshal her thoughts, as well as her fading strength. She gazed down into Pharikian's dearly loved face, seeing the worry lines etched under his closed eyes, the papery quality of his skin. Although he had lost his earlier haunted, collapsed look, he would never fully heal until he knew Aeyron was home. Releasing a deep, bone-weary sigh, she opened her mind to Pharikian and felt for the cocoon of his psyche.

There was no resistance. He was an empty shell. His spirit, his psyche, his mind; all were wrapped and insulated from stray thoughts and external stimuli. He heard nothing, felt nothing. But she could see within to where he lay, where his spirit only awaited release before completing its destructive wish to dive into the Void of oblivion.

She recognized the signs, for she had once felt the same. He was a Senior Master, the same rank as she. She wasn't physically able to prevent him from carrying out his desire. In her current depleted state, she barely had the power to release him.

There was someone he would heed, someone who did possess the power to reach Pharikian's desperate soul, though with the power of love rather than mind. Before beginning her work, she gathered Aeyron's life force and used it to shield and conceal her own so that the first thing Pharikian felt would be the yearned-for touch of his son's psyche.

Aeyron offered no resistance. She was part of him now, completely accepted into his life and soul even as his father was. He let her work through him, her touch sure and gentle despite her great weariness. She felt his father stir.

Rising from the bed, she removed her hand from Pharikian's brow. She turned his head toward his son, who was already gazing at his father's face. When Pharikian's eyes finally opened and she saw his incredulous smile of love, she slipped unnoticed from the room.

⁜ ⁜ ⁜ ⁜ ⁜

If Taran thought he would be released once he had told Elias everything he knew, he was sadly mistaken. He had to endure Elias's endless questions, most of which he was unable to answer. Blaine asked questions too, and Taran suffered a bad moment when the General demanded to know how Sullyan had overcome the spellsilver on her wrists, as well as that within the circle, in order to prevent the catastrophe the Baron had set in motion.

He answered as best he could. "I wasn't there, sir, so I didn't see. You'd have to ask Sullyan. I may now be Adept-elite, but I won't pretend to understand how she did it."

It was true enough and Blaine had to be content, but Taran could see the General suspected he held something back. This final secret of Sullyan's was not for Taran to divulge. He would respect her wishes and leave that one to her.

Finally released from the King's inquisition, Taran searched the camp for Cal. His belly was growling with hunger. Blaine had offered him food, but he was anxious to rejoin Sullyan. Eating could wait till later. He simply wanted to thank Cal and say farewell.

As he walked through the camp, a troubling sense of unease crept over him, making his skin crawl. He halted and glanced around. His eyes met Robin's. The young Major was staring balefully at him from a campfire not ten yards away, his arms folded over his chest.

Taran hadn't spared Robin a thought, so intent was he on finding Cal. He felt his face redden with shame and was immediately furious with himself. He had nothing to be ashamed of. If anyone, it ought to be Robin who was shamed. He was the one who should be caring for Sullyan, especially in her condition.

Taran briefly imagined himself marching over to Robin and telling him about his child. His unborn child who had already served his King, and indeed the whole world, by saving them from destruction. Then the image of Sullyan's face came into his mind, and he knew he could not. It was none of his business. Robin wouldn't believe him anyway.

He tore his gaze away from those eyes so full of pain and anger, and moved on.

Taran finally found Cal with Dexter. The two captains sat surrounded by their command, laughing and joking among themselves and seeming more at ease than any of the other men. Their help and support of Sullyan, and the outcome of that aid, had raised their spirits and lightened their hearts. They welcomed Taran with much backslapping and rough pride, and he felt it like a balm to his soul. He had not realized how much he'd missed Cal.

They sat and spoke together for a while, Cal persuading his friend to eat with them. They all demanded the story of the Princes' rescue, and Taran couldn't deny them. When he eventually rose to go, Cal stood with him and sent one of his men to fetch Taran's horse.

"When will you be back?"

Taran replied honestly. "I don't know. When Sullyan returns, I suppose. She needs me now, Cal. She'll need me until all this is sorted out, until Robin realizes what a fool he's been. How long that will take, I just don't know. And then there's Elias. I imagine he'll apologize and reinstate her, but whether she'll accept, I can't say."

He saw Dexter's expression and thought the other captain would protest, but Dex closed his mouth without speaking. Taran turned back to Cal. "Give my love to Rienne. Tell her I'm looking after Brynne. She'll know what I mean."

Cal gave him an old-fashioned look. "Oh, yes? What else is going on, Taran?"

He grinned, shaking his head. "Just give her the message. I'll keep in touch. You take care."

They clasped forearms before Taran mounted Morlech, taking the reins from Cal's man with thanks. The dark-skinned Apprentice sat back down as Taran rode off, a thoughtful look on his face.

The last thing Taran heard as he headed off through the trees was Cal's longwhistle playing one of their favorite folk tunes.

Chapter Two

Taran gained immediate entry to the Citadel. He gave his name to the sentries and rode through the encircling Gwayeth forces to the sound of cheers. Ephan must have told them what he and Sullyan had done. The Velletian Guard opened the western gate to his call, and he rode up to the palace through streets thronging with townspeople celebrating the return of the Heir. Aeyron was beloved by his people and Taran probably would have been mobbed by the delighted crowd had they known who he was.

He gained the palace courtyard unmolested and gave Morlech to the grooms. He would have to arrange for the horse's return if he remained here any length of time. For now, it could wait. He entered the palace and made his way to the private suites. On the way he caught sight of Norkis, Pharikian's personal page, sitting in a corner with his head bowed. The boy was weeping as if his heart would break.

Fearing the worst, Taran knelt beside the sobbing boy. "Norkis. What's happened, what's wrong?"

The face the boy turned on him was radiant with joyful tears, and from the lad's somewhat garbled version of events, Taran gathered that Norkis's lord and master had awakened and reunited with his son.

Relieved, Taran asked after Sullyan and then left Norkis to regain his composure. The corridors were silent and empty as he made his way to the suite Sullyan always occupied when staying in the palace. Those concerned with the welfare of the royal family were ministering to them; all others respected their need for privacy and rest.

He halted outside the door to Sullyan's chambers and stood irresolute. Norkis had told him she had gone to her rest some time since. She would surely be asleep by now, as she had been so exhausted. He only wanted to check on her, but if he knocked on the door he might wake her, and he didn't want to do that.

He had just made up his mind to leave her in peace when he heard her soft call.

"Come in, Taran."

Hoping he hadn't disturbed her after all, he opened the door.

Sullyan was sitting cross-legged on the huge bed in the sleeping room. Her face was ashen, making the dark smudges under her eyes stand out in stark contrast. She wore her beloved old green shirt and was carefully toweling dry her mass of tawny hair. He should have known she would take a bath at the first opportunity.

He closed the door and crossed the floor toward her. Sullyan laid the damp towel aside, flaring her tumbled hair over her shoulders and back. It was coming on for evening, but the early summer air was still warm. All traces of thunderclouds had left the sky. The large windows of the sleeping chamber stood open to the warm breeze, but heavy drapes had been pulled across them, dimming the room to dusk.

Taran dropped his jacket onto one of the chairs and regarded her.

"I thought you'd have been asleep long before this. How on earth can you keep your eyes open?"

"I was waiting for you. I knew you would come."

"I only came by to make sure you were all right. Have you eaten anything? Has anyone checked that head wound?"

Sullyan waved a weary hand toward the remains of a meal on a bedside table. "Deshan was here earlier and he checked me over. The fracture is not serious and will heal in a few days. He brought the food and sat over me like a nursemaid while I ate it, damn him. I thought I would be sick. But then I sent him packing. Aeyron needs him more than I do."

Taran could see that even this short conversation had drained her. She pushed herself back against the pillows, stretching her legs out in front of her. The ugly slash in her thigh where Izack's sword had caught her had been tended and was already healing. Her face, although unhealthily pale, also looked better for her bath, less swollen and bruised.

"I'll let you get some rest," he said. Her eyes flicked to his and he read something strange in them. She didn't want him to go.

In a voice low and strained, she said, "I cannot seem to rest just yet, Taran. Would you stay and talk awhile? That is, unless you are too weary. You must crave sleep too."

Hardly able to credit that she didn't want to slip beneath those inviting sheets and sleep for a week—it was what he felt like doing, and he hadn't been through half what she had—he sat on the edge of the bed.

"I hear you awakened Pharikian," he said, and told her about Norkis.

She smiled, a genuine expression despite her great weariness. "Yes, father and son are reunited. Timar will be well once he regains his strength. I imagine Deshan will allow him up tomorrow, if only for a short while. And Idrimar can now concentrate on her twins, instead of fretting after her father and brother. Marik has been so concerned for her."

Taran heard an echo of grief in her voice and thought he knew why she had asked him to stay. But he couldn't just blurt it out, and besides, it would only give her more pain.

Instead he said, "I was detained by the General when you left. He wanted me to tell the King about Eadan's rescue."

She nodded, her expression wary. "Yes, I thought he would. How did Elias take it?"

Taran told her, also relating the King's fury over Reen's treachery, and his desire to apologize to her. "He said he'd wait until you returned."

Sullyan's eyes filled and a single tear slid slowly down her cheek. She stared at her hands in her lap. "And did you … did you see Robin?"

Taran's uneasy silence was all the answer she needed. Another tear followed the first. She was forced to take a steadying breath.

"Taran, I do not intend to return."

He had been afraid of this. She had hinted as much to Bull after she had left the Manor. "What, not ever?"

He was aware that her hybrid blood enabled her to live in either realm without suffering any ill effects, and, of course, Pharikian had already offered her a home at the Citadel. Now, it seemed she intended to take up his offer.

She raised her eyes to his, her face white and strained. "I have decided to stay here until my son is born. After that, well, we shall see."

He turned his head away, not wanting her to see the hurt this decision caused him. She sensed it anyway and leaned toward him.

"How could I return to the Manor? You saw Robin's face today when we rode in together. He *still* believes me false. He does not want me back. And no matter what the King says now, no matter what his state of mind at the time, he still stripped me of everything I have ever held dear. He threw all my loyalty and all my years of service back in my face and declared me a traitor. How can I return there? It is not the place it was. It is no longer my home. There are too many painful memories."

17

She slumped back into the pillows, spent. "Here, at least, I have something that feels close to a family. I was born in this room, in this very bed. My parents stayed here, my mother died here. I feel I am close to them while I am here. And I need that, my friend. I need that very badly."

Her voice had fallen to a whisper. She looked so forlorn, so lost, that Taran found it hard to equate this tearful, abandoned girl with the confident young woman who had been so strong for Aeyron, who had fought Izack so viciously, and who had hunted and captured Kethro and Corbyn so ruthlessly. That, he knew, was the core of her contradiction. She could be immensely strong for her friends and the causes she believed in because she had lost so much that she loved.

She deserved happiness, she deserved stability and love. She had earned it. And he had so much love to give her, if only she would let him. As he watched her, the tears fell more freely from her eyes, and then he could stand it no longer.

"Oh, Brynne."

He moved onto the bed beside her and gathered her slight form into his strong arms. Ignoring her initial resistance, he felt the tremble of her body caused by exhaustion and deep sorrow. He felt her give way to her emotion and grief as she sobbed against his chest.

"I miss him, Taran. I need him and miss him so much that it hurts, and I hardly know how to bear the pain."

He held her ever tighter, trying, with the depth of his love, to give her tortured spirit some ease.

They sat this way for some time, resting against the deep, downy pillows of the great bed, simply sharing comfort. He murmured soothing words into her glorious hair and, slowly, her shuddering eased. Cradled and comforted by his masculine presence and the sincerity of his solace, she drifted into exhausted sleep. Careful not to disturb her, he drew soft sheets over them both.

✣ ✣ ✣ ✣ ✣

The ruby sun set in a wash of crimson, and the inevitable could be put off no longer. The pavilion had been erected. Chairs, a table, and a fire were set within. The incongruously normal aromas of food and fellan permeated the balmy summer air.

It was almost too normal, thought Mathias Blaine sourly as he prepared for the awkward meeting to come. The purple and gold of the Hierarch's colors flying over the pavilion's tented roof spoke eloquently of summer soirees, music, and dancing—not crisis talks and hints of surrender. Yet he appreciated the gesture Anjer was making and hoped its nuances were not lost on Elias.

The King seemed to have recovered his normal mental faculties with the return of his son, and only a vague distress was visible behind his eyes. That could be due to any number of things: Reluctance to admit he'd been wrong, the Baron's treason, the probable betrayal of his wife, even the casually brutal dismissal of his most trusted and loyal servant. Blaine thought it was probably all of these and more. There were times when he was heartily relieved to be a general and not the King.

Yet there was steel in Elias Rovannon of Albia, and under it beat a generous heart. Bluff, he could be—abrasive, even—and certainly ruthless in the defense and furtherance of the interests of his realm. But he was no fool, and he recognized a wrong when he was capable of seeing it. So although he could not take back what had gone before, he could, and would, do everything in his power to make amends.

At the appointed hour, Anjer sent a herald to Elias's encampment to invite the King to the meeting. Elias hadn't wanted to leave his son, but it was inappropriate to take the baby. Eadan

19

was left, well wrapped and asleep, in a makeshift bed under the stretched leather shelter with two Kingsmen standing guard.

Elias beckoned to Blaine, Robin, and Valustin, who waited under the russet glow of the evening sky, and followed the herald toward the pavilion. Anjer was waiting for them, Commander Barrin at his shoulder. Both men stood at the wide entrance to the pavilion, no guards around them. At Blaine's suggestion, Elias also had eschewed guards, and he made another ostentatious gesture of trust as he halted before Anjer. He deliberately unbuckled his sword belt and directed his companions to do likewise.

Anjer raised his brows as Elias handed an Albian swordsman his weapons, retaining only his eating knife. Blaine, Robin, and Valustin did the same. Then Elias turned to face the Lord General.

"There has been more than enough mistrust and misuse between our realms these past few weeks, my Lord Anjer, and blame for much of it may be laid squarely at my feet. Let there be no more. I hereby pledge you—and through you as his representative, the Hierarch of Andaryon—that I will do everything in my power to ensure there is no more. To prove my sincerity, I come to this meeting unarmed and with an open heart, as a symbol of future trust and honesty in all our dealings."

Anjer stood impassively, hands on hips, watching the King's face as if assessing Elias's intent. Blaine suffered agonies during those few crucial seconds. Anjer's reaction would make or break their fractured alliance.

He needn't have worried.

The huge man snapped his fingers and the herald stepped closer. Unbuckling his own sword belt, Anjer handed it to the man, staring pointedly at Barrin until the Commander did the same. Then he turned back to Elias and held out his hand.

"Let us put behind us the wrongs of this situation, your Majesty. There is blame on both sides and an accounting to be sought. Grief and loss drive many a man to unaccustomed action, and to judge blindly is to risk misunderstanding. Let us sit now and talk, with no recriminations and no harbored grudges, and let us repair the damaged link between our realms."

Elias took the proffered hand and was led inside the pavilion. Blaine followed, breathing a silent sigh of relief. Barrin stuck close to Anjer, eyeing Robin suspiciously. The Lord General may be prepared to forgive and forget, but it appeared his Commander was not. Blaine was pleased to see that Robin, who appeared to be in a very strange mood, gave Barrin no notice, nor cause for offense.

Wine was served by the herald and the meeting began. Anjer was as good as his word. He made no accusations and brought no grievances. The Albian invasion, such as it was, had caused little actual damage, and Elias was quick in offering gold and manpower to put right what hurt had been caused.

Loss of life in the battle itself had been light, although the unnecessary nature of it was galling to both sides. Here, however, Anjer and Elias had a just target for their wrath, and Blaine gave Robin the nod to have their captives brought in.

Both Corbyn and Kethro had been kept in chains, the son held apart from his father. Not only did Blaine not wish them to have the comfort of the other's presence, he also wanted to ensure they had no opportunity to plan together. Also, Kethro's absence was surety for Corbyn's submissive conduct.

Not that he was acting submissively right now. Despite his hands being bound behind his back, he stalked into the pavilion ahead of his guards as if he were the one who was wronged. He completely ignored the Albian King.

Halting before Anjer's chair, he declared in a ringing voice, "I demand you obtain my release and that of my son from these outland barbarians! By what right do they hold me? I am a subject of the Hierarch. I am certainly not answerable to an invading alien race. It is preposterous that I should be held like this on our own soil. I demand to be released at once!"

No one in the pavilion had risen at Corbyn's entrance, and this insult wasn't wasted on the furious renegade. Neither did they react to his demands. Elias simply gazed at Anjer, his arms folded across his chest.

Anjer heaved his deceptively agile bulk to his feet, towering impressively over the thin and wiry Corbyn.

"Preposterous? You *demand*? From what I can see, you're in no position to demand anything." He pointedly eyed Corbyn's chains.

Corbyn's face turned purple and his pale eyes flashed.

"Are you going to let a rabble of outland barbarians tell you what to do, Anjer? They've invaded our territory! They've captured our towns! They've ravaged our people! And you just sit and *talk* to them? Have you lost your mind, man, or just your courage?"

Anjer's face paled dangerously and his eyes snapped black fire. Blaine found himself thankful they had all put aside their weapons. He wouldn't care to face an armed and enraged Anjer.

"I would be very careful if I were you, when you speak of ravaging and invading. You are not blameless in that department yourself."

Corbyn responded hotly. "I merely exacted retribution for their raids on my lands. You can't deny I'm entitled."

Anjer's brows drew together. "Are you telling me you deliberately sanctioned raids into Albia?"

His tone was deceptively mild but Corbyn was too incensed to see the trap.

"Well, *you* wouldn't do anything. They have you in their pocket, Anjer! *Someone* had to defend our people."

Anjer drew himself up. "Then you stand condemned out of

22

your own mouth, for you have just admitted before witnesses that you knowingly went against the Hierarch's decree."

Corbyn's face drained of color and he stared in disbelief at the Lord General. Anjer, however, was looking at Elias.

"Your Majesty, what do you term such an act in your realm?"

Elias smiled coldly. "We call it 'treason,' Lord Anjer."

Anjer nodded. "And what is your ultimate penalty for such an offense?"

"Death."

Anjer stared at Corbyn, his lips curling under his black mustache. "Indeed? Well, it just so happens that death is our ultimate penalty, too. It can also be extended to any of the perpetrator's accomplices."

Corbyn subsided. The threat of the death sentence had stunned him, even more so because of its implications for Kethro. Disgusted by his treachery, Anjer waved him away, and Robin ordered him taken back to the Albian encampment.

Once Corbyn had left, the King asked Blaine to relate what they knew of the Baron's scheming, and what Taran had told them regarding the two Princes. Anjer listened gravely, his face betraying his emotions. He then reciprocated by recounting the events at the Citadel, beginning with Aeyron's abduction. He told them what he, Marik, and Sullyan had learned from Lord Rand, and what they had surmised from Corbyn's actions. It was agreed that a more detailed accounting was needed, and preferably in both Corbyn's and Reen's own words.

More wine and fellan were served while they discussed the practicalities of removing the Albian presence from Andaryan soil. The healers from the Manor had recently arrived from Andeno, where they had not only remained safe but had actually endeared themselves to the townsfolk by contriving to save the life of the chief elder's wife, who had suffered a near-fatal heart seizure brought on by the imprisoning of her husband.

As soon as they arrived, the Albian healers began working. Human and demon alike were treated by healers of both sides. All the injured would be able to travel by morning. It was decided that the dead of both races should burn on pyres side by side, so the smoke would mingle and rise entwined into the night sky.

Anjer and Elias concluded their business amicably, with the King agreeing to hand Corbyn and Kethro over to Anjer for trial in their own lands. In his turn, the Lord General assured Elias that they would be kept alive in order to provide evidence at the Baron's trial, if necessary. The King also gave a solemn promise to meet with the Hierarch at his convenience, to discuss reparation and the future course of their alliance.

These necessities out of the way, Anjer, Elias, and Blaine refilled their glasses, ready to sit talking into the night. Robin, Barrin, and Valustin were excused to go about their duties. Robin was the last to leave. As he turned to go, Anjer caught his eye.

"That was a spectacular entrance your wife made today. You must be immensely proud of her, Major. When I think what she went through—what you both went through—two years ago, I can't imagine how you must be feeling at this moment."

Blaine held his breath, watching Robin. The young man clearly couldn't think of a thing to say. Even Elias had the grace to look shamed. Blaine wondered what the Major would do; it was an awkward moment.

"Proud?" managed Robin in a strangled tone. "Oh yes, my Lord, my *wife* can always be relied upon to do the right thing."

He flung himself out of the pavilion.

✤ ✤ ✤ ✤ ✤

Taran woke sometime in the dark hours. He didn't know what had roused him. He only knew he was warm, safe, and deliciously comfortable. He was still dressed in his shirt and breeches, and a light cotton sheet covered him. The night air was cool with a soft breeze from the open windows, and it was fragrant with the scent of flowers from the garden outside.

No, it wasn't the scent of flowers. It was the scent of soft, luxuriant hair. His nose was buried in its tumbled masses and it was this clean aroma that had woken him. He breathed in deeply and smiled.

He could hear other breathing besides his own, and feel its gentle rise and fall beneath his hand. She was snuggled close against him, her back to his chest, and he had one arm curled protectively about her slender body, cupping a small breast in the palm of his hand. She fitted into his embrace as surely as if she belonged there.

He lay staring into the balmy darkness, feeling the increasing tempo of his heart. He listened to the soft chirring of night insects and the faint sound of her slumbering breath. How many times had he fantasized about the two of them lying together like this? A large and comfortable bed, soft, downy pillows, smooth sheets, and the beloved and much-desired slim and sensuous body snuggled against his. His breathing quickened.

She lay so still, so trusting. One of her legs had twined with his and he could feel the smooth silkiness of her skin against his bare foot. He longed to run his hands over her body and feel the softness of her under his touch, but he was loath to move for fear of waking her.

He lay there in the peaceful darkness, letting his love for her wash through him. His heart was beating ever faster. He could almost hear its incessant urging. Passion was building in his veins.

Unable to resist, he brushed his lips across the back of her neck. She made a soft sound and stirred beneath his hand. She still wore the green linen shirt, but it was old, softened and thinned with much use. It did nothing to disguise the contours or scent of her body.

He caught his breath, feeling his skin flush with heat. She had asked him to stay. What did that mean?

It meant she needed to be held.

To be loved.

He was suddenly sure, with an intuitive clarity he had never experienced before, that if he turned her toward him now, if he ran his hands over her supple body, if he kissed her as he longed to kiss her and offered his love, then this time—oh, this time—she wouldn't refuse him.

Passion leapt to fire in his loins and the heat of his desire was almost unbearable, fanned by his certainty. She would allow his desire. She would take his love and take comfort from it. And he knew he would never see reproach in her eyes, knew he would never have cause to shy from silent recriminations or soured friendship. She would take him in the spirit of his offering, and love him for it. He was sure of it.

And yet....

Despite the heat of yearning, despite this being his heart's most fervent desire, he couldn't do it.

It wasn't that he was incapable. Far from it! His eager body was capable to the point of discomfort. No, that wasn't the problem. If he allowed his body the release it craved—if she turned to him and accepted him inside her—then, once the moment was over, once they had shared the love and comfort they both desired, she would never—*ever*—be able to forgive herself.

He knew it with a total and utter certainty that cooled the heat of his loins. And he could not bear that thought.

Tears welled from his eyes, running across his nose to soak the pillow beneath his head. How could he give her such pain? It was inevitable now, whatever he did. She needed him so badly, yet he must refuse her. This aching desire, this act of love he had craved for so long and which he was sure she would now grant him, he could not allow. It was his turn to be strong. The pain he was feeling, a physical pain as well as a soul-deep yearning, was better—lesser—than what they would both suffer if he gave way.

He closed his eyes briefly, fighting the fire, fighting for strength. Gently, slowly, he slid his hand from under her soft breast and moved away from her body.

Already his soul screamed for the loss. He felt cold for her absence. He slipped from the sheets and stood for a moment, trying to see her slender form through the blur of his tears. Then he walked across the room and opened the door of the suite, never looking back.

✣ ✣ ✣ ✣ ✣

A deep, shuddering sigh sounded in the darkness, muffled against her pillow. Was he suffering more heartache than he could bear? Had he understood what had just happened, or had the trial been too much? She had thought he was ready, and there would never be another opportunity as natural as this. The trial was necessary to his continued growth, and they would have had to endure it at some point. It was inevitable. That it would cause him pain was inescapable. What she hadn't expected was the depth of pain it caused *her*.

She gave a small moan of anguish. What had she done to deserve this? She was so alone, so bereft, more so now than at any other time in her life. Taran had been quite right; she badly needed his love. She had even half-hoped he would be unable to control himself, that he would have given her an excuse to give way to her loneliness and grief.

Oh, but that was so unfair, so ungrateful of her! She knew, deep down, that despite her physical need, her surrender would not have eased the burden of grief in her heart. Rather, it would have increased it, and she would never have found peace.

The trial had been so hard for him. It was understandable, given the depth of his feelings. But the time had been right, and she owed him this chance to prove himself. He had passed the test, as she had been sure he would, and now it only remained to be seen whether he understood, whether he could forgive her. If not, if their friendship suffered, she would be more alone than ever.

She failed to stop the sob that threatened to burst the floodgates of her sorrow. Her hands slid to the barely perceptible swell of her belly, but she could take no comfort even from the thoughts and feelings of her unborn son. He would enter a world full of heartache and pain, and it would never end. She didn't know if she could stand it.

She stared long into the warm summer darkness, her spirit and soul in shreds.

Chapter Three

The Albian camp roused early in the gray-pink dawn. The men who had been left behind to guard the two towns Elias had captured had arrived under their Andaryan escort during the early hours. Robin and Valustin went round the camp, organizing the Albians into sections ready for the journey back through the Veils.

The healers and the wounded would go through first, followed by the King and the General, and then the rest of the men by their sections. Robin would be last to leave, as he would collapse the tunnel.

The King and General Blaine had sat long into the night talking with Anjer. Despite the awkward circumstances, Anjer and Elias got along surprisingly well. The Andaryan Lord General was bluff and uncomplicated, and Elias could appreciate that. They had much in common, and Blaine found himself regretting once again that Elias's instability had prevented him from agreeing to talks with the Hierarch's representative before things went too far. At least they were talking now.

They had even touched on a raw subject without too much friction: namely, Sullyan's dismissal from Elias's service. The King had regained his composure and common sense far enough to admit he'd made a grave and uncharacteristic error when he had rejected her advice. Anjer had nothing but admiration for her. Through the Lord General's recollections of how she had dealt with her abuse at Rykan's hands, its near-fatal consequences, and her successful challenge to him, Elias remembered his own high regard for her. He was coming to rue his savage treatment of her deeper by the hour.

Anjer promised to do everything he could to persuade Sullyan of the King's deep regret, and also his desire to make amends. Elias had bowed his head in grateful thanks. He had not expected such support.

They had retired for the night as allies, if not yet actual friends. Thanks to Anjer's hard-headed realism and reluctance to retaliate over Elias's ill-considered invasion, what could have become a bloodbath had turned into a salvageable situation. Mathias Blaine, for one, was intensely relieved.

The General was roused by the camp's first stirrings, but he left his monarch to sleep a little longer. Elias was stretched out on a camp bed, his son cradled in his arms. The look of strain he had worn since Eadan's disappearance had finally vanished from his normally youthful features. The little Prince was happy to be reunited with his father. He had lain snugly and contentedly by his side throughout the dark hours. Blaine granted them peace and privacy for a little longer.

The General employed his rarely used metaphysical powers to contact Bull. He expected to have to wake the big man, but to his surprise, Bull's psyche showed no signs of him having been recently asleep. Blaine caught a note of concern behind Bull's mental tone, but the big man didn't seem to want to speak of it.

Bull reported that once Colonel Vassa had been apprised of the cessation of hostilities, and also the capture of Lord Corbyn, he had suspended and recalled the extra patrols, and was ready to begin dismissing the militia. Blaine agreed he should commence this, and advised that those men who had journeyed the farthest should be the first released. He also advised Bull on how much they should be paid. The King had been more than generous in allotting pay. The return of his son and his shame over his mistake had made Elias doubly magnanimous.

Bull promised to pass on Blaine's orders and broke the link, leaving a faint trace of disquiet in the General's mind.

Blaine went looking for Robin and found him with the wounded, making a last check to ensure they were all capable of surviving the transition through the Veils. As he received Robin's report, Blaine studied the Major's pale face and tight expression, deciding against questioning the young man until they were back on home soil. Although things had turned out well enough, the campaign had been a great strain on them all, not least on Robin, who had been required to bear arms against his friends. Blaine hoped Robin's distress was due only to that.

Yet as he linked with the Major, preparatory to opening the Veils, he sensed how Robin shielded and hid his thoughts. Sighing with concern, Blaine let it go. Now was not the time.

The tunnel was quickly established and opened out onto the pleasant little valley with its meandering stream, which was situated below the ridge on the Manor's extensive estate. Once it was stable, Robin sent the healers and wounded through with a small contingent of guards.

The King went next, and Valustin oversaw the filing through of the other troops while Robin maintained the tunnel. It took some time.

Anjer and Barrin stood to one side, their men well away from the substrate construct as they watched the Albians leave their lands. Blaine had already handed over lords Corbyn and Kethro, and they had been escorted, none too gently, back to the Citadel. Corbyn had been rigid and outraged, his son cowed and frightened.

Blaine saw Anjer watching the departure of the Albian troops with satisfaction. Both generals were pleased with the way things had gone, although if Sullyan had failed in her task Blaine dreaded to think what this dawn would have looked like. He knew Elias would never have given up. His malady of mind would have driven him to greater and greater lengths in order to procure the impossible release of his son.

The resulting carnage would have affected both realms deeply, and for many years to come. The two races would probably have been pushed back to the old days before Morgan Sullyan's sacrifice, when Andaryan nobles would raid Albia with impunity. This would have opened an irreparable and permanent split which would have precluded any thoughts of trade or alliance. Albia and Andaryon owed Sullyan for much more than the return of the two Princes.

Just before entering the tunnel, Blaine accorded Anjer an Andaryan-style salute. The huge man returned it, his black eyes glittering. Blaine turned away and Robin silently followed, collapsing the tunnel as he went.

Blaine rode behind Elias back to the Manor to the acclaim of those men still in residence. It was now past midmorning and the departure of the militia was well underway. Colonel Vassa came forward to greet Elias as he and Blaine drew rein in the open space before the Manor house. He held the roan stallion's bridle while the King dismounted. He wore a stern expression.

Chief Healer Hanan, looking careworn, arrived to relieve Elias of his son. She would have none of the King's assurances that the babe was well. She intended to give the little boy a thorough examination. The Chief Healer was a formidable force when exercising her professional skills, and Elias didn't demur for long.

Vassa handed the reins of the King's horse to the stablemaster and approached Blaine, closely shadowed by Bull. Both men bore troubled expressions and Blaine knew he was about to hear the reason behind Bull's unease. The King came closer to hear what was said and Robin also joined them.

Vassa's deep voice was full of concerned indignation. "General, your Majesty, it pains me to tell you that we have harbored a traitor here at the Manor. Baron Reen has had one of our own in his pay, and the spy has done much damage. Hal Bullen made the discovery early yesterday morning, but under the circumstances I decided not to burden you with it. Now that you have returned, however—"

Elias's expression was thunderous. "Have you apprehended this traitor? Who is it?"

Vassa shook his head. "It's Captain Parren, your Majesty."

Blaine swore. "Where is he?"

Bull clenched his fists. "We can't find him, sir. He should have gone out on patrol at dawn yesterday morning, but contrary to every regulation, he ordered his militia command to leave without him. They knew no better than to do as he said. He told them he'd catch up with them later, but he never did. They straggled back on their own around midday.

"He was already under suspicion due to certain events that had occurred the day before, and a report I received early yesterday morning confirmed he'd been spying for the Baron. We had a reception committee ready to apprehend him when he returned from patrol, but when we discovered he wasn't with his men, we carried out a full search of the Manor. I have to report that his room's been cleared and his horse has gone. It looks like he's deserted."

Blaine was furious and demanded to know why they had suspected Parren. His rage only deepened when Bull told him about Ozella's murder and Tad's grave condition. As Bull spoke, all traces of blood drained from Robin's face. He turned and bolted toward the infirmary without asking leave of the General. Blaine let him go. He knew of the strong attachment between Robin and the young cadet.

Bull finished the tale by revealing who had finally confirmed Parren's treachery. Blaine, who had already guessed, sighed in frustration and shook his head.

The King, however, covered his face with his hands. Despite his frustration, Blaine sympathized. Elias had so much to apologize for; so many amends to make. The sheer scale of his errors and the depth of his astonishment over Sullyan's unwavering loyalty in the face of his unfeeling rejection and flagrant mistrust threatened to overwhelm him with remorse.

Leaving Elias to his distress, Blaine asked what Vassa and Bull had done to discover Parren's whereabouts. The Manor and its grounds had been extensively combed. Search parties had been sent to the surrounding villages. Vassa had sent out patrols with express orders to apprehend Parren at all costs. He was wanted as a traitor to his King and country, as a deserter, and also as a murderer. There was only one possible penalty for such heinous crimes.

Fuming, the General dismissed them. He wished he had dealt more firmly with Parren over his illegal duel with Robin two years ago. He also knew he should have forced Robin to bring charges against Parren over the damage he had tried to cause at the siege of Hyecombe. But done was done and couldn't be changed now.

Leaving orders that he was to be kept informed of Tad's condition, Blaine invited the King to join him in his private apartments. His valet, Hyram, was dispatched to organize hot food and fellan, although whether either of them could stomach it right now, he didn't know.

✣ ✣ ✣ ✣ ✣

Bull went to the infirmary, where he found Robin on his knees by Tad's bed. The Major clutched the boy's pale, cold hand, swearing with the most vicious and binding oaths to personally tear Parren's living heart from his breast with his bare hands. Tad lay unresponsive to Robin's promises.

Rienne stood behind the Major, watching him attempt to pour his own strength and life force into Tad's pathetically still body. Bull moved to stand beside her.

"How is he?" he murmured.

She glanced at him sadly. "No change. He's hanging on, although how he's doing it, I just don't know. Despite our best efforts, he doesn't have nearly enough blood, but we can't give him any more just yet without harming his mother. His wound's not healing because of his body's depleted resources, and I dread to think what effect all this has had on his brain."

"Can't he have someone else's blood?"

Robin heard Bull's question and glanced wildly up at Rienne with red-veined eyes. "He can have mine, he can have it all! Just save him, Rienne, I beg you. It's my fault he's like this."

Bull frowned. "How is it your fault?"

Robin stared at him, almost unrecognizable in his grief. "You know how Parren hated me! Before we left for Andaryon he begged me to get Vassa to change his mind about his duties. He was desperate to go with us."

Bull shrugged. "Well, you spoke to Vassa, didn't you? He refused."

Robin's breath hissed sharply. "Yes, yes! But do you really think Parren believed that? He knew I didn't trust him. He'd have thought I was pleased he was being left behind. And because he couldn't take his rage out on me, he took it out on Tad."

Robin's eyes filled with tears as he gazed down at the lad's limp form. "He knew how Tad felt about me, and he knew I'd be devastated by this. I know he's a vicious bastard, but I still can't believe he'd kill a child just to get back at me."

Rienne laid a hand on the Major's arm. "Tad's not dead yet,

Robin. He's a fighter. He won't die, not if I can help it. But I can't risk giving him your blood. I can't take the chance he'll react badly. His heart couldn't take any more strain just now. In another day or so we can take more from his mother, but until then, we just have to keep giving him strength. Be strong for him. Parren's not killed him yet."

Robin shook her hand away. "He killed poor Ozella, though, didn't he? Oh, you can say what you like, but all of this is down to me. If I hadn't been so lax about pressing charges against him for what he did two years ago, none of this would have happened. He'd have been dismissed and wouldn't have been able to pass secrets to the Baron. And Tad wouldn't be ... he wouldn't be ..."

They left him sitting by Tad's side, willing life into the boy, and moved out into the corridor to give him some privacy. As they did so, Cal arrived and swept Rienne into his arms, kissing her soundly. Bull watched their reunion with wistful pleasure. He'd never had the comfort of a life mate, and now that he was growing older, he felt the lack. It was one of the reasons why he was so angry with Robin for throwing away his relationship with Sullyan.

Cal and Rienne parted at last, each smiling into the other's eyes. A small sound intruded on their pleasure and they turned to see Robin in the doorway, his face white and strained, his eyes dark with pain. There was a strange look on his face and, fearing the worst, Rienne gasped and made to push past him. Robin stopped her.

"He's just the same," he said, his voice dull and toneless. "I'm doing no good here. But I can't just sit back and ignore what's happened. If I can't help Tad by giving him my blood, I'll avenge what's been done to him by giving him Parren's. I'm going to hunt that bastard down like the vermin he is and make him pay for all the hurt he's caused. I should have done it long ago. Now, I'm going to put that right."

They stared at his grim determination. Cal folded his arms.

"Well, you're not going alone. Vassa's just told me we're on a rest tour now, so I'm coming with you."

Bull moved forward. "Me, too."

Their assertions drew a glare from the young Major.

"What, you think I need a nursemaid? I can take care of myself, thank you, and Parren for that matter. I don't need the two of you blundering along behind me. Just leave me to deal with it."

"No," said Cal.

Bull saw the look of surprise Rienne gave him. He was growing in confidence and stature daily. His training, and his association with the men of the Manor, was bringing out a new maturity in him.

Bull grinned mirthlessly. "Looks like you have no choice. We're coming, and that's that. Rienne, get word to the General about where we've gone, will you? He'll understand."

Robin seethed, but there was nothing he could do. "Oh, very well," he spat. "Just don't get in my way."

He stormed off. Cal shot Rienne an apologetic look and blew her a kiss as he turned. She smiled back, shaking her head, and returned to the sick boy's side.

Bull and Cal followed Robin down to the horse lines. Robin was yelling for Solet long before they got there. The irascible stablemaster had all the horses of the invasion forces to check over and was in no mood to be gracious.

"If you want horses, Major, you'll have to fetch them yourself. Can't you see I'm run off my feet? Find me another twenty cadets to cope with this lot, if you want to be useful. If not, you'll have to fend for yourselves." He stumped away, muttering curses.

Robin swore, but there was no help for it. The three men grabbed what halters or ropes they could find and strode down to the pasture where Solet kept the riding stallions. Robin couldn't take his chestnut, Torka, as he had ridden him in Andaryon and the beast deserved a rest. Instead, he haltered Tobias, the dark bay colt he was training up to be Torka's replacement.

Bull collected his usual stocky bay and Cal took Thunder, the dark bay usually ridden by Taran. His own iron-gray was as in need of a rest as Torka.

Having caught their own mounts, they were obliged to brush them down and saddle them too, as the horse lines were seething with scuttling stable boys and tired horses. Robin had Tobias harnessed in short order. He didn't wait for Bull or Cal, but leaped into the saddle and rode out into the lane, leaving the other two men to follow as best they could. They glared at his back and exchanged long-suffering looks.

They caught up with him before he left the Manor grounds, and Bull asked him how he intended to conduct the search for Parren. "He does have a day's start on us, you know."

Robin's temper flared. "I do know that! I intend to run the bastard down wherever he's fled to, so if you can't keep the pace, Bull, you'd better stay behind."

"But where will he have gone?" asked Cal as they spurred out of the Manor gates, heading north.

Robin stared grimly ahead between Tobias's dark ears. "If he was in the pay of the Baron, he'll be running to his master. I doubt he knows the Baron's been imprisoned. He'll get a nasty shock if he reaches Port Loxton ahead of us, but I don't intend to let him get that far. I'm going to search the Loxton road all day and all night if necessary, and if you two really want to help, you'll keep your eyes peeled and your mouths shut.

"Now, *ride!*"

✣ ✣ ✣ ✣ ✣

It was around midmorning when Sullyan was woken by a tap at

her door. She opened her eyes to a shaft of sunlight that slipped through the gap in the heavy drapes at the windows. She blinked, amazed. She hardly ever slept past dawn, but the events of the previous day and her lack of sleep for some hours after Taran had left her could take the blame.

She sat up, calling an entry to whoever had knocked and trying to summon some composure in case it was Taran.

It was Norkis, with fresh fellan, bread, and honey.

"I'm sorry if I woke you, my Lady." The page bowed as he deposited the tray upon the bedside table. He took up the one Deshan had left the night before.

Sullyan was arrested by his tone and form of address, which were unusually polite. Norkis had the same mischievous temperament and penchant for practical jokes as Tad. It was rare to see him follow court protocol so strictly. Today, although cheerful, he seemed unusually respectful.

"Is everything all right? Is Aeyron recovering? And his Majesty?"

The page smiled. "Oh, yes, my Lady, both will be well. His Majesty asked me to convey his very best wishes, and he asks that he be allowed to attend you once you are refreshed and dressed."

Sullyan frowned. "Why such formality? This is me, remember, not some visiting foreign monarch. Be off with you, and you may tell Timar I will be very happy to meet with him in his rooms in an hour or so. And you can take that fawning humility off your face!"

Norkis gave her a huge grin, which transformed him back into the jocular imp she knew so well. "I think you might find things have changed a little, Lady Brynne!"

He was gone before she could demand an explanation.

Sighing, she slid out of bed and poured herself a cup of fellan, feeling the pull of her thigh wound and muscles not yet recovered from her ordeals. She still had a headache from her skull fracture, but the split lip and the bruises on her face were all but healed. She headed for the bathing pool for a long soak to deal with her other hurts.

While luxuriating in blood-warm water, she used her metaforce to soothe her muscles and the throbbing in her head. Yet she couldn't control the pounding of her heart as she recalled how close she and Taran had come last night to giving in to the release they both craved. Goosebumps prickled her skin. Would he understand? Would he realize why she had allowed things to go that far?

She hadn't really intended for it to happen just then, but the opportunity had presented itself and the timing was right. Better to deal with it now, before the high from Taran's achievement in the stone circle faded. She could only hope he would take the time to sort through his feelings and realize exactly what had occurred during the night.

She had always been acutely aware of the depth of Taran's feelings for her. They had worked and trained closely together over the past two years, and because Artesans were naturally passionate and emotional beings, hiding such an intense emotion as the love they both felt was impossible. He knew she shared his deep attachment, and it would be a short and easy step from their present strong friendship to a full physical relationship. And that could be very damaging to them both.

Under normal circumstances, with Robin's love to surround and satisfy her, she was well able to keep her other feelings in check. Without his abandonment of her, she would have handled last night's close call much more calmly. She was under no illusions about her own emotional state now that she had lost her life mate's love and support—not to mention the effect her pregnancy was having on her.

But she was bound to Robin, and her vows had not been taken lightly. Whatever Taran thought he had sensed last night, she had no intention of proving false to them, no matter Robin's current opinion. Fortunately, her judgment of Taran's new capability to control the Fire of his deeper passions had proved well-founded. Despite her low energy levels and her stricken soul, she hadn't lost her touch.

Still, she would have to face him soon and offer her apologies for not preparing him for the ordeal.

Emerging from the pool, she dried herself and donned clean clothes. She chose a simple royal blue gown rather than her combat leathers. They were becoming a little too tight now that her belly had finally begun to swell. Soon she would be unable to wear them at all.

Taking a last swallow of fellan and a final morsel of bread and honey, she left her rooms.

She encountered a few servants and retainers on her way to Pharikian's rooms. Without exception, they bowed most respectfully to her; unusually so, she thought. Was this what Norkis had hinted at? She supposed that as Aeyron's rescuer, along with Taran, she was experiencing the gratitude they felt. Smiling graciously at each one, she continued on to Pharikian's suite.

Norkis was back on duty at his master's door. He grinned at her as she approached, sweeping her a full courtly bow with an elegant flourish.

"My Lady Brynne, his gracious Majesty, the Hierarch of Andaryon, awaits you within."

Playing along, and grateful for his lighthearted tone, she returned a graceful curtsey, thanking him prettily. She was pleased when he couldn't keep the blush from his cheeks as he ushered her inside Pharikian's drawing room. He closed the door behind her.

The room was warm and bright with sunlight, the windows

open to the summer breeze. Through them, the blowsy heads of roses could be seen in the garden outside. Their rich and heady scent pervaded the air. Deshan, who had been sitting by the window, turned in surprise and stood as she entered. He crossed to her, extending his hands in greeting.

"Brynne, my dear! It was Timar's intention to call on *you* this morning. How are you feeling? Are you sure you should be out of bed? That was a very nasty crack on the head you took."

She was glad Deshan could still address her as he always did, but narrowed her eyes at him all the same. His spoken concern was for her injuries, but his eyes lingered just a little too long on her belly.

"You need not fuss, Deshan," she said, giving him a smile to take the bite from her tone. "I am perfectly able to look after myself, you know. It is Timar and Aeyron who need you now. I would not distract you from them."

The door to Pharikian's bedchamber opened and the Hierarch came into the room. He looked healthier than she had seen him for some time, and the welcoming smile on his lips melted her heart. The love she felt for this tall, majestic man was the love she would have given her father had he lived. She stepped into his offered embrace as if she were coming home.

Deshan withdrew to the window and stood admiring the view while they shared an intimate reunion. Both could feel the tremor of the other's body, brought on by intense emotions. Pharikian radiated love, relief, and admiration, as well as a deep and heartfelt gratitude. Sullyan's emanations were more complex because she kept secrets from this much-loved man, and had suffered losses with which she had not yet come to terms. Yet she felt so safe and natural in his arms that she knew the time for secrets was over. She badly needed his support and approval.

He held her away from him at last, the better to study her face.

He examined her bruises and the faded swell of her lip, and then she felt his request for contact so he could satisfy himself as to her spiritual well-being. She could never refuse him that, and so her pupils dilated as she allowed him access to her metaforce.

Finally satisfied, he drew her to the table and bade her sit, both of them bathed in the warm sunlight. There was a crystal flagon on the table and three glasses. Deshan poured the clear, red liquid for them all. Sullyan raised her fine brows at the physician. He knew she did not normally drink alcohol.

"Take it, my dear. It will do you good."

Suspecting him of covertly trying to medicate her, she sipped at it, but it was only a refreshingly light and fruity cordial with a faint hint of herbs. He grinned unrepentantly at her look.

Pharikian was still watching her. "My dear Brynne," he said, his voice husky with emotion, "I can't begin to thank you for what you have done. My entire realm is in your debt. The deed will never be forgotten."

"I did not do it alone, Timar," she demurred. "If not for Taran's rescue, both Aeyron and I still might have perished at the Baron's hands."

"Yes, so I have heard," he replied. "I have had brief words with your Adept this morning. He seemed rather preoccupied, I thought."

She cast down her eyes, coloring slightly. Perhaps Taran had not understood after all. She would have to speak with him and explain.

"He has also been through much recently. I am deeply in his debt for his care of me. He rescued the King's son too, you know, with the help of two friends."

"Yes, child, there is much to be told concerning what happened in Albia. But that can wait." He fixed her with a loving yet compelling look. "Brynne. Do you not have something to tell me? Something of significant importance?"

She cast down her gaze yet again, unable to meet his eyes. "Ah, Timar, you see too deeply."

She missed his fleeting smile, but she heard the echo of it in his voice. "I fear you overestimate the scope of my abilities. I have also had some speech with my son this morning, and he has told me part of the tale."

She looked up quickly, concerned. "How is his Highness?"

He patted her hand. "He is doing very well, thanks to you, and I will not be sidetracked!"

She couldn't help but smile. "You do not need me to tell you, though, do you?"

"I would have it from your own lips, my dear. As would Deshan."

"Ah, yes," she said archly, turning an accusing eye on Deshan. "I gather you were always of the opinion that I would heal well enough to conceive, Master Physician. Yet you did not think it politic to inform me?"

He spread his hands, unrepentant. "How could I so jeopardize my reputation, Lady? But I need not have worried. You have proved me right yet again."

Pharikian leaned toward her, taking her hands between his. "So it is true, then? Aeyron was not deceived or confused? You truly carry a child?"

The tears that shone in his eyes were mirrored in her own.

"Yes, Timar, it is true. Robin will be a father in a little over two months' time."

The men exchanged a look and Deshan eyed her slim form. "Are you quite sure about that, my dear? You have barely begun to show."

With a wordless sigh, she held out a hand to the physician. The expansion of her pupils told Deshan that he would be

44

permitted an examination. Both she and the Hierarch sat in silence as Deshan used his deft hands as well as his metaforce to verify her words. Finally, he released her and stepped away.

"You're quite right, my dear." There was wonder in his voice. "You will give birth in around ten weeks' time. The babe is very small and delicate, but he's perfect." He grinned. "However, I think I should warn you. I sensed that he's getting ready for a spurt of growth. You should resign yourself to wearing gowns from now on."

She smiled back, relieved to hear him confirm what she already knew. The Hierarch, quite overcome, folded her yet again into his embrace, murmuring words of congratulation and pride.

The conversation then turned to the events in the stone circle at Port Loxton. What Aeyron had so far been able to relate to his father was sketchy at best, and so she sat awhile, drinking the cordial which she was sure had been laced with one of Deshan's herbal restoratives, and told the two men, as succinctly as she could, everything that had transpired since she had been forced to cocoon the Hierarch within his own psyche.

He listened in silence. Regret showed openly in his yellow eyes when she was done.

"I'm so sorry I wasn't stronger. I failed you when you needed my support. You must have felt very alone once the King had cast you out."

"I had other good friends, Timar. I was very fortunate. Without them, I do not know what would have happened."

"Yes," mused the Hierarch, "we really must see about some kind of recognition for Taran Elijah."

"I have a suggestion to make on that subject." Sullyan got no further because there was a tap on the door and Norkis pushed his blond head into the room.

"Excuse me, Majesty, but his Highness has awoken once more

and is asking for the Lady Brynne. Her Highness the Princess is concerned that he will overexert himself if she doesn't come."

Sullyan stood at once, looking expectantly at Pharikian.

"No, my dear, go on your own. I will see Aeyron presently. It's you he needs now."

Slightly puzzled by his words, she dipped a graceful curtsey and followed Norkis from the room. She barely saw the significant look which passed between the two men at the table.

Chapter Four

Norkis escorted Sullyan along the corridors, although she knew her way well enough. As she neared the Prince's private rooms, she saw a tall, lean figure with a long face coming toward her.

Her eyes lit up at the sight of him and he returned her smile. To her astonishment, and before she could speak or react, Marik cast himself upon one knee before her and raised her right hand to his lips. He then stood and swept into a lavish, courtly bow.

"Ty, whatever are you doing?" she exclaimed, clasping his arms as he straightened.

He grinned at her with his usual pleasure and hugged her to him. "Oh, Brynne, I'm so pleased to see you. I've been hearing such tales about what you did. There's not a man in all the realm who wouldn't fall at your feet for gratitude."

She shook her head. This was all becoming too much. "Ty, why is everyone behaving so strangely? The Heir has returned and the Hierarch is restored. Can we not all go back to normal?"

"Ah, but what is normal?" he said, annoyingly enigmatic.

She glared at him. "If you will not answer me one simple question in a simple fashion, then I will not tender you my apology."

That got his attention and he dropped his strange manner. "Apology? What on earth for?"

Now that she had come to it, she felt abashed, but she would not allow herself to turn from it. He had a right to know, especially as he had really been the first one to guess.

"Your instincts were correct, my friend," she said. "I apologize for ever doubting you."

He frowned, and she realized Aeyron had not told everyone of her condition, nor had the Hierarch spread the news. She was grateful.

"You were right, Ty. On the day Aeyron's ransom note arrived, you believed I was pregnant and I told you I was not. I was wrong. You were very perceptive."

Marik's pale eyes opened wide and he stared at her in shock. "Then what you said ... about Rykan ...?"

"Oh, that was true enough. But it seems my body has healed itself of that blemish, and quite without my knowledge. And it did so some time ago, for I am nearly seven months pregnant."

An incredible smile broke over his face. For once, the instant reaction was not to stare in disbelief at her still-slim form, but to crush her to him in a glad and tearful embrace which left them both gasping. They struggled with their emotions while Norkis waited impatiently a few paces away.

Marik finally released her. "Oh, I'm so happy for you!" he said, wiping his eyes. "This just puts the final shine on it. Does Timar know?"

"Yes, he knows. But it is still not common knowledge and I would beg you not to spread it around just yet. There are others I need to tell first, and I would rather they heard it from me than from gossip. You may tell Idrimar, but no one else.

"Ty, there is more to this than you know. I cannot say more just now. Aeyron has called for me and I must attend him. I will speak with you later, if I may. Can you wait?"

He was struck by her serious tone and the unfathomable look in her eyes. His pleasure and excitement dimmed a little. "Yes, yes, of course. Whatever you say."

She squeezed his hand and moved on.

The Hierarch's page led her into Aeyron's bedchamber and left her there, closing the door in his wake. There was no one in attendance on the still form in the bed, and she wondered at that. She had expected his sister or squire, at least, if not one of the healers. Instead, the Prince lay alone, breathing quietly, his body covered by a single, snowy sheet. He appeared to be asleep.

She moved toward him and ran her fingers lightly down his cheek, watching his face. He stirred slightly at her touch and opened his eyes. She immediately saw the fear of loss in them and gave a gasp of pain.

"Oh, Aeyron, you are not alone! I am here with you. You are safe now, you are home."

He held his good hand out to her in a silent plea and she bent to him, gathering his gaunt frame into her embrace, careful of his strapped ribs. She could feel every bone in his body through his thin night robe.

She barely heard his whisper. "I thought you'd left me."

Her heart contracted. Had his mind been affected by his ordeal? She murmured comforting words into his hair as she held him and felt the tension leave his body. He began to tremble violently. She stroked his back and face as he let his emotions run their course. Her soul ached for his pain.

She remembered how it felt to be in terrible pain and in terror of dying under torture, never to see loved ones again, never to breathe the air of home. In what he had believed to be his final hour, Aeyron had been granted a friendly presence. He had clung to that presence like a lifeline, only to be faced with the possibility of seeing that friend tortured and broken beside him, consigned to the same fate.

Despite that trial, he had been able to offer her comfort, and they had shared many intimate secrets in those dark and desperate hours. They were inextricably linked now, bound by suffering and by love, and neither would ever be the same again. Small wonder, she thought, that he should take some time to come to terms.

His shuddering gradually calmed and she was able to lay him back onto his mound of pillows. She looked him over, pleased to see that his wounds had been properly tended by Deshan and were covered by clean, soft bandages. The room smelled of fresh linen and flowers.

"Deshan tells me you saved my hand." Aeyron's voice was husky, his pale yellow eyes damp.

She smiled gently down on him. "I am glad, Highness. Taran and I did all we could. You will be well before you know it, and when you are ready, I have some exercises in swordplay that will strengthen your muscles and teach you how to compensate for your injury. It might even become an advantage for you, as any opponent would think you reduced in skill. I can show you how to convince them otherwise."

He responded to the encouragement in her voice and stretched forth his left hand again. She sat by his side in order to take it. Physical contact seemed to be very important to him just now.

"Please, Brynne, you must not call me 'Highness.' I have already asked you to use my name. Your position here among us has changed because of what you have done. You are one of us, now."

She was almost overcome by his words. "Oh, Aeyron. That is the nicest thing anyone has said to me for a long time. And I confess I have been feeling very alone lately. You know the reason why. But the fact remains that I have no real home now. I am a hybrid. I belong nowhere."

The Prince's eyes fixed hers with an odd gaze. "Then we must change that, mustn't we?"

She smiled at him, grateful for his attempts at comfort.

Not wanting to tire him, she changed the subject and they spoke of easier topics. She had no desire to burden him with her troubles. He needed love, care, and peace, not to listen to the extent of her sorrow and loss. By the time his eyes were closing with fatigue, he looked like a man who had made a decision.

Sullyan rose and kissed him lightly on the brow. "You should sleep now. Do not fear. I will be within call. Should you need me, at any hour of the day or night, just reach for my pattern. I will always be open to you."

Comforted by her presence and her words, he was asleep before she reached the door. She slipped out of the apartment, closing the door soundlessly behind her. As she turned to go, she came face to face with Taran.

✣ ✣ ✣ ✣ ✣

The Adept had spent the dark hours since he had left Sullyan's bed deep in thought. Once his tears had dried and he'd been able to unclench the arms he had wrapped about his sore heart and aching body, a startling realization had come to him.

His feelings for her had changed.

Oh, she was still the most precious thing in his life, still the person he loved more deeply than anyone he had ever loved before, but now—finally—he was able to control it.

The utter shock of this revelation gave him pause. What was different?

It wasn't just his heartfelt desire to spare her any more pain, although that was a strong consideration. And it wasn't his highly-developed sense of right and wrong that had stayed the hand which had longed to caress her into gentle and loving fulfillment. Those feelings were just as strong and they caused an awakening of arousal within him even as he considered them.

No. It was his power over them that had changed, and it hit

him like a blow between the eyes. He was now Adept-elite, albeit unconfirmed, and he had achieved influence over Fire. As she had told him before, his passions were a form of Fire, a very strong form, and that Fire was part of his makeup. It was part of his spirit and his soul, but a part that he could now channel and control.

Then, hot on the heels of this understanding, came the shocking realization of what she had done for him, the tremendous risk she had willingly taken. It crashed over him like a thunderous wave and he wept afresh. The true depth of her love for him was suddenly revealed, and he couldn't believe she had found the strength to do what she'd done in her exhausted and grief-wracked state. He couldn't quantify the debt of gratitude he owed her.

He had sat on his bed, alone in the dark, trying to recover some composure. How could he face her now? But then his new-found confidence, his new control, assured him that he could. Instead of his usual embarrassment, he felt a deep and uncomplicated gratitude. If anything, his love for her had intensified, but it had also settled into something less strident, something more akin to a merging of souls. He would never again feel the shame and sense of inadequacy that had been his father's unwitting legacy.

And now here she was, standing before him, searching him for signs of understanding or of hurt.

"Taran," she said, holding his gaze, "can you ever forgive me?"

"*Forgive* you?" he cried, coming close and taking her by the shoulders. "You give me the most precious gift in the whole world and ask me if I can *forgive* you?" He shook his head in disbelief and was relieved when she smiled at him. "But you took a huge risk, you know."

She shook her head. "No, I did not. It was no risk."

"You had that much faith in me?" He frowned. "But those

feelings were so strong! How could you possibly have known I'd be able to control them?"

Now she did look away, unable to deal with the intensity in his eyes and unwilling to let him see her own reaction to the depth of his feelings.

"I saw what you did at the circle, remember? I sensed your struggle. I know what you overcame in order to pass through the Fire. You did not just contend against your own perceived strength, my friend; you wrestled with your deep-rooted insecurity, your lack of self-confidence, of self-esteem. And you won. I always knew you would, one day. Oh, how proud your father would be to see you now! But you must know that the intensity of your feelings for me and your inability to deal with them were stunting your growth. Even had it been possible for us to be to each other what you desired, that intensity would have hampered your development. You called it a risk, but I always knew we would have to face that trial someday, that we would be forced to confront the depths of our passion and the strength of our friendship. I am so glad I was able to help you accept it. It is an integral part of who you are, and now, you will find it easier to stretch and grow. You will be able to call upon the vast well of your love and emotion to strengthen your powers, instead of running away from it. This was the one thing I could not teach you. You had to work through it yourself."

Her liquid eyes gazed up at him and he found he could return her regard without shying from the ache of his desire. He had assimilated it and accepted it. Instead of trying to shut it out and turn from it, he was able to gather it to him and use it, with no shame or reservations.

He stepped closer to her and took her into his arms. She entered his embrace willingly, letting him feel the warmth of her approval. She accepted the wash of his devotion with no reproach.

"Taran," she said, pushing away at last, "I believe Timar has questions still unanswered which only we can satisfy. I also would hear his suggestions as to how we proceed in the matter of the Baron and Lord Corbyn. Will you accompany me to his rooms?"

The Adept nodded. They linked arms as they walked companionably back to the Hierarch's private suite, finally completely at ease with each other.

✤ ✤ ✤ ✤ ✤

Riding at speed for the rest of the day, Robin allowed only the briefest of halts to breathe the horses. He was poor company, being single-mindedly engrossed in the pursuit of his prey, and the other two soon gave up trying to talk to him. The grunted replies they got when he deigned to answer at all did nothing to encourage conversation.

They had little energy for anything but the ride anyway. Robin kept up a fast pace, only slowing when he thought he spied an area where they might find tracks. All the Manor horses bore iron shoes, and all those shoes were marked. The senior officers' mounts all bore unique scores, but the majority of the horses bore shoes with one nick on the off hind and two on the near fore. And in the early afternoon, at the ford of a small stream, Cal spotted recent hoof prints bearing these marks.

Robin smiled in grim satisfaction and set off again at an even faster pace.

Since then, they had seen the distinctive spoor twice more; once in the softer earth of a plowed field that bordered the road, and once at a stand of trees where the horse's rider had obviously stopped for the same reason Bull had. That, the big man reflected, had been a fortuitous comfort break.

It was coming on for dusk, yet Robin showed no signs of stopping for the night. Tired and hungry, the other two swapped glances, each vying not to be the one to voice the question. It eventually fell to Bull to say, "Robin, where do you intend to stop tonight? We can't track him in the dark, you know. He could be nearly there by now, and if he is, breaking our necks or our horses' legs in the dark won't help anyone. Least of all young Tad."

Robin turned a savage look on him. "I'm not stopping, Bull. If you want to, go right ahead. It makes no difference to me."

Bull sighed. "You'll do yourself no good. If you drive yourself all night and catch up with him exhausted, how will you take him? I bet Parren's not pushing himself half so hard."

The young man sneered. "If he isn't, he won't be nearly there, will he? All the more reason for me to hurry. I don't want him there ahead of me, Bull. I want to catch him out in the open, alone and friendless, like he caught Tad and Ozella. I don't want him to have any other choice but to fight me. He's not getting away with it this time."

A dreadful certainty entered Bull's mind. "You're going to kill him, aren't you? You've no intention of taking him back to the Manor to be tried by the King. You're going to slaughter him."

"Does he deserve any less?" yelled Robin. "Does he deserve the King's justice after what he's done? What chance did Tad or Ozella have? What justice did he give them? None! He slaughtered Ozella. Now I'm going to show him how that feels."

The tears in the Major's dark eyes prevented Bull from remonstrating with him further. The big man gave Cal a resigned look and they rode on into the night, following Robin's rigid and unresponsive back.

Despite his words and driven state, Robin did finally call a halt around an hour after midnight. There was no moon and the road was hard to see. He wouldn't risk Tobias's legs, no matter how incessantly his soul screamed at him to keep on riding until he ran Parren down. He stopped in a small stand of trees, unsaddling the sweaty colt and rubbing him down without a word to the others. They followed suit and broke open the meager supplies they had found time to grab before following Robin to the horse lines.

It was a cold meal. Robin refused everything except water. He was too keyed up to eat. He cast himself down upon the ground and was asleep in minutes. Weary though he was, Bull didn't want to sleep. He thought there was a good chance that Robin would ride off without them come the dawn. However, he knew that he and Cal were too weary to set watch, so he tried to lay out tendrils of metaforce as he slipped into slumber, hoping they would alert him if Robin tried to leave alone.

The big man simply could not let Robin face Parren on his own. Now he knew the young Major intended to settle old scores with Parren, he feared that Robin's sense of honor would bind him to promises he shouldn't make. Bull intended to ensure this didn't happen.

It could have been either his powers or his military training that alerted him the following morning as soon as Robin stirred. Nudging Cal with his foot, he climbed to his feet, stretching cramped and aching muscles. Robin again refused any food and saddled Tobias in stony silence. The unappealing prospect of yet another grim ride in morose company faced the other two men.

Around midmorning, more tracks were found. "He's moving slowly," said Cal, measuring the strides with his eyes. "Maybe he's not sure of his reception at Port Loxton, or maybe he's heard of the Baron's arrest."

He got no reply. Robin was staring fixedly ahead, a hungry gleam in his eyes. Bull's gaze was unfocused, a sure sign he was communing with someone.

The big man shook his head to clear his thoughts and turned to his companions. "The King's returning to Port Loxton today and

Blaine's going with him. The General has to stay close to Elias to take him to Andaryon when the Hierarch's ready for their talks, so Vassa's in charge at the Manor. We have orders to take Parren before the King in Loxton if we manage to apprehend him."

Robin made no response and Bull frowned. "Did you hear me, Major?"

Robin glowered at him but didn't speak. Bull continued. "The Baron will be put on trial as soon as the King has all the facts, but he wants to get his apology to the Hierarch out of the way first. And the timing of that will depend on the recovery of Prince Aeyron and the trial of Lord Corbyn. I expect Elias will ask that Corbyn be brought here afterward, to speak at the Baron's trial."

There was still no response from Robin. Bull tried again, more gently this time.

"Rienne reports that young Tad is still holding on. They risked taking more blood from his mother this morning, and she thinks he's getting a little stronger. He's got more color in his face now. He'll be all right, Rob, you'll see. He's a tough kid, that one."

Robin thumped his heels into the colt's flanks and the horse squealed in startlement as it bounded forward. Bull just saw the glitter of tears in Robin's dark eyes as the horse bolted away. Sighing, Bull and Cal spurred after the Major.

During a very brief stop around midday to water the horses and give them a little food, Robin finally gave in to his hunger. He must have known that weakness due to an empty belly would do him no favors. Bull was sure they must be very close to their quarry now. Loxton Forest was only twelve miles away. When they rode on again, Robin took a short detour up the side of a small hill. From its crown, they could see the dark mass of the forest on the horizon. More importantly, they could also see the rest of the road as it wound toward the green canopy.

A lone rider on an unmistakably fine horse was just visible in the distance, riding purposefully toward the trees.

Robin pumped a fist triumphantly. "Yes!" He turned to Bull. "How far away do you reckon he is?"

Bull shaded his eyes against the sunlight. "Two, maybe three miles?"

Robin almost purred. "And around ten more to the forest." He stared at his companions. "Are you still willing to help?"

They gave him startled glances tinged with irritation. "You know we are!" Bull said. "We have orders to take him."

Robin ignored the comment. "Then this is what we'll do. I'm going off across country to work my way around in front of him. I don't want to take the chance of losing him in the forest if he runs for it. You two follow him and close up if you can, but do it without him seeing you. I'll let you know when I'm in position and then we'll show ourselves."

"And then what?" pressed Bull, trying to force Robin into accepting Blaine's command.

Robin refused to be cornered. "That'll be up to Parren," he said curtly, and set his heels to Tobias's flanks. The young stallion wheeled away and bore Robin down the western side of the hill at great speed, the Major lying along his neck.

Bull shook his head as he stared after Robin. "I don't like this, Cal. I've no love for Parren and normally I'd have no qualms about watching someone spill his guts, but we have specific orders and I don't intend to disobey them. Robin has been in enough trouble over the years on that score anyway. Parren obviously carries vital evidence against the Baron, and if Robin kills him, it might help Reen's case. It certainly won't help ours! We're going to have to do everything we can to convince him to heed us."

"Agreed," said Cal as they made their way off the hill and back to the road. "But don't forget, I'm still under his command. We may be off duty, but I can't disobey a direct order from him, no matter what the General's said. It'll be up to you to sway him if he won't listen."

Bull pursed his lips. Cal was right, but that wouldn't help them if Parren turned nasty or—gods forfend—managed to kill Robin.

"Let's just catch up with him and see what happens," said Bull. "Maybe Robin'll come to his senses once we've actually caught the treacherous bastard."

Bull and Cal followed the road at a good speed, never catching sight of Robin off to their left. They came to a bend in the road and saw their quarry not a mile ahead. He was loping along at a hand-canter, his horse burdened with saddle packs, and he wasn't looking behind him. Nevertheless, the two men stayed out of his sight and Bull reached for Robin.

The Major had pushed the colt hard and gone as straight as he could, cutting corners off the winding road. He had managed to gain about two miles on Parren. He was letting the colt blow when Bull contacted him. Yet Tobias had been bred for stamina, and he was young. He soon regained his wind.

Receiving Robin's acknowledgement, Cal and Bull stepped up their pace and came out onto the road in full view of Parren should he turn. They had covered half the distance between them before Parren's gray swiveled its ears and alerted its rider to company. The renegade captain thumped his heels into his beast's sides as soon as he realized he was being followed. He whipped the gray to a gallop.

He was staring over his shoulder at his pursuers when his stallion swerved abruptly, nearly throwing him from its back.

Parren wrenched on its mouth, hauling its head back, and the battle-trained beast skidded to an earth-showering stop. Robin sat Tobias nonchalantly in the middle of the road. He stared expressionlessly at the thin man before him.

Bull and Cal slowed their pace and came up behind, cutting

off Parren's retreat. He spared them one venomous but dismissive glance before turning all his attention on Robin.

The Major sat his horse casually, one hand lightly on the reins, the other resting on his thigh. He regarded Parren steadily with cold, unflinching eyes. Parren stared insolently back, betraying no sign of nervousness or fear.

"So, what's this, Captain?" said Robin, his voice deceptively mild, his bleak eyes roving over the packs attached to the gray's saddle. "Not *deserting*, are we?"

Parren gave him a sneer. "I don't desert those who have my best interests at heart."

"That'd be Glinn Parren, then," Bull quipped, drawing a snigger from Cal and a look of pure poison from Parren.

Robin's mental voice crashed into Bull's mind. *Shut up, Bull! Leave this to me.*

The big man winced with the force of Robin's reprimand and gave him a reproachful look. It was ignored.

Parren was unaware of the silent exchange. "You're very brave, Tamsen, coming three against one." There was outright challenge in his pale eyes. "But it's only what I'd have expected. You never did have the skill to take me on your own."

Robin remained cool. "Oh, I won't need any help, Parren, believe me. I wasn't the one who had to resort to dirty tricks the last time we fought, if my memory serves. Needed your lap-dogs at your heels that day, didn't you? What does that say about *your* skill and courage?"

Parren's already sallow face turned paler, the long scar down his right cheek standing out lividly against the drained skin. "They were only there as backup in case you resorted to witchery!" he snarled. "I didn't need anyone else that day, and I don't need anyone now!"

"Careful," advised Robin, still using that maddeningly

reasonable tone. "You might just end up with a scar on the other cheek to match the one you already have. It might even balance your face. It certainly couldn't make you any less attractive to the ladies."

Parren's breath caught raggedly in his throat and his face turned a mottled purple, a most unpleasant sight.

"And who was it gave me that scar?" His voice was low and savage. "Your pet witch, wasn't it? Not you! You've always needed a woman to do your fighting for you. Always hiding under her skirts, weren't you? Never man enough to stand up for yourself. Well, she showed her true colors in the end, didn't she? First she goes off with that demon lord, then she sleeps with the peasant from Hyecombe! There's loyalty for you. What's the matter, *Major*? Not man enough to satisfy her? Not even as good as a demon outlander or a peasant farmer, that's what I heard."

Now it was Robin's turn to redden in rage. Parren saw he had hit a raw nerve and laughed. "All over Port Loxton, it was, so Denny told me. They were laughing at you in the King's barracks, just like they've always done. Oh, we all knew why you were brought to the Manor from that run-down garrison in Garon. Nothing to do with your battle skills, that's for sure! More to do with your pretty face and that other weapon you hold in your hand. Only you failed there too, didn't you?"

Robin was thoroughly enraged now. "Shut up, Parren!" Bull hissed at him to calm down, but he ignored the warning. "How dare you speak like that? How *dare* you insult my wife? I'll make you rue the day you ever set eyes on either of us, you foul-mouthed bastard!"

Parren smiled lazily. "Me, foul-mouthed? I'm not the one who's resorted to swearing."

"Get off that horse," snapped Robin. "We'll have this out here and now, unless you're too scared to face me."

61

Parren gave a harsh bark of laughter. "What, and have you turn your unnatural powers on me? Not bloody likely! I can't trust you to fight fair—not with these two thugs at your back."

Robin calmed abruptly and Bull could see his resolve stiffening. The big man eyed him warily. Robin was formulating a plan, and Bull knew he wasn't going to like it.

Robin dismounted slowly, keeping his hands away from his sword hilt. His voice was tightly controlled. "A duel, then, Parren. Like before, only this time just you and me. Bull and Cal will stay well back and leave us to it. It'll be your skill against mine, as fair as we can make it. What do you say? It's the best and only chance you'll get. We've been ordered to take you before the King, but Bull and Cal will honor my word once it's given. Which would you rather, Parren? My justice or the King's?"

Parren snorted. "Justice? What justice?"

He eyed Robin icily, weighing his options. With Bull and Cal at his back and the Major before him, Parren must know he stood very little chance of escaping. Even if he spurred away and got past Robin, Cal and Bull would pursue him. He would be unlikely to lose them in the forest. Besides, the opportunity to kill Robin must be very tempting. If he succeeded, Bull wouldn't put it past him to attempt the same with him and Cal.

"If I agree to this," the Captain said, "what's the deal?"

"A straight duel, no deals. Just you and me. No interference. Either I kill you or you kill me."

Parren shook his head in disgust. "And if I do, your two thugs will jump me. Not good enough, Tamsen."

Before Bull could step in, Robin added, "I give you my word that neither Bull nor Cal will touch you. I'll even send them back if you won't take their word. Is that good enough for you? You get to ride away from here unmolested if you win. That is, if you still can."

Parren held Robin's gaze. "And what of your treacherous mind powers? Swear not to use them, will you? How can I trust that?"

Robin spread his hands. "I don't know how to convince you, but I can't use them and fight effectively at the same time. Surely you've heard that before? Why else do you think we fight with steel if we could just stand back and blast our enemies with Fire or Earth power? It takes too much concentration, too much energy. We'd be cut down before we could gather enough force to protect ourselves. All I could do would be to use it to numb the pain of any wounds and maybe staunch the bleeding. I'll give you my word not to do that, but I can't make you believe me. Now, are we going to stand around jawing all day, or shall we settle this once and for all?"

Chapter Five

Parren sat a moment more before dismounting, eyeing Bull and Cal suspiciously as he did so. Robin curtly beckoned them down and Bull gave him a flat stare.

"Major, don't do this."

"Shut up, Bull."

"You heard the King's orders. We're to take him in, not kill him! What about the evidence he holds?"

"Bull, you'll obey me or suffer the consequences! I'm going to do this, whatever you say. I've had enough of his poison and it's time he got what he deserves. Now take the horses over there and leave us to it. If you don't, I'll make you. You too, Cal."

Bull held his stare as long as he dared, though Robin's threat to use his superior powers on them told Bull just how determined he was. The hurt and fury in the Major's heart were plain to see, and this duel was the only way he could think of to alleviate the pain. He was ready to risk the King's wrath, being maimed, or even killed, just to have the satisfaction of carving some recompense out of Parren's scrawny hide.

Resignedly, wondering what on earth Blaine would say—not to mention Elias—Bull dismounted, took Tobias's reins, and led the horses over to the side of the road. Cal followed him.

Parren led his gray to the other side and tethered it to a tree. He shed his jacket and loosened his sword in its scabbard. Robin did the same, rolling up his shirt sleeves. He and Parren moved to face each other on the hard-packed dirt road.

"This is for Ozella, and Tad, too." Robin's voice was hard, his cold blue eyes locked firmly on Parren's. "Even if you survive this duel and decide to return to your treacherous master, Tad will live to tell his tale. You'll be hunted down like the vermin you are. There'll be no hiding place, Parren. Blaine will send others after you, and maybe Sullyan will come herself. The Baron will be no protection then."

Bull noticed Parren's confidence slip a little at the mention of Sullyan's name, but he recovered well. "You let me worry about that," he snapped, and suddenly came for Robin, his sword ringing free of its scabbard as he aimed a hard cut across Robin's chest.

The Major had been expecting such a move and was ready with a block. Their blades rang together as the first blows were struck.

Bull and Cal stood uncomfortably by the horses, watching the struggle before them. This bout was inevitable—it had been brewing for many years—but the outcome was by no means certain. Parren was a highly skilled and ruthless swordsman, and he had the added incentive of his freedom to urge him on.

Robin was no mean fighter himself, and he had the benefit of years of Sullyan's training behind him. She knew tricks Parren had never seen, and she had passed them on to Robin. The Major was young and fit, healthy and strong, and he was fighting for a cause, and for love. The maturity he had accrued over the last few years, whilst still not sufficient to completely erase his hotheadedness and hitherto unsuspected jealousy, was nonetheless deep enough to make him an opponent worthy of respect.

Parren would not make the mistake of underestimating him.

The day was warm and the fight vicious. Both men were soon sweating freely and bleeding from numerous wounds. Robin was keeping his promise not to use his metaforce, and Bull found himself wishing the Major wasn't quite so honorable. The loss of blood, although not currently serious, would inevitably sap his strength.

The big man pursed his lips, thankful that his saddle pack contained a full emergency medical kit. It looked like they would need it.

Robin and Parren fought across the dirt of the road, never letting up, giving no quarter, their lunges and parries, cuts and ripostes constantly testing each other's reflexes. Neither had received a deep or serious wound as yet, and Bull remembered their previous duel and how evenly matched they had been until Parren's corporal had tripped Robin.

It seemed the same applied now. Neither man could gain the upper hand; neither could get past the other's guard. Bull wanted to call out encouragements or warnings to Robin, but had been ordered to silence. He and Cal could only watch in anxious helplessness.

Robin found an opening and got in under Parren's guard, ripping a slash down his opponent's torso. Blood welled and Parren gasped in pain, but instead of being weakened and falling back with the shock of the wound, it seemed to enrage him all the more. He lunged at Robin, catching him off balance. The first three inches of Parren's blade sank into the big muscle of Robin's thigh. He staggered.

Bull and Cal gasped aloud and Bull took a step closer, catching himself before going too far. Robin recovered his footing and managed to avoid a second swipe from Parren that would have severed his arm. The sallow Captain's lunge took him past Robin and the Major got in a light cut across Parren's left upper arm.

They pursued each other relentlessly back and forth. The day was waning and Bull began to wonder how much longer they could last. The sound of rasping, pain-filled breaths was loud in the air; their movements grew slower, less graceful. Both were exhausted and nearing the end of their endurance. Soon, one of them would make a fatal mistake. He just prayed it wouldn't be Robin.

✣ ✣ ✣ ✣ ✣

Stinging sweat was running into Robin's eyes, blurring his vision. His initial rage and righteous anger had burned cold now, centering in his breast like a fist of ice. There was no room for thought, no sense of justice now. He was fighting for his life, pure and simple. There was only Parren and his deadly blade. Only dodge, survive, lunge, and attack.

He hadn't used his powers once. If he won, he wanted to know, wanted to be able to tell himself that he had stuck to his word. He would prove to himself that he was the stronger man, the more skilled fighter, without recourse to arcane powers. Yet he was weary. He was so weary he could hardly think of his next move. He couldn't hold on much longer.

✣ ✣ ✣ ✣ ✣

Parren saw the weariness in Robin's eyes. He was no less exhausted, but he'd be damned if he let the witch lovers see that. He would show them all! He was worth ten of these so-called Artesans. He could outfight them and out-command them, and he needed no arcane forces to do it. He had Robin on the run now, on the defensive, and he moved in for the kill.

✣ ✣ ✣ ✣ ✣

Parren's attack was vicious, and Robin stumbled on his wounded leg. He went down, even as he had been tripped two years ago. Parren stepped in close, seeing his opening. His sword flashed out toward the stricken man's throat, just as it had two years ago. The coincidence wasn't lost on either man, and Parren allowed a savage grin to stretch his lips as he put all his weight behind the killing thrust.

Unfortunately for Parren, this was not two years ago. This time Robin had feigned the stumble. Caught up in his thirst for blood, Parren had committed too soon, and he was unable to regain his balance as Robin, gambling that his adversary would be unable to resist the coincidental temptation, pivoted away from the deadly lunge. At the same time, his own blade swept around behind him, severing the tendons behind Parren's knees.

With a scream of agony, denial, and rage, Parren went down.

Robin stood over his downed opponent, his lungs heaving in air. The point of his sword was at Parren's throat, just as two years ago Parren had stood triumphantly over him. The sallow-skinned man stared up at his nemesis with hatred and loathing in his eyes. Robin's blade never wavered.

"I don't think anyone's going to come and save *you*, Parren," he wheezed. "I was lucky back then, I'll admit. But I know I was gaining the upper hand when you had your corporal trip me, so I look on it as justice rather than luck. You would have killed me if Sullyan hadn't come when she did. But she's not here today, is she? What do you think she would do if she were? Would she stay my hand? I rather think not."

"But you'll never know, will you?" rasped Parren. "She's off with her peasant lover, isn't she? Or maybe she's found yet another man better able to satisfy her than you were. After all, there must be plenty of them about."

Robin's eyes darkened with anger and pain. His breathing grew more ragged and he stared hotly down at his victim.

"Major!" hissed Bull, coming up behind him, trying to cut through the red mist of his fury. "Robin! Leave him be. You've defeated him. You've had your revenge. Let the King's justice finish him now. They'll stretch his neck for what he's done. He's no use for anything else now you've crippled him. Just think of the satisfaction you'll get when he's dangling from the gibbet for his crimes. You've done enough. Leave it."

He put a hand on Robin's shoulder, but Robin threw it off. Blood oozed from his many wounds, not least the deep gash in his thigh, but he took no notice. His sword point still hovered over the pit of Parren's throat, where the pulse jumped erratically under the skin.

"Go on, then, *Major*," sneered Parren, gasping for breath. "But you can't do it, can you? You can't satisfy a woman and you can't kill a man in cold blood. You're useless, Tamsen! Is that why you took up with a young boy? A young and pretty lad? Is that how you like them? Too weak to fight back? Well, I think you're pathetic, and it seems your witch does, too. It's no wonder she left you, no wonder she preferred that animal Rykan over you. Is it true that he raped her four times? Have you thought that perhaps she enjoyed it, Tamsen? Do you think she begged him for it? Can't you just imagine her begging him? Well, at least he could manage it!"

Robin's expression grew blacker and blacker as Parren's vicious tirade went on. Tears of loss, betrayal, and fury poured unheeded down his face. He couldn't even see Parren lying bloody on the ground. The ugly words spilling from his mouth smacked into Robin's mind, reminding him forcefully of those he had thrown at Sullyan during their one and only argument. He suddenly understood, with a soul-wrenching pang which threatened to burst his heart, how deeply they must have hurt her and how false they clearly were.

No wonder she had lost control so thoroughly that she had turned her superior metaforce on him. He couldn't believe it had taken Parren's evil mouth to make him see what a terrible thing he had done. Even if she was guilty of betraying their marriage with Taran, she didn't deserve that.

He had rescued her from Rykan's dungeons. He had seen her dreadful injuries, both physical and mental, and he knew, with an intimate depth of insight, the hideous pain and suffering she'd borne. Only her faith that he would come for her had allowed her to last as long as she had, and he couldn't believe he had flung that back in her face.

He had almost been ready to heed Bull's words, had almost decided to remember his duty, to step back and let the big man take over. But Parren's taunting and his own shocking epiphany snapped his control.

"You foul-mouthed, evil, lying bastard! This is for Sullyan! This is for Tad! But most of all, this is for *me*!"

"No, Rob!" cried Bull, making a desperate grab for Robin's sword arm. He was too late. Robin thrust the point of his sword through Parren's windpipe, his spine, and deep into the earth below.

The thin man's eyes bulged and his blood gurgled around the blade. His eyes, still locked with loathing on Robin's, glazed over as his life leaked away.

Robin lurched a few steps to the side and collapsed, loss of blood, shock, anger, and exhaustion finally claiming their price. Cal looked from Bull to Robin and then to Parren's corpse, his face white with concern. Bull turned away, punching one fist into the palm of his other hand in furious frustration.

"Oh, *bugger*!"

✣ ✣ ✣ ✣ ✣

Cal went over to where Robin lay in the dirt, supporting himself on one elbow, his other hand clutched to the gaping wound in his left thigh. He was so exhausted he had very little energy left with which to staunch his wounds and stem the bleeding.

Cal crouched down beside him. "Come on, Major, those wounds need seeing to. Let's get you into the shade of the trees."

He took Robin's arm over his shoulder and helped the semi-conscious man over to the trees where Parren's horse was tethered. Bull joined them, glancing in disgust at Parren's lifeless corpse lying abandoned in the gory dirt. He had fetched a waterskin and his medical kit. Without a word, he stripped Robin of his soiled and sweaty clothing and proceeded to wash his wounds. He made no concessions to Robin's pain, nor did he offer to lend the young man any strength. As far as Bull was concerned, Robin had brought this on himself and could deal with the consequences.

He poured a small quantity of firewater brandy over the deep gash in Robin's leg and saw Cal glance in sympathy at the Major's white, pinched face. Robin was too weak even to gasp in pain, and Cal could stand it no longer. He offered Robin his own strength and received a flicker of gratitude from the Major's pain-filled eyes.

Bull then pulled a needle and thread from his pack.

"Leave it," Robin gasped, trying to bat Bull's hand away.

Bull stared at him coldly. "It needs stitching. You're in no state to heal it yourself and we've a long ride back. Grit your teeth and put up with it."

His unfeeling tone made Cal frown. Even Robin, in his state, recognized the censure in the big man's tone. He closed his eyes.

"Go easy, Bull," murmured Cal. "You know what bad blood there's been between him and Parren over the years and what he's gone through lately. Give him a break."

This, finally, was too much for Bull. "Give him a break?" he snarled, swinging round on Cal. "What do you think I've been doing these past few weeks? I've given him so many 'breaks' I've lost count! He's brought all this down on himself, Cal, and I've

71

just about had enough. Give him a break? I ought to break his bloody neck!"

Cal held his peace as Bull applied himself angrily to the torn flesh of Robin's thigh. Despite his words and his anger, he was no rougher than he needed to be, and Cal's flow of metaforce was sufficient to numb most of the pain.

When it was done, Bull left his flask of brandy for Cal to hold to Robin's bloodless lips. He packed away his kit and stowed his pack. He even brought Robin's spare clothes over, though he left Cal to help Robin dress again. Then Bull stalked toward Parren's lifeless body.

He stood staring down at the shell of the bitter young man, remembering the abrasive, cocky cadet he had once been, the spiteful practical jokes he had played, and the trouble he had caused Sullyan when she'd finally received Blaine's permission to train. It was Parren who had taunted her with the unlikelihood of her ever being permitted to take the King's Oath, shattering her dreams of service, and Bull vividly recalled the day he had come across her deep in the woods, sobbing as if her heart would break. He had spent an entire afternoon trying to console her, and then had gone straight to Ardoch to persuade him to throw his weight behind Bull's as they endeavored to convince Blaine to offer her to the King. Not that Ardoch had taken much persuading.

Bull knew she was aware of what they'd done, but what he didn't think she knew was how close both he and the swordmaster had come to rescinding their own Oaths because of her. Fortunately, both Blaine and the King had seen sense, and also her worth. Parren had been furiously jealous and critical.

Now, however, he had finally reaped the consequences of his cruelty and spite. Bull shook his head. Such a waste. The man could have gone far and become a well-respected officer if not for the innate vindictiveness in his self-absorbed nature. And although he had finally received the justice he deserved, his death would cause yet more trouble for Robin. The Major had knowingly defied a direct order from his General and his King, and that was insubordination of the worst kind. No mitigating circumstances—especially revenge—would be considered.

Bull didn't condone what Robin had done, but he did understand it. Would the General, though? Would Elias?

Sighing heavily, Bull wrenched Robin's sword from the corpse, cleaned it on Parren's shirt, and tucked it through his own weapons belt. Then he picked up Parren's limp arms and dragged the body over to his horse. The animal stirred nervously, but soon quieted under Bull's hand. It was battle-trained and used to the scent of gore. With Cal's help, they got the body over the saddle and tied it in place. Cal then helped Robin up onto Tobias and took the colt's reins, as Robin was barely conscious and in no state to guide his own mount. Bull took charge of the gray and they began the journey back, apprehension filling Bull over the inevitable meeting on the road with the King's party.

They only went as far as the inn where Taran and Sullyan had spent their last night before arriving in Port Loxton. Robin was too exhausted and weak from blood loss to ride far. Bull requested a room large enough for the three of them and, while their packs were taken up, he and Cal wrapped Parren's body in a large sheet of oiled leather and put it in an outhouse. They helped Robin into bed and he was asleep in minutes. Bull felt he was safe enough, and so they left him, spending the rest of the evening in the inn's comfortable common room.

Neither of them felt like talking. Parren's killing had sobered Cal, and Bull was anxious over the King's probable reaction to Robin's disobedience. Not to mention its possible consequences. He didn't know how much concrete evidence there was against the Baron, but he fervently hoped Elias hadn't been counting on

Parren being the lynch-pin of their case. He struggled with it for a while before giving up. He couldn't change what had happened. They would just have to face what came.

There were no Artesans left at the Manor for Bull to contact, so he could get no news of Tad. Cal was sometimes able to reach Rienne, but he got no response this time. If the healer was busy or preoccupied, she wouldn't sense his contact. He was still only Apprentice-elite and his military training had recently taken precedence over his Artesan skills. Once he was confirmed a captain—and with Parren dead it was inevitable, even without Cal's exemplary record—he could once again concentrate on strengthening his powers.

The two men sat in silence until they finally retired to bed.

✣ ✣ ✣ ✣ ✣

The following day Robin was stronger. A long sleep and a decent breakfast had replenished his energy, and he was able to channel more of his metaforce into healing. The wound in his thigh was stiff but not incapacitating, and he was able to take control of his own mount.

He was quiet and withdrawn, and Bull knew there was more to his unhappy reticence than Parren's killing. It was more even than worry over what the King might do. Something had changed within Robin, something had altered him on a profound level, and Bull wondered what it was. That it was connected to Parren's vicious taunting, he was sure, but as Bull didn't know the details of the furious row between Robin and Sullyan, he couldn't guess why Robin seemed so deflated, so soul-sick.

He tried to approach the younger man mind-to-mind, but the Major was shielded. Bull gave up. He had tried countless times to help Robin since Sullyan had left, and he had been rebuffed every time, sometimes vehemently. He could only do so much.

Frustrated, furious anew with the hotheaded young man for his stubborn resistance, Bull concentrated on the ride.

It was late afternoon before they met with the King's party, camped by the side of the road. General Blaine took one look at Robin's pale face and Bull's closed expression and strode immediately over to Parren's shrouded corpse. He twitched the leather away from the gray face beneath, then glared up at Robin.

"You have some explaining to do, Major."

One of Valustin's men took Tobias from Robin. Bull and Cal were left to take care of their own mounts. Robin was led over to where the King rested, his son in his lap, in the scant shade cast by a few scrubby bushes. He was offered no seat or refreshment. Bull heard the General demanding to know why Parren was hanging lifeless over his horse's saddle instead of being brought before them bound and alive.

It was much to Robin's credit, thought Bull, that the Major made no attempt to deceive the King. He told the story straight, although in a lifeless tone, and spared himself no shame as he recounted the duel. He took full responsibility for the outcome and completely exonerated his two companions. He didn't hold back when asked why he had not stopped at crippling Parren, and related his reasons for killing him. Bull had to admire his resolve.

The dispassionate way he spoke did nothing to disguise the obvious pain in his heart. Not even Elias, who was unaware of the full tally of Parren's long and vicious record where Robin was concerned, could doubt the absolute lack of conscious choice Robin had experienced.

There was silence when the Major had finished. Bull and Cal had joined the men, standing just close enough to hear Robin's lackluster tone. They watched the faces of the King and the General. Elias's expression, at first furious, was now closed and hard to read. His own recent experiences had left him less willing than he might have been to judge another man's deeds committed under duress. Blaine, who knew the history behind the event, regarded Robin with frustration akin to Bull's.

"I wish you'd brought charges over the Hyecombe business when you had the chance, Major," he said coldly. "You had the support of both Baily and Dexter to back you up. If you had acted then, none of this would have happened."

Robin made a halfhearted attempt to defend himself. "I know, sir. There was just too much going on at the time. I didn't have the strength. I had other things on my mind."

That was the grossest understatement, thought Bull. Robin's whole world had been on the point of collapse, and if Rienne and Deshan hadn't been able to guide Sullyan's lost spirit back home, Robin would have found it impossible to continue with his military career. His heart would have broken.

Not that he was much better off right now. Bull wondered when Elias would speak. Before he could, Robin pre-empted him, glancing at his monarch for the first time.

"Would his evidence have been so vital, your Majesty?"

Elias seemed to give himself a mental shake, as if emerging from some unpleasant reverie. "I'll know more when we reach the castle. Until I've spoken with those concerned, I cannot say." Turning to the General, he said, "My Lord Blaine, if you agree, I'm happy for the Major to continue back to the Manor to recover from his injuries. We will leave any disciplinary matters until later. I see no reason at present to curtail his freedom or relieve him of his duties."

He swung back to Robin, who was openly surprised. "Major Tamsen, you are to hold yourself ready to answer my summons and come to the capital if commanded. Any knowledge you have of this affair will be required of you. If the cadet Tad regains consciousness, you are to find out what he can tell us of Captain

Parren's recent behavior, and any connection he knows of to the Baron. If he is still too weak to travel at the time set for the trial, you will give evidence on his behalf as his proxy. Is that clear?"

Robin saluted his monarch as best he could given his astonishment and stiffness.

"I cannot say yet when the trial will commence," continued Elias, "as we are reliant on the gathering of evidence and the timing of my forthcoming diplomatic visit to Andaryon. Until then, Major, I strongly suggest you review your actions to date and reconsider your future. You acquitted yourself well during our recent campaign, and your loyal service to me during that time is the only reason I am not ordering you detained for disobeying my direct command. But do not make the mistake of thinking that your defiance will be overlooked. Much has occurred over these past few weeks that is displeasing to me, and I intend that it should all be put right as soon as possible. Do we understand each other?"

As Robin stared into Elias's piercing blue eyes, Bull realized the King wasn't just referring to Robin's insubordination and the feud with Parren. He was also referring to Robin's split from Sullyan. He could see Robin realized it too, and the revelation shocked the young man. Just how much did the King know? Bull caught the look Blaine gave Robin and saw his emphatic nod. Robin reddened and turned away.

"Yes, your Majesty."

The King's party rode on, leaving the three men watching Elias's receding back. Robin turned Tobias's head and rode ahead of the other two. Cal had the reins of Parren's horse. The body would be returned to the Manor to be searched and then burned with no ceremony or honors, as befitted a blackmailer and a traitor. He had no family to inform and so would simply cease to exist, his name expunged from the Manor's records.

Chapter Six

Over the next few days, while she and Aeyron recovered some of their strength, Sullyan's mood was often quiet and pensive. Her waking hours fell into a regular pattern. Her mornings were spent with the garrison. Despite her pregnancy, she rose at dawn as usual and went out to train. Taran always accompanied her. They had become closer than ever since his trial of passion and Fire, and they were easier together than they had ever been.

Once training was over and they had bathed and changed, Sullyan spent her time with Aeyron. The Prince was growing stronger by the day. Rest, good food, the love of his family, and Sullyan's comforting presence all worked to heal the wounds of his body. Worry over the maiming of his right hand and its implications for his future could always be seen behind his eyes. Because of this—and maybe other things—his confidence had not returned.

He was unwilling to go about the palace alone, always requesting Sullyan's presence. Taran trailed along behind them like a faithful guard dog. The Prince had also taken to wearing leather gloves, and though these hid the wound in his hand, they could not conceal the one in his heart. Pharikian tried to hide it from his son, but there was often concern in his eyes as the elderly ruler watched Aeyron's progress.

Their evenings were spent with the royal family and their

immediate friends, which usually meant Anjer and his wife Torien, Marik and Idrimar, General Ephan and Lady Hollett, Deshan, Baron Gaslek, and the widow Falina. The plump woman had taken a shine to Taran and he usually found himself sitting by her side during supper. He didn't mind too much. She could be good company and her friendship was uncomplicated. She was content in her widowed state, and besides, Taran was human. She could flirt and share saucy jokes and innuendoes with him and he could return them with an easy heart.

Her only irritating habit was her penchant for matchmaking. Aeyron was her godson and she was concerned about his single status. When she wasn't speculating on Aeyron's possible future wife, she turned her attentions on Taran. It was amusing at first, but the novelty soon faded.

At one such supper, once the remains of the meal had been cleared away and the musicians had begun to play, Pharikian drew Sullyan and Anjer to him. Aeyron had been persuaded to leave Sullyan's side for a while by Falina and Taran, and the plump widow was playing the spinet and encouraging Aeyron to sing for her. Sullyan glanced in query at Pharikian's serious mien as he gestured to her and the Lord General. He drew both of them into a quiet corner and began with no preamble.

"Brynne, I'm very concerned about Aeyron's mental state. It's obvious that his experiences in Albia have affected him deeply, and I want you to know how much I appreciate your constant support."

Sullyan smiled fondly at the Prince, who had now persuaded Taran to join the song. "It is my pleasure, Timar. I will do anything in my power to help restore him."

Pharikian nodded, smiling also, although his yellow eyes remained troubled. "My dear, my own experiences during that dreadful time have not left me wholly unaffected either." Alarm spread over her features and he hastened to reassure her. "Oh, it's nothing to worry about. It's only that I have come to realize I'm not getting any younger. Ty Marik made a fine job of being Regent while I was … unavailable, and that has given me pause for thought. I have talked it over with Gaslek and Anjer, and I intend to start handing over many of my daily duties to Aeyron. It is my wish that we should eventually share the throne. What do you think, Brynne? Will Aeyron be able to cope with this? I'm hoping the extra responsibility and the overt show of my faith in him will help restore his self-confidence."

Sullyan considered his words, glancing over at Aeyron, who was now trying to learn the raunchy Albian folk tune Taran was laughingly teaching him. She was aware of Pharikian studying her as she watched his son, and thought she sensed some other intention behind his eyes. There was an undercurrent of anticipation—almost excitement—that didn't entirely fit with what he had told her.

"I think it would be good for him. Provided it is done carefully. Once he realizes he is as capable as he ever was, his confidence will return. I am sure of it. He knows in his heart how you value him, and this overt acknowledgement will not only bolster his courage, but will also show your people unequivocally how you feel."

Pharikian nodded, pleased. "Gaslek and Anjer are of the same opinion. Very well. To that end, I intend to order a festival day and host a gathering at which my intentions to share the throne with my son will be declared. The lords of the land will be required to attend, and they will publicly proclaim their fealty to the joint throne once the decree is in place. I can think of no clearer gesture to announce my faith in Aeyron."

"A good choice, Majesty," asserted Anjer, grinning at his ruler with a gleam in his eye.

Sullyan noted it, though she did not comment on it as she gave her wholehearted agreement.

✣ ✣ ✣ ✣ ✣

The festivities were scheduled to take place in four days' time, to allow the lords from the more distant provinces time to assemble. During that time, Pharikian ordered the trial of the renegade, Lord Corbyn. He knew he could put off no longer the meeting between himself and Elias, and Elias might need Corbyn's testimony to lend weight to his case against Baron Reen.

Corbyn and his son, Kethro, had been held separately in the garrison's secure cells. They were comfortable rooms and befitted a lord of Corbyn's standing. Yet they were still cells and were closely-guarded. Corbyn and Kethro had been permitted no contact with each other since being installed there, and neither even knew if the other was being held in the same building.

Pharikian ordered Lord Kethro brought to him on the day before his father's trial. It had been Marik and Anjer's opinion that, given the opportunity, the young lord might tell them much that his father would not want revealed.

The Hierarch received the young man in his formal audience chamber. It was a huge and impressive room, Sullyan thought, as she watched from her seat to the side of the dais. The ceiling was vaulted and decorated with painted and gilded timbers and bosses, depicting the Hierarch's tangwyr symbol and the colors of the major ruling Houses. The marvelously carved columns lining the central aisle were wonders of the stonemasons' art and were reflected in the highly polished marble floor. The Hierarch's dais was at the top end of the aisle, and where it had formerly borne one ornately carved throne, now it held two.

Pharikian and his son sat side by side, wearing almost identical golden robes over which flowed the imperial purple of their ceremonial mantles. Sullyan's gaze fell to where Aeyron's hands lay on the arms of his throne. It had taken much persuasion by his father to convince Aeyron to leave off the black leather gloves under which he had been concealing his disfigurement. The wound was healing well, but openly showing his maimed hand had been almost a rite of passage for the traumatized Heir. Once he had taken that initial step, however, a measure of confidence had returned to him. Sullyan had dropped him a deep curtsey, then caught and kissed his hand when she had seen it that morning. He had blushed bright crimson and then hugged her hard, tears standing in his pale eyes.

Sullyan herself was arrayed like a princess for this important interview. Her fire opal fillet, a wedding gift from Pharikian, nestled in her unbound hair. Her long gown was a soft velvet-green trimmed with gold, the narrow girdle at her waist accentuating the swell of her pregnancy.

Deshan had been right; her baby had indeed put on a spurt of growth. Sullyan, pondering this, was of the opinion that her final acceptance of her state and her contact with her unborn son in the stone circle had triggered this development. It was almost as if the baby had been waiting for her to acknowledge his existence in some way before he could truly begin to grow. Now she wore her pregnancy with as much grace as she could muster.

The four men of the Velletian Guard at Pharikian's back stirred as the double doors at the far end of the audience hall opened. Lord Kethro was brought in, unchained but closely guarded by four more of Barrin's men. His face was white and pinched, and he appeared very frightened. He was brought to the foot of the platform where he fell on his knees, his face pressed to the floor, awaiting words of judgment from his sovereign.

Pharikian regarded him expressionlessly, while Aeyron's face was tight and unreadable. There was sympathy in Sullyan's eyes as she turned her head to regard the Hierarch. He accepted her unspoken plea.

"Lord Kethro," he said, making the lad start, "you will rise and stand before us."

Kethro struggled to his feet, the tremble of his limbs clearly visible. He couldn't meet the Hierarch's gaze and his eyes shied from Aeyron's closed countenance. He fixed them instead on Sullyan's face, seeming to draw some measure of courage from her serenity.

"My Lord," continued the Hierarch, "before we proceed, I want to assure you that you are not on trial here. This is not an officially convened judiciary. We merely wish to speak with you in order to clarify events before your father's trial. Do you understand?"

Kethro nodded, his face a pale mask of apprehension. He was clearly terrified of saying the wrong thing, especially without his father to prompt him, and Sullyan recalled how protective Corbyn had been of him after Aeyron's abduction.

She leaned toward Kethro, her lilting voice a balm to the terrified boy's ears. "My Lord Kethro, we already know of your father's association with Baron Reen of Albia. We know he was responsible for the attack on Lord Marik's parley party, and we also know he led the force which attacked both Commander Barrin and King Elias in the woods east of Medinia, which caused the battle to be joined. We are aware that Lord Corbyn was associated with both Lord Rykan and Lord Sonten, which, presumably, is how he first came into contact with Baron Reen. We know that your father considered Lord Sonten a rival. All of this is established fact and will be presented to your father at his trial. It is irrefutable and a matter of record."

She caught his nervous gaze and held it. Softly, she added, "My Lord, I have to tell you that it is evidence enough to hang him for treason."

Kethro's face turned gray and he staggered. One of his guards stepped forward and caught him by the arm to prevent him from falling.

Sullyan appealed to the Hierarch. "Majesty?"

He nodded. "Fetch a chair for Lord Kethro."

One of the guards brought over a plain chair from the side of the hall. Kethro collapsed into it, his face bloodless, his eyes haunted and wild. They gave him a moment to recover.

"My Lord," murmured Sullyan, recalling his attention, "do you understand the implications of what I just said? If your father refuses to admit and abjure his perfidy, he will surely hang as a traitor to the Crown. This means that you will be disinherited, as all his lands and wealth will be forfeit to his Majesty. But more than that, Kethro"—she leaned forward again, using his name to appeal to him on a more personal level—"if he refuses to repent of his crimes, all those suspected of complicity in his treachery could hang alongside him."

Kethro stared at her numbly, unable to take it in. He was alone and he was frightened; he didn't know what to do. He was very young—just seventeen—and had never had to face anything like this before. They knew so much already and he clearly felt he was being required to make decisions the import of which he was ill-equipped to understand. He swallowed.

"Wh-what do you want me to do?"

Sullyan smiled kindly and leaned back in her chair, her hands folded in her lap. "Just tell us your own version of events and what you know of your father's involvement with Rykan, Sonten, and Baron Reen."

He stared at her unhappily.

"You are not condemning him, Kethro. I have already told you that. This is your chance to redeem yourself. His Majesty is no tyrant, but he will not tolerate disloyalty and treachery. Just tell us what you know. Tell us all and give yourself over to his mercy. You may be surprised at the outcome."

Pharikian raised his brows at this and turned a look on his son. Aeyron's pale yellow eyes were fixed on Kethro's face, no doubt wondering what part this terrified youth had played in his abduction. Pharikian turned his attention back to Kethro. Sullyan had made no promises, after all.

Kethro sat a moment, trying to marshal his thoughts. He had little choice other than to comply with Sullyan's request. The alternative was too awful to contemplate. He drew a deep breath.

"For as long as I can remember, my father has been—was—a friend and supporter of his Grace Lord Rykan." His voice was low and trembling, and he kept his eyes fixed on his hands as he spoke. "He made many visits to the Duke's palace. I don't know what they talked about. I was never allowed in their meetings on the rare occasions he took me with him. Then one day, about three years ago, Lord Sonten introduced his nephew, Jaskin, to Rykan's court, and his Grace's attitude toward my father began to change.

"It was nothing sinister and he never actually broke with my father, but their relationship never recovered. My father felt used and slighted and he was furiously angry with Lord Sonten. He also absolutely hated Jaskin. It was my father's fervent hope that Lord Rykan would take me under his wing and agree to train me as an Artesan, as his level of skill was far above anyone in my father's court, but it seemed that Sonten had conceived the same idea. He wormed his way into his Grace's favor and managed to discredit my father at the same time. I don't know what methods Sonten used to persuade Rykan, but in the end it was Jaskin who benefited from Rykan's tutelage, not me. I believe he was even considering making Jaskin his Heir."

Sullyan added this knowledge to her understanding of affairs surrounding the Staff. They had often wondered how a lower-ranking Artesan such as Jaskin had managed to usurp the Staff and turn it to his own ends. But if the young noble had had intimate contact with Rykan's psyche, had maybe even seen the Duke working with the Staff, that would go far toward explaining it. She turned her attention back to Kethro, who was still speaking, his unsteady voice fearful and apologetic as he recounted Corbyn's treachery.

"My father had intended to support Lord Rykan's challenge on the Crown, and his Grace had been paying him a retainer on that understanding. He told my father that in return he would throw his weight behind our own challenge on Lord Tikhal's lands and power. But Sonten's currying of Rykan's favor, and the Duke's spurning of my father's friendship, caused him to withdraw his offer of troops, and I know my father was fearful of what might happen in the future. He wasn't ready to take on Lord Tikhal by himself, and was worried Tikhal would learn of his plans. If he could no longer count on Rykan's backing, then he was in a very vulnerable position. So he pulled all his troops back to Quarlock and forbade any of his nobles to leave the province. Instead, he sent his personal spies to report on Rykan's affairs.

"My father knew of Rykan's association with the Albian Baron before Lord Sonten usurped his place. I gather Sonten didn't approve of Rykan's alliance with a human, and I know he counseled the Duke against it. In principle, my father didn't approve either, but he could see the advantages of what the Baron was offering, and I know he was excited by Rykan's plans.

"I only learned of it later, but it seemed that between them, Lord Rykan and the Baron had formulated some scheme for creating a device that could steal and store metaforce. My father called it a 'Staff.'"

Kethro paused in his narrative and glanced nervously up at the impassive Hierarch, who said, "We know all about the Staff, Lord

Kethro. Continue your tale."

Kethro swallowed.

"I didn't really understand it at the time, Majesty, but my father recognized the Staff's potential in terms of conquest—bearing in mind my own underdeveloped Artesan skills—and he was eager to learn more. He took me with him on our final visit to the palace, before his split with the Duke, and he gained Rykan's permission for us to meet his allies."

Kethro faltered in his narrative, his face a study in pity and disgust. Sullyan hardened her heart. Her opinion of Kethro would be set in stone by his next words. He remained unaware of the intensity of her gaze.

Kethro continued, speaking as if he had tasted something unpleasant. "We met the Baron in Albia, in a house somewhere. I don't know where it was. It was at night, and I wasn't the one providing access through the Veils. That was Huw, the Baron's Artesan. I'd heard Lord Rykan speak of him, but I was shocked when I finally saw him. He was immensely powerful—more powerful than I'd ever imagined an Artesan could be—but he was also very strange.

"He was a little older than me, but he was like a little child. It was obvious right from the start that there was something very wrong with his mind. He was physically deformed as well. He had a hunch back, odd-colored eyes, and a club foot. And he dribbled all the time. The Baron also had a personal guard with him, an evil brute of a man, and Huw was clearly terrified of him. This guard only had to look at him and he cringed, and once I even heard him cry out as if he'd been whipped, but the man had only gripped him by the arm. He was frightened of the Baron, too. I saw Reen slap the lad once and he burst into tears like a baby.

"I felt very sorry for him; he was a pathetic sight. I wondered why on earth he didn't use his powers against his tormentors, as neither the Baron nor his guard could have stopped him, but I came to the conclusion that his mind was too damaged. He didn't seem to understand anything that was going on. He just sat huddled in a corner, gabbling nonsense to himself and drooling."

Sullyan's eyes filled and she was finding it hard to breathe. The specter of Huw's lost potential had come back to haunt her. Kethro glanced at her, but probably saw only sympathy for a deformed and disabled boy.

He carried on. "We only met them that one time in Rykan's presence, and I wasn't privy to the plans they discussed. It was soon after this that the Duke lost interest in my father, and we never went to the palace again. This infuriated my father on many levels, and also frightened him, I think, not least because he had no way of knowing what would become of us if Rykan gained the Crown by using the Staff. He was terrified that Sonten would poison Rykan's mind against us and that Rykan would take our lands, or worse. That's why he sent his spies to the palace to report on Rykan's challenge, and to forewarn us of any plans. But then the Duke was killed."

Kethro's eyes flicked briefly to Sullyan before sliding uncomfortably away. "And the Staff he'd helped to create was destroyed, along with Sonten. I can still remember the terrible headache I suffered when that substrate tunnel imploded.

"My father rejoiced at Sonten's death, for had he succeeded in recovering the Staff, neither of us would ever have been safe. Even without its powers, Sonten would have remained a threat. But he was not so gladdened by Rykan's fate. I think he had always hoped to rekindle their friendship once Rykan had taken the throne.

"But with Rykan dead and the Staff destroyed, my father was right back where he started, still subordinate to Tikhal and with no prospects of increasing his standing. He was desperate to find a new ally."

Kethro paused once more. He glanced up at the Hierarch, his face pale and strained. Notwithstanding Sullyan's earlier assurances, he probably still felt like a traitor, blurting out his father's secrets as if he could not wait to see him condemned.

Pharikian, angered though he was by the depth of Corbyn's perfidy, recognized Kethro's discomfiture. His severe expression softened at the plea in Kethro's eyes, and they could all hear the sincere regret in the young man's wavering voice. Pharikian waved his hand. "Go on, lad, tell us the rest."

Kethro hung his head. "That first time we met with the Albian Baron, my father was careful to let him know we'd be as willing to ally with him as Rykan had been. Once the dust had settled after Rykan's death, my father was desperate to regain contact with the man, as he was certain they could aid each other's plans. But I'd never learned Huw's psyche, so we had no way of reaching him. We never knew where Rykan used to meet with the Baron, and even if we had I'm not skilled enough to influence the emergence of a tunnel or portway. There was nothing we could do.

"It was nearly a year before contact was re-established, and the approach came from the Baron himself—or rather, from Huw. I didn't think that the poor boy knew my psyche pattern any more than I'd known his, but he must have learned it somehow from that first time we met. Anyway, once I got over my surprise at the contact and told my father what they wanted, he agreed to meet with them at once. We crossed the Veils into Albia."

Kethro paused, misery plain on his face.

Sullyan shifted slightly. "Go on, Kethro."

The young man sighed.

"During that first meeting, the Baron, still accompanied by his guard, told us he'd formulated a new plan and gave his reasons for contacting my father. He said he needed thirty pounds of reverse-polarity spellsilver, and in return for our help in obtaining it, he would support my father in whatever way he wished—even in challenging for the Crown as Rykan had done."

The Hierarch leaned down from his throne, his voice cold. "And did Lord Corbyn want that?"

Kethro regarded the Hierarch unhappily. "My father didn't specify a price for his aid in my hearing, Majesty. All he did was assure the Baron of his willingness to help obtain the silver. The Baron wouldn't tell us what his own plans were, and when my father asked, he cut the meeting short. They parted on amiable terms, and it wasn't until some weeks later that we met with him again.

"This time, I wasn't involved in their discussions. My father and the Baron closeted themselves alone, and I was left with Huw and that brutal guard of his. From then on, that was the way it went every time my father met them. I was always kept out of the way and never allowed to hear what they discussed.

"Then one day my father called me into his office and told me things were going to change. He said he intended to challenge Lord Tikhal for Morvaigne and overlordship of the North, and he'd thereby finally gain the standing he deserved. I wasn't asked for my opinion. He just took it for granted I'd do as he said. And really I didn't have much choice. I don't have my majority yet, and I'm still duty-bound to obey him. But even if I had been old enough to speak against him, he'd have found a way to force me. He's very good at that."

Kethro's voice was bitter, but he didn't expand on his thoughts.

"He told me the Baron was going to lend him men, enough to support his overthrow of Morvaigne, but before that could happen we had to support the Baron's plan. I was to mesh with Huw and we would send men through into Albia. In return, the Baron's men would come here, to pose as raiders against our realm."

He raised his eyes. "Majesty, the raids he told you Quarlock suffered were all fabricated reports, but those suffered by his vassals were real enough. My father complained to Lord Tikhal about his losses so frequently and so forcefully that Tikhal was obliged to contact you. My father knew you would invite him here to air his grievances in person. All I was told was that while we were here, my father would suggest that Prince Aeyron and I go hunting. He gave me precise instructions as to where we should go. I think he was taken aback when Lord Tikhal decided to accompany us, and I know he never intended for Lord Rand to be included in our hunting party. But once Lord Tikhal heard of it, it was impossible to refuse him without arousing his suspicions. After all, Rand and I have been friends for years."

Pharikian's eyes narrowed. "Did Corbyn say what would happen on this hunting trip?"

Kethro looked away. "Not in my hearing, Majesty."

He began to tremble again and suddenly broke down into sobs, his dreadful situation proving too much for him. He slid from the chair to his knees, spreading his hands before the throne.

"Please, Majesty, Highness, you must believe me! I would never have agreed to it if I'd known what they intended. I was told they just wanted the Prince kept out of the way for a few days. I never guessed they were going to *take* him! All I was told was where to lead the party, and to inform Huw when we reached a certain position. I *swear* to you on my life, Majesty, I never knew what they were going to do!"

Chapter Seven

Kethro's face was ashen, his lips bloodless. His eyes slid pleadingly from Aeyron to Pharikian, begging them to believe him. He had been instrumental in the abduction of the Prince, and if he couldn't convince them of his unwitting involvement, he would hang beside his father.

"That's why they came for me and Rand with spellsilver, Majesty," he blurted. "Not only so that Rand couldn't warn anyone here, but also to prevent me from betraying the Baron. Once I regained consciousness here in the Citadel, my father made me swear never to breathe a word or I would get us both killed. He told me that something must have gone wrong and that someone else must have abducted the Prince, but later on, once I heard about the ransom note and the theft of the spellsilver, I guessed the truth. I've been terrified we'd be found out ever since. But before that I truly had no idea that the Baron planned to carry off the Prince. I swear it!"

Pharikian chose to ignore Kethro's outburst. "And after the abduction?"

Kethro hung his head. "I was required to take and send more messages regarding the movement of troops and the planning of attacks on the human forces. I was frightened, and I tried to persuade my father to break with the Baron, but he was too deeply mired in his plans. He grew furious with me and ordered me never to question his motives again. I was to do as he bid me and hold my tongue.

"You may think I've been spineless and craven, Majesty, but you don't know my father. He can be very ... forceful. I really had no choice but to obey."

An awkward silence followed his words. Sullyan broke it.

"Kethro, during your stay here, did you or your father take one of his Majesty's seals?"

The young man nodded unhappily. "My father ordered me to take one from Baron Gaslek's office. He kept Gaslek talking one day while I slipped inside and took one of the spare ones from the box. We sent it to Baron Reen."

Kethro fell silent once again. The trembling of his body was still evident. His anxiety over both his fate and his father's was clear in every nervous glance.

Pharikian said nothing at first but communed with his son. Sullyan remembered Kethro's air of fear during Rand's questioning after Aeyron's abduction, and also the way Corbyn had hovered over him under the guise of a protective father. She thought Kethro was probably telling the truth. If the Hierarch doubted the young man's story, there was a simple way to be sure.

The Andaryan ruler sigh heavily. "You have been very naïve, boy. You have allowed yourself to be used. I accept that you were following your father's orders and filial obedience is to be commended. But you were aware long before the abduction of my son that what was being planned amounted to treason, and duty to the Crown takes precedence over obedience to your father. You know this. You signed the Declaration of Fealty when you turned fifteen years of age. You are culpable, Kethro. You cannot claim to be an ignorant child, even though you have not yet attained your majority. In light of this, I simply cannot ignore your complicity in this matter."

Kethro gasped and turned white.

Sullyan stirred. "Majesty—"

The Hierarch held up a hand and she fell to silence.

"Remove him," said Pharikian curtly, and the guards stepped forward, hauling the young man to his feet. "Lord Kethro, you will be returned to your quarters where you will remain under guard. We acknowledge the service you have given us by relating these events frankly and of your own free will. Tomorrow we will hear your father, and you may well be required to speak at the trial. Lord Corbyn's own testimony will dictate its outcome, and with it, your ultimate fate. Now leave us."

Kethro staggered unevenly between his guards, staring back at Sullyan from desperate, pleading eyes. She looked up at the Hierarch, who was regarding his son. Aeyron was pale and uttered not a word. There was a faraway look in his unfocused eyes.

"I believe him, Timar," said Sullyan softly. "Whatever else he is guilty of, he had no knowledge of the Baron's plan."

Pharikian was silent, his lined and weathered face still turned toward his son. Aeyron continued to hold his peace and, eventually, the Andaryan ruler sighed again.

"Yes, child. I, too, believe him. I am glad. It would grieve me sorely to hang father and son side by side. And maybe Corbyn will give me reason to mitigate his own sentence, although I doubt it."

✣ ✣ ✣ ✣ ✣

The next day, Lord Corbyn was brought before an official judiciary to be tried for the crime of treason. The main trial hall was packed. Most of the Hierarch's nobles had attended, interested in seeing one of their own brought to account for his conduct.

The Hierarch himself did not try Lord Corbyn. That task was undertaken by Baron Gaslek, the Hierarch's secretary. Taran was surprised to see how efficient and stern the normally fussy Gaslek became when he donned the purple and black of the Primary

Magister's office, and his manner throughout the proceedings was formal and dour.

The royal family had their own box to one side of the hall, and Sullyan accompanied Aeyron, as usual. Marik sat beside his father-by-marriage with Lord General Anjer behind them, a dark and brooding presence in his black uniform. Princess Idrimar was nowhere to be seen.

Prince Aeyron, still gaunt from his ill-usage during his captivity, looked subdued and gray. He was facing one of the men who had wished him great evil, and who had been instrumental in condemning him to the dreadful torture he had endured. Taran saw how tightly Sullyan clasped the Prince's hand as she constantly whispered words of encouragement.

When Lord Corbyn was brought into the trial hall, manacled, chained, and escorted by six Velletian Guardsmen, the room erupted in malice. It took the trial officials some minutes to restore order. Throughout the tumult, Lord Corbyn stood in silence, staring stonily to the fore. He spared his white-faced, sweating son one brief, malignant glance. Apart from that, he betrayed no emotion.

Once calm was restored, Gaslek had the charges read out. Corbyn refused to acknowledge them and remained silent even when Gaslek gave him the opportunity to speak for himself. Taran thought he was going to stand in stubborn silence and force them to condemn him unheard. But the chance to air his grievances proved too tempting, and Corbyn finally stood forth to address those assembled against him.

It was more a rant than an address, and Kethro covered his face with shaking hands when he heard his father haranguing the ruler of Andaryon, condemning himself out of his own mouth and sealing his fate for sure. There was no remorse in Corbyn, no attempt to justify or deny his crimes, and Taran supposed Corbyn already knew he was doomed. There were simply too many credible witnesses who could be brought to speak of his treachery for him to waste breath trying to spare himself the ultimate penalty.

Gaslek allowed the wiry lord his allotted time, and the Hierarch heard Corbyn's catalog of accusation and complaint with expressionless eyes. Aeyron was forced to sit and endure Corbyn's disparaging comments about his suitability to rule now that he was 'crippled.' Corbyn's deliberate use of this word caused Aeyron's face to drain of blood. Sullyan's eyes turned midnight black as she poured supportive strength and love into him.

Eventually, Gaslek had had enough. Under Andaryan law, traitor or not, Corbyn had the right to speak as he would and none could refuse him, but the stream of disaffection and disloyalty that he flung at the ruling House of Andaryon was too much to stomach, even for such a staunch defender of the law as the Primary Magister.

"Silence!" thundered Gaslek, striking the table with the flat of his hand. The resulting crack echoed sharply through the hall.

Corbyn obeyed. He had done his worst. He glared at Gaslek, daring the Magister to utter his death sentence.

The small man drew himself up to full height. He glanced over at the Hierarch, who nodded once. Gaslek cleared his throat.

"My Lord Corbyn, the Crown brings no witnesses before this assembly to speak against you, for out of your own mouth you stand condemned of treason, the penalty for which is death."

He turned to the hall. "Before sentence is pronounced, is there anyone who doubts the judgment of this Court? Is anyone willing to speak in defense of the traitor?"

There was silence but for the rustling of cloaks, the shifting of feet. No one stood forth for the condemned man.

No one but his son.

Slowly, fearfully, Kethro stepped forward. A soft intake of

breath echoed round the Court. Taran raised his brows and the Hierarch's gaze sharpened. Gaslek turned his attention on the lad and frowned.

"My Lord Kethro, is there something you wish to say before the Court?"

Kethro licked dry lips. He didn't glance toward his father, whose eyes were fixed scornfully on his son's unsteady figure.

"My Lord, I wish to sue for clemency."

Kethro's voice was faint and quavering and those at the back of the hall could not hear him. They all heard Corbyn's derisive snort, though.

Gaslek's frown deepened, but his tone was a little kinder. "Lord Kethro, you are young, and this, coupled with your relationship to the condemned man, must excuse your error. I fear there can be no clemency under Andaryan law for one found guilty of treason."

Taran had to admire Kethro's spirit. Still shaking, he faced the Hierarch and said more clearly, "Nevertheless, Majesty, I ask it."

He went down on one knee but did not relinquish Pharikian's gaze. The tremor in his limbs was visible to those who stood near him, and none could fail to be moved by his plea. Even Aeyron regarded him with surprise.

"You stupid, spineless boy!"

Corbyn's outburst raised gasps around the hall. His words hit Kethro like a knife in the back, and he turned to stare at his father. Taran saw the resolve in the lad, long repressed by his domineering parent, but released now by fear and by love.

"Spineless and stupid I may be, Father, but I am no traitor. And whatever you have done, however you have conspired and plotted to gain your own ends, I am still your son and I do not wish to see you hang. If I can obtain some measure of mercy for you, I will, though you turn your face from me for it."

Not a soul in the hall remained unmoved by Kethro's loyalty. Taran saw Sullyan smile in approval, and even Pharikian had an evaluating look in his eye.

All attention then centered on Gaslek, to see how he would respond to Kethro's petition. The plump little man shared a glance with his ruler before turning to address Corbyn once more.

"My Lord Corbyn, you have heard the appeal for mitigation entered by your son. What say you? Is there any reason for us to accede to Lord Kethro's request?"

Corbyn's hand cut the air sharply. "*Lord* Kethro? The boy is nothing but an adolescent idiot with no ambition and fewer brains! I always did consider him a lightweight, and now he has proved it. Make no mistake, you who sit in judgment. He knew what we were doing. He followed my orders and did what he was told. Don't be fooled for one moment into thinking he is some innocent child, ignorant of our purpose. But if he has neither the faith of his convictions nor the courage to accept his fate, then I want nothing more to do with him. He is no son of mine. I have no son. I disown him."

Gasps of shock and outrage sounded throughout the hall, not least from Kethro himself. He went white and had to support himself with one hand on the floor. Corbyn's damning words had signed his death warrant.

Yet instead of calling for the guards to confine Kethro in chains, Gaslek smiled. "Well said, my Lord, well said. I hereby Witness your words."

Corbyn frowned, his moment stolen, and Taran wondered what Gaslek meant. He caught the satisfied gleam in Pharikian's eyes and shot a glance at Sullyan. She was talking quietly to Aeyron. Marik also seemed to know what was going on. The Adept turned his attention back to Gaslek.

"Lord Kethro," the Magister said clearly, "arise and approach."

Kethro staggered to his feet and approached Gaslek, his gait unsteady. Taran saw his terror and the glitter of unshed tears in his pale brown eyes. He clearly expected to be branded a traitor.

Gaslek looked down on him. "My Lord, your father has formally disinherited and disowned you before this Court. He has been duly heard and Witnessed. As you have not yet attained your majority, you are now officially an orphan. You have no lands, no affiliations, and no means of support. As is my right under the powers granted this office by his Majesty the Hierarch, I claim you for the Crown. I have pleasure in declaring you a ward of his Majesty."

He paused to allow Kethro a moment. Then he said, "So now I must ask you. Will you pledge, before these assembled Witnesses, your duty and unquestioning loyalty to his Majesty, Timar Pharikian, Hierarch of Andaryon, and to the ruling House of Andaryon for the duration of your life hereafter?"

Kethro's eyes stretched wide. Gaslek's last words formed part of the Declaration of Fealty, which Kethro had signed under his father's seal when he turned fifteen. Yet Gaslek's question was couched in terms appropriate for one who has not previously declared an allegiance, and Kethro had the wit, despite his circumstances, to realize that something of import was happening here. He swallowed.

"I s–so swear, my Lords," he stammered, barely managing to remember the correct form of reply. "L–let those assembled bear Witness."

Gaslek gave him an approving nod as the entire hall, with the exception of the royal family and Lord Corbyn, came to their feet, crying, "Heard and Witnessed!"

Once the echoes of the ringing phrase died away and they returned to their seats, Gaslek raised his right hand. "Then, my Lord Kethro, this Court declares that you are disassociated from the taint of treason which would otherwise accrue from the crimes of this man before us. It also decrees that your fate and your future shall be decided by his Majesty the Hierarch. Do you agree to be bound by those terms?"

Kethro raised his own right hand, although he still seemed to be in shock. "I do, my Lord."

Gaslek waved him aside and turned once more to the defiant traitor, Corbyn.

"Corbyn of Quarlock, you are condemned by your own admission and are hereby found guilty of the crime of treason against the Crown. The penalty for this is death and I now pass such judgment upon you."

Corbyn stared at him and spat. Gaslek ignored the insult.

"The sentence shall be carried out at his Majesty's convenience. Before this takes place, however, you are to be taken to the realm of Albia at the request of High King Elias Rovannon, and there will give evidence at the trial of Baron Reen. The date for this trial has yet to be announced."

Taran thought Corbyn might protest, but he must have realized it was futile. He contented himself with a defiant glare. Taran also wondered briefly whether Corbyn entertained the idea that the Baron might be able to help him in some way. The Adept found himself hoping that Corbyn's guards would be extra vigilant on the journey through the Veils.

Gaslek continued. "On your return to the Citadel, the sentence laid upon you will be carried out. The usual method of execution for traitors is to be hanged by the neck outside the walls of the Citadel, the corpse to be left for seven days to serve as a warning to any who think to conspire against the Crown."

There was a stir from Kethro, and his eyes filled with tears. He turned a look of supplication upon the Hierarch, but Gaslek wasn't done.

"However, there has been a plea of clemency lodged here today by one who has the right, and it is our pleasure to grant this plea."

Corbyn stiffened—whether in hope or disgust, Taran couldn't say—and Kethro's face betrayed his hope. Gaslek, however, crushed it.

"While we cannot and will not repeal the sentence of death for such crimes as yours, we can and will offer a less shameful execution. Corbyn of Quarlock, we pronounce that you are to be beheaded by the sword. Your body will be given to Lord Kethro to dispose of as he sees fit."

Kethro hung his head, grieving that his plea had not saved his father's life. He should be thankful, thought Taran, that Corbyn wouldn't suffer the humiliation of a public hanging.

Corbyn himself made neither move nor comment, and Gaslek ordered him removed. There were jeers and cat-calls from the public benches as his guards hustled him away. Then Gaslek concluded the proceedings and the trial officials began clearing the hall.

Taran left his seat and moved nearer to Sullyan. She had come down from the royal box to commiserate with Kethro, who stood confused and dejected on the floor. She was followed by Prince Aeyron, and Kethro fell to his knees when he saw the Heir approaching.

The Prince was still pale, but appeared more composed now that the ordeal was over. He regarded Kethro while Sullyan drew away to stand beside Pharikian. The Hierarch put an arm around her shoulders.

"My Lord Kethro," said Aeyron, "you may rise."

Kethro stood, still unable to meet Aeyron's gaze.

"I'm so sorry, Highness," he said. "I—"

Aeyron reached out and rested his hand on Kethro's shoulder, causing the lad to flinch. "I forgive you," the Prince said, drawing a look of amazement from Kethro. "You have shown us your mettle today and I appreciate how difficult it was for you to do what you did. I admire your courage. I also accept your assertion of innocence in the matter of my abduction. Your crime, if any, was a lack of judgment and a reluctance to disobey your father, even though you knew what he did amounted to treason. But you have no father now and you have sworn your life to our service before witnesses. Kethro, was your oath sincere?"

Kethro knelt again, taking the Prince's maimed hand in both of his and kissing the Imperial signet.

"It was, Highness, I have never been more sincere. I pledge to you my fealty, my loyalty, and my life."

Taran noted the effort it cost Aeyron not to snatch his disfigured hand away. Somehow, he found the strength to smile down at Kethro.

"Then I claim a price from you to demonstrate the truth of your oath."

A look of fear came into the lad's pale brown eyes, but he replied stoutly enough. "Highness, name it."

Aeyron held his gaze. "The fiefdom of Quarlock lies undefended now that its lord has deserted it." Kethro's gaze widened. "It will need a firm hand after the mismanagement of its former lord, and one that is dedicated to the service of the Crown. This is my price. Will you hold Quarlock for the Hierarch and protect its people? Will you return it to its former state as a loyal subject land, and will you pledge troops from its people to answer your sovereign's call? What say you, Lord Kethro? Will you accept this charge?"

Stunned, Kethro stared up at the Prince. Belatedly realizing a response was required, he managed to stammer, "I–I will, Highness. I so pledge myself."

"Then rise, Lord Kethro of Quarlock. The Throne of Andaryon accepts your pledge."

Chapter Eight

Just after dawn on the day before the festivities planned in honor of Prince Aeyron, Timar Pharikian went down to the garrison to forbid Sullyan use of the training ground.

He and Deshan had held long discussions over when they should do this. They both expected her to resist them, knowing how she valued her exercises in both swordplay and her independence. Although she was still slimmer than a woman nearly seven months pregnant had any right to be, Pharikian had grown more and more concerned that she continued to risk herself in training. This morning, he decided, the hour had come.

As so often happened, however, he found himself pre-empted.

He came across her at the training ground, as he had expected, Taran by her side. Though she had her father's blade in hand, Pharikian could immediately see she had no intention of using it in any kind of bout with the man standing before her.

For one thing, she wasn't wearing her combat leathers. Instead, she had dressed in a simple gown of russet velvet, gathered lightly at her increasing waist by a thin belt of gold silk. Her tawny hair was woven into a long braid which fell down her back to her waist. She did wear her sword belt, which should have looked out of place on the russet gown but somehow did not. Otherwise, she was dressed for court life, not the military.

For another thing, the man she was instructing this morning was not one of the garrison swordsmen.

Pharikian stood back out of sight, watching fondly as Sullyan demonstrated the various ways in which Aeyron could compensate for his maimed right hand. He felt a deep rush of gratitude as he observed the casually caring way the young woman he now thought of as his foster-daughter instructed his son. Aeyron was understandably sensitive about his disability. Anything approaching pity would have offended and embarrassed him. There was nothing of pity in Sullyan's manner, or in Taran's as he helped her demonstrate what she wished to convey. Aeyron was totally engrossed in what they were doing, and Pharikian's troubled heart was suddenly relieved, freed of the terrible burden he had been carrying for so many days.

He now knew, with absolute certainty, that his son would overcome his shameful disfigurement and would eventually return to the confident, strong young man he had been before his dreadful ordeal. Tears of love pricked at the elderly Andaryan's eyes. They owed her so much. He could only hope that what they had planned for the next day would go some way toward showing her how deeply they valued her love and generous spirit.

Silently, without showing himself, he left.

✣ ✣ ✣ ✣ ✣

Sullyan called a halt to the session before Aeyron was ready to stop.

"Enough," she said firmly when he begged her to continue. "Remember, neither your ribs nor your hand are yet fully healed. Work gently at the beginning or you will strain yourself. You are using different muscles now and they must be built up carefully. I will not let you overtax yourself until you are completely recovered."

Aeyron glared in mock ferocity, and she smiled.

"You have made a good start today. Keep up those strengthening exercises I showed you, twice every day, and we will train again the day after tomorrow. But for now, Taran and I need to wash and then I must contact Bulldog for news."

"Are all your friends coming to join the celebration?" Aeyron spoke casually as he sheathed his blade, turning to stroll beside her as they made their way through the strengthening sunshine back to the palace. In a few weeks' time it would be Midsummer Day, and Andaryan summers were dry and hot. The early morning was the only time comfortable enough for training, and even then exercise left them dripping.

Aeyron's casual tone didn't fool Sullyan. Her face paled and the Prince immediately regretted his question.

"No, not all," she responded quietly. "The wounded cadet, Tad, is still gravely ill and Rienne may not wish to leave him. I need to speak with Bull and find out how he does."

She walked on ahead and Aeyron hung back to speak with Taran, knowing it hadn't been Tad or the healer on her mind.

"Have she and Robin still not spoken?"

Taran shook his head sadly. "I think it's too late, now. Too much time has passed. Neither knows how to approach the other. At least, that's how she feels. I can't speak for Robin. For all I know, he's still convinced I've stolen her from him."

Aeyron snorted in annoyance. "But what about the baby? He'd come if he knew she was pregnant, surely? Doesn't the father have a right to know?"

Taran fixed his concerned gaze on Sullyan's slender back as she neared the palace doors. "Perhaps, but would *you* be the one to tell him?"

Aeyron frowned, realizing the dilemma.

"Not even Bull knows yet," continued Taran, "although he soon will. She'll wait for him to arrive before she tells him, and then she'll order him not to tell Robin."

"Order him? Why?"

"She wouldn't want anyone else to do it, and she'll not do it herself. And yes, Highness, I've thought about going behind her back and telling him, but I'm Robin's least favorite person right now. I'd probably make matters worse. But even if I didn't care about angering Robin, I wouldn't want to risk upsetting Sullyan. Would you?"

Aeyron understood, though he felt it wasn't right, and he fumed inwardly that he was helpless to give her ease from the awful weight of blame, shame, and regret that burdened her spirit.

They could all see it. She was contented enough among them. She had good friends here, and her self-appointed task of showing the Heir how to relearn his weapons skills gave some immediate purpose back to her life. She had accepted her pregnancy, but they could tell she took no special pleasure in it. Her split from Robin meant she felt no eager anticipation for the coming birth, such as Marik and Idrimar experienced.

Aeyron's heart was sore. She was missing out on so much that should have been delightful. He remembered Torien and Anjer's reactions when the Lord General's wife had fallen pregnant. They had never thought to have children. Anjer had always been too afraid of losing Torien in childbirth, as she was so tiny and he so huge. Sullyan had convinced them it would be all right, and she had been proven correct. Little Brianne, named for Sullyan, was a joy to her parents and loved by all.

Sullyan was being denied all that pleasurable anticipation and it showed. All she experienced was sorrow and anxiety over the future, and it shadowed her eyes and blighted her heart. Anyone who knew her well could see it. They also saw how she strove to hide it without success. Aeyron wanted to heal that blight, but there was only one man who could.

✣ ✣ ✣ ✣ ✣

When Taran caught up with Sullyan later, she had bathed and changed and had spoken with Bull. Her mood was lighter than it had been for some time at the prospect of seeing her friends again, and she asked Taran to go and meet them on the Citadel Plain when they arrived later that afternoon. She gave him special instructions concerning Bull.

At the appointed time, Taran positioned himself well outside the southern Citadel gate and awaited Bull's signal. There would be three people coming through: Bull, Cal, and Rienne.

Taran knew Rienne was torn between her desire to see Sullyan again and her duty of care for Tad. She had labored many long hours over the young cadet and supervised the three infusions of his mother's blood they had been able to give him. They could do no more for now. His mother wasn't strong enough to part with any more of her precious life fluid. It had been enough to sustain Tad through the worst of his weakness, and his chances of survival were consequently much improved.

He still hadn't regained consciousness, although he now had a steady heartbeat and some color in his cheeks. They would simply have to wait to find out whether his injuries had affected his brain. Rienne now felt able to leave him for a day in Hanan's capable hands.

Taran saw the characteristic blossoming of the end of a substrate tunnel, and silently thanked the Master-ranked Anjer for his help in guiding the structure. Bull didn't have the strength to direct it himself, and no one would ask Robin. So Anjer had offered his services and Bull, Cal, and Rienne rode out onto the Plain half a mile away from the city walls. Taran stood where they could see him as they rode up, a broad grin on his face and pleasure swelling his heart.

Rienne was the first off her horse and Taran was amazed that she had felt able to come at all. She was pregnant too, although not far along, and this was a delicate time for her. She had been worn down by Robin's grief and Tad's care, not to mention distress over Sullyan's situation and worry for Cal's safety during his time in Andaryon with the King. Taran could see how strained and pale she was. Still, a happy smile came to her face and lit up her soft gray eyes. He took her gladly into his embrace as he grinned up at Bull and Cal.

They dismounted and their horses were taken by members of the Velletian Guard. It was Taran's intention that they should walk through the lower town and up the Processional Way to the palace in the warm summer sunshine. They had much to say to each other on the way.

Taran learned that General Blaine was still in Port Loxton with the King, and that Elias would soon be making his obligatory penitential visit to the Hierarch. Blaine had reported that the King was engaged in gathering evidence against the Baron, who was still being held under house-guard at his mansion, and interviewing everyone at the castle time and time again. Both Ardoch and First Minister Levant had been closeted with him on more than one occasion, as had Lieutenant Major Denny. Taran wasn't surprised to learn that both he and Lady Jinella would be required to attend the trial.

The King's reunion with his Queen had been a private but stormy affair. Bull had heard that their raised voices had been audible throughout most of the central parts of the castle, and they had not been together since. Elias was morose and angry most of the time, the exception being the hours he spent with his son. The Queen, too, was furious, and no one dared approach her. The fact that she wasn't permitted access to Eadan without the King's express permission and one of his men in attendance probably had much to do with her fury.

Then Rienne turned the conversation to Tad's condition and

voiced her concerns for Robin.

"He's spending all his free time with the lad, and it's wearing him down. He keeps pouring his own life force into Tad to help him recover. It's as though he feels personally responsible for his condition—as if his hand had wielded the blade. I dread to think what'll become of him if the lad doesn't recover."

Taran understood her worry, and also Robin's feelings. If blame could be apportioned to the Major for not speaking out and denouncing Parren sooner, then, technically, he was in some measure responsible for what had befallen Tad. Certainly, no one would convince Robin otherwise.

By the time they reached the palace, Taran had heard all the news from the Manor. Rienne was impatient to see Sullyan, but Taran stayed her. He turned to Bull, trying to sound casual.

"Brynne has something she wants to tell you, Bull. She asked me to send you to her rooms. We'll see you both later, at supper." He turned to Rienne and Cal, forestalling Bull's inevitable question. "Come on, I told Marik we'd drop by when you arrived. He's dying to see you."

✤ ✤ ✤ ✤ ✤

Bull stood alone at the door to the private suites, a tight knot of worry paining his chest. He forced it away. Taran's demeanor hadn't hinted at a problem, and he knew he shouldn't imagine the worst. It was just that what with everything that had happened lately, it was hard not to. All he could hear right now was Sullyan's voice telling him she might not ever return to the Manor. He watched the others walk away before making his way to Sullyan's rooms, a measure of dread in his heart.

The door to her suite was open and she sensed his approach. He heard her call of welcome as he entered the suite and closed the door behind him.

She was seated by the window, dressed in a loose gown of royal blue, her hair caught back from her face and flowing over her shoulders. She stood to greet him, holding out her arms, and almost fell into his bear-hug embrace. They both had damp eyes when they broke apart.

Bull held her at arms' length to study her. His eyes narrowed, then widened in shock. "Sully ...?"

She smiled a little sadly. "Hal, I cannot tell you how pleased I am to see you. I do hope you can forgive me for this. I so dearly wanted to tell you sooner, but.... I would never willingly have kept something like this from you, you must know that. I had my reasons."

He stood and stared open-mouthed, unable to take it in. She took him by the hand and drew him to a seat opposite hers, by the open window. Cooling breezes from the ornamental garden washed through the sunlit room.

"I only found out myself three weeks ago." She sought his gaze. "It was Rienne who discovered the miracle had actually happened. But that was only two days after ... after Robin and I—"

She stopped and looked away. Bull reached for her hand and she grasped his tightly, making him recall other times when she had taken comfort from his large and soothing presence.

"Was that what sparked the argument?" he asked, remembering how Robin had forced Taran to leave the Manor. A dreadful thought occurred to him and he blurted, "Oh gods, Sully, he never thought—"

She cut across him, not wanting to even hear that thought given voice. "No, Hal. The baby had nothing to do with it."

"Then ... I just don't understand how he could have let you go!"

"Hal, you were not the only one I did not tell." She sighed and looked out into the garden, unable to meet his gaze.

He stayed silent. He knew she was imploring him to speak, but he did not. When she was forced, finally, to look him in the eye, she was dismayed by the tears coursing down his cheeks.

"Oh, *Hal*!"

He folded her once more into his arms and she gave way to the tremendous burden of grief and hurt within her. The release had been pressing for some time, and so it took some time to clear.

Once she mastered herself, she pulled away and dried her eyes.

Bull's expression was serious. "Sully, you *have* to tell him."

She shook her head emphatically. "No. Not like this. I could not bear it if he felt obliged to return to me just because I carry his child. There are unresolved issues that need to be addressed first."

Despite knowing he was courting her temper, he persisted. "You're not being fair."

"Not fair?" she exclaimed, suddenly angry. "This whole situation is not fair! Not fair on either of us. I never asked to be pregnant, I never planned it. I had just come to terms with being barren, only to learn I will give birth in less than ten weeks' time! How do you think that felt? How fair is that?"

Bull couldn't hide his amazement. "Ten weeks? Why on earth did it take you so long to find out? Did you never suspect?"

"Why should I? Have you ever been pregnant? Do you know what it feels like? No? Well, neither did I!"

Clumsily, he placed the image of a pregnant waddling bulldog in her mind. It cut through her acerbic mood and she stifled a snort of laughter. She was too weary with strain and worry to sustain her anger, and she sighed in resignation.

"I never suspected because I had been told it was not possible. It took Rienne to discover the truth, but by then it was too late."

"You still have to tell him."

She glared at him in annoyance. "This is between Robin and me. It is our business and no one else's. I will tell him when I am ready."

He shook his head. "You're wrong. How can it be between you and Robin when he knows nothing about it? And you can't say it's no one else's business when your friends love and care about you." He met her glare unflinchingly, ignoring her displeasure. "I'm sorry, Sully, but this is one time when I can't—I *won't*—obey you. You can rage and shout at me all you want, but unless you tell him first, I'm going to tell him the minute I get back to Albia. Someone has to. Now, are we going to fall out over this?"

He could see she wasn't happy, but she had lost too much already to risk falling out with him. They had too much shared history and knew each other too well. She needed him, and on a very fundamental level, he needed her, too. There were times when he felt like her father, and others when he felt more like a husband. But always, whatever the confusion of his inner emotions, he was her truest, staunchest friend. Nothing would ever alter that, and they both knew it. She had told him what she wanted and he chose to deny her. So be it. He wasn't going to hide it, and she wouldn't try to sway him. They left it alone.

✣ ✣ ✣ ✣ ✣

Aeyron's inauguration as co-ruler of Andaryon was a splendid affair. It was held in the formal audience chamber, which was a vast room to begin with. Huge removable panels in the walls on the right-hand side of the main colonnade were stowed away to give access to the enormous ballroom next door, and the result was a cavernous space which under normal circumstances would have dwarfed a horde.

These, however, were not normal circumstances.

The place was packed. When Taran, Bull, Cal, and Rienne

arrived at the doors, they agreed they had never seen so many people gathered together under one roof. The Manor could house around three thousand souls at full capacity, but they were never all in the same place at the same time. Taran thought there must be at least that many here today, maybe more. If it were not for the tall windows at the far end of the ballroom, which were thrown open to the breeze, the air would have been unbreathable.

It seemed that every noble who held title or lands had attended, accompanied by their families and trusted retainers. Taran never considered trying to find out who they all were. There was no point. They were all gathered for one reason, and the expectancy in the air was electric.

There were minstrels playing in the ballroom and servants circulating with refreshing drinks. Tables along one wall of the ballroom would later groan with food, but for now they stood empty. Taran and his three friends moved among the press of guests, sticking close together, drinking in the sights and sounds.

They didn't feel too out of place, as they had all been given new clothing for the occasion as gifts from the Hierarch. Each man had silken trousers, a fine lawn shirt, and a flattering doublet, all of rich, muted, colors. They had received new sword belts too, with buckles of gold, the leather tooled and finely worked.

Rienne was resplendent in a flowing sleeveless gown of deepest sapphire satin, and she also wore the heavy silver necklet which had been her wedding gift from Pharikian. Cal could hardly take his eyes from her.

They had been admiring the finery of the various guests and watching some of the court ladies unfavorably comparing each other's gowns for about an hour when the trumpeters at the doors sounded a flourish. All conversation hushed. Gowns rustled like a sighing silken wind as the crowd pushed forward into the audience hall to gather around the platform and dais. Bull used his size to full advantage to secure his companions a good view.

There was an honor guard in place around the dais, headed by Barrin. Rienne was pleased to see that Norkis, the Hierarch's page, was on door duty, although his resemblance to Tad sent a pang of sorrow through her.

The four trumpeters sounded again, and Norkis threw the heavy doors wide. To a stirring paean the royal party entered, led by Lord General Anjer and General Ephan, resplendent in black uniforms trimmed with purple and gold.

Pharikian and his son walked directly behind the generals. They both wore ceremonial robes of white and gold, over which flowed silken purple mantles emblazoned with the tangwyr symbol. Pharikian moved with his old supple grace. His lined face bore a proud smile and his eyes shone. Aeyron bore himself quietly, but a greater measure of confidence now hung about him and he, too, wore a glad smile.

His Grace the Lord Marik, Duke of Kymer and Cardon, came next, and on his arm was his heavily pregnant wife, the Princess Idrimar. She was arrayed in maroon satin as a compliment to her husband's family colors. The strong, unforgiving hue did her pale complexion no favors, but she carried it off as best she could. Marik was bursting with visible pride in his much-loved wife.

Last came Sullyan, escorted by the dapper Baron Gaslek. She wore a glorious satin and velvet gown of rippling amber with a light overmantle of forest green. Her hair, held back by her fire opal fillet, streamed over her shoulders and down her back. She bore the gentle swell of her pregnancy with regal pride and paced quietly at Gaslek's side, her hand on his right arm.

As the little party reached the dais, the trumpeters climaxed with a ringing fanfaronade that slowly faded to silence.

Taran regarded the dais as Pharikian stepped onto it. There were three other thrones on it in addition to the Hierarch's and his

Heir's. Marik and the Princess would surely occupy the two thrones at Pharikian's left hand. Aeyron's throne, identical to his father's, was on the Hierarch's right. But who would occupy the fifth throne, the one set to the right of Aeyron's?

It was slightly smaller than the others but was as elaborately decorated and richly upholstered. Taran wondered whether Aeyron intended to announce a betrothal today, for his wife would certainly merit the place at his right hand. Taran hadn't heard that the Prince was considering a bride, but he knew that Pharikian had often pressed him to it. Recent events would have made the elderly Andaryan even more determined to see his Heir settled and a son produced. Perhaps today, from all the nobly-born ladies here, Aeyron would announce a choice.

Pharikian ascended the dais alone and came to stand before his throne, in full view of the hall. Cheers accompanied his appearance. Anjer and Ephan still flanked the rest of the party, and someone had provided a chair for Idrimar. Marik hovered protectively by her side. There was another ringing fanfare on a single silver trumpet, and then the Hierarch began to speak.

He welcomed his people and greeted each major noble House. He thanked them for their loyal support of his family through a difficult time, and asked them to voice their opinion of the homecoming and returning health of his son and Heir. The resultant cheers were deafening.

He then said a few words concerning the misguided invasion of their realm by King Elias. He called for forgiveness and understanding. There was more inclination to accept this when he described Elias's state of mind over the abduction of his own son. He told them of his proposals to strengthen ties with Albia and exhorted them all—especially those with younger, hotheaded sons—to remember his dictate against raiding into Albia.

Then he fell silent and his mien turned sober. He regarded the throng before him, and they waited expectantly to hear what he would say next.

"My friends, the distressing events of the past few weeks have had far-reaching and very nearly tragic consequences. My son was sorely wounded, suffered great torment, and very nearly lost his life. Caught in the helplessness that breeds anguish and despair, I also suffered and could well have died. That both of us were spared this fate and survived to stand before you is due to friendship, to loyalty and selflessness, to skill and unconditional love. But more on that later.

"Since recovering from this traumatic affair, I have realized a very important fact. My friends, the years continue to advance upon me."

His smile was wry and gentle as murmurs of anxious protest rustled through the room. He shook his head ruefully.

"I know, I know. It's obvious. But it often takes these life-changing events to make us realize that time is precious and not to be wasted. My daughter, the Princess Idrimar, will soon be delivered of twins, and it is my fervent hope to live to see them grow and to spend time with them while they are young. To that end, my friends, I hereby propose an amendment to the Hierarchy, as is my right under Andaryan law."

More murmurs, this time of real unease. Many thought he meant to abdicate. He held up his hands and silence fell once more.

"No, my friends, I do not intend to relinquish the throne just yet, but I do wish to devolve some of my duties onto my son, who has proven himself of suitable mettle to rule."

He gestured to Aeyron. The young man stepped up beside his father and faced the throng.

"My people," continued the Hierarch, "it is my will that my son become co-ruler of Andaryon and occupy the throne in his own right. Will you accept him and serve him as you have his father all these years? Will you accord him the honor that is his due? Will you accept and uphold his decrees? What say you, nobles of Andaryon? Will you accept Prince Aeyron as your sovereign Lord?"

The nobles of Andaryon would. In fact, they indicated their willingness in noisy fashion and their joy was contagious.

Chapter Nine

harikian gestured to the trumpeters and the horns sounded yet again. The crescendo of adulation died down. Pharikian led his son by the hand to his throne and personally seated him upon it. The Hierarch then assumed his own throne, thereby symbolizing their intent to share power. The room was somber and silent as the crowd witnessed this historic act.

Baron Gaslek approached the platform, bearing a purple satin pillow upon which was set the royal Crown of Andaryon. There were gasps of astonishment all around as Sullyan took up a second pillow bearing an identical crown and moved to stand behind Gaslek. Taran exchanged incredulous glances with Bull, and Rienne's gray eyes were shining.

The Baron ascended the platform, followed by Sullyan. However, she remained there while he continued on toward the Hierarch. He stopped a few paces away and bowed low.

"Majesty, I bear to you the Crown of Andaryon."

Pharikian stood and accepted the crown. It was light, fashioned of gold and set with silver, and bore the tangwyr crest of his House on the band. He took it and faced the crowd to speak the formal words.

"My people, it is the will of your Hierarch that Prince Aeyron be acclaimed as rightful co-ruler of this realm in perpetuity. Is it the will of the people also?"

A ringing "Yea!" echoed around the hall and the trumpets spoke again. Pharikian bowed very slightly at their affirmation and turned back to his son.

"Prince Aeyron, do you accept the burden of co-rulership over the realm of Andaryon?"

Aeyron bowed his head. "Majesty, I do."

"Do you swear to uphold its laws, to defend its justice and honor, and to deal fairly and swiftly with its enemies? Do you swear to spend your life in the service of our realm and to lay it down in that service if so required?"

"Majesty, I so swear."

"Then, Prince Aeyron, accept this crown as the symbol of your right to rule, and accept the service and acclaim of your people."

He set the crown upon Aeyron's head and the trumpets sang with joyful notes. Aeyron rose to the raucous rejoicing of the throng, tears standing in his eyes.

Sullyan stepped forward with the pillow bearing the other crown. She smiled radiantly at the Prince, and the look he turned on her would have melted any heart. There were many ladies there that day who would have given their all to have that regard turned on them. No one could hear what the two said to each other, but all could read their expressions.

Aeyron accepted the crown from her and she stepped back to stand with Gaslek. The Prince approached his father, who had seated himself on his throne. Aeyron did not bend the knee, nor did he bow. He was now co-ruler and, as such, his father's equal. He merely bent forward and placed the crown on the Hierarch's head. His father extended his right hand and Aeyron clasped it warmly. He resumed his seat on the throne next to the Hierarch and they sat side by side while the trumpets blared and the people celebrated.

It took some time, but the noise finally died away. Marik and Idrimar took their places on the dais beside Pharikian. Gaslek and Sullyan retreated to the marble floor, their duty done. Taran saw her wave to him and he urged Bull to help make a way for them to reach her. They made it just as yet another horn call sounded for silence.

Pharikian was on his feet again and Lord General Anjer had moved to stand behind the throne. The babble of voices died away and Pharikian spoke.

"Taran Elijah, would you please step forth."

There was cheering from the crowd, and Taran started and flushed. No one had warned him of this. He approached the dais, glancing at Bull, Cal, and Rienne. They all shook their heads, as bewildered as he. Gaslek grinned at him and guided him onto the platform.

He stood there, unsure what was to come. Then the Hierarch also called Sullyan's name and there were more cheers as she moved gracefully to stand beside the Adept. She smiled encouragingly at him and he relaxed.

Pharikian addressed his people once more. "My friends, many of you will have heard the tale of my son's succor and rescue from those who would have taken his life. I present to you the two people who were instrumental in restoring my son and Heir to me and to the Crown of Andaryon. I owe them more than words can say. I ask you all to acknowledge them and give thanks for their inestimable service to our realm. I present to you the Lady Brynne Sullyan of Albia, King's Envoy and Artesan Senior Master, and Taran Elijah of Albia, Artesan Adept."

The room erupted into hails and rejoicing and Taran flushed bright red. He didn't know where to look. Sullyan smiled and waved to those she knew.

Once the cheering faded, Pharikian turned to Taran.

"Artesan Elijah, please approach the throne."

Taran mounted the dais, falling to one knee before the throne. The Hierarch turned to Anjer, who passed him a long box clad in

121

deep purple velvet from where it had lain concealed behind the dais. Pharikian took it and stepped closer to Taran.

"Adept Elijah, you have rendered exceptional service to one who was in grave need and in peril of his life. In so doing, you imperiled your own life. That this service was rendered to one who was not even of your race makes your deed doubly selfless. I want you to know that we stand forever in your debt. There are yet other ways in which we hope to show you our deep gratitude, but for now, we ask that you accept this small gift as a token of our indebtedness and a sign of our lifelong friendship."

He held the box out and opened it as the confused Adept took it in his outstretched hands. Taran gasped aloud and the nearest among the crowd craned their necks to see. Lying on a bed of gold silk gauze was the most beautiful sword he had ever seen. It was light and long and exquisitely worked. He glanced up in bewilderment at the elderly Andaryan ruler, who said gently, "Take it up and rise with our heartfelt thanks, Artesan Adept Taran Elijah."

Taran drew the sword from the box to murmurs of envy and admiration from the assembled throng. Light flashed along the perfect blade. It fitted his hand as if made for him and he suddenly realized that it had, in fact, been crafted especially for him. There was a pattern engraved about the hilt and he started at its familiarity. He caught the impish gleam in Sullyan's eye.

"Yes, my friend," she murmured, "it is a representation of your psyche."

Taran shook his head in wonder. This was a gift beyond price and he didn't know how to respond. The problem was solved for him by Aeyron, who came forward and embraced him warmly. The crowd raised their voices yet again.

Taran was eventually released to rejoin his companions. Bull and Cal were eager to get a closer look at his priceless gift, as were many others around him. There was much backslapping and praise. Then Rienne nudged them for their attention, and when they glanced back up at the dais, they realized Sullyan had not yet been released by the Hierarch.

There was an air of tension about him and his son, and also Marik and Idrimar, who watched the tableau intently. Taran suffered a shiver of premonition, as if some life-changing event were about to take place. At a signal from Aeyron, the single silver trumpet blew again, commanding silence.

Sullyan stood on the platform, looking enquiringly from Pharikian to Aeyron. Aeyron stepped forward to the edge of the dais. He pitched his voice to carry.

"My Lords and Ladies, nobles all, my friends, my people. Today is a very special day. That I have lived to see it is attributable to two very remarkable people. Taran Elijah aided my rescue from the clutches of Baron Reen, an Albian sworn to the eradication of Artesans and the destruction of our race. It was this Baron who backed the traitor Rykan in his unsuccessful challenge of the Hierarch two years ago. Without the selfless bravery, the skill, and the care of Adept Elijah, I would not be here today, and you have seen him rewarded and acknowledged by the Crown.

"But my greatest debt of gratitude is owed to the Lady Brynne Sullyan. Not only did she share my confinement and torment, but by her strength and love she was able to offer me comfort and companionship in my darkest hour, despite her own pain and grave injury. She gave me the strength, the courage, and the will to live through what we were certain would be our final hours. She was also fully prepared to sacrifice both her life and the life of her unborn son in an attempt to save our world. For Baron Reen had set in motion an apocalyptic explosion of Earth force intended to shatter the Veils, so rending the fabric of our world and casting it into oblivion. Against all the odds, she succeeded."

Murmurs ran through the crowd as the gathered nobles and their families realized the enormity of the threat they had been under. Taran, who was watching Sullyan closely, could see she had no idea where Aeyron was going with this. Whatever was coming was something momentous.

"My people, these are the acts of one who has a deep and filial attachment to those she serves. It is true that the Lady Brynne has Andaryan blood in her veins, though she is essentially human. It is the blood of the Hierarch, and as such, it is also my blood. Lady Brynne has no known Albian kin. Her mother died birthing her and her father died soon after. Morgan Sullyan proved himself a true and faithful friend to the realms of Andaryon and Albia by willingly sacrificing his life to broker the pact which united our noble Houses to end wholesale raiding into the human realm. Thus, the name of Sullyan stands proudly in our history and will do so for all eternity."

Aeyron paused while the swelling acclaim of the crowd found expression. He smiled down at the woman who stood bewildered but proud on the platform below him.

Yet still she had no notion of what was to come.

Aeyron hushed the crowd once more. "My people, it is traditional at such ceremonies as these, and also my right as co-ruler of Andaryon, to issue a decree, a point of law. I wish to do so today, to mark this special occasion and to do what honor I can to a beloved and true friend. This will be my first official act under the Crown, and I have the blessing and the wholehearted agreement of my father and my sister. My friends, hear these words and remember them well."

✤ ✤ ✤ ✤ ✤

Sullyan's mind was blank. She had been taken rather unawares at Taran's gifting. The sword had been as much a surprise to her as to

Taran. What Aeyron was about now, she had no idea. She had allowed herself to hope that they would content themselves with a private expression of their thanks and leave it at that. She would vastly have preferred it to this very public display. She could not, however, deny Aeyron his right to stand before his people and say his piece. If nothing else, it proved his returning confidence.

She tried to still the tremble of her body. A strange feeling had come over her, as if some bird of momentous omen had suddenly settled on her shoulder and was waiting for Fate to pronounce.

The tall Prince approached her and held out his hands. She raised hers and he took them, looking deeply into her eyes. A profound hush descended on the crowd.

"Brynne Sullyan, you have been without family, without kin, and unclaimed for too long. It is our desire, our earnest wish, that you accept our claim upon you. Brynne, we wish to formally adopt you into our House. You bear the blood of the Hierarch in your veins as surely as it runs through mine. I claim that blood, as is my right. I claim that you are my kin, through the blood of my father. I acknowledge you. I claim you as my sister, dear and beloved. Brynne Sullyan, do you acknowledge my claim?"

The room was silent. Sullyan couldn't speak. She was incapable of coherent thought. Her heart was so full she had no room for breath. She simply stared at him from unseeing eyes. Her throat was tight, her chest painful. She didn't see Idrimar approaching her. She hardly felt the Princess take her numb and trembling hands from her brother.

"Brynne Sullyan," the Princess said, a gentle smile on her face, "for the love you have shown us, for the service you have done us in supporting my father and returning my brother, whom I love more dearly than life itself, I claim that you are my kin through the blood of my father. I acknowledge you. I claim you as my sister, dear and beloved. Brynne Sullyan, do you acknowledge my claim?"

A single tear escaped and rolled unheeded down Sullyan's face. Timar Pharikian was coming toward her now, and he held something that glittered. Idrimar moved back and her father halted before Sullyan, taking her unresisting hands in his. He smiled, trying to lend her some strength. She still couldn't utter a sound, and all her muscles were quivering uncontrollably.

The Hierarch spoke, almost in a whisper. "Brynne Sullyan, my dear, dear child. I have wanted to do this for so long. I owed your father so much that I could never repay, and then, out of nowhere, in duress and in torment, you came to me. You appeared here, in this very hall, like a revenant out of time, and gave to me the same love, the same service, the same loyalty that your father gave. And you asked for nothing in return. You have given me friendship, hope, and strength. At great personal cost, you helped me retain my realm, which was under the direst threat it has faced since the sacrifice of your sire. And now, most precious of all, you have given me my son again, whom I feared was lost forever. What we do here now can only in small measure repay the debt we owe you."

He went on, raising his voice in a clear and unmistakable call to his people. "Brynne Sullyan. I claim that you are my kin by right of my blood which passes through your veins. I declare that you are a true daughter of my body, sister to my son, Aeyron, sister to my daughter, Idrimar. I declare that you are a legitimate scion of the House of Pharikian and a Princess of the royal line. Brynne Sullyan, daughter, accept this claim and accept also this Seal of our House. Princess Brynne, come take your rightful place among us."

So saying, he slipped a delicate golden ring onto the little finger of her right hand. It bore the tangwyr crest of Andaryon's ruling House, and it circled her finger as if it had always rested there.

The rapturous tumult that erupted at the Hierarch's declaration failed completely to impinge upon Sullyan's awareness. She stared at Pharikian, blinking in bewilderment and awe. The pain in her chest threatened to overwhelm her and her brimming eyes could hold no more. Her body trembled violently and shimmering tears streamed down her face as she stood in stunned silence. She was unable to move, unable to speak. Never before had she been so totally overcome. It was all too much, too mind-numbingly wonderful, and she had no idea what to do.

Few among the crowd had ever witnessed anything as incredible and strange as this. People crowded toward the platform, Bull, Taran, Cal, and Rienne foremost among them, all with tears of joy in their eyes and smiles on their faces. Anjer stood nearby, trying unsuccessfully to hide the evidence of his own emotion, and Marik was weeping openly. Yet still she could do and say nothing.

Aeyron glanced in concern at his father. Had they gone too far? It had not been so long, after all, since she had suffered a cracked skull, and although it was healed, she was not at her peak of fitness.

Pharikian knew she was only overwhelmed. He took pity on her. Instead of insisting on the traditional response, he simply enfolded her warmly into his embrace. The physical contact, along with the inevitable sharing that occurred between two Artesans upon such contact, snapped the bonds that held her captive, as he knew it would. She broke down completely under the soothing balm of his love, and sobbed freely into his breast. She uttered the only words she could find breath for, and he was the only one who heard them.

"Oh, *Father!*"

The trumpets rang and rang as Pharikian led her, still dazed and uncomprehending, up to the dais. They rang as she was seated on the throne, Aeyron doing her the additional honor of placing her between himself and his father. They rang as the delicate fire opal fillet was replaced by an equally delicate representation of the Andaryan Crown, worked in red gold and studded with fire opals. They rang as Pharikian, Aeyron, and Idrimar all did her homage as befitted a Princess of the royal line. And they rang as the entire throng, over three thousand souls, bent the knee, acclaimed her as the new Princess, and accepted her into the House of Pharikian.

They would ring in her heart forever.

✣ ✣ ✣ ✣ ✣

To give her time to come to terms with what had just happened, Pharikian sent word that the minstrels should strike up again. The servants had filled the tables while Aeyron's ceremony was under way. Slowly, encouraged by Gaslek and by Barrin's men, the audience hall began to empty as the nobles and their ladies moved into the ballroom. The air was charged with the sounds of gossip. The Hierarch's court—and probably the entire realm—would be buzzing with this news for days.

On the dais, Sullyan was slowly recovering from the deepest shock she had ever suffered. This was as momentous, and in many ways far more traumatic, than her discovery that the Hierarch had been intimate with both of her parents, people of whom she had known nothing whatever. Now, incredibly, she had a family, and it contained people she loved with the depth of her generous heart and the whole of her soul.

Surrounded only by her friends now, she was able to master herself by degrees. Her pupils dilated as she drew on her inner resources to garner the strength she needed to compose herself. It would all eventually have to be paid for, but she could worry about that later.

Under their gentle and loving ministrations, she was soon able to smile again. Still seated upon Aeyron's cushioned throne, she gazed around them all, wondering how on earth she could ever respond to such selflessness, such unconditional generosity and love. It was impossible, but she did the best she could.

She fixed them all with a straight stare and said, as sternly as she could manage with a voice that still shook, "After today, if any one of you so much as considers addressing me as 'Highness' on anything less than a formal State occasion, he or she will find my sword at their breast!"

Bull roared with laughter. He was joined by Anjer. The unnatural emotional hiatus was broken and now they could all be themselves again. Any attempt to put such intense feelings into words would have failed miserably. Barring Idrimar and Gaslek, they were all Artesans. They all knew how powerful and overpowering these deep emotions could be. It was the source of strength, as well as the curse, of the Artesan. Controlling and channeling life force necessarily intensified the emotions, and the effect was inescapable.

Now that Sullyan was able to speak again around the lump in her throat, normal conversation was possible. Pharikian and Aeyron seated themselves on either side of her and Marik brought his and Idrimar's seats closer. Barrin's men brought chairs for Sullyan's friends, and also Anjer, Ephan, and Gaslek.

Norkis appeared bearing a tray loaded with crystal carafes of golden wine. There were also goblets and platters of food. Toasts were drunk to friendship, to love, to family, and to those not present. Strangely, Sullyan felt the presence of her parents very strongly tonight, as if they had witnessed and approved the day's events. This seemed both fitting and ironic, considering she now had a new family.

Or maybe it was as natural as breathing since, in a very real way, Pharikian *was* her father. Maybe not in seed, but certainly in blood and expedience. If not for his selfless gift to her mother, Sullyan would never have been born. She held his gaze with her own as that particular toast was drunk. Intuiting her percipience, Pharikian raised his goblet with hers and their thoughts mingled in his memories of Morgan and Bethyn.

Later, Sullyan felt able to join the throng in the ballroom. The music was welling out and calling to her, urging her to the dance. Escorted by a happy and confident Aeyron, she led the rest of her family and her friends out onto the dance floor. They were swallowed into the crowd and gave themselves over to the festive mood.

✣ ✣ ✣ ✣ ✣

The hour was growing late and the guests were beginning to leave. Rienne, Cal, Taran, and Bull sat on chairs in the ballroom, listening to Sullyan's haunting voice. The new Princess had long since joined with the minstrels and was playing a lap harp and singing Andaryan folk tunes.

Pharikian and Aeyron sat by themselves, watching their people revel in the joy of the day and feeling content. The Hierarch had covertly watched his tall and handsome son—still thinner than usual but regaining muscle daily—and noted how Aeyron's gaze rarely left the slender figure of his newly-adopted sister.

Pharikian had watched her also throughout the evening, concerned in case the shock they had unwittingly inflicted upon her should manifest itself in unwanted ways before the day was out.

The Hierarch finally stirred beside his son. "Aeyron, I know we have spoken of this before, but you must forgive me if I raise it again. In the light of recent events, you really must give some thought to finding yourself a bride."

Aeyron never moved, never took his eyes from Sullyan's glowing face. She was serene and content, playing with her eyes closed. The tiny gold signet flickered on her finger, echoed by the wedding band on her left hand.

The Prince sighed deeply. "I know, I know. But how can I? And especially now. Look at her, Father. Wherever will I find another like her?"

Pharikian's heart sank. He had been afraid of this. "You won't, my son, you know that. She is unique in so many ways, and if you give her your heart, I am afraid you will be hurt. You know she is already wed to the mate of her soul, despite their present circumstances. She is also mainly human, regardless of our family's blood flowing within her."

He laid a hand on Aeyron's arm. "You love her, I know, but you still need a mate. You need someone to share love with, someone to share your bed. You need a woman of our race to bear you sons and daughters. Could you not find room in your heart for another?"

Aeyron tore his gaze away from Sullyan and read the concern in his father's eyes. "We spoke of this," he said. "In the circle. We talked of many things, shared many secrets. I told her that the women of our race are not encouraged to think for themselves as are the women of Albia, my mother and my sister being rare exceptions. I told her I would never take a mate unless I could find one such as they."

Pharikian's eyes glittered. "And what did she say to that?"

"She told me I should start a revolution."

The Hierarch smiled and Aeyron's eyes narrowed. He glanced back at Sullyan. "Do you know, I might just do that."

✤ ✤ ✤ ✤ ✤

The evening, full as it had been, held yet one last surprise, one last honor. Most of the invited guests had gone to their lodgings. Now, only the royal family and their immediate friends were left, a party of around fifty in all. They had gathered at the far end of the ballroom where the wide-flung windows gave on to the rose garden, and the heady scent of blossoms pervaded the cool night breeze. Some talked softly among themselves and some, including Taran, were silent, listening to Sullyan's sweet voice as she sang ballads into the moonlit night.

The last quivering notes finally faded as she laid her hands on the strings to still them. Taran saw her glance at Pharikian, who inclined his head.

"Well, my friends," she said, laying aside the harp, "this has been quite a night."

There were murmurs of agreement and one or two reluctant yawns.

"We have spoken much of service and of the duty of love tonight," she continued, "and reward has been meted out where it was due. In some cases, far in excess of what might have been expected!" She smiled lovingly at her new family. "But one achievement has been left unacknowledged. This attainment, long desired, long thought inaccessible, was finally gained through love and great effort, and also through disregard for personal peril."

They all watched her now, but only a few were aware of what she intended. Taran became aware she was looking at him. He froze, recognizing himself in her last words, and guessed what she meant to do. He flushed crimson.

Yet it wasn't Sullyan who uttered the ritual words. It was Aeyron.

He spoke quietly, making Taran jump nevertheless. "Taran Elijah, Artesan Adept. Are you feeling strong tonight?"

He hesitated. He wasn't feeling strong—far from it. Then the pleasure and pride he had felt at his achievement, so swiftly repressed due to the urgency that followed it, came flooding back to suffuse his psyche. He had actually attained the exalted rank of Adept-elite, the rank his father had held and which Taran had been convinced he'd never reach. It had taken Sullyan's love to show him he shouldn't be afraid of the Fire of his passion, that he should use it and channel it, not run from it. And now, although it was stronger than ever and would become stronger still, he was in control. He could call it up or damp it down at a moment's thought, and he no longer felt helpless under its influence.

His smile as he gazed into her eyes was frank with the knowledge of this passion. She blushed as she perceived his thought, but she also smiled back with pride.

Taran replied to Aeyron, though he still held Sullyan's gaze. "Yes, Master Artesan, I am feeling very strong tonight."

The three of them—Aeyron as Master and Pharikian and Sullyan as Senior Masters-elite—would confirm him in his rank, an unprecedented honor in the history of their kind. Aeyron called Fire at Taran's feet where it danced and writhed on the polished marble floor, and Taran reached down for the portion of his psyche that paralleled the element of Fire. As he immersed himself in it, he was amazed at the changes it had undergone since he'd broken through the fiery circle. He had not had the leisure to examine it since, but he had been aware on a subliminal level of its evolving.

Now he saw how much more complex it was, how the loops and spirals, whorls and helixes had increased, how they had intertwined and become more convoluted. He would need to familiarize himself with its new configuration very soon, but for now he just accepted it. He reached for it and merged with it, felt the flow of Fire through his veins, and accepted the surge of strong passion that suffused every part of his body. He felt no trace of embarrassment, just pride and joy in what he could now achieve.

The Fire at his feet suddenly blazed with white intensity and leaped for the rafters. He heard Sullyan's gentle laugh and knew she was remembering her own early experiences with Fire. He heard Rienne's gasp of astonishment and saw Cal's dark eyes widen with awe. His old master had grown out of all recognition.

Taran damped the Fire with ease, let it fade from his body, and even sent it back through the substrate. He saw Sullyan's approving nod of satisfaction and he subsided, shivering from the effort. All power had its price, and although he now knew how to use it, he still needed to build his strength.

Realizing they were waiting for him, he cleared the Fire from his eyes and thoughts and approached the three powerful Artesans before him. He dropped to one knee and gave them the obeisance which was their due.

"Taran Elijah," intoned Pharikian solemnly, the gleam in his eyes betraying his sober tone, "you have proved yourself well able to influence Fire. In passing this test, you demonstrate your capacity to support being raised to the next level of your craft. Artesan Elijah, you are an Adept no more. I pronounce and affirm that you hold the rank of Adept-elite. Rise and well done, my friend."

Sullyan was the first to embrace him, tears of joy sparkling in her eyes.

Chapter Ten

It was a fine morning and none to see it but those on guard duty. Many had sore heads, and no one who could help it rose early. Sullyan and Rienne, who had shared Sullyan's suite, had not lain down to sleep until they had talked themselves out the previous night, despite the late hour. Even Sullyan didn't wake until well after dawn. Once she and Rienne had bathed and dressed, a page was dispatched to fetch breakfast and to see if the men were awake.

They all gathered around the table before the open windows, drinking fellan and eating new bread with cold meat, cheese, or honey. The previous day's incredible events were talked over once again and congratulatory remarks were reiterated, both to Sullyan and to Taran. Neither Bull, Cal, nor Rienne missed the meaningful glances shared by Taran and Sullyan, but as they were not explained, the others were left to make of them what they could.

The three visitors had already given Taran and Sullyan all the gossip from the Manor. One piece of news, however, had yet to be told. Bull hadn't wanted to inform Sullyan of Parren's death through the substrate as he wasn't at all sure how she would take it.

For her part, she had guessed he had something on his mind, but she knew he would approach it in his own way. She listened in silence as he finally related the tale, and her face was pale when he'd finished.

"How is he recovering from his injuries, Rienne?" she asked, betraying none of her thoughts over the rights or wrongs of Robin's actions.

The healer shrugged. "Well enough, I think. He seems to regard it as some kind of penance for disobeying the King's order. He won't let me touch him. Luckily, Bull did a neat enough job of stitching the flesh at the time, so there won't be much of a scar when it's fully healed."

"It was only meant to be temporary until Rienne could get a look at it," grumbled Bull. "Silly sod won't let anyone near it. It'll serve him right if it puckers."

Sullyan fixed him with a stricken stare.

"It's all right," he added hastily, "it won't. But he really should have let Rienne see to it. It was pretty deep."

Sullyan sighed. "He should know well enough whether it needed attention. At least Parren did not kill him as he would have done last time."

Bull huffed in disgust, unwilling to comment further.

Sullyan asked after Tad and received a detailed account of his condition from Rienne. Her expression was grave when the healer was done.

"His situation is still serious, then?"

Rienne nodded unhappily. "Robin sits by his side every minute he can spare, holding his hand, talking to him, pouring strength into him. If Tad survives, it will be because of Robin's determination, I'm sure of it."

Sullyan nodded. "And you found no evidence of Parren's treachery on his person or in his rooms?"

Bull answered. "None. If he'd had anything incriminating, he must have destroyed it."

"Has anyone checked Tad's or Ozella's things?"

Bull frowned, reddening. "Do you know, I don't think anyone has?"

She gave him a stern look. "Then I suggest you see to it the moment you return. Parren attacked them for a reason. Either they overheard him talking to the Baron or a messenger, or they saw something incriminating. Either way, it was enough to convince Parren they were a deadly threat."

She stopped, struck by a memory.

"You know, while we were at the horse fair in Loxton, the King told me he had received a message from Ozella's father saying that his two daughters had gone missing. He suspected an abduction and was waiting for a ransom demand. He asked Elias not to tell Ozella, but as far as I am aware, a ransom demand never arrived. I wonder if that was the hold the Baron exerted? How easy to tell Parren of it and let him threaten Ozella with his sisters' lives unless he cooperated. Parren would pass any information he gleaned to the Baron—he could even have used the King's own runner service—and that would have cleared the Baron's hands of any blood over the affair. Perhaps Ozella confided in Tad and they challenged Parren with it."

Bull gasped. "Oh, gods! I told young Tad to work on Ozella! I told him to try to find out what was bothering the boy."

He turned to Sullyan, a desperate appeal in his eyes. "You know how distracted Ozella had been. I told Tad to befriend him. I thought the lad might be able to get through to him. I never thought ... gods, Sully, I never intended them to go *that* far!"

Sullyan laid a hand on his arm. "It was not your fault, Hal. And we do not know what actually happened. You know what Parren was like. If he even thought they were a threat, he would have acted. They may not have challenged him."

"But if they suspected something, why didn't they come to *me*? I would have listened. Tad knew that!"

She sent him a flow of soothing thought. "We will just have to wait until Tad can tell us the story. Do not upset yourself. Done is done."

137

She changed tack to distract Bull from his self-reproach. "Did Parren have any extra coin over what he should have had?"

Bull sighed, still unhappy. "Yes, he had a tidy sum in one of his packs, about a years' worth of pay."

"Blood money from the Baron, no doubt," she said, staring out into the garden. "Well, Parren is gone, and dead men make poor storytellers. Robin can consider himself fortunate that the King did not order him confined for his disobedience."

Bull sighed heavily and changed the subject.

✤ ✤ ✤ ✤ ✤

The time for the three Albians to leave had arrived. Colonel Vassa needed Bull's assistance in running the Manor, and Rienne was anxious to return to Tad. So, late in the afternoon, they assembled at the Citadel's southern gate to say their farewells.

Sullyan, who had seemed distracted for much of the afternoon, pulled Rienne aside. They stopped just out of earshot of the men. Sullyan turned, hugging herself and looking into Rienne's eyes. She spoke diffidently.

"Rienne, I have a favor to ask of you."

Rienne's gaze sharpened, but she smiled easily. "Anything, Brynne, you know that. What is it?"

Sullyan seemed uncomfortable as she looked off into the distance. "You may not know, but in many ways I feel very alone here."

Her voice was barely audible, not much above a whisper. Rienne had to strain to catch her words. What she heard surprised her.

"But I thought—"

"Please, let me finish. Yesterday, when they … when they adopted me, I had the strangest feeling. I felt as though my parents, especially my mother, were watching over me. I have never felt that before. Perhaps if I knew where they came from, I might have a similar feeling if I visited where they lived. But this is the only place I know where they came and where they stayed, and the knowledge that I live in the very room they shared and sleep in the very bed where my ... where I was born, gives me a measure of comfort, a sense of closeness to them. I intend for my own child to be born in that bed."

The healer's eyes brimmed and her heart held deep sorrow. She could hear the depth of Sullyan's loneliness, could see it behind her eyes, and her heart yearned to comfort her.

"What can I do, Brynne? How can I help you?"

"Dear Rienne, you mean so much to me. Do you know that I think of you as the first true friend I ever had?"

Rienne's eyes widened. "Me?"

Sullyan smiled gently. "You and I met under difficult circumstances and you did not like me much at first. No need to protest. I could see it within you! You were almost afraid of me. You were certainly very nervous around me. I have seen it before and I recognized the signs."

Rienne blushed. It was true. She had never been an overly confident person, and meeting such a gifted, beautiful, powerful, and confident young woman as Sullyan had completely thrown her. It hadn't taken her long to catch a glimpse of the lonely soul beneath the poised exterior, and they had become firm friends from that moment on.

"There is no need for shame," Sullyan assured her. "I think we are very similar beneath the veneer of what life and experience has made of us. I certainly feel very close to you, especially as you often perceive my thoughts and moods."

Rienne smiled wryly. "If that were so, then I should have an idea of where you're going with this, but I'm afraid I don't!"

"I apologize. I am skirting the point." She sighed. "In a few weeks' time, my child will be born. I have to admit I am nervous. I have never lived with other women. I have not had the benefit of older sisters, cousins, or aunts from whom to learn about childbirth. I have no idea what to expect. In a very real way, I have only been pregnant for a few weeks and I am still not used to the idea. Too much has happened to allow me the time to assimilate it properly. I could talk to Torien, or Hollett, or any of the other ladies, but I am not close to them as I am to you. At this time, the person I really yearn for is my mother—the one person I cannot have.

"I know you have to return today. You have Cal and your own duties. Above all, it may harm you or your child if you stayed here too long. But when my time comes"—Sullyan's voice cracked a little—"will you return here? Will you be with me through this? I know you have not experienced birth yet either, but you are a healer. You know what to do. I would trust Deshan with my life and I know he would help me, but he is a man. I need a woman by my side. If I cannot have my mother, I would have you. Will you come?"

Rienne's cheeks were damp. "Of course I'll come! You didn't need to ask; I was going to come anyway. I wouldn't let you go through this alone, you must know that. All you need is to send for me whenever you want me. But you really mustn't worry, you know. You're in very good health, you're fit and strong. With your Artesan skills, you'll have the easiest birth there ever was. It'll be a wonderful experience, I promise you. And when you hold your baby son in your arms, knowing that you've given him life, it'll be the most incredible feeling you'll ever have. And if you get worried in the meantime, or if you want to talk, just send someone for me. You know I'll always come."

Sullyan nodded wordlessly, tears traversing her pale face. She tried to smile her thanks, though the haunting sadness didn't leave her eyes. Rienne's heart bled for her pain, but she didn't know what other comfort she could give. Damn Robin for his unreasoning jealousy! She felt a great surge of anger and forced it down as she embraced the slender woman.

They returned to the others. Bull was ready to leave. He was giving Taran needless instructions for looking after Sullyan.

"I'm not leaving her, Bull," Taran assured him. "As long as I'm taking no hurt from staying in this realm, I'll be here. I'll see this through to the end, whatever that may be. Just call me if you want news."

"Well, don't forget that you'll most likely be required for the Baron's trial," cautioned Bull. "You were the one to rescue Prince Eadan, after all."

"I didn't do it alone," said Taran, but Bull was right. It was only to be expected, especially considering the lack of tangible evidence against the Baron.

Bull and Cal took their leave of Taran and the big man turned to Sullyan.

"You take care, my Princess," he rasped as he took her hands. His big fingers stroked the ring that had belonged to Jessy, Robin's sister, before he'd given it in betrothal to Sullyan. She smiled up at him as she stepped into his embrace.

"I will, Bull. You, too. And you, Cal. Be sure to look after your lady! She is very precious to me. And I hope you are giving some thought to names for your daughter."

The three Albians mounted their horses and Sullyan opened the Veils for them. Familiar country appeared at the far end of the structure. Rienne saw her and Taran standing side by side, watching their friends ride through, before the construct was collapsed and they were gone.

Chapter Eleven

Bull rode into the stable yard, a grim expression on his face. He had not mentioned again his determination to inform Robin of Sullyan's pregnancy, but he still had every intention of doing so as soon as possible. He knew Robin would be off duty in the middle of the afternoon. As all the Major's free time was currently spent with Tad, Bull knew exactly where to find him.

Their horses had been taken care of and Cal had gone up to the Manor, taking all three packs with him. Rienne wanted to go straight to the infirmary, so Bull accompanied her there.

He didn't ask Rienne what Sullyan had said to her before they'd left. He had a pretty good idea what it was. He knew she was lonely, and wonderful as Pharikian's gesture had been, her heart still resided here. The keeper of that heart needed to know a very important piece of information.

Bull had no doubt this would be a turning point. Robin couldn't possibly ignore news like this. Fired with determination, he strode purposefully toward the infirmary, quite outpacing Rienne. She caught up as they arrived at the door to Tad's room. They could both see the desolate figure within, seated by the cadet's bedside. Robin's eyes were closed and there were lines of strain on his pale and handsome face. He had one of Tad's hands clasped in his, and the unease of his breathing told them he was linked with Tad's weakened psyche, trying desperately to will it back to strength.

Rienne's lips pursed in concern. "He'll kill himself if he goes on like this."

Bull agreed. "We can't stop him, though. If we deny him this and Tad doesn't pull through, he'll never forgive himself. He'd never forgive us, either."

Rienne nodded. She moved silently into the room and placed two fingers on the pulse at Tad's neck. She turned to smile briefly at Bull. He gazed at the young lad lying so still, so unnaturally quiet. His breathing was shallow. His face was still pale, though not bloodless and gray as it had been. He was strong enough now to accept liquids and thin soups, and Rienne had also given him some of the powders Deshan had once made for Sullyan when she had lain in a similar condition.

Tad was holding on and they were fairly sure his body would mend. As to his mind, they had no such certainty.

Rienne placed a hand on Robin's shoulder, softly calling his name. The young man startled and his eyes opened. They were dark with worry and exhaustion. His recent exertions over his fight with Parren, his nasty wound, and the King's displeasure had all combined to sap his strength. His labors over Tad were taking a heavy toll on what was left.

"Robin," she said, "go rest awhile. I'm here now, let me take over. I'll call you if there's any change."

He nodded and rose, still stiff on his wounded leg. He gave Tad's hand a final squeeze before he let it go, but there was no response. Disconsolately, he walked from the room.

Bull caught Rienne's eye. "I'm going to tell him now."

She frowned. "Do you think that's wise? He's in no state to hear it."

"When will he be? He deserves to know. He has a right. He can't undo the damage until he knows. I appreciate how low he is, but I have to think of Sully. I have to tell him."

Rienne stared at him and he sensed the pit of doubt opening in her stomach. She was almost sick with worry. Unable to do anything about it, she turned her attention back to her patient.

Bull followed Robin out. The Major wasn't looking where he was going as he wandered away from the Manor. That suited Bull. He had no intention of blurting this out where others could hear. He followed silently as Robin made his slow and unsteady way toward the nearest pasture, where he stopped by the fence and slumped onto the rail. Exhaustion and despair were written plain in every line of his body.

Bull came up beside him and leaned his bulk on a fence post. He stared across the field, watching the horses crop grass. Robin gave no sign he'd noticed Bull.

The silence stretched on. When it was obvious Robin wouldn't speak, Bull said, "I've just come from seeing Sullyan."

Robin stirred uneasily. "What are you telling me for?"

Bull's eyes tightened but he held his temper back. "Aren't you at least going to ask me how she is?"

"Why should I? I'm sure you're going to tell me anyway."

Bull's temper snapped. "Maybe you don't bloody well deserve to know!"

Robin turned his head, staring the big man directly in the eye. "Just tell me this. Is she still with *him*?"

Bull's eyes flashed. "If you mean Taran, then yes! He's looking after her. He's doing what *you* should be doing!"

"Then she's made her choice." Robin spun angrily. "Let him take care of her. See how long she stays with *him* before she tires of him!"

He pushed away from the rail and stalked off. Bull stared after him, hands clenched on the wood, wanting to scream in fury at Robin's pointless and damaging jealousy.

"You bloody young idiot!" he raged. "Don't you even care anymore? She's bloody *pregnant*, damn you! Doesn't that mean anything to you?"

Robin froze. His whole body stiffened and he stood rooted in place. Bull couldn't see his eyes or his face, but he saw the sudden shudder that unlocked the rigid muscles. Robin spun on one heel, his face a mask of white fury, his eyes spitting sparks.

"Why should *I* care? What's it to me if she's carrying that peasant's child? Why should *I* care about another man's bastard?"

With no warning and no hesitation, Bull crossed the paces between them. Too swiftly for Robin to react, he lashed out with all the force and trained experience of his mighty muscles. Boiling rage, fear, and frustration powered the fist he swung at Robin, and Robin never even saw it come. One minute the big man was looming before him, a red mist in his eyes. The next, Robin was lying sprawled on the ground, moaning and clutching at the fiery agony of a cracked jaw.

Bull stood over him, massaging his fist. He didn't say a word. The hurt and rage within his breast were too vast for words. He stared in disgust at the young man beneath him, bitterly regretting the day he had ever set eyes on him.

He turned on his heel and left, leaving Robin lying there, one hand to his bloody jaw, tears of anger and betrayal in his eyes.

✤ ✤ ✤ ✤ ✤

After the incredible events of Aeyron's coronation, the next few days followed much the same pattern as those that preceded it. Sullyan continued the Prince's rehabilitation, spending a couple of hours with him in the cool of early morning before going to change into formal attire more fit for official duties.

Aeyron was gradually taking on more of his father's responsibilities. He spent a large part of each day hearing petitions, settling disputes, and granting claims. He had quietly begun the revolution he'd spoken of to his father by requesting that Sullyan sit in on these sessions at his right hand, thus paving the way for when he found an Andaryan noblewoman strong-minded enough to aid him in his rule.

During these sessions and, more worryingly, during Aeyron's weapons training, Sullyan was often distracted, a pall of sorrow seeming to hang over her. Although he would never ask her, Taran was sure he knew what had caused it. She had told him of Bull's determination to tell Robin about her condition, and Taran could see how desperately she hoped the news of her pregnancy would bring Robin to her side. As the days passed and he didn't come, she grew more and more withdrawn.

Under normal circumstances she would have found an outlet for this heartache in her weapons skills. Hard physical exercise, coupled with the ever-present threat of injury required total concentration. Working her body to the point of exhaustion often seemed to leach away her emotional pain with the sweat of her exertions. In her present physical condition, however, such anodynes were denied her.

Pharikian noticed her distraction and quizzed both Taran and his Master Physician over the state of her health. Deshan assured him her body was well; the babe was growing as he should, although she would never grow as large as most women did. Her child was very small and delicate and her muscles were strong and held him firm. She rarely even felt him kick. For the malady of her spirit, though, only one man held the remedy.

✣ ✣ ✣ ✣ ✣

There came a morning when the Prince and Pharikian were closeted together on business that did not require Sullyan's presence. Feeling displaced, she spent the morning with Marik and

Idrimar, accompanied by Taran, as usual. They ate together at noon, keeping up a pleasant discourse, although her heart wasn't in it.

Once the meal was over, she felt a desire to climb the palace tower and walk on the battlements awhile. Her heavy spirit often goaded her to walk if she could not fight, as if she could leave her depression behind. Taran readily agreed to accompany her and they made the long and arduous ascent together. It was a measure of her heavier state that she had to stop and rest twice on the way up.

They eventually emerged from the stairway and moved toward the parapet. Despite the chill of the breeze, the air was crystal clear and afforded a fine view of the land around for many miles. The Hierarch's standard streamed above them, snapping in the frisky wind. Sullyan drew her shawl about her and paced around the walls, staring silently out over the land.

She was reminded of the battle with Rykan. She and Robin had watched much of the conflict from this vantage, and from here she had seen and helped counter Rykan's last ploy to break through Anjer's battle lines.

To the south was the area where she had fought and killed Rykan, the spot unmarked by any remembrance but burned indelibly onto her mind's eye. She halted for a long time, just staring at the place. Then her gaze traveled east, to the mounds left by the pyres of the dead, their soft grassy coverings now studded with wildflowers.

To the north, the megalith-crowned hill was visible, the site of her farewell to Torman Vanyr, who had proved such a true and loyal friend, and without whose selfless sacrifice she almost certainly would have died. The hill held other memories as well, memories which would have been joyous had they not been marred by jealousy and anger. Slow tears fell as she gazed to the north.

She was still standing there when she heard movement over by the double tower doors. Timar Pharikian had climbed the steps and was walking slowly toward them.

"My daughter, are you not cold standing out here in the wind? Will you not come inside where it's warmer?"

She gave him a weary smile. "No, Father, I am well enough. I needed to see the sky and the space around me. I have felt caged these past few days."

Pharikian frowned. "You have been working too hard. We must arrange a hunting trip or a picnic soon. We have carriages you can use. I will speak to Aeyron about it."

She nodded and silently resumed her contemplation of the land below. Pharikian hesitated before speaking again.

"I came to find you for a reason. There is someone here who earnestly desires speech with you. I think it would be good for you to hear what he has to say."

Sullyan turned to stare at him, a mixture of dread, anxiety, and hope too intense to bear kindling within her.

He returned her look unhappily. "He will come to you here," was all he said. He turned to leave, gesturing to Taran with an unmistakable request to give her some privacy.

She could see Taran had no intention of leaving her alone. Not until he knew for sure who it was, anyway. He merely moved farther along the parapet, remaining just within earshot.

The Hierarch passed through the tower doors. She heard his voice as he spoke to someone inside. Sullyan turned to stare at the doors, as if by the intensity of her regard she could bring him to her. Her hands clutched her shawl feverishly and she began to tremble. She struggled to swallow her rising emotion.

There was another noise by the doors and then he was there. The unbearable knot of pleading hope that had clenched Sullyan's heart broke apart, leaving her bereft. It was not Robin who stood there framed by the doorway.

It was Elias.

She turned away, the blood draining from her face. She stood disconsolate, staring blindly down at the land spread below her like a carpet. Elias, dressed in his state robes for the embarrassing, uncomfortable, but entirely necessary visit to the Hierarch, stood immobile, as if stunned.

Eventually, hesitantly, he approached.

Taran watched from the other wall, and she was glad of his presence. She was quivering with emotion and wondered how she would bear this meeting. Elias had wounded her deeply.

The King moved to her side, clearly determined to say his piece. He put out a hand as if to touch her, but dropped it back by his side.

His voice was hoarse. "Ah, my Lady. Such sorrow and grief. Can they ever be assuaged?"

She stiffened, striving for control. She had to swallow some of her pain before she could speak. She stared out over the land, unwilling to meet the King's gaze.

"Are you so surprised, my Lord? Do you not know that grief is the price we all must pay for love? The deeper the love, the greater the grief. And I, my Lord … I have loved deeply indeed."

Elias hung his head. Then, to Sullyan's shock, the High King of Albia fell to his knees before her, catching her right hand in his.

"And I betrayed that love. I know it. I set it at naught and cast you out when all you ever did was render me loyal service. I have hated myself for it. I have come here to seek your forgiveness, if you can find it in your heart to grant it. Can you, my Lady? Can you ever forgive me?"

She stared down at him, eyes wild. Glancing hastily about, fearful lest someone should see his unprecedented action, she clutched at his hands.

"My Lord—your Majesty—Elias, rise, *please*! This is most unseemly."

He stubbornly stayed put. "Unseemly? I'll tell you what is unseemly. What I did to you was unseemly. It was the basest thing I have ever done, and if you never can forgive me it will be less punishment than I deserve. I wasn't in my right mind. I didn't know what I was doing. That is the only way I can explain it, the only reason I can find for my dishonorable and shameful actions. When I think of what I did to you … how I humiliated you …"

"And now you would compound it by doing so all over again! I ask you again, Elias—I *beg* you—please rise!"

As she stepped back to urge him to his feet, she lost her hold on her shawl. It fell back from her body. The fullness of her figure was revealed for the first time and shock drained the King's face of blood. His mouth fell open and he gasped, the full import of what he saw striking him like a bolt from a bow.

"What's this? You are with child! I didn't know of this! Why wasn't I told?"

She dropped his hands and drew herself up, gathering the shawl once again across her body. "It is my own business, my Lord. You have no call upon me now. I am not answerable to you."

She turned from his kneeling figure and resumed her scrutiny of the land below. He stared uncomprehendingly at her stern and unbending back before slowly rising and moving closer. She did not deign to look at him.

"I deserved that." His voice was low and shaky. "I cannot deny your right to rebuke me. But will you tell me, please, why you didn't inform me of this sooner? Do you think I would have treated you so harshly if I had known you were pregnant? Do you consider me such a monster?"

She sighed deeply, her flash of irritation vanishing. She was too weary and heartsick to sustain it.

"Oh, Elias, of course not. I did not tell you sooner because I did not know myself. I only found out the day before ... before you ..."

"Before I made the greatest mistake of my entire life?" He raised both hands to cover his face, his despair plain. "Are you telling me that you were dealing with the shock of finding yourself pregnant as well as my crass and irrational behavior?"

He dropped his hands and shook his head. He was trembling.

"How did you manage it? How did you find it in your heart to continue serving me after what I did to you? You put your life and that of your unborn child in jeopardy to rescue Eadan and Prince Aeyron. None of us can ever repay you, you know."

"I do not ask for repayment," she said, her tone acerbic, "and I did not do it just for you. I did it because I knew what a threat the Baron was to all of us. I did it for Timar." Her voice dropped to a whisper. "I did it for love."

The King was silent, unable to speak. Seeing his slump-shouldered figure and sensing the utter desolation in his soul at the things he had done, she relented.

"I know you were not in your right mind at that time. You would never have done what you did otherwise. And my love, as with all true love, is not conditional upon circumstances. My life and my skills were sworn to you years ago. I would never go back on that."

Elias winced. "Ah, Brynne, you shame me so!"

He turned away from her, unable to meet the steady regard of her golden eyes. She put out her hand, touching him lightly on the arm.

"There is enough grief and regret already in my life. I cannot add yours to the tally. You are forgiven."

She spoke softly, but the effect on the King was electric. His shoulders shook and she heard him sob. Sullyan took the King in

151

her arms to soothe and comfort him, seeing Taran turn away, uneasy at witnessing Elias's emotion.

When Elias mastered himself, Sullyan drew him away from the parapet to sit on one of the low stone buttresses that provided wind-breaks for anyone on watch detail. Elias put a hand to the pocket of his doublet and drew forth something that caught the light. He extended his hand to Sullyan.

"I have something that belongs to you." Her rank badges and battle honors glittered on his palm. His expression was hopeful, but also fearful, as if he doubted her desire to have them back. And indeed, she looked down at what he held and made no move to take them.

His face paled as he searched her eyes. "Have we not both been punished enough? I was wrong, Brynne. Now I'm asking— no, *begging* you to accept their return in the spirit with which I offer them: A deep respect, an unworthy love, and a truly penitent heart."

She lowered her head, tears blurring her sight. Elias placed the badges in her hands, folding her fingers over them. She gripped them tightly, remembering how bereft and naked she had felt without them. They had come to symbolize the meaning of her life.

Elias shifted on the stone beside her and her face fell in dismay as he once again knelt, very deliberately, at her feet. He caught her stricken gaze to forestall her protest and reached into his doublet yet again.

"My Lady Brynne. I know that nothing I could ever do or say could wipe away the memory of the great wrong I did you. Nor could I repay your selfless service in restoring my precious son to me. So I ask that you accept this token as a gift, given as it is from my heart, and wear it as a sign of my deepest affection for you and my everlasting regard and respect."

He took hold of her left hand and slipped a ring onto her third finger. It had obviously been made especially for her. It was a representation in miniature of her Artesan rank badge, the one denoting her Senior Master status which Elias had designed himself and which incorporated his own seal and symbol of a sun-circled Crown.

She stared down at it sparkling on her finger, next to her simple wedding band. She could find no words to say. Elias raised her hand to his lips and lightly kissed her palm. She started at the strange electric tingle that coursed down her spine.

Elias noted her reaction.

"Ah, Brynne," he said huskily, "would that I had known you before I married Sofira. What a queen you would have made me! We would have been invincible, you and I."

Sullyan's eyes widened and she snatched back her hand. "Elias, for shame! You should not say such things to me. You are already wed. *I* am already wed!"

"Aye, and to a man who deserts you and reviles you even as you carry his child!" Elias seemed to have completely forgotten they were not wholly alone. He stood, glowering down on her, though she was not the object of his wrath. "You just wait till I see him! You know he's killed Captain Parren? He cut him down in the dirt, even though he knew the man carried vital evidence against the Baron, and against specific orders to bring the renegade before me. And to think I was lenient with him for your sake! I should have had him confined to the cells at the least. That's nothing to what he'll endure when I return, believe me."

Sullyan leaped to her feet. "No, you must not! I beg you to forbear. Robin knew nothing of the child until five days ago. Please, you must not do anything rash."

He stared at her. "What do you mean, he only knew five days ago? How could you keep something like that from him? He's the father of your child!"

She remembered then that Elias knew little of what had passed between her and Robin these past few weeks. If she desired his mercy for Robin's actions, she would have to tell him the full story. Drawing him back to the stone beside her and gathering her wits, she told him everything.

When she was done, drained and exhausted from reliving the pain, he sat in silence, just looking at her. His eyes held understanding, sympathy, and an even greater measure of respect than before. Finally, he stirred and smiled sadly.

"Your life has held much of sorrow lately. We will have to see what can be done to alter that. I understand that Timar Pharikian has already begun the process. He tells me you are now a member of his family, a Princess of the royal line. So I was right earlier. You would have been more than a fine match for me."

She turned her head away, her blush betraying her wish that he would move on from this subject. She was uncomfortable with this aspect of him and not least because he was an extremely attractive man.

"I have been most fortunate."

He gave a snort. "That's a matter of opinion."

She met his eyes again and saw he had sobered. "Brynne, there is much I would discuss with you concerning what occurred on the Baron's estate. If we are now friends again, can I prevail upon you to speak of it? But please, can we at least go somewhere more comfortable? It's so damned cold up here! I thought Andaryan summers were meant to be hot, but it's warmer in Loxton than it is up here."

His pitiful look and mock shiver made her laugh. Their crisis was broken. Perhaps now they could return to their old relationship. Or maybe not, she thought, seeing shame twist his features as he noted the careful grace with which she stood, her body showing the swell of her babe.

"Of course," she said. "I am sure you are quite frozen beneath that flimsy mantle." She glanced impishly at the heavy state cloak hanging from his shoulders. "You should have brought a warmer one, as I did."

Drawing the delicate shawl about her, she took his offered arm and they moved toward the stairs.

Elias looked over his shoulder. "You are welcome, too, Taran Elijah, especially since you have been such a faithful guard dog today and kept your mistress from any harm I might have done her."

Taran flushed. "Your Majesty, I didn't mean—"

"Come, man, I'm teasing you! I owe you as great a debt of thanks as I owe Brynne. You rescued my son and I'll never forget that. I have had the story from Master Ardoch and he paints a much more flattering picture of your bravery and skills than you did. I would be honored to call you my friend."

Taran's embarrassment tested his newfound control over the Fire within him, but it held, allowing him to smile easily back at his sovereign. He made a courtly bow.

"Then I accept your invitation, your Majesty, for it's about time we put an end to the Baron's scheming."

Elias raised his brows and grinned at Sullyan. "My word, you've trained him well."

She smiled back. "I pick my friends carefully, Elias. They are all skilled and strong."

Laughing together, finally at ease again, they descended the stairs to find a warm room and some much-needed fellan.

Chapter Twelve

Another surprise awaited Sullyan at the base of the tower stairs, although, she reflected, she really should have known. Mathias Blaine stood there, anxious to know how Elias's apology had been received. It seemed the General had one of his own to offer, and if she had accepted the King's she could hardly refuse his.

He needn't have worried. Her generous spirit embraced his shame as it had Elias's and smoothed any awkwardness away. Blaine could see the forgiveness in her eyes before he spoke. She heard his apology for not openly supporting her against Elias, and then simply stepped into his arms, effectively closing the topic.

No one had informed the General of her condition, but he merely widened his eyes at the evidence and smiled.

"Pregnancy suits you," he said. She smiled her thanks.

They held their discussions in Sullyan's suite, since she had the afternoon sun through her windows. The unseasonable chill of the east wind had permeated the corridors of the palace and the warmth of the sun was welcome.

Assembled there were the three ruling monarchs, General Blaine, Duke Marik, Baron Gaslek, Taran, and Sullyan. Norkis was kept busy supplying them with fellan and platters of food. The brisk chill air had made Taran and Elias, at least, ravenously hungry.

Elias asked Sullyan for the full tale of what had happened

since she left the Manor. Sullyan stared into her fellan, casting herself back to that unhappy time. She stripped the tale of everything except the bare facts, and encouraged Taran to join in and relate those parts he had been involved in. It took some time. When they were done, Elias told them what his investigations at Port Loxton had yielded.

He had interviewed all the men who remained at the garrison under Lieutenant Major Denny, as well as Denny himself. He had spoken at length with all the castle servants, especially the Prince's nursemaid, Bessie. The poor girl had been in a terrible state ever since Taran had taken the Prince away and would be no help in their quest for evidence against Reen.

Elias recounted his interviews with Ardoch and also Lord Levant, and said he had personally conducted a thorough audit of the treasury and all its accounts. His furious expression when he told them of the depletion of the treasury reserves left them in no doubt as to his feelings.

"Don't concern yourself on our account, Elias," said Pharikian considerately. "We can wait a short while for the settlement."

The King regarded the Andaryan monarch sourly and Sullyan surmised Elias had been forced to make an offer of significant recompense over his ill-advised invasion. She wondered whether the Hierarch had also been able to wring more advantageous trade concessions from him. She thought he probably had; it was what she would have done.

"And what of Queen Sofira?" murmured Sullyan, voicing the question no one else dared to ask.

Elias's mood soured further. "She denies any wrongdoing, of course. She maintains that the large sum paid out of the treasury reserve went to her father's lands, and that as Keeper of the Treasury she had every right to gift him the gold. I have someone looking into the letter from Lerric, but as her father will almost certainly back her up, it will likely be impossible to prove or disprove after so long.

"She is adamant that the Baron rescued my son from the Andaryans who abducted him, and insists he should be hailed as a national hero instead of being confined under suspicion. After all, there is no doubt that it was Andaryans who took him. Sofira exonerates Reen of all blame and has even provided him with an alibi for all those times when he could have been accused of plotting against me. She cites his vehement and publicly-aired opinions of outlanders as evidence against any suggestion that he would ever countenance dealing with them.

"She has implored and then commanded me to release him from his confinement, and she has even convinced the Minster to support her. Arch Patrio Neremiah has joined his voice to hers, and he holds much sway with the populace. Together, their demands grow louder by the day. They attempt even now to raise the city against me. If I don't try Reen soon and have firm evidence to convict him, I'm afraid he'll walk free."

Taran inhaled sharply. "But he was holding your son captive in his mansion! Ardoch and I saw it. How can he deny it? He took Prince Aeyron and Sullyan captive and had them chained in the circle! I myself heard his declaration that the Queen was protecting him. How can he defend all of that?"

Elias looked disgusted. "He's been very clever. He swears he was holding Eadan for his own safety and had set guards over him to prevent another attempt on his life. He claims he didn't tell the Queen of Eadan's whereabouts for fear a spy might discover where he was. Bessie still believes this whole-heartedly, and Sofira maintains that if she, who was there at the time, isn't accusing him of abducting her son, how can I, who was not? As for your testimony, Taran, Reen maintains that Artesans—Sullyan in particular—have been trying to undermine me for their own ends.

He swears that Artesans were behind the abduction of my son, which is truth, in a way, for someone gave those Andaryans access through the Veils. He has issued an accusation, through the Queen, of murder and abduction against the two of you."

Taran started. "*What?*"

Sullyan laid a soothing hand on his arm. "It was inevitable, my friend. You killed Patrin, and I killed Izack. He will try to implicate us both in Eadan's abduction by pointing out that we took him from the safety of the Baron's home and exposed him to terrible danger. We did, after all, take him across the Veils into the realm of Elias's so-called enemies. Given his opinions concerning Artesans, this is a gift to him. The Queen will probably back him in this, too. She has no love for our kind either."

She turned from the anxious Taran back to Elias. "What does he say about the death of Huw?"

Elias pursed his lips. "He claims Huw was trying to protect him. He says Huw was unarmed, but you killed him because you were trying to get through him to Reen." Elias paused, adding reluctantly, "It was your knife that killed him, wasn't it?"

Sullyan's eyes blurred at this travesty of the truth. It filled her with impotent rage to think that Reen should claim Huw's protection when he had terrorized the lad for years. Yet she had no proof of this now. And part of his statement was true.

"Yes. It was my blade that took his life."

She fell silent, lost again in the memory of that dreadful night. Her thoughts had grown no easier to bear, and she shook herself out of them once more.

"What has he to say about the attempts on your life, Elias?" she asked, her eyes still haunted with sorrow.

He held her gaze briefly, as if trying to convey his compassion, and then sighed.

"Of the accident during the horse race, he says the same as

before. You were responsible for the Earth shift, which was clearly the work of an Artesan. Unfortunately, we cannot dispute that."

"Indeed." She turned to Taran. "You were by the rails of the course that day. How close was the Baron to Huw when the earth heaved?"

Taran's brows creased in thought. "Not very close. Jinny had made me move away from him. She said she was afraid of the boy. Huw was standing by himself. No one seemed to want to be near him. "

Sullyan's face tightened. "Would you say Huw could have heard the Baron speak at that distance?"

He shook his head. "Not without everyone else hearing as well."

"What about some kind of hand signal or gesture?"

"I didn't see one, but I wasn't really looking at the Baron. I was watching the race."

She looked grim. "As, of course, was everyone else." She turned back to Elias. "What does he say about the attack on our party when we returned to the Manor? The day Lord Fiann died?"

Elias's eyes clouded with the memory and he scowled. "He's had the temerity to use *me* as the perfect alibi for that one. He knows I saw he had no contact with the raiders. Once again, he blames you for it, saying you must have called them. And how can I speak against that? Though you fought against them, he says that was for appearances' sake. And I can't deny you weren't close enough to me to have saved me from the Andaryan's blade. He claims you made a show over Lord Fiann's death to hide your anger that I was still alive. But that aside, how could I possibly accuse Reen of involvement when the attack was patently the work of an Artesan?"

"That storm was the work of an Artesan," she allowed, "but there was no Artesan present at the time. Except for Taran and me, of course. Reen was not directly responsible for calling the raiders, perhaps, but someone gave the signal for them to attack at that precise moment. And Reen was certainly unmolested by them. His decision to wear distinctive clothing that day was more than opportune."

She shook her head in frustration and her eyes lost their focus as she delved within her mind.

"What are you thinking, Brynne?" Elias asked.

"I need to speak with Lord Kethro," she murmured. "I need to reread those archives Gaslek found. There is something very strange going on here."

She would say no more about it and Elias didn't press her.

The Hierarch spoke into the uncomfortable silence. "Then, as experienced Artesans will be looked upon with suspicion, it seems Lord Corbyn and your gravely-ill cadet are the only ones who might be able to irrefutably impeach the Baron."

Elias threw up his hands. "As yet, we don't even know that young Tad can produce any damning evidence." He sighed in frustration. "If the traitor Parren had succeeded in killing him, we'd have no reason even to suspect Parren was the Baron's spy. It's only because Parren acted suspiciously when he realized Tad wasn't dead, and because he then deserted and was so obviously trying to reach Loxton when he was … apprehended that we guessed at all. Now that he's dead, we only have hearsay evidence that the two were in league. Brynne, I don't suppose Reen spoke the name of his spy when he was gloating over his plans in the circle?"

She shook her head. "I guessed, and he was angry. But he did not confirm it was Parren."

She had been watching Aeyron intently as Elias and the Hierarch spoke. The Prince's face was deathly pale and his eyes were haunted as he returned her regard. She didn't share aloud what she was thinking, but it didn't please Aeyron.

The Hierarch was still speaking. "Elias, the traitor Corbyn awaits your pleasure whenever you require him. I know that his testimony will count for little under Albian law, but his presence might just force the Baron into making an admission. Corbyn is already a dead man. You have our blessing to do whatever you please to persuade him to denounce his ally."

"Thank you, Timar. I am very grateful."

"How grateful?" enquired the Hierarch with a sidelong glance.

Elias stiffened and stared at the elderly Andaryan. He was about to open his mouth to protest when Sullyan's sharp tone cut across him.

"Father!"

Pharikian smiled at her. "Very well, daughter," he said fondly, waving his hand. "And anyway, King Elias and I concluded our business very satisfactorily earlier on. Did we not, Elias?"

"Indeed," replied the Albian King heavily, looking with suspicion from Sullyan to the Hierarch.

She smiled sweetly back, giving him to know that, forgiven as he was, he would be made to pay for his past mistakes in many different ways. He sighed and shook his head.

Aeyron spoke for the first time. "When do you anticipate holding the trial, my Lord?"

Elias turned to him. "I wanted to wait as long as possible to give the injured cadet time to regain consciousness. In truth, I don't think I can hold off much longer. The more I delay, the more time Sofira has to raise public opinion against me and the more time she can spend scheming with the Baron. I think the trial must be held within the week, whether the cadet recovers or not."

Gaslek stirred. "Is it wise to allow your Queen to meet with the Baron if this gives them the opportunity to plot together?"

Elias glared at him. "She is still a ruling monarch, my Lord

Baron. She is not on trial, although if I can prove she has conspired against me or undermined me in any way … but I cannot forbid her access to her countryman while his guilt is still unproven. Can you imagine the public outcry she'd raise if I tried?"

Gaslek muttered about the inadvisability of allowing women to rule in their own right, but he subsided immediately when he caught Sullyan's predatory gaze. He reddened and looked away.

They worried further at the problem, but there was no escaping the fact that there was no hard or non-partisan evidence of the Baron's perfidy. Elias left Taran in no doubt that he would be required to attend the trial, and it was plain he would have liked to order Sullyan to attend also, but her condition and his unassuaged shame over his earlier actions prevented him.

She was also the legitimized Princess of a royal House—even if she had accepted back her Albian rank badges, he had no authority over her now. Neither could he ask Prince Aeyron to give evidence. Under Albian law, the word of an outlander carried no weight. And besides, Aeyron had already been through enough. Neither the Prince nor his adopted sister volunteered their services.

As the afternoon drew to a close, Pharikian offered Elias and General Blaine rooms for the night. Elias, however, didn't want to stay. He was far too concerned over what his Queen and the Baron might be planning in his absence. He also still seemed uncomfortable here in the Hierarch's palace among the very people he had declared war on only a few weeks ago.

Pharikian understood and was happy to let him go. He was content with the concessions he had obtained from Elias and, in truth, the Albian King had come off lightly considering what he had done. Elias knew it too, despite his earlier sourness.

Elias and Blaine took their leave. Sullyan and Taran accompanied them out into the chilly sunshine of the courtyard, where their horses were being held by grooms. Sullyan was pleased that Elias had chosen to ride Darius for the trip, and the young mahogany stallion whinnied in recognition when she whistled to him. Elias walked with her as she went to handle the beast. Blaine and Taran stayed prudently out of earshot.

The King watched her breathing nose to nose with the horse. "What will you do now, Brynne? Will you return to the Manor? It is still your home."

She heard the wistful note in his voice and was silent. Her head was bent while she communed with the horse, taking comfort from his familiar presence. She was forbidden to ride at present and missed the feel of Drum's powerful muscles beneath her and the wind of speed in her hair.

She sighed.

"No. Not yet. I intend to stay here for the birth of my child. After that, who knows? Much will depend upon circumstances which are out of my control."

Elias knew she was referring to Robin and began to speak. She shook her head vehemently and spun to face him.

"No, Elias! I will not beg you this time, I will command you. I want no interference, no pressure brought to bear on him. Bulldog has already gone against my express wishes and told Robin about the child, and what good did it do? Do you see him here? No. He does not wish to come, that much is evident, and I will not have him forced against his will. Keep out of this. It is my business, not yours. The outcome is unclear and I must bide by whatever comes. My life has already changed with the existence of this child, and that would have been the case even had I remained at the Manor. Maybe the time has come to change it in other ways too. I do not know. All I can say at present is that I will be here until my son is born."

She calmed herself and continued. "You had better leave or you will be traversing the forest at dusk, one of the riskiest times. I trust you have arranged an escort for the journey?"

He looked down at her with grieving eyes. He didn't want to lose her—not as his colonel and not as his friend. Yet there was nothing more he could say to her and nothing he could do, except abide by her wishes. He had done her enough harm already; he wouldn't compound it now.

Taking up her left hand, the one that now bore the ring of his crest, he bowed low over it and kissed it tenderly. That same electric tingle shivered down her spine and it was all she could do not to pull away.

"Farewell, Highness," he said sadly, looking deep into her eyes. "I wish you nothing but good. You will be much in my thoughts over the coming weeks. Never fear, I will heed your wishes in the matter of the Major, and I pledge you, he will suffer no recriminations from me. My deepest desire is that you should return to us—to me—and I will grieve if you do not. But if it is not to be, then the wish of my heart goes with you in whatever you may do. Farewell, my Lady Brynne."

She watched him mount the glossy mahogany colt, but the strong lines of his body blurred as her eyes brimmed with sorrow. Blaine cast her a glance and a wave as he followed the King, his anxiety plain on his face. She gave him a smile and returned his salute as they rode out of the courtyard and down into the town.

By the time they reached the open Plain and the General prepared to open their way back to Port Loxton, Sullyan was watching from the tower battlements. Her sore and pleading heart traversed the Veils to Albia with them.

Chapter Thirteen

S ince throwing the punch that cracked Robin's jaw, Bull hadn't spoken to the Major again. Indeed, he had actively avoided him. Bull's generous heart had been ripped in two by Robin's terrible accusations, and Bull just couldn't bear to look at him.

For his part, Robin had no wish to meet Bull again, either. He'd never really had a falling out with a friend before, and Bull's ferocious assault had wounded him deeply.

He bore the bruising on his face and the fierce ache of his cracked jaw like the stigmata of martyrdom. He stomped around in a rage. How the Void had Bull *expected* him to react? He knew very well the child she carried couldn't be his. She would never have left the Manor—would never have left *him*—without telling him something so precious. Would she?

Would she?

And anyway, she couldn't be pregnant. She was barren. They'd had two years of unrestrained lovemaking and never had to use their Artesan's ability to prevent conception. Rykan's abuse and the poison of his seed had taken care of that. Or so she had led him to believe. Her alleged condition could be nothing more than a despicable ploy for garnering sympathy.

How had it come to this? How had it all gone so wrong? She had been all and more than he'd ever wanted, and she had felt the same. He *knew* she had. They couldn't share their minds and feelings the way linked Artesans did without seeing each other's deepest thoughts and emotions.

Why—*why*—had she gone with Taran? He'd always known she loved the Adept the same way she loved Bull. She had never hidden that side of her. And Taran, to give the bastard his due, had never hidden his love for her, either. So had it just proved too strong for them? Or had Denny been lying after all?

But why should Denny lie? What would the Lieutenant have to gain? If it had just been Denny's word that something had happened in Port Loxton, Robin might have laughed it off. But all the Loxton men had known. And Denny had had the truth of it from Taran's own mouth.

No, thought Robin angrily, whatever had happened to cause Sullyan to break her vows, the facts were undeniable. Bull could shout and bluster and use his fists all he liked—he couldn't change hard fact.

Robin was deep in his depressingly circular personal agony when he heard his name being urgently called.

The shout came again and he strode to his office door, flinging it wide. One of the healers was rushing toward him, shouting his name. Robin's heart missed several beats and he felt sick. It could only be Tad, he must have—

"Major, young Tad's regained consciousness!"

The first genuine smile to cross his lips for weeks transformed Robin's careworn face. For one instant he was again the joyous and handsome young man he'd been when he wed his soulmate. Then his eyes clouded.

"When did this happen?"

"Just now, sir, and Healer Arlen says it may not last. She thinks he'll respond better to you than anyone else, so she sent me to fetch you. Thank the gods you weren't out on patrol."

Robin ran ahead of the man to the infirmary and skidded to a stop at the door to Tad's cubicle. Rienne was sitting by Tad's side, holding the boy's hand and talking softly to him. She looked up as Robin arrived.

She stood as he came hesitantly into the room. He couldn't quite believe what he saw.

"Go easy with him, Robin," she said, her voice low. "He's only just woken and he's weak and confused."

Robin ignored her frosty tone, too full of the miracle of Tad's recovery. Besides, everyone was using that tone to him lately and he'd become used to it. He took Rienne's place on the bed and clasped the boy's cold hand. Tad's pale gray eyes, bleary from his coma, fastened on Robin's with a dreadful intensity, but he seemed too weak for speech. To spare him the effort, Robin laid his other hand on the lad's clammy brow and reached for Tad's psyche.

The reaction stunned his senses.

He was instantly gripped by urgency and desperation so strong, so compelling, that he gasped aloud. Rienne heard and came swiftly forward.

"What is it, what's wrong?"

Robin couldn't reply. His mind was held in thrall. He was caught in the maelstrom of Tad's terrible memories and was experiencing the full horror of the lad's encounter with Parren.

✠ ✠ ✠ ✠ ✠

Rienne watched helplessly as a feverish tremble took hold of Robin's body. Sweat broke out on his brow. She recognized the signs and knew he was communing with Tad, but something wasn't right. Tad was only an Apprentice and Robin a Master. The boy shouldn't be able to snare the Major so thoroughly.

Rienne didn't know what to do. Should she try to separate them? Would that hurt Tad, or Robin?

In the end, she did nothing but watch. Apart from a bleached face and a rapid heartbeat, Tad seemed to be coping with the strain. Rienne guessed this was something he needed to do. He must have been desperate to tell them what had happened to him, and once he had, he'd be better for it. Drained and even weaker, maybe, but better able to recover.

At least this proved Tad's brain was definitely functioning.

Finally, Tad's eyes glazed and his lids sagged shut. Robin fell forward with a soft moan, and Rienne was forced to catch him. He was still bound up in what he'd seen. The horror of it stared out of his unfocused eyes. To try to anchor him, Rienne took him into her arms. He was shaking still. He'd had all Tad's desperation thrown at him, the fear, the horror, and the pain, and his shock had rendered him completely vulnerable. It took him a few minutes of clinging unawares to Rienne's embrace before he could master himself.

When he did, he was embarrassed by their proximity. He was aware of Rienne's current opinion of him, and to find himself held in her arms was not something he could cope with right now. Still, she had done her best to help him and he was grateful. He pushed away gently and she let him go, watching him carefully.

"All right now?" she asked, her voice less cold, more concerned.

He nodded, breathing deeply. "Yes, thank you, Rienne. That was ... quite unexpected."

"I take it he was showing you what happened to him. Was it Parren's doing, as we thought?"

Robin nodded, the pallor of his face telling her that the experience had been harrowing in the extreme.

"Give me the details later, will you?" Rienne turned from him to re-examine Tad. She was reassured by his even breathing and normal pulse. She even thought he had a better color now. "Well

169

done, Robin," she said, and meant it. She glanced over at the Major's pale face where the bruises of Bull's fury were fading, the cracked jaw healed by Robin's own metaforce. "I think that was just what he needed."

"Will he be all right, though? He must have used a week's worth of energy to do that and he can't have had much to begin with."

"He'll be fine. I think he'll mend quite quickly now. He knows he's passed on vital information, and the fact that he's passed it to you will comfort him even more. You ought to go rest now. You look exhausted."

Robin shook his head. "I want to stay here. He might wake again."

"I don't think he will, not for some time. He's drained himself, but he's sleeping now. He hasn't slipped back into a coma. He needs this. It's the most healing thing he can do. He's out of danger, Robin. You've pulled him through. Now go and rest or you'll be no good to him when he does wake. And that's an order!"

Her tone made Robin glance up in surprise. In matters relating to the infirmary, the healers took precedence over every other rank at the Manor, including General Blaine. The Major couldn't refuse a direct order from Rienne. Yet it was the way she'd said it, almost as if she'd forgiven him....

Then the shutters came down over her eyes and their gentler light was extinguished.

"Really, he'll be all right now. You can see him again in the morning. I expect he'll want to talk then. And you must need to tell someone what he's shown you."

Her voice had that cold edge again and he heard her mild rebuke. He turned to go.

"Take care of him, Rienne."

She snorted, unsmiling. "Of course I will."

✣ ✣ ✣ ✣ ✣

Back in his rooms, Robin reviewed what he'd been shown. He sat on the settle in the living room, his head in his hands, and shut out all other sights and sounds. He immersed himself in Tad's memories and relived the boy's terrifying last conscious moments.

Through Tad's eyes, he saw the two boys searching Parren's rooms. He saw them run and guessed they'd heard someone coming. He saw the wild, triumphant ride down to the stream in the woods and the purloined parchment as it was smoothed out and read through. He saw it with Tad's eyes and realized what a find it was. He experienced Tad's exultation and excitement, tinged though it was by a healthy fear. He felt the lad's frustration with Ozella's reluctance, although there was nothing in Tad's mind at that moment to reveal why the foreign lord had been so fearful. He saw Tad pounce on the sentence in the letter which referred to the Baron's "powerful benefactress at court" and agreed with his conclusion that it had to mean the Queen.

It was then, with Tad and Ozella arguing the pros and cons of telling Bull or Vassa what they'd found, that Robin heard mention of Ozella's sisters.

Kidnap and blackmail, he thought angrily. No wonder poor Ozella had been so distracted. Robin's spirit grew heavy with the thought of that dreadful burden borne alone for so long, and he was suddenly fiercely glad he'd killed Parren.

Then the traitor appeared in Tad's memories. Robin felt the sting of terror that shot through the lad's heart as he saw Parren's steel jutting from Ozella's chest. Tears glimmered in Robin's eyes as he saw the sword appear in Tad's hand. He was only fourteen and a raw cadet. Parren had been twenty-six and a well-trained veteran of many fights, but the lad was prepared to take him on.

Robin's senses screamed at him to yell, *Run, Tad! RUN!*

But, of course, it had already happened. Nothing could avert the dreadful events Robin was about to witness all over again.

He forced himself to review the fight, if "fight" was the right word for Parren's calculated, taunting play. He recognized the embryonic skill in Tad's untutored hands which, one day, would allow him to become a fine swordsman. He felt the upwelling of Tad's rage-filled grief at Ozella's senseless and casual slaughter. He was caught up once more in the boy's desperate need to hurt Parren, to make him pay for Ozella's death. Then the rage burned out, replaced by naked fear and the certain knowledge of Tad's own death.

Robin pulled back, sweating. He simply couldn't live through Tad's final memory again. It was far too raw and painful.

Shivering, he stood and walked about the room, his arms hugged to his chest. What Parren had done was unspeakably evil. Not even Robin would have thought him capable of such cold cruelty. In his grief and anguish he fervently wished he had carved out Parren's living heart and squeezed it, quivering, before those pale, uncaring eyes.

In his blind pacing, Robin's foot struck the harp that rested by the side of the settle. Its familiar tones rippled into the air, startling Robin into a cry. The harp spoke of Sullyan so vividly that he could almost smell her scent and hear her move. He nearly looked over his shoulder to see her even though he knew she wasn't there.

Robin clamped his hands on the harp strings to silence them. Their sweet ringing was more than he could bear. He wanted nothing more right now than her beloved body in his arms and the comfort of her presence.

Fighting back sobs, he made for the little cooking room and put water to heat for fellan. He had a duty to perform and needed a clear head if he was to contact General Blaine at Port Loxton. He would have to relate Tad's story to Blaine and then, no doubt, he'd be summoned directly to the city. Baron Reen's trial was to start in two days, and Tad's evidence would be vital.

Chapter Fourteen

The Baron's trial took place within the castle at Port Loxton in direct opposition to the stridently-expressed wishes of the Queen. As Elias had feared, the whole thing went badly from the start.

He had gone reluctantly to see his Queen, whom he had avoided since his return from Andaryon. This, however, she had a right to know. So he had stepped within her solar, tersely told her what he intended to do, and then endured her raucous, screeching protests.

Her voice, never the softest even when calm, tore at his eardrums. The term "fishwife" passed through Elias's mind, but it was not a phrase he felt it politic to utter at that point. His arms folded across his chest, his face immobile and stern, he waited for her to take a breath and then coldly reiterated his intentions. Then he turned on his heel and left.

Something heavy crashed against the door as he closed it, and he thought of the solid marble statuette on its plinth by her table. He winced. He now knew that whatever the outcome of the trial, his relationship with his wife, loveless at best, was irretrievably wrecked. He sighed deeply and returned to his chambers, where he chewed over the known facts of the case yet again with General Blaine and Lord Levant.

Robin's news was received with no little relief. Blaine instructed the Major to make his way with all speed to the castle.

As it was, Robin wouldn't arrive before the trial commenced.

Blaine was of the opinion the proceedings would last more than one day, so Robin's late arrival would not be damaging. The Major would have preferred to wait in order to speak with Tad properly before leaving, but he understood the importance of his information. He merely expressed the wish that they could have had the parchment Tad had seen.

He reported that a thorough search of Parren's clothing, room, and belongings at the time of his death had yielded only his store of gold. No other incriminating evidence was found. The small pile of ashes in his cooking room grate had not been investigated at the time, but after Sullyan's admonition to Bull and Tad's revelations, another, much more careful, search of Parren's rooms turned up a tiny corner of unburned parchment in the cold grate. Robin's heart fell when he saw it. They still had no firm evidence.

Elias had decided the trial should not be public. The city was divided in its opinion of the Baron. Lord Neremiah, Arch Patrio of Loxton's Matria Church, had done his best to sway the populace against Elias, and although he had been partially successful, the fact that Elias had returned safely from Andaryon with his baby son seemed to justify his declaration of war in many people's eyes.

The Arch Patrio had also worked hard to raise the Baron's standing as the true rescuer of the Prince, and had condemned Elias's conduct over the thwarted abduction as the unnecessary and unbalanced reactions of a monarch sorely in need of sober guidance. Reen was portrayed as a loyal and misunderstood advisor who only had his Queen's and his country's best interests at heart. With Sofira publicly supporting this view, the populace were understandably confused by the conflicting opinions they heard.

In this light, Elias decided a closed trial would be best. He could do without those nobles who had been won—or bribed—to support Reen causing unrest during the proceedings. When the city heard the news there was outspoken dismay and protest, most notably from Reen's so-called supporters, but the King was adamant. The trial would remain closed.

It would be held in the castle's main council chamber. Reen would be brought under guard from his mansion and kept close-confined in a suite of rooms by himself. At Elias's order, not even Sofira was granted leave to see him, an edict for which she bitterly and loudly reproached him.

Elias remained unshakable. He knew Levant had been unable to prevent Sofira from visiting Reen at his mansion while he was in Andaryon, but he had no intention of allowing her to plot with him now. She had already been closeted with Neremiah for the whole of the day before the trial, although the given reason was for spiritual guidance and comfort.

Elias had a different word for it. He called it "scheming," and he could do without them passing the results of this on to the Baron. No matter how forcefully Sofira protested, she was unable to change her husband's mind.

✣ ✣ ✣ ✣ ✣

Taran arrived in the city on the morning of the trial, bringing Ardoch's gray, Morlech, back to his master. The Adept had reluctantly taken his leave of Sullyan earlier that day. He hadn't liked leaving her. She grew more withdrawn as time went by with still no word from Robin. Taran knew she spoke frequently with Bull, but despite this much-needed contact, she was deeply homesick and lonely.

Yet he couldn't refuse the King's summons, or the opportunity to put an end to the Baron's threat. Sullyan herself opened the Veils for him, sending him just to the south of Loxton Forest, and sped him on his way with a kiss. She admonished him to be careful.

He reached the city's Forest Gate in good time and was recognized by the guardsman stationed there. It was Fergus, one of the men who had given them escort through the forest the night both Princes had been returned to their fathers. Taran acknowledged his nod as he rode up through the city.

The castle gates were guarded by a man Taran didn't know. He was expected, though, and was waved through. Dismounting in the garrison compound, he gave Morlech to one of the grooms. He was then given directions to the council chamber.

The castle was strangely quiet as Taran walked its halls. Few servants were in evidence, and they seemed unusually subdued. He met no one else on his way up to the council chamber, but many people had gathered in the hallway leading to the chamber doors, all awaiting entry. He was hailed immediately by Master Ardoch, who had been watching for his arrival. Ardoch shoved his way toward him and clapped him on the shoulder.

"Taran, lad, 'tis good to see you. How are you? How's our lassie?"

"Well, Ardoch, my thanks." Taran felt unwilling to discuss Sullyan's current situation in the crowded hallway and neatly sidestepped the question. "I've brought Morlech back. He's in the compound. I'm grateful to you for lending him."

Ardoch grinned. "Ach, lad, you're welcome. I won't pretend I've not missed him. So, are you speaking today against yon Baron?"

"I imagine so. You?"

"Aye, we'll have to give our stories, right enough." Ardoch sobered. "It doesn't look good, I don't mind telling you. Yer man's very thick with the Queen and she doesn't want to lose him. The Minster's backing him too, I've heard, so unless there's some hard evidence to convict him, I fear he'll walk free."

Taran feared so, too. "The King said the same thing. The

trouble is, Ghyl, none of us has solid evidence that can't be refuted. It's our word against his. Who can prove he kidnapped Eadan for his own ends if the boy's mother says otherwise? If the Queen has no suspicion concerning his loyalties, how can anyone else?"

Ardoch eyed him sourly. "Whose side are you on, lad? Aye, though, you're right enough. He's been very clever, has our man. But Elias is no fool. He'll find a way to trip him. Look sharp, we're going in."

The doors to the council chamber opened and the crowd filed in. It was a large rectangular room, wood-paneled, with high windows on one long side. Banners and tapestries hung on the walls depicting Elias's family emblem, the sun-circled Crown, as well as the various devices of other noble lords. There were tiered benches along three of the walls and a section of richly-upholstered private boxes at the top end of the chamber. The King, General Blaine, Lord Levant, and Lord Kinsey already occupied the foremost of these.

All those who entered were ushered toward the royal presence by members of the King's Guard. Taran looked about for Denny, but couldn't see him. Neither could he see the Queen, and that puzzled him. Surely she would attend?

They made obeisance to the King, who stood stern-faced to receive their homage. He was dressed in his state robes, imposing in a black satin doublet over a scarlet silk shirt and black breeches slashed with scarlet and gold, and over that was his heavy silk and velvet mantle. His thick gold chain bearing the symbol of his House hung around his neck, and Albia's crown of red gold glittered on his head.

Lord Levant, who sat on his left, wore his family colors of dark blue, and General Blaine on his right was attired in his russet dress uniform. Lord Kinsey, who sat just below the main royal box, was dressed in brown and gold.

General Blaine caught Taran's eye and directed him and Ardoch toward benches very near the royal box, on the right-hand side of the chamber. From there, Blaine could speak quietly to Taran without being heard by anyone else.

Once he was seated, Taran took stock of the people in attendance. There were more than he'd expected for a closed trial. Elias was attended by two pages, and Lord Kinsey was there presumably to put the sovereign's questions to the Baron and generally conduct the trial. He had a scribe by his side ready to record the proceedings.

On the benches opposite Taran were four men, all dressed in Elias's colors of red and gold. In answer to Taran's whispered question, Ardoch told him they were the treasury clerks. Next to them was a group of church officials and clerics, including the Arch Patrio of Loxton's Minster.

His Immanence, the Lord Neremiah, was a short and wiry man in his sixties with a balding head, a pockmarked face and a purple-veined nose. His hands were liver-spotted beneath his wealth of gold rings. His dark brown eyes darted over the assembled company with acute clarity. He wore simply-cut yet lavish robes of heavy black velvet trimmed with gray silk, belted with a thick silver chain from which hung the wheel symbol of the Matria Church, Albia's primary faith.

The only other people present were the Attestors, twenty of the Baron's peers picked by sealed ballot from the lords of the land. Attestors sat in judgment on all trial proceedings and were always selected from the same class as the accused. They were required to hold silence throughout the trial and were never addressed by the court. If the guilt or otherwise of the defendant could not be clearly proved, the Attestors were required to write their findings and verdict on a parchment which was then sealed and handed to the senior court official—in this case the King—to aid him in making his decision. Their responses were never disclosed.

Once they were all seated and quiet, a small noise sounded from the side of the room nearest the King. A door had opened just to the left of the royal box. Lieutenant Major Denny, Lady Jinella, and the baby Prince's nursemaid, Bessie, were escorted into the chamber by members of the King's Guard. Taran's heart turned over when he saw Jinny, and this reaction surprised him. He hadn't thought much about her since he and Sullyan had left Albia.

Now, looking at her pale but composed face, her slim and graceful body, her shining blonde hair and green eyes, Taran's heart spoke to him.

Jinella had dressed carefully for this day. Her gown was of wine-red satin trimmed with black velvet. She wore a rope of pearls around her neck rather than the diamond necklace her uncle had gifted her. She had gold rings on most of her fingers and also wore gold at her ears. She bore herself soberly and seemed intent on comforting Bessie, who was visibly trembling at her side and seemed on the verge of tears.

Jinella looked up once, caught Taran's eye, and smiled briefly, causing his heart to skip a beat. He would have to contrive to speak with her later.

Denny halted before the royal box and saluted his monarch. Jinny curtseyed elegantly and Bessie tried to do the same. The King acknowledged them all and they were shown to seats along the side of the chamber next to the churchmen. Taran noted a group of castle servants being ushered in behind them.

Once the noise of their arrival and seating died down, there was a stir at the far end of the chamber. The doors were thrown open. A single trumpeter blew a short and strident sequence and the entire company rose to their feet, including Elias. Pacing sternly, looking neither right nor left, Queen Sofira entered the room.

She held herself rigidly straight, her slender body appearing hard beneath her robes of pale gold silk. Her face, always colorless, was bleached and wan, and her cheeks were more sunken than ever. Her honey-blonde hair, the only hint of softness about her, was drawn severely back from her prominent cheekbones and fastened atop her head. Her brittle gray eyes stared balefully into her husband's as she paced the length of the chamber, followed by her attendant ladies.

As she passed, those assembled bent their knees in genuflection or curtsey. When she reached the royal box, Elias accorded her a stiffly formal bow.

"My Lady Queen."

Sofira made no response. She ignored Elias's page, who was holding open the door to the royal box. Instead, she directed one of her ladies to open one of the lesser boxes, to the King's right. She entered it and sat down, her attendants arranging her gown around her feet.

It was a deliberate rebuff, an unmistakable and damning indictment of the charges brought by her husband, and a clear indication of her loyalties.

Elias went white with fury at this public snub, but he said not a word. He seated himself and gestured curtly to the Guardsman on his left, beside the single door. The man disappeared through it and they all waited.

Footfalls were heard and the Baron appeared. He was flanked by four of the King's Guard, all of whom held their swords naked in their hands. Composed, unhurried, and confident, Reen walked between them as if they were an honor guard. He was dressed somberly in black breeches, snowy linen shirt, and black silk doublet. He never glanced at the Queen, nor at Elias, but kept his eyes suitably downcast. Even so, Taran could swear there was a glitter of malice in them.

He was led to the center of the chamber where stood a platform surrounded by iron railings. He was directed within, and his escort positioned themselves at the four corners, their swords held at the guard. The Baron then turned to face the King and bowed respectfully. Elias, who had not risen, acknowledged him with a bare nod of his head.

Lord Kinsey rose and called the court to order. Taran watched the Baron assessing those gathered against him and noted the especially venomous look he directed at his niece. Fortunately, Jinella didn't see it.

Kinsey's voice rang out. "Your Majesties, my Lords and Ladies, nobles and members of the court. We are here to ascertain the guilt or otherwise of this man, Baron Hezra Reen, on the charge of High Treason. My Lord Baron, do you understand why you are here?"

Reen stared at him coldly, his voice harsh in the silence when he answered, "Of course I do."

Taran thought he detected a glimmer of warning in the Queen's eyes and guessed she didn't want the Baron to appear overconfident. Whether Reen saw her or not, Taran couldn't tell.

Lord Kinsey continued, ignoring the Baron's curt manner. "Hezra Reen, you are hereby charged with High Treason against the Crown of Albia. It is alleged that you have assayed two separate attempts on the King's life, that you have fomented insurrection against the Crown, that you have allied yourself with dissidents and traitors from the demon realm of Andaryon, and also that you did abduct his Majesty's son and Heir, using demons as your agents, in order to force his Majesty to declare war on and invade the realm of Andaryon. You thereby hoped to cause the collapse of his Majesty's treaties with that realm, thus bringing about an end to trade between our two peoples.

"You are also charged with attempts on the lives of Artesans from the King's College, and the murder of the crippled boy known as Huw. My Lord Baron, how do you respond to these charges?"

Taran was interested to note that no mention was made of the abduction, imprisonment, and torture of Prince Aeyron, nor of the attempted destruction of the Veils. Of course, most of the court members were ungifted. Perhaps the Artesan-related matters would be dealt with later on.

He had also noticed that there was as yet no sign of either Lord Corbyn or Robin, and he didn't know whether the King intended to call upon them or not.

The Baron, standing at the rail before him, looked Kinsey in the eye as he responded confidently and clearly.

"Your Majesties, my Lords and Ladies, nobles and members of the court, I aver and swear that I am innocent of each and any of these heinous and ludicrous charges, and I demand to know by what evidence I am so charged."

Lord Kinsey stared right back. "My Lord, you will hear the evidence and witnesses of this court, and you will be granted the opportunity to speak in your own defense against them."

Kinsey turned to the King, presumably to allow Elias to indicate where he wanted to start, but before Elias could reply, Queen Sofira rose to her feet and turned to face her husband.

Elias regarded her through narrowed eyes. "Madam?"

She replied in icy tones. "My Lord, I wish to make a statement before the court."

Elias pursed his lips. "This is not the time for statements, Madam."

"Nevertheless, my Lord, it is my right."

Elias was clearly furious at her breach of procedure, not least because it took control away from him. Yet he could hardly refuse her request before the entire court. He gestured curtly. "Very well, Madam. Make your statement."

She nodded once and turned to the court.

"Nobles and members of the court," she began, and no one missed her deliberate exclusion of her husband, "before these ridiculous proceedings get underway, I wish to make a clear and unreserved statement of support in favor of the man before you. I wish it to be known and noted"—she glared down at Kinsey's scribe, who was annotating furiously—"that I do not hold with the charge of abduction relating to my son, Prince Eadan. It is not I who accuse the Baron of such an act. I wish to state unequivocally that I have utter faith in his loyalty to my person, to the Crown, and, indeed, to Albia. In fact, I refute all the charges brought against him and I believe you will all come to see how spurious they are. Members of the court, that is all."

She sat back down, smoothing the silk of her gown. Murmurs of surprise ran through the court. The Baron wore a self-satisfied smirk and the Arch Patrio smiled in beneficent approval. Elias, on the other hand, wore a stormy expression which told plainly of his fury at the turn this trial had taken before it had properly begun.

Elias stood, trying to regain some control over the proceedings. All eyes turned to him.

"My Lord Kinsey, if we might now proceed with the trial?" At Kinsey's bow he turned to the Baron, who regarded him from hooded eyes. "Baron Reen, you will hear the reasons for the charges brought against you and you will hear witnesses speak. You will have your chance to answer their allegations, but unless you satisfy us fully and completely as to your total innocence of all perfidy against the Crown, you will stand convicted. Do you understand me?"

"Your Majesty, I do." Reen's tone was flat, his face an

expressionless mask.

Elias nodded to Kinsey and sat down, his mantle flaring about him. His hands gripped the arms of his chair.

Lord Kinsey stood once more. "My Lord Reen, the Crown maintains that for many months—possibly as long as two or three years—you have been working to undermine the policies of his Majesty, and that to this end you have associated with outlanders for the express purpose of obtaining goods and exchanging information that could be used against the rulers of both Albia and Andaryon.

"It is commanded first that you answer the allegation that you had dealings with the demon Lord Rykan, the deceased Duke of Kymer, who was a challenger of Timar Pharikian, the Hierarch of Andaryon. What have you to say to this?"

The Baron stiffened his spine. "I utterly refute that I ever had any dealings with outlanders. My views on the subject of treating with them are well known. I have no means of contacting them even should I wish to, and I have never dealt with this Lord Rykan, whoever he was. I also take exception to the charge that I ever undermined the policies of the Crown."

Kinsey held the Baron's glare. "Yet you cannot deny that you did most vehemently disagree with his Majesty's policy of interaction with the Andaryans. You made no secret of the fact that you disapproved of his trade alliance with the Hierarch of that realm."

"Indeed!" responded the Baron. "And I was right to disagree, was I not? See what damage has been wrought by courting their favor. The little Prince was stolen away and might very well have been killed if not for the timely intervention of my men. And since when has disagreement constituted insurrection? If we tried for treason everyone who ever disagreed with his Majesty, this court would never conclude."

There was a muted ripple of amusement along the benches. Taran saw the Arch Patrio smile coldly. Elias's face was stony.

Lord Kinsey ignored the Baron's last words. "So you maintain you never had any dealings with the Andaryans. Will you then tell the court how it was that you managed to rescue the King's son from their clutches?"

Taran watched Reen carefully as the Baron replied. His tone was unpleasantly smug.

"It was due to the vigilance of my own guards, nothing more. I had set them to warding the Queen and her children, as his Majesty had seen fit to strip the garrison of all its able men, leaving his family and the city defenseless. It was just as well I did. The loyalty and watchfulness of those guards allowed us to thwart the outlanders' plans before they could spirit the Prince away to their own realm, where, I have no doubt, he would have been lost for good. I'll admit they were duped initially into allowing him to be snatched from his nursemaid, but no one could disagree that they more than redeemed themselves by foiling the demons' plans. My experienced and trustworthy commander, who has since been most foully murdered"—Taran stirred indignantly and felt Ardoch's hand on his arm—"was selflessly brave in fighting them off. If not for the base and vicious actions of the traitorous Artesan woman, Sullyan, I would be nominating Izack for a knighthood, and there would be none of this unwarranted suspicion!"

"My Lord," said Kinsey sternly, "we will examine the abduction of Prince Eadan in detail later. For now, we wish to concentrate on the two attempts on the King's life. The Crown maintains that you were responsible for orchestrating these attacks. In this court today are those who were present at the time and who witnessed both incidents. Captain Elijah and Lieutenant Major Denny, will you both step forward, please?"

Taran stood and walked toward Kinsey. Denny joined him and

they stood shoulder to shoulder before the court.

"Gentlemen, the Crown requests that you tell this court what you witnessed, both on the day of the horse fair and also during the subsequent journey to the Manor, when the King's life was put under threat."

They both did so, as concisely as they could. Denny spoke from a military viewpoint and Taran added his insights and knowledge as an Artesan. Brief and to the point as they were, this still took some time. There were no interruptions and Kinsey nodded his thanks when they were done.

"So, gentlemen, you both agree that the Baron was perfectly placed and had ample opportunity to orchestrate either attack?" They nodded agreement. "Very well, you may return to your seats. My Lord Baron, how do you respond to these accusations?"

Reen spluttered angrily. "Good grief, man, they are clearly quite preposterous! The first incident was indisputably the work of one of these cursed Artesans. Even his Majesty would not refute that. The earth was caused to heave beneath the King's horse, throwing it to the ground. It was purely good fortune that our sovereign wasn't killed or seriously injured in the fall. At the time, I tried to tell his Majesty who I thought was responsible, and my counsel was rejected.

"The second occasion was much the same, although the perpetrator was more subtle that time. Someone with these unnatural powers called up a vast rainstorm which allowed a substantial group of demon raiders to come upon us largely unobserved. I pointed out to his Majesty that the person responsible was right by his side, but again, he refused to heed me. She even got his permission to hold some meaningless rite of honor over the dead body of one of the cursed outlanders. She was more concerned with honoring this alien being than she was for the King's continued safety.

"My Lords, both these attacks were clearly and irrefutably organized by Artesans, and yet you accuse me. I do not understand why I am here instead of the Artesan woman, Sullyan. *I* have no such powers, yet she makes a parade of hers! My Lord Kinsey, I wish it to be noted by the Court that I am convinced this Sullyan has cast some kind of occult glamour over our ruler's eyes so he cannot see his own danger. This causes him to mistrust those of us who have only his best interests at heart."

Kinsey ignored the Baron's request and did not even glance at Elias as he continued.

"It is alleged, my Lord Baron, that you had control over an Artesan, whom you forced to do your will. It is further alleged that you instructed this person to cause the ground to heave beneath the King's horse at precisely the right moment, and that you called on him to release the raiders on the King's party when the storm you had compelled him to raise was at its height."

Reen sighed heavily. "Oh, really, my Lord, this is pure fantasy and nonsense. How on earth could I possibly have controlled an Artesan? Aren't they supposed to have powers we lesser mortals don't enjoy? Why should one of them do my bidding? Who is it I'm supposed to have controlled, anyway?"

"We will come to that later, my Lord. You deny all involvement, then?"

"Of course I do! His Majesty knows full well who orchestrated those attacks. He just doesn't want to admit the truth."

Elias stiffened, but made no comment. He gestured to Kinsey to continue.

"My Lord Baron, will you now relate to us the reason why you included yourself on the journey to the Manor that day? The King went there in order to inaugurate his new College of Artesans. If you are as opposed to them as you say, why did you go?"

Taran saw the Baron's eyes narrow. This could be awkward

for him. His dislike of Artesans was well known, and he couldn't deny that his going was out of character. Taran wondered how he would defend it.

He didn't have to. Reen was spared the task of replying by Sofira, who rose to her feet.

"My Lord, I believe I can best answer that point, if you will allow."

All eyes turned to her and Elias's lips thinned in displeasure.

"The Baron accompanied the King at my request," she said coldly, her eyes hard. "My royal husband does not always see fit to give me detailed reports of his dealings on these excursions, and so I am forced to use agents of my own to keep myself informed. I am not at liberty to travel as freely as does my Lord; *I* have responsibilities that tie me to the castle. However, the Baron graciously agreed some while ago to be my agent and he reports most faithfully to me. Does that answer your question, my Lord Kinsey?"

No one missed the censure in her tone or the criticism she implied. Elias's face darkened. He was unable to rebuke her without causing a scandal.

Kinsey glanced at him and then recovered well. "I thank you for your clarification, your Majesty." He bowed and Sofira sat.

"So, my Lord," he continued, "you traveled to the Manor at the request of the Queen to be her eyes and ears?"

The Baron leaned forward. "Do you doubt her Majesty's word?"

"Indeed not, but if that was the case, can you explain to us why you did not attend the ceremony for which the King had gone and on which you were charged to report?"

The Baron seemed momentarily at a loss. The Queen couldn't help him here. He hadn't attended because he was sickened by the King's approval of Artesans. Yet he could hardly say this before the Court. Instead, he relied upon a half truth.

"I was unwell that day. The shocking events of the attack on the King and the rigors of the journey had taken a toll on my health."

Kinsey wasn't convinced. "And yet you recovered well enough to attend the King when he addressed the men later?"

"It was a mild upset, no more. A short rest put matters right."

Taran noted the glint in Kinsey's eye. "You did not then, use the time during this "mild upset" to plot with your associate at the Manor? For we know you had one."

Taran watched the Baron keenly. Had Kinsey caught him out? Surely Reen must have been expecting them to raise this at some point. The slight start he gave was covered well and he regarded Kinsey with hurt innocence. "Associate? What do you mean? I don't understand."

Kinsey pursed his lips. "Oh, come now! We know you passed messages to and from the Manor. We know you paid King's gold to a certain Captain Parren in order to persuade him to inform you of events there. What have you to say to that?"

The Baron feigned puzzlement. "Well, of course I sent messages to her Majesty while I was resident at the Manor. That was my duty to her. But I certainly did not part with any gold—the King's or my own—and I know of no Captain Parren. Where is this fellow? What does he say about the matter?"

Kinsey again glanced at the King before replying. "Captain Parren was killed three weeks ago. He murdered a Beraxian lord who had been staying at the Manor, and he also attempted the murder of a young cadet. He did this because they found him out. He was killed because he was deserting and running here to *you.*"

Reen drew himself up. "I can assure you that I do not associate with murderers and deserters! What makes you think he was coming here? Such a desperate man could have been fleeing anywhere. If he was deserting, then it's much more likely he intended to join with the brigands who plague the forest. Their numbers seem to grow each year. I have often offered his Majesty the services of my men to help clear them out, but there, too, I have been refused."

The Baron's sigh of regret was a trifle overdone. Taran saw the Queen shoot Reen a warning look from frigid eyes. He wasn't finished, though.

He appealed to Elias, speaking in reasonable tones. "Really, your Majesty, I must protest at this treatment. I cannot imagine what I have done to offend you that you so accuse me. There can be no evidence to support these claims, for I have never done you anything but service. Yes, I'll admit I was against your policies of treating with outlanders, and in the light of what has happened you cannot deny I was right. But these other allegations are tenuous in the extreme and I wonder at your willingness to be deceived by them. I truly believe you have been the victim of some manipulative spell or glamour cast by your enemies.

"When I heard you had cast out the Artesan woman, Sullyan, I rejoiced, thinking you must have seen through her plots and schemes at last. I even heard you'd accused her of High Treason, so how is it that *she* does not stand here before you?

"It was *I* who saved your son from the demons, although I do not ask for recognition. It was my duty to protect your Heir and I was proud to have done you that service. Your Lady Queen understands and supports what I did, so I cannot understand why you persecute me this way."

This reproving speech severed the King's patience. Elias leaned forward in his chair. "Be silent!" he snapped. This drew a look of furious protest from Sofira, but he quelled her with a glance. "You will get your turn to speak when you have heard all our evidence. Until then, I remind you that every denial is being recorded even as you utter it. If you are found to be guilty of falsehood at any time, I will hold it enough to convict you. So I suggest you hold your tongue and issue no more opinions on the actions or fitness of your sovereign. Speak only to answer Lord Kinsey's questions, and restrict yourself to the truth. It will go better for you in the end."

Elias took a deep breath. Furious as he was with the Baron, he had nevertheless raised a subject that Taran knew Elias had to face at some point. It seemed the King had decided it was best he do it now, before them all. His Queen wasn't the only one who could publicly declare her trust.

"Nobles and members of the court, I have to inform you now that my accusation of Colonel Sullyan was unjust and in error. I fully retract any charges leveled against her. I have made a full apology to her and reinstated her unreservedly, for she has proved her worth and her loyalty against bitter and desperate odds. It was a malady of the senses brought on by the abduction of my son that caused me to forget myself, and I hereby state that my accusation of treason against her was false."

The King's voice dropped to a low and menacing growl as he turned to Reen once more. "But let me assure you, my Lord Baron, that when your complicity in these acts is proven, I will show you no mercy. Think on that and beware. You anger Elias Rovannon of Albia at your peril."

Chapter Fifteen

The King called an adjournment, as it was well past midmorning. The Baron was removed from the court and servants moved around the room, offering refreshment. There was hushed conversation among the Attestors concerning the Baron's claims, but the rest of the room stayed quiet, musing on what they'd heard.

Taran caught the General's eye, but there was no request for contact. He wondered when Robin would appear, and when the King would call on Lord Corbyn to confirm Reen had dealt with the Andaryans. Corbyn's evidence probably wouldn't be heard by the Attestors, but surely his presence and testimony couldn't be denied by the Baron, blatantly, in front of the King?

When the court reconvened, the Baron appeared calmer and more in control. He had heard no firm evidence against him yet and had even managed to reiterate his suspicions concerning Artesans. Taran expected him to play on their influence over the King should he get the chance, despite Elias's threats.

He had the appearance of a man beginning to feel safer. Would he fear the testimony of Taran or Denny? Taran thought not. Neither of them had anything irrefutable. It was simply a case of their word against his. Taran doubted even Ardoch caused the Baron anxiety. The finding of the Prince in Reen's own mansion had already been covered. He could afford to relax a little. With Sofira prepared to back him against her husband, and the weight of the Minster behind him, how could he lose?

Lord Kinsey stood and the court came to order. He faced Reen. "So, my Lord Baron, to briefly recap, we have heard you categorically deny any involvement in either of the attempts on the King's life, any dealings whatsoever with outlanders, and you also maintain that it was you and your men who rescued Prince Eadan from his demon abductors. Is that correct?"

Reen inclined his head. "It is, my Lord."

Kinsey turned to his scribe. "Enter that in the records as the Baron's sworn statement. Now, my Lord, I believe we need to hear what occurred on the day the Prince was abducted. His senior nursemaid, Lisbeth, is here and will speak to us. Come forward, Lisbeth."

Bessie turned pale and began to shake. She seemed incapable of rising from her seat. Jinny, who was sitting next to her, whispered encouragingly in her ear, but the poor girl was terrified, clearly still believing the King blamed her for the Prince's abduction. Her fear held her rooted to her seat.

Kinsey grew impatient, but his urgings made Bessie worse. Eventually, Jinella stood.

"Your Majesties, my Lords, the girl is overcome with fear. She believes she is blamed for what happened to the Prince and fears she will suffer some dire punishment for it. Your Majesty, I think a soft word or two from you might help relieve her terror."

Elias sighed, regarding the shaking maid with irritation, though he spoke gently enough. "Bessie, my dear, can you look at me?"

The nursemaid raised her eyes, tears rolling down her cheeks. Elias smiled at her. "I am not angry with you, Bessie. We've spoken of this before, don't you remember? No matter what anyone else might have told you, I do *not* hold you responsible for what befell my son. No one's going to punish you. All these people here have heard me say so, so you're quite safe. We just need to hear what happened that day. Now, do you think you can tell us?"

Bessie nodded, but refused to let go of Jinny's hand. Kinsey saw this.

"Lisbeth, you may speak from there. The Lady Jinella will stay beside you. Just tell us what you remember of that day."

Swallowing, encouraged by Jinella, Bessie began to speak.

"I'd taken his little Highness out into the park in his carriage as it was such a lovely day." Nervousness made her almost inaudible, but Jinny spoke to her and she raised her voice. "Her Majesty told me it would be all right. I had two guards with me; the Baron's men, they were."

Kinsey stopped her. "The Baron's men, you say? Not garrison swordsmen?"

"No, sir. Most of the garrison men had gone to war, so my Lord Baron offered his personal guard to her Majesty to watch over her and the children."

"I see," said Kinsey. "Go on."

"We were walking in the park, sir. The two guards were talking to each other and I was singing to the little Prince, to try to get him off to sleep. It was very peaceful. But then there was a commotion by the castle gates. We'd come down the avenue and were near that large grove of trees. The gate wasn't far away. I looked over when I heard the noise and I think it was some merchants who were trying to get in. They were being difficult. That poor backward boy, Huw, he was there too, and he was shouting at the merchants, which didn't help. There was only one guard on the gate, and so the two with me told me to stay where I was while they went to help."

"Was the guard on the gate from the garrison, or was he one of the Baron's?" asked Kinsey.

Bessie frowned. "I don't know, sir. I didn't look that closely and I don't know them all."

Kinsey turned enquiringly to Denny, who shook his head. "He wasn't one of mine, my Lord. Her Majesty had instructed me to relieve my men of all duties within the castle grounds and to concentrate on the security of the city. She said she trusted the Baron's men to guard her."

"And how did you react to that, Lieutenant?"

Denny looked disapproving. "I protested. I told her that his Majesty had sent me back expressly to guard her and the children, and that the Baron's men were not as well-trained as mine. But she was adamant and I could hardly disobey her."

Sofira stirred with a rustle of silk. "I should think not, Lieutenant, as it was a direct order. And you had recently been injured, as had many of your men. My Lords, I objected to being warded by the dregs of the King's Guard as if my safety were of no importance! When my faithful Baron offered the services of his fit and trained men, I accepted gladly. And well that I did, for the Lieutenant's men wouldn't have been able to chase down those demons before they got away with my son."

"Thank you, Madam!" rasped Elias. The Queen fell silent, smiling at the Baron.

Kinsey continued. "So, Bessie, the guards left you to go and deal with the disturbance at the gates. What happened then?"

Bessie swallowed. "I stood where I was, sir, like I'd been told. I sang to the Prince while I waited for the guards to come back. I suppose that's why I didn't hear the demons. They must have come out of the trees while I was singing and crept up on me." Tears gathered in her eyes and her voice quavered. "There were two of them, sir, and one grabbed me and covered my mouth while the other took the little Prince from his carriage. I was so frightened! I wanted to scream, but I couldn't. They dragged us into the trees and then the one holding me pushed me to the ground and let me go. I screamed and screamed then, but they'd run off. The guards came running and dashed into the trees, and I couldn't see what happened. There was yelling and crashing, and I just stayed where I was and covered my face with my hands."

She turned to the Queen, tearful and afraid. "I was so scared, your Majesty! I'm sorry I couldn't stop them. They were just so strong and quick."

Sofira's severe expression never altered and she waved her hand dismissively. This did nothing to reassure Bessie, who turned back to Kinsey.

"I was so frightened, I just ran for the castle. I was still screaming for the guards and some of them came when they heard me, my Lord Baron among them. They galloped for the trees and I ran to her Majesty. I told her what had happened and she ordered me to my room. I went there and hid in my bed. I was so scared we would be overrun by demons. But later, when I'd got over my fright and tried to leave my room, I found my door was locked, though I hadn't heard anyone turn the key. I was terrified the demons had stormed the castle and taken everyone. My room has no window, so I couldn't see anything. And no one came until the Baron let me out the next day."

Bessie's near-hysterical voice fell into silence, her hands covering her face. Jinny put a comforting arm around her shoulders and handed the girl a cloth. When she was calmer Kinsey said, "Can you tell us what happened after the Baron let you out?"

Bessie sniffled and wiped her nose. "He told me the Prince was safe, but he wasn't going to let him stay at the castle for fear the demons would try again. He said the whole city was in uproar after the attack and that's why I'd been locked in my room, to keep me from harm. He said their Majesties would blame me for not keeping Eadan safe, but I could fix that by doing exactly what he told me. He said he'd take me to the little Prince so I could look after him until it was safe to bring him back. He took me in a carriage to his mansion, and there was his little Highness, none the worse for his ordeal. I was told to keep him in the sewing-rooms and we had two of the Baron's men as guards, one on the door and one who stayed inside with us. I was told not to make a sound and to make sure the little Prince was quiet, because it was a secret where he was.

"I tried to do as I was told, but I couldn't stop Prince Eadan crying once or twice. The Baron came to see us sometimes, but he said it wasn't safe to go back because the King was still away fighting. He said we'd have to stay hidden until the war was over.

"But then Master Ardoch came with that other gentleman, and he said even the mansion wasn't safe anymore. He said we had to go with him. I didn't want to, but Mistress Jinella said it was all right, and they took me and the Prince to Master Ardoch's house. And when I woke the next morning, the little Prince was gone, and they told me that the other gentleman there had taken him away."

Bessie fell silent and stared accusingly at Taran. Jinny whispered soothingly in her ear.

Kinsey thanked Bessie and turned back to the Baron.

"My Lord, can you tell us how the nursemaid came to be locked in her room?"

Reen spread his hands. "As she said, it was for her own safety. She wasn't the only one. As soon as I realized demons had gained access to the castle grounds, I gave orders to shut the whole place down. Many doors were locked. It was unfortunate she was forgotten. It was only when I knew I'd have to take the Prince to the safety of my mansion that I thought to release her."

"I see." Kinsey sounded unconvinced. "And once you'd installed the Prince and his nursemaid in your mansion, why then did you did not see fit to inform her Majesty as to his whereabouts?"

The Baron drew himself up. "I didn't tell her because I couldn't guarantee the security of the castle at that time. The demons had got in somehow, and for all we knew they could have been hiding somewhere just waiting for the chance to strike again. The whole city was unsettled and fearful, as the nursemaid has said, and I couldn't be sure that demons or their agents were not concealed among the populace, just waiting for us to drop our guard. I couldn't even trust the castle servants for fear that some of them were in the demons' pay. I tightened the security around her Majesty and the Princess, but I feared that if I told her Majesty where her son was, or even that *I* knew where he was, the demons might get word of it and none of us would be safe. I thought that if she seemed distraught, any spies that might be lurking about would be convinced she had no knowledge of his whereabouts.

"It was for this same reason that I didn't send the information by letter to the King. If a messenger had been waylaid on the long journey to the Manor, all of our efforts would have been wasted. I and my men had risked our lives to rescue the Prince. I wasn't going to imperil him again."

"Yes, very laudable," commented Kinsey. "But it was convenient, was it not, that you were on hand with a saddled horse just when news of the abduction reached the garrison courtyard? How was that, my Lord?"

The Baron raised his brows. "Convenient? Yes, I suppose you could call it that, although I prefer the word 'fortunate.' But it was not so surprising. I'd given orders that horses should be kept ready at all times in case of emergency—we were at war, after all—and my men were faithful to their duty. I was just about to ride the grounds, as I frequently did to ensure the security of the parklands, when I heard the news. And it was just as well. Otherwise, the outlanders would have escaped with the Prince."

Kinsey let it go and spent some time questioning the group of castle servants. They all told the same story, many of them praising the Baron for his care of the Queen during the King's absence. Taran could see Elias growing weary and irritated by the constant stream of patently-rehearsed statements. He soon gestured for Kinsey to halt that line of enquiry. Reen had plainly had far too long to plan his own defense.

Kinsey then called upon Ardoch to recount the tale of the Prince's rescue. The old swordmaster related the events sparingly. He described how they'd entered the Baron's mansion with Jinella's help, how they'd found the Prince's hiding place, and then taken both him and the nursemaid back to his own house.

"And how did you know where to look for the Prince?" asked Kinsey.

Ardoch glanced at Jinny. "It was Lady Jinella who suggested we search the mansion, my Lord. She'd heard the sound of a baby crying in the servants' quarters one day and, knowing her uncle's stricture against servants' bairns in the house, she became suspicious, especially as this was after the Prince's disappearance. The lady had already begun to question her uncle's allegiances, for she'd heard something else which had aroused her suspicions, and she told us about it before we went looking for the Prince."

Kinsey thanked Ardoch and dismissed him, and the old Torlander resumed his seat next to Taran.

"Let's see yon traitor wriggle out of *this* one!" he growled as Jinny, pale but composed, was called to speak to the court.

It was now late in the afternoon and Taran wondered whether Jinny's evidence would be the last they heard that day. He had expected Robin to appear before now, and although he was highly uneasy about seeing him again, he was concerned by the Major's absence.

To Taran's mind, Reen had definitely had the best of the proceedings so far, what with Sofira's unshakable support and the lack of tangible proof against him, and he could only hope that Jinny's tale would go some way toward redressing the balance. If not, everything could hinge on what Robin and Corbyn might say.

Jinella stood before the court and, in a calm clear voice, briefly told how she had come to live in Port Loxton and of her life in her uncle's mansion. Then she moved on to the day of the horse fair and how her uncle had ordered her to wring information out of Taran, and how he had threatened her inheritance if she refused to obey.

Lord Kinsey frowned at this. "And why did the Baron want this information?"

Jinny shrugged. "He didn't give me a specific reason, my Lord, but his hatred of their kind is well known. He'd do anything to cause them hurt." She glanced at her uncle and saw his poisonous expression. Taran admired her unruffled air, but guessed it was probably a front.

Jinny continued her tale. "I owed a debt to Captain Elijah and Colonel Sullyan. They fought off some brigands who attacked my coach in Loxton Forest the day before the fair, and they almost certainly saved our lives. The ruffians had already knocked out our coachman and killed our guard, and I dread to think what they'd have done to Lily and me if the Colonel and the Captain hadn't run them off. Taran—I mean Captain Elijah—was badly wounded in the fight."

Jinny's words weren't strictly true, but Taran decided against protesting. It would serve no purpose.

Jinny carried on. "My uncle was furious when he discovered he was beholden to two Artesans. He charged me to find out as much as I could about them, hoping, I suspect, to find something he could use to sway his Majesty against them."

"And did you do as he bid you?"

Jinny had the grace to look sheepish. "I didn't want to, but I couldn't afford to lose my inheritance. I was cross with my uncle because I'd taken a liking to Captain Elijah and I didn't want to repay him for his bravery by betraying his secrets. So I decided to partly obey and only pass on what I thought would be harmless. In the end it didn't matter, because his Majesty had his accident and my association with Captain Elijah ended."

She finished there and Kinsey seemed about to move on, but Reen wasn't satisfied with the part-truth she had told.

"That's not all there was to it, though, is it?" he rasped. Jinella turned pale.

"What do you mean by that?" demanded Kinsey.

Reen shot Taran a gloating look before turning back to his reluctant niece. "Go on, Jinella, tell them. They were behaving improperly, weren't they? Under the King's roof, too!"

Elias stared at Reen, then at Taran, who was trying to control a furious blush. Not this again! He should have known the Baron would bring it up.

"Explain, my Lord," commanded Elias.

The Baron bowed and Sofira smiled.

"They were carrying on a liaison right under your nose, your Majesty," said Reen. "This man here and that Artesan woman, Sullyan. My niece saw them together late one night in a state of scandalous undress, obviously just having indulged in a clandestine adulterous assignation!"

Elias's brows drew down and he turned a look of suspicion on Taran. "Is this true, Captain?"

Taran stood. "As regards the allegation of an affair, your Majesty, no. Absolutely not." He tried to remain calm. A vehement disclaimer now would only serve to suggest his guilt, and he blessed his new-found strength and control which dampened the Fire in his cheeks and allowed him to rule his temper. "Lady Jinella did see us together that evening, but what she saw was misconstrued. Much harm has come from her misunderstanding, as I believe you already know. The Colonel and I did have a meeting late that night. Sullyan had heard the disturbing news of human raids into Andaryon and we discussed this between us. But it was nothing unusual and certainly nothing clandestine."

Elias studied Taran's honest expression, dismay in his eyes. Taran knew Sullyan had told Elias some of the details of her estrangement from Robin, but she hadn't gone back as far as this. She had known of the forthcoming trial and hadn't wanted to add more prejudice to Elias's mind than was already there. Knowing the Baron was also at the heart of this trouble inflamed Elias's already wrathful soul. The King glared at Reen and the Baron's swarthy face paled.

"What did you do with this unfounded suspicion, my Lord?"

The Baron feigned innocence. "Nothing. I do not stoop to scandal-mongering."

Jinella gasped in outrage. "But you paid Lily to spread the gossip around the servants and the garrison! You made very sure everyone knew of it."

Reen's eyes blazed. "You prove that, you ungrateful girl! Bring the maid to testify! Oh, but you can't, can you? Because you found she had stolen that gold from *you*, and you dismissed her yourself. It was nothing to do with me!"

He leaned forward against the rail and glared at her. "I rue the day I ever took you in, you trollop. You took my hospitality, made use of my connections, ate my food, and spent my gold. What have you ever done for me in return? Turned on me like the common little tramp you are! Well, you've done it once too often, my fine young lady. You'll never see a copper bit of your inheritance now. You can go back to your whining mother, if she'll have you."

Jinny's eyes filled and she dropped her face into her hands. The King regarded her with sympathy.

"Lady," he said, "if it turns out that you have served me well, you will not go unrewarded. I will match whatever your inheritance would have been and you will receive that and more. Let me assure you, if you are innocent of wrong, you need not fear for your future here."

Jinny's head came up and she took a shuddering breath, ignoring her uncle's presence. "I am guilty only of indulging a foolish girl's hurt pride, your Majesty, and I intend to put right what wrong I have done. But I thank you for your kind words."

Seeing her composed once more, Kinsey said, "My Lady, Swordmaster Ardoch mentioned that you'd heard something which aroused your suspicions about your uncle. Could you tell the court what that was?"

Jinny nodded. "I happened to come across my uncle speaking with his commander, Izack. I didn't hear their words exactly, but I'm sure they were talking about someone being abducted. I got the impression the person concerned was the demon prince."

Kinsey frowned. "And why did that seem suspicious to you?"

"Because it was the day *before* the message about it arrived from the King."

The court went silent. Taran stared at Reen, who glared at his niece. "More lies!" he spat. "She didn't hear *exactly*; she *thinks* we were talking about an abduction; she 'got the impression' it was the demon Prince. Come on, my Lords! Isn't it convenient that the person I'm supposed to have had this conversation with has been murdered? None of these statements can be proven. All come from the imagination of a gold-digging girl who thinks she's been slighted—"

"Enough, my Lord!" Kinsey's hand waved curtly and Reen fell silent. The chamberlain then asked Jinny for her version of the tale of the Prince's rescue. She told it calmly. There were murmurs of admiration for her bravery when she related her encounter with

Izack and how she had distracted him, and Taran felt an unexpected rush of pride in her.

"You were under no illusions about why your uncle had secreted the Prince in his mansion?" asked Kinsey.

"No, my Lord. Not after what he'd done and what I'd heard. That is why I agreed to help Captain Elijah and Swordmaster Ardoch search the mansion for the Prince."

Kinsey inclined his head to her. "It was a very brave thing for you to do, my Lady. So, you went with them and you found and rescued the Prince. What happened then?"

"Taran—I mean Captain Elijah—left us to go and look for Colonel Sullyan. He said she was trapped somewhere on my uncle's estate. The swordmaster and I returned to his house with Bessie and the Prince, and we waited for the Captain and the Colonel to arrive."

The Baron snorted derisively at Jinny's mention of Sullyan's plight, but he was ignored. Kinsey released Jinny to her seat and Taran sent her an encouraging smile. Her face lit up when she saw him and Taran's heart turned over.

Kinsey then called for a break. Taran was surprised, as it was getting late and he'd thought the day's proceedings were over. They were only given time for refreshment, however, and the chamberlain's pointed glance gave Taran to know he would be called upon again when they reconvened.

Once the servants had left, the Baron was brought back once more. His face was tight, but he didn't appear too concerned. He had still heard nothing which constituted proof of perfidy.

Taran's name was called and he wondered what he would be asked now. The chamberlain turned to him, his manner more deferential now that the details of Taran's actions had come to light.

"I think it might be helpful, Captain, if you would recount to the court the sequence of events which led you and Colonel Sullyan to suspect that the Baron was behind the attacks on his Majesty and the abduction of his son. The hour grows late and we must soon adjourn for the day. But before we do, and in the light of what we have heard so far, some detailed background will give us all something upon which to base our thoughts as we leave. If you would be so good?"

Taran nodded. "Of course, my Lord, but I'm not the best person to ask. Colonel Sullyan could explain it better."

Kinsey waved a hand. "I understand, Captain, but the Colonel isn't here. Just do the best you can."

"Very well, but I'll have to go back two years to when this all started—for me, at least. I hope you'll bear with me. It all began with a disastrous plan of mine to obtain tutoring from an Andaryan Artesan ..."

Taran recounted the tale as briefly as possible, keeping to the facts as they emerged and telling Sullyan's theories and suspicions as faithfully as he could. He told them how he and Sullyan had left the Manor and joined up with Ardoch, and how they'd gone their separate ways to follow different lines of enquiry once they were inside the city.

"So," said Kinsey, "it was purely from this chance meeting with the Lady Jinella that you decided to search the Baron's mansion?"

"It was that, my Lord, together with the Colonel's discovery of the stone circle on his estate and what Ardoch and Lord Levant had seen in the dungeons beneath the castle. We believed Prince Aeyron, the Heir to Andaryon, had been held captive there. All our suspicions seemed to be correct up to that point. And then, once we had rescued Prince Eadan, I found the Colonel and the Andaryan Prince chained within the circle on the Baron's lands."

"Ah, yes, the abduction of the Andaryan Prince." Kinsey

206

swept the entire court with his gaze. "We have not yet touched upon this. It is on this that the involvement of the Baron with renegade outlanders hinges, does it not? For if he had no dealings with them, as he claims, how did Prince Aeyron end up in a dungeon beneath the castle and then in a stone circle on the Baron's lands?"

Kinsey fixed the Baron with a glare. Everyone else watched him, too. Reen just stared back, unmoved. The Baron knew they had no proof of his personal involvement. None of the witnesses here had seen him with the Prince, and the fact that the circle was on his land meant nothing. Neither Aeyron nor Sullyan were here to accuse him, and even if they did come forward, he would still feel safe. Aeyron was an outlander, so his testimony wasn't legally admissible. The Baron had already planted doubts as to Sullyan's impartiality, so they were hardly unimpeachable witnesses. Taran noted Reen's confident smile.

Kinsey turned to Elias. "Your Majesty, may I suggest we adjourn for the day?"

Elias nodded and stood. The room rose with him, all bowing respectfully as he left the chamber. The Queen, however, ignored him. She was busy watching the Baron as he was led away by his guards, and the look she gave him was full of expression. She swept out of the chamber the way she had come, ignoring the bows and curtseys she received.

Taran shivered at the icy look she shot him.

"Don't fret, laddie," said Ardoch kindly, resting a hand on Taran's shoulder. "You did just fine today. Let's hope yon Baron trips over his own slippery tongue tomorrow. Come on, I need some ale."

Taran gave him a smile that didn't quite reach his eyes and they made to leave the benches. The General, who had remained behind after the King had left, stopped them before they got too far.

"It's not going too well, is it, sir?" Taran said by way of greeting. The three of them were alone in the echoing chamber.

Blaine shook his head. "Reen's a wily one, that's for sure. We were hoping the weight of evidence against him might weaken his resolve and cause him to make a slip, but the Queen's staunch support is keeping him confident. I'm beginning to think we won't win against her. Elias was hoping to catch her in the same net, but it doesn't look too likely. The Baron can hardly be convicted of treason simply because he disinherited his niece for no good reason, and we've no solid proof of any of the other charges. Major Tamsen's proxy evidence won't further our cause much either, unless the Baron betrays himself. Even if the cadet wasn't still too weak to travel, we've only his word of what was on that parchment, or that it ever existed. If Captain Parren hadn't destroyed it, it would be a different story, but there's no proof whatsoever of Parren's involvement with Reen.

"So, with no firsthand witness evidence and no statement from Sullyan, I'm very much afraid the Baron will go free. Worse, the Queen will consolidate his position beside her and demand a minister's post for him in recompense. Elias's hands will be tied."

Taran stared at the General in disbelief. "What do you mean, sir? What about Lord Corbyn? I thought the Hierarch had agreed to send him?"

There was a rueful twist to Blaine's mouth. "He did, but Elias is loath to call on him. He feels he can't put himself or the realm under further obligation to the Hierarch, especially for so little potential gain. Corbyn's testimony is inadmissible as evidence and there's only the smallest chance that what he could tell us would cause the Baron to slip up. No. This is an Albian matter and Elias wants it kept that way. He won't be beholden to Pharikian any more than he can help. And you can both keep that bit of information to yourselves!" He fixed Taran and Ardoch with a grim stare.

Taran was unable to credit that Elias would pass up this chance. "Wouldn't it be worth it to convict the Baron, even if the chance is small? And what about Sullyan? She'd come if he asked, I'm sure of it."

The General sighed deeply. "She's a sore point with Elias at the moment. Since returning from seeing her, he won't even mention her name. Elias is a very proud man. He's taken some heavy blows. The abduction of his son and what his reactions caused him to do have changed him, lessened him, and yet he now knows that his suffering was nothing compared to hers. He'd never ask Sullyan to relive any of that again, not even to rid himself of the Baron."

He took another deep breath. "There's not much more we can do, I'm afraid. Corbyn's under sentence of death, so he won't be around to cause any more trouble. And with that poor boy Huw dead, Reen has no way of contacting any other Andaryan allies he might have had. He'll be restricted to creating mischief here. Perhaps now, with Elias warned against him and aware of his close ties to the Queen, Reen will behave himself."

"But, General, he plotted to have his Majesty assassinated! Who's to say he won't try it again? Sullyan said he told her he planned to rule through the Queen once she was Regent. I know he was going to blame the killing on the Andaryans, but how can he be left loose around the King after admitting something like that?"

Blaine briefly closed his eyes. "You're right, of course. If he does get off, there will have to be some fundamental changes to Elias's personal guard. I will have to come here and see to it myself. I've always resisted moving my command center from the Manor to the city, but I can't see any other solution now. It'll mean the end of the Manor as we know it, but that can't be helped. Jerrim Vassa can run it as an outpost."

Blaine shook himself to cast off the melancholy the day's

events had engendered. "Anyway," he continued with the ghost of a smile, "I wanted to tell you that you did well today, Captain. Elias intends to reward you for your part in the rescue of his son, no matter what the outcome of the trial. You deserve it. I also wanted to ask you how Sullyan is."

His tone had turned wistful, if such a gruff voice could be described so, and Taran smiled.

"Why don't you contact her yourself, sir? She holds no grudges, you must know that."

"Just tell me if she's well, Captain."

Taran spent a few minutes reassuring the General as to Sullyan's state of health. He didn't feel it wise to mention her loneliness or depression.

Once the General had left, Ardoch repeated his invitation to go in search of intoxicating liquor. Taran waved him away. "You go on, Ghyl. I've a few things to do before I join you. But get one in for me and I'll match you. My throat is parched."

Ardoch looked at him narrowly, but left without a word. When he was alone at last, Taran seated himself once more on the bench and stilled his mind, emptying it of the day's events. The chamber was silent now, the doors closed, the members of the court gone to refresh themselves or to deliberate on what they'd heard.

Taran quested for contact. It came at once. He passed the information requested of him and committed to memory his instructions. Then he went looking for Jinny.

Half an hour later, he was matching Ardoch glass for glass.

Chapter Sixteen

The next morning, the preliminaries of the previous day repeated themselves. The court convened early and the Queen once again shunned her husband's company and occupied the lower box. This time, however, she invited the Arch Patrio to join her and sat talking softly to the senior cleric while the court came to order. Elias watched them with an unreadable face.

The Baron was led forth under guard and installed once more within the railed platform at the chamber's center. His face bore a tight smile and the bow he directed toward the Queen was full of confidence. Taran, seated once again on the right-hand side of the chamber, hoped to see that condescending smile wiped from his lips later in the day.

Ardoch had not yet made an appearance, as the swordmaster was following up on a request Taran had made the evening before. The errand had caused him to raise his brows, but as no explanation followed, the old Torlander had grinned and agreed. Taran awaited his return with impatience.

Lord Kinsey stepped forward to open the proceedings. He began with a recap of the previous day's revelations and how the Baron had countered them. Taran noticed Sofira whispering to the Arch Patrio throughout, although her eyes never strayed from the Baron.

The Adept also watched the King, who looked strained and careworn. Elias was facing another humiliating defeat. Another enforced, public, and all-too-embarrassing apology was staring him in the face. This one would hurt him just as deeply yet cost him dearer than his amends to the Hierarch or his emotional meeting with Sullyan. Its implications could also be far wider reaching. Taran pursed his lips in sympathy.

Then Kinsey called out the name Taran had been both dreading and expecting to hear. He was aware that Robin had arrived in the city during the early hours of the morning, and knew the Major must have ridden hard and forgone sleep to have made such good time. Now he was to give his evidence, and Taran did his best to calm his thumping heart. The memory of Robin's menacing stare on the battlefield of Andaryon refused to be banished from his mind. He schooled his features with some difficulty as the door nearest the King opened and Robin entered the chamber.

The young man wore his russet dress uniform, which displayed his rank insignia and battle honors. He bore himself calmly, no sign of his feelings showing on his face. Taran, though, could see how pale and drawn he was and that the youthful spring was missing from his step. Robin came before Lord Kinsey and made his obeisance to the King, who acknowledged him with a nod. He then took his place on the benches and kept his eyes on Kinsey. He never even glanced at Taran.

"Major Tamsen," said the chamberlain, "I believe you are standing as proxy for a young cadet named Tad Graylin, who holds evidence relating to the Baron's involvement with the deserter Captain Parren."

"That is correct, my Lord." Robin's level voice carried clearly in the chamber. "The boy is still suffering from the effects of a near-fatal wound and cannot yet travel. He has told me his story and I swear to relate it to this court faithfully, just as I heard it."

"Very well, Major. Please begin."

Robin stood and drew a breath, his gaze skating across the Baron's face. He briefly described Tad's call to him in Andaryon, and how Bull's search party had found the boys. He then detailed what Tad had told him of Parren's blackmailing of Ozella, and how he had forced Ozella to spy for him. When Robin reached the part about Ozella persuading Sullyan to take him to Andaryon the day before Aeyron was abducted, the King stirred. Robin fell silent.

Elias was staring hard at the Baron. Kinsey turned to his sovereign enquiringly.

"My Lord Baron," said Elias, "you were present at the Manor the day Colonel Sullyan's party left for Andaryon. And it was that very evening that you interrupted my meeting with General Blaine to tell us of your niece's … indisposition. You were so desperate to return to Loxton that you commandeered the General's carriage and drove through the night, despite the danger of footpads or demon raids. Is that not so?"

The Baron licked his lips and his eyes darted to the Queen. Yet he maintained an outward calm and his voice was steady and controlled as he replied, "It may have been, your Majesty. I cannot remember precisely."

"Can you not?" Elias's voice was heavy with irony. "Well, I can assure you that it was. We have already heard the Lady Jinella say that she was not, in fact, indisposed, but that you had told her most emphatically to pretend that she was. And if I recall correctly, you told me that it was the Queen herself who had summoned you. You even showed me a parchment bearing her seal. How do you explain that?"

Elias leaned forward in his chair, his piercing eyes boring into Reen's. The Baron turned a little pale and spared his niece a vicious glance.

"Your Majesty, you are correct. I did receive a message,

purportedly from her Majesty, informing me that Jinella was grievously ill. And I, understandably, was desperate to return to be by her side. When I arrived that morning and found my niece as healthy as ever, I became suspicious. Even more so when I discovered her Majesty had no knowledge of the parchment I had received. We could only surmise that the whole thing was a ruse to get me away from the Manor, although we were unable to fathom why. My own theory is that the Artesans at the Manor felt threatened by my presence, knowing how I distrusted them, and they wanted me out of the way."

His voice gained strength as he continued. "I decided to call their bluff and told my niece to pretend she really had been ill, in order to convince whoever had sent the message that I wasn't suspicious. In hindsight, it was a mistake on my part not to tell her the reasons behind such a strange request, but I believed that as a close family member and her guardian, she would trust my motives and obey me without question. At the time, I thought it best if she knew nothing of my misgivings, as I did not want to place her in danger. I should have considered the possibility that her ... association with Captain Elijah might have turned her against me. Your Majesty, I have been most cruelly deceived by the pair of them."

Jinella opened her mouth to protest, but Elias raised his hand. Taran saw her green eyes fill with tears and longed to put his arm around her for comfort.

Elias's hand cut the air. "Enough! We will hear no more condemnation of your niece. Now, I suppose it is too much to ask if you still have the parchment that summoned you so falsely back to the capital?"

"I do not have it, your Majesty. I believe I destroyed it."

Elias glared at him. "Of course you did." The Baron breathed again as the King said gruffly, "Major Tamsen, kindly continue."

Robin inclined his head, cleared his throat, and went on with his tale.

"As I said, Parren was blackmailing Ozella. Ozella was terrified of what might befall his sisters if he told anyone other than Tad, so the boys decided to search Parren's rooms for hard evidence. The result of their search was a letter, written by the Baron to Captain Parren, setting out the details of their arrangement. It even mentioned a 'powerful benefactress at court.' Your Majesty, my Lords, I swear on my Oath those were the exact words on the parchment."

Gasps of shock and outrage ran round the chamber and Sofira's face blanched. She stared icily at the Baron, who seemed momentarily frozen. Taran had to give him his due; the man knew how to throw confusion on things. Recovering well and not returning the Queen's accusing glare, he rounded on Robin.

"That's a base lie! I demand to see this letter!"

His enraged shout echoed in the chamber. Blaine and Elias both wore resigned looks. They already knew the Baron demanded the impossible. Without the parchment, Robin's evidence was worthless.

Robin knew it too, yet he answered calmly. "I regret this is not possible, my Lords. I saw it myself through Tad's own eyes, but a search of Captain Parren's rooms after his death yielded only a few ashes and a tiny scrap of parchment in his grate."

Before anyone else could speak, the Baron sneered, "So once again, we have only words as evidence, and no proof. And they are the words of yet another Artesan! He saw it 'through Tad's own eyes.' Really, my Lords, what use is that? Can no one else see the conspiracy that is staring us in the face? How convenient that this damning parchment was destroyed. How strange that only Artesans discover these purported treacheries. Open your eyes, my Lords! Can you not see their plan? Are you all so blind?"

Robin glared at him. "Are you questioning the sworn word of an officer of the King's forces, my Lord?"

The Baron stared defiantly back, his expression triumphant. "Would you care to tell us, Major, what became of this traitor, this murderous deserter?"

Robin faced him squarely, a bleak and soulless look in his eyes. "I killed him, my Lord. I killed him for the damage he did to me and mine, and for the murder of Ozella and the attempted murder of Tad. And for deserting his duty. He deserved to die."

Reen folded his arms and glared at Elias. "Yes, yes, very convenient. More false accusations, your Majesty, more unsubstantiated allegations. I don't doubt for an instant that this deserter murdered and wounded the boys. I don't doubt he was blackmailing one of them for information. But I utterly refute that I had anything at all to do with him. Why would I? Yes, I was at the Manor when Colonel Sullyan left for Andaryon, but I had nothing to do with forcing Lord Ozella to accompany her. What would I want with information on Artesans? But mark my words, your Majesty, *they* wanted *me* out of the way. That's why they sent that false message, knowing I'd play into their hands. They wanted you to think I was guilty, and you have fallen into their trap. This is yet another ploy to implicate me and impugn my good name. Can your Majesty not see? They fear me because I see through their little schemes. It is *they* who are the traitors, *they* who seek to undermine your good sense. They have you under some kind of charm, your Majesty. They have been working their will upon you for years, to earn your favor and strengthen their hold in this realm.

"You should have trusted your instincts when you branded the Sullyan woman a traitor and cast her out. Their hold on you had slipped, your innate good reason had surfaced, and you acted on it. But I very much fear they have you under their spell once again, and you cannot even see it."

"Silence."

Elias spoke the word levelly, without inflexion. The Baron obeyed, but the look he cast the Queen was tight with satisfaction. Sofira herself had recovered her aplomb once she knew the damning parchment wouldn't be produced, and she returned to whispering with the Arch Patrio.

Elias turned to Robin, thanking him for his evidence and the effort he had made in order to attend the court.

Robin bowed. "Your Majesty, do I have your leave to return to the Manor? I have told all I came to say. I'm still very concerned for the health of the cadet, Tad, and I should be by his side. The boy is my Apprentice and we have a strong bond. I fear his recovery might suffer if I'm not there."

Taran's heart twisted. It was imperative that Jinny and Denny should speak with Robin and tell him the truth about the rumors that had so blighted his and Sullyan's lives. He couldn't leave Port Loxton without hearing what they had to say. Yet Elias was granting his permission, and Robin turned to leave. The Baron watched him go with a mixture of triumph and distaste.

As Robin made for the door to the left of Elias, Taran signaled frantically to Jinella. Thankfully, she seemed to understand. She touched Denny on the arm and whispered urgently to him. The Lieutenant glanced up at Taran and then to the door through which Robin had departed. He nodded reluctantly and stood.

He approached Lord Kinsey, murmuring to the chamberlain. Kinsey replied, and Taran sighed with relief as the Lieutenant and Jinny left the chamber together, Jinny casting a glance over her shoulder at Taran as she went.

Once the noise of their departure died down, Kinsey addressed the court.

"My Lords, we will now turn our attention to the events leading up to, and subsequent to, the confinement of the Baron within his mansion. My Lord Levant, stand forward, please."

The First Minister obeyed. He glanced at the Baron from shrewd eyes and Reen stared maliciously back. Without Levant's raising of the garrison, which not even the Queen could overrule, he wouldn't have had to suffer the indignity of languishing under house confinement. Levant ignored him, unimpressed by the tacit enmity.

"My Lord," said Kinsey, "would you tell us, please, of your conversations with Swordmaster Ardoch, and describe the events leading up to your instructions to the King's Guard which led to the Baron being held within his own dwelling?"

Levant proceeded to relate his initial interview with Ardoch and his agreement to look through the treasury records. He told what he had found there and it was confirmed by the chief of the treasury clerks, who also produced the letter purportedly from Sofira's father, King Lerric, asking for a vast sum of gold to help repair a section of coastline damaged by earthquakes.

Kinsey called on Taran, in the continuing absence of the swordmaster, to explain why they had suspected such a sum would be missing from the treasury. He did so, reiterating part of his story from the day before. He had to make an effort to drag his thoughts away from the painful interview he hoped was taking place somewhere within the castle. It took some doing.

When he was done, Elias gestured to a man standing in the shadows by the door. He was dressed in runners' livery and he held a parchment. This was given to Lord Kinsey, who compared it to the letter from King Lerric.

"My Lords," said Kinsey, "it is impossible to tell from this whether the first letter was indeed written in King Lerric's hand. There are similarities and there are discrepancies. King Lerric himself, however, does confirm that he asked for and received such a sum from her Majesty, drawn on Albia's treasury. More than that, we have not had the time or opportunity to investigate."

Sofira stared pointedly at the chamberlain. "Do you doubt the word of my father, Lord Kinsey?"

"Indeed not, your Majesty," he assured her, glancing swiftly at Elias's disgruntled expression. He put both letters aside and turned from the topic.

"First Minister, would you now tell us what occurred after you discovered this payment to King Lerric?"

Levant related how he and Ardoch had investigated the dungeons. His description of the cell they had found drew murmurs of disgust and pity from the court.

"Yet there were no clues as to who this prisoner was, or who had incarcerated him?" pressed Kinsey.

"None, my Lord."

Taran noted the Baron's smug look. Only Reen himself, his Commander, Izack, and the Queen had known of Aeyron's imprisonment. Izack was dead and the Queen supported her countryman thoroughly, so once again, there were no witnesses to connect the Baron with the dungeons. Taran's face grew hot with anger for Aeyron's suffering and pain.

Kinsey, however, wasn't done. "What happened then, my Lord?"

Levant looked grim. "I was more than half convinced by then that Master Ardoch's suspicions concerning the Baron were correct. What I'd been told was corroborated by the evidence of my own eyes. Ardoch said he was going to search the Baron's mansion for Prince Eadan while the Baron was attending the Minster the next day. He hinted that he and his associates expected the Baron to proclaim himself the rescuer of the King's son, and that he would use this both as a lever to further his career and also to convince the populace of the inadvisability of his Majesty's alliance with the Andaryans.

"It was much later, after I had returned to my suite, that Ardoch came to me once more. He was in a state of high anxiety and told me that Prince Eadan had indeed been found at the Baron's mansion and that Ardoch had taken him and his nursemaid to his own house for safety's sake. He begged me to turn out the garrison and to place the Baron under house confinement."

Kinsey nodded. "How did you react, my Lord?"

"I was convinced by Ardoch's manner and by his account of finding the Prince that something was badly amiss. I freely admit I have never fully trusted Baron Reen, but I have known Master Ardoch for more years than I care to remember. I did trust *him*. I knew he would never be involved in any kind of plot against our King, and he would never have come to me with his suspicions if he hadn't been convinced of the Baron's guilt. I thought it best to follow his suggestion and confine the Baron. If it did turn out he was innocent, he would have suffered nothing more than a little indignity. But if he was guilty, I would be doing the Crown, the Prince, and my King a service which was no more than my sworn duty."

"And what was her Majesty's opinion of your actions?"

Levant grimaced. "Queen Sofira was ruling in her own right during his Majesty's absence. I could not, in all conscience, go behind her back. So I sent for Lieutenant Major Denny and gave him my instructions, and then I sent a message to the Queen."

Levant hesitated and risked an ill-advised glance at Sofira's furious expression. "Her Majesty was … less than happy with my actions," he admitted. "She ordered me to rescind my instructions at once and to step down from my post. I refused to do either."

"That was very courageous of you," said Kinsey. "You must have been very sure of your facts."

Levant frowned. "I knew that unless or until the King should be pronounced dead on the field of battle, her Majesty had no power to relieve me of my post. And I have already told the court why I acted as I did. So I held my ground and let my orders stand. I sent Lieutenant Major Denny to apprehend the Baron and his men.

"I ordered Denny to leave sufficient men to guard the Baron and to let no one in or out. But, of course, her Majesty was free to come and go as she pleased, and I believe she visited the Baron on several occasions. That's all I can tell you, my Lord."

Kinsey released the First Minister, thanking him for his evidence. He needed to call upon Denny once more, but the Lieutenant had not yet returned to the chamber. As the morning was advancing, the chamberlain announced a recess.

Chapter Seventeen

Jinella and Denny left the court chamber and strode down the hallway, following the route Robin must have taken. Jinny almost had to run to keep up with the Lieutenant's long strides. She could swear she felt the urgency of Taran's will in the pounding of her heart—or maybe it was just her own apprehension.

Yesterday's events had taken their toll on her. She was in two minds as to her feelings over what was happening to her uncle, and the lack of firm evidence against him had allowed doubts to slip into her mind. He was so cleverly refuting every charge brought against him, and overnight it had dawned on her that she really only had Taran's word that Reen was, in fact, guilty. That and what she had seen and heard for herself. She wondered how she'd be feeling now if she hadn't seen Izack unloading that cart, if she'd never heard the baby cry, and if she hadn't overheard that snippet of conversation between Izack and Reen.

She and Denny rounded a corner and caught sight of Robin ahead. He was walking swiftly, no doubt eager to be gone. Jinny clutched Denny's arm.

"Major!" he called.

They saw Robin hesitate then turn. He frowned, looking annoyed, and waited for them to approach.

"What is it, Lieutenant? I'm in a hurry."

"I can see that, sir, and we don't want to hold you up. But we have something to tell you, something of importance."

Robin sighed irritably. "Can't it wait? Send me a runner."

"With respect, sir, we can't do that."

Robin glared at Denny, who shifted uncomfortably.

Jinny reached out to touch Robin's arm. "Major, you really do need to hear this."

He looked down at her, noting the glisten of tears in her eyes. "Oh, very well. But make it quick. I'm in no mood to linger here."

"We can't talk in the hallway, Major." To Robin's growing irritation, she pushed open a nearby door. It gave onto a small solar. "This will do," she said, "we'll not be disturbed in here."

She ushered the two men inside and closed the door. Robin gave her a look of exasperation.

"What is this? What's so urgent you have to detain me now? I warn you, I'm not in the best of moods."

"Won't you sit down?" pressed Jinny, taking his arm to diffuse his mounting anger and leading him over to a group of chairs clustered near the room's single window. Robin suffered himself to be led and sat, glaring at the two of them as they seated themselves in chairs facing him.

"Well?"

Jinny looked at Denny, who refused to meet her gaze. He found it hard to look at Robin, too. The Major abruptly lost his fragile temper.

"Either one of you spits it out *right now*, or I'm leaving!"

Alarmed, Jinny held out a hand to him. "Major, you must understand that this is hard for us. You have been wronged, your life has been blighted, and it's our fault. Well … mine, really."

Robin's eyes hardened as he stared at her. His face, pale and drawn already, took on a sickly hue. "What do you mean?"

Jinny took a deep breath. "It goes back to the horse fair," she said, gazing down at her hands twisting in her lap. "I expect you know how Colonel Sullyan and Captain Elijah rescued me and my maid from brigands in Loxton Forest?"

His lips tightened. "I heard about it."

Awkwardly, Jinny went on to relate the events that had followed her rescue. As she spoke, the despair seemed to deepen in Robin's eyes. Denny remained motionless at her side. She managed to continue until she came to the moment she decided to visit Taran in his chamber.

She raised her eyes to Robin's, seeing the tight white grip of his hands on the chair, the desperate look in his eye. She leaned forward, appealing for his sympathy with her actions that day.

"Major, can you imagine what it's like for a young girl who has set her heart on someone? I felt spurned, cheated. How dare he extoll the virtues of another woman all day when he was supposed to be escorting *me?* It was demeaning, Major. It was ungallant of him, and I'll admit I was jealous. However, I finally decided I'd been harsh on him—the King had nearly died, after all—and so I made up my mind to call on him before he retired."

Robin made no move or sound. He sat frozen, his eyes glued to her face. His stillness was unnatural and she began to fear how he would react when he heard the truth. Yet she had gone too far to stop now. Besides, she had Denny to protect her, and Taran was relying on her. Taking a deep breath, she told him the rest, ending with her discovery of how Lily had spread the scandalous gossip.

"So you see, Major," she said, holding Robin's wild gaze, "I really didn't see anything at all. Taran explained it to me later, when we met up again. He told me how my jealousy had caused you to believe they'd … been together. He told me how the men of the Lieutenant's command had spread the gossip around the Manor. He told me how you and Colonel Sullyan had become estranged."

She spoke urgently, leaning toward Robin and putting out a hand that never quite touched him. "But, in fact, none of those rumors were true. It was only my jealousy, my stupid pride, and my uncle's malice that led you to believe what they said. Colonel Sullyan was never unfaithful to you. And Taran would never—*ever*—do anything like that. I know him so much better now and I know with all my heart that he would never betray your friendship and trust like that. I had to tell you, Major. I just hope and pray it's not too late."

✢ ✢ ✢ ✢ ✢

Robin sat motionless, his eyes locked on Jinny's. His heart strained in pain, his mind was in turmoil. Not too late? When his whole world had already been shattered? When he had caused his life mate to turn her own vast powers against him in the worst, most unforgivable transgression that could ever be committed by one Artesan upon another?

Not too late?

He turned woodenly to Denny. The Lieutenant paled visibly at something he saw lurking in Robin's eyes. Robin swallowed with an effort. "But you said …" He faltered, tried again. "On the way to the Manor, you said …"

"That Taran confessed to it?" Denny hung his head. "I was wrong. What he actually said was that you knew about them. He never said anything about … sleeping with her. That was my own interpretation, formed after I'd seen the way he watched her and heard the rumors going around the men. All Taran really admitted to was loving her. And then while I was in the infirmary—before Healer Arlen threw me out—I had a visit from Captain Parren."

As Denny pronounced the name, a terrible rage began building in the icy fortress that had once been Robin's heart. Denny didn't see it as he continued, his gaze flicking around the room, avoiding Robin's.

"He seemed eager to talk, and the conversation got round to the subject of the Colonel. Well, you know that I trained with Sullyan at the Manor, as did Parren. Trouble always followed him. He was forever playing pranks and trying to get others blamed for them, especially Sullyan. He was intensely jealous of her, of her skills, of her rapport with the other cadets, and he did whatever he could to hurt her, to make her appear less able. He even attempted to force himself on her once, after she'd continually refused his advances. He tried to blame her for that, too.

"Speaking of that led us to the topic of affairs. I won't repeat what Parren said about her, but he said enough to convince me that the rumors I'd heard the men spreading were true. Added to what I thought I'd heard Taran Elijah say—well, perhaps it's understandable. Parren also accused her of being responsible for the King's accident, although we didn't get the chance to discuss that because Healer Arlen came in just then and Parren left. When I was alone, I had nothing to do but think over what he'd said. I should've known better, but somehow it all made sense. And that was the same day you came to see me."

Denny fell silent. Robin's face felt cold and bloodless. A tremor had begun in his body that he couldn't control. He had felt the same when Denny had confirmed the ugly rumors concerning his life mate. The numbness in his muscles was in direct contrast to the agony in his soul, and Robin didn't know how much more he could take. He had believed his beloved life mate had utterly betrayed his deepest trust with another man who was his close friend. So much so that he'd cut himself off from them. Now he was hearing they were both wholly innocent. He could hardly breathe for the pain in his heart.

"Are you telling me it was all false?" he rasped, his voice strangled and strange. "All those vicious rumors, all that ugly gossip? Not one word of it true? You're telling me this *now*? That

Taran never told you he'd slept with Sullyan? Because you told me quite categorically that he had!"

Denny hung his head, his face red with shame. "I know I did. I've already told you it was my own interpretation of what he said, colored by the rumors I'd heard among my men. I was wrong. I should have known better. I should have enquired more closely for the truth. I'm sorry. What else can I say?"

"What else can you say?" Robin's voice was toneless, the terrible anger in his soul boiling toward the surface. A painful pulse throbbed in his temples and he could hardly focus his eyes. His mind threw chaotic images at him: Sullyan's shock when he'd accused her of infidelity with Taran, her severe distress when she'd been forced so far out of her legendary control that she had turned her immense powers on him, the ice in her voice when she'd told him to go.

Then, too fast for him to control, came other nightmare images: Taran's terror when Robin pinned him to the wall, the desperate anguish in Sullyan's eyes when he'd seen her at the gate after Elias had declared her a traitor, Robin's own shock and anger as he'd seen her ride away with Taran. And last—and maybe most terrible of all—the red mist of fury behind Bull's eyes when he'd broken Robin's jaw for suggesting Sullyan's pregnancy was Taran's doing.

This last revelation caused Robin to drop his head into his hands with a deep moan of bereavement. For if none of the accusations were true, then neither was his belief as to her baby's parentage. And *that* meant....

He groaned in anguish. "Oh gods. Oh dear gods, no." The true enormity and horror of what he had done rushed through him.

He barely heard Jinny's timorous voice. "Major ... Robin ... are you all right?"

He couldn't control his shuddering. The full realization of the injustice of his actions and thoughts over the past few weeks crashed into his beleaguered brain. He had no room for anything else. He felt dizzy, he felt sick. Somewhere within his mind he was aware of Denny and Jinella watching him in concern, but he possessed no power to move or to speak. He was held locked within the parade of ghastly memories and he couldn't break free.

He saw Rienne's dismay when she'd realized Sullyan had left without imparting some kind of revelation to him. At the time he'd wondered what she meant, but he hadn't had the will to pursue it. An ice cold finger of dreadful suspicion trailed its way down his spine. His eyes narrowed behind his hands and his face grew hot with anger as he recalled Parren's clumsy attempts to persuade Robin he'd only held his grudges against Sullyan, never Robin himself. How Parren must have laughed at the anguish he had helped to create.

A roar of rage threatened and Robin swallowed it with difficulty. He now knew the reason behind Parren's request to accompany him into Andaryon. He had no doubt that had Vassa not refused that request, Parren would have found ample opportunity in the confusion of battle to slide a sly dagger through Robin's heart.

The image of Parren's pale, scarred face brought painful memories of Tad's ordeal flooding into Robin's overburdened soul. He gasped in pain. Parren had caused so much hurt, so much anguish. Why had he harbored such deep hatred? Why hadn't he been dealt with before? Why, *why*, hadn't Robin found the strength to bring charges against Parren for his actions at the siege of Hyecombe? For if he had, none of this would have happened. Tad wouldn't have been injured and Ozella would still be alive. Robin heard again the cold censure in Bull's tone when he had contacted the big man after Tad's despairing cry for help. It wrung his tormented soul.

The memory of Bull's steadfast support of Sullyan and his many attempts to get Robin to see sense were the final straw. A great sob wracked his body and he let out a cry of deepest pain, dropping to his knees and clenching his fists to his breast. All he had ever wanted in his life and more—so much more—was now completely beyond his grasp. He'd had it all and he had thrown it all away. He had done it on a tide of pathetic jealousy he'd never even known was there, dormant until Parren's cruelty and a featherheaded woman's imagined slight brought it rampaging to vindictive life.

His cry of anguish was too much for Jinny. She leaned forward and placed her hand on his shoulder, murmuring softly. Robin couldn't bear it, not from her. *Especially* not from her. He leaped to his feet, startling her into a frightened cry. He didn't care.

"Get out!" he thundered, his eyes spilling unheeded tears, his face taut with pain. Jinny stared at him, terror in her eyes. "Go on, get out! Leave me alone. Haven't you done enough damage? I can't stand any more!"

"Steady, Major," warned Denny, moving to stand between Robin and Jinella. "This wasn't easy for her, you know. It took a lot of courage for her to tell you this."

Robin rounded on him. "Well, she's told me now, though no good will come of it!"

He wanted to scream. His anger, his despair, and his anguish were now turned against himself. He didn't know how he would live with what he had done. He could never face any of his friends again. He could certainly never go back.

Denny stared at Robin, looking as if he feared Robin might strike him. His uncertainty turned Robin's white-hot fury to ice. Emotion washed out of his soul, replaced by a deeper, more frightening rigid control. Adrenaline leached from his muscles, his body sagged. Denny saw that the danger of violence had passed, but what was in its place?

He opened his mouth to speak just as his name was called in the corridor outside. It seemed the court hadn't finished with him.

Robin glared at him. "You'd better go, Lieutenant."

Denny traded glances with Jinny. "But what about you? I don't like to leave you like this. Will you be all right?"

Robin's hand cut the air. "I'll be fine. You've done what you came to do. I'm obliged to you. Now go."

Denny hesitated, but he had no choice. The call came again; he couldn't keep the King waiting. He held out his arm to Jinny. "My Lady?"

She stared at Robin, her green eyes wide with distress. "It'll be all right, Major," she said, her voice weak and small. "You just need to talk to her—"

Robin's harsh voice cut across her. "*GO*!"

Denny frowned. "Come, my Lady," he said, steering her firmly toward the door. She went, casting a last tear-filled look at Robin over her shoulder.

The door swung shut and their footfalls faded. Robin stood staring at the door, unheeding of the trembling that continued to shake his body like a palsy. It grew stronger—so strong, in fact, that he could no longer stand. He collapsed into the chair, his head cradled on his arms, his heart burning with pain, with rage, with despair. The uncontrollable storm of weeping that clenched him in its grip swept through his agonized soul like fire.

✣ ✣ ✣ ✣ ✣

Taran watched intently as Denny and Jinella were ushered into the chamber. Jinny made for the benches and glanced at Taran as she took her seat. He could see her distress and knew that the interview with Robin hadn't been an easy experience. Explanations would have to wait.

As Denny stood forward to answer Lord Kinsey's questions, Taran saw Ardoch finally enter the council chamber. He came quietly and made his way to Taran's side. He didn't speak, but merely nodded as the Adept raised his brows.

Taran sighed. He had now done everything he reasonably could to aid the successful outcome of this whole sorry mess. The rest was up to others.

Kinsey addressed Denny. "Lieutenant Major, will you tell us what you witnessed on the night you received the First Minister's order to detain Baron Reen?"

Denny's voice at first was rather shaky, but it soon regained its usual strength. He related how he had gathered his men and followed Swordmaster Ardoch's advice as to where they would likely find the Baron. He continued uninterrupted until he mentioned seeing the stabbed body of Huw lying upon the ground.

"Did you see who stabbed him?" asked Kinsey.

Denny shook his head. "He was already on the ground when we arrived. But Captain Elijah went to his side as soon as Colonel Sullyan killed Izack. He took some sort of collar off the boy's neck."

Kinsey turned to Taran, who stood once more. "I removed a ligature of spellcord from Huw's neck, my Lord. The Baron had wound it tightly about the boy's throat and was restraining him by it while he taunted Colonel Sullyan, trying to get her to release Izack by threatening the boy's life. When he heard the Lieutenant's men pursuing his own and realized his cause was lost, he stabbed Huw in the back and left with his men. I will swear to the truth of this, my Lords. I clearly saw him do it."

"That's a lie!" snarled the Baron. The Queen shot him a furious glance and he fell silent, his face purple with rage.

Kinsey ignored the outburst, his attention still on Taran. "Captain Elijah, I think you had better tell us of the events leading up to this moment, if you would."

Denny was released back to his seat and Taran stayed where he was while he related his discovery of Sullyan and Aeyron within the burning circle. When he spoke of releasing them from their chains, Kinsey asked, "Did you see any indication that the imprisonment of Colonel Sullyan and the Andaryan Prince was the Baron's doing?"

With all his heart Taran wished he had. "No, my Lord. But I had the word of the Colonel and Prince Aeyron. The Colonel told me the Baron had come to gloat over them before he forced Huw to activate the circle. He told her that he intended to destroy the Veils, the links between the realms, to prevent any further traffic between them. It was his belief that the Veils provided the power that Artesans use to travel the realms, and that by destroying them he would render all Artesans powerless. Sullyan tried to tell him he was very wrong and that he risked destroying the entire world, but he refused to listen. It was his intention that she and Prince Aeyron should die within the circle when the explosion took place."

"And what happened after you released them both and attempted to leave the estate?"

Taran briefly related the fight between him and Patrin, Sullyan and Izack, and ended with the Baron threatening to use Sullyan's knife to end Huw's life.

Kinsey frowned. "How did the Baron come by the Colonel's knife?"

Taran shrugged. "He must have taken it from her when she was chained within the circle."

"So what happened then?"

"As I said, the Baron threatened to take Huw's life if Sullyan didn't release Izack. That's when we heard the sound of Denny's men approaching, and the Baron stabbed Huw in the back. He didn't have time to take Huw with him if he wanted to escape the

Lieutenant's men, and he didn't want Sullyan to be able to question Huw. So he stabbed him."

"This boy, Huw," said Kinsey. "If he was an Artesan, as you claim, why didn't he fight back? Why did he let himself be used by the Baron? Couldn't he have stopped the Baron from using the knife?"

Taran was glad Sullyan wasn't here to relive Huw's torment as he told the court why Huw couldn't have resisted the Baron, and how Reen had used the lad's terror of violence to control him.

Kinsey's tone held sympathy as he said, "So he died of his wounds. You could do nothing?"

Taran sighed. "We tried, my Lord. Sullyan tried her hardest. But she was powerless to save him. He died in her arms."

Chapter Eighteen

"Oh, how very touching."

Elias glared at Reen. "How do you answer *these* accusations, my Lord? I would hear how you defend yourself in this instance. The imprisonment of one of my most trusted officers, torture and abuse, the abduction of a royal Prince, the murder of a disabled and innocent boy. Explain yourself!"

Reen countered hotly, staring Elias in the eye. "I don't have to, your Majesty. It's all lies to cover their conspiracy. What do I know of this ... this spellsilver, these stone circles? How could I have abducted an Andaryan Prince when I had no way of laying hands on him? I have never tortured or imprisoned anyone! All I know is your son was once again snatched from a place of safety by Artesans and a demon. Artesans led, moreover, by the same woman you yourself accused of High Treason and cast out of your forces. Both she and this Captain Elijah are murderers. You have just heard him admit it from his own mouth!

"My faithful manservant Seth saw Ardoch and Captain Elijah stealing the little Prince away from my mansion and he very sensibly sent for me at once. I came as quickly as I could and found my two men trussed like chickens—the Commander also suffering from a severe blow to the head. Their stories matched that of my servant about who was responsible. I set them to searching the grounds while I went to send for the rest of my men. When I finally caught up with Izack, the Artesan woman, Sullyan, was about to murder him, a man who was only following my orders! He'd been told to apprehend her so she could answer to you for her crimes, but she had no scruples about killing *him*. Captain Elijah had already murdered my other man, Patrin, also quite needlessly. By the time I arrived, the crippled boy, Huw, was already lying on the ground and I really couldn't say how or why he was there. But we have already heard he had *her* knife in his back, and I can only surmise that he got in her way. And then the Lieutenant's men came charging up, unlawfully pursuing my guards. One of them, when he saw the danger I was in, most bravely stayed to take me onto his horse and he bore me away to my home, where we found ourselves penned and confined.

"And that's the truth of it, your Majesty. Now ask Captain Elijah what they did with your son, and where they were taking him! To the demon realm, your Majesty, to your enemies, that's where. How can you say I was wrong to oppose them?"

Elias's face was white with rage. "If their intention was to deliver Eadan to my enemies, Baron, why did they bring him straight to *me*?"

Reen was unfazed. "Obviously, your Majesty, because they thought the demons were losing the battle! They could see you would win the day and so they turned their coats once again and pretended they had rescued your son."

General Blaine stirred beside Elias and whispered urgently in the King's ear. Reen watched this with narrowed eyes and stared with suspicion as Elias turned to him once more.

"Baron Reen, do you still claim that you rescued my son from his Andaryan abductors before they were able to slip him through the Veils?"

"I do, your Majesty, for that is what happened."

"And you maintain you secreted him within your mansion for his protection until he was removed from your custody by Captain

Elijah and Swordmaster Ardoch?"

Reen huffed. "I have already said so."

Elias smiled nastily and Reen frowned.

"If what you say is true, my Lord," snarled Elias, "how do you explain the message I received informing me of the abduction of my son? It bore the seal of the Hierarch, if you remember. *But he never had him, did he?*"

Taran had to grudgingly admire the Baron's nerve. Despite the draining of his face, he never faltered. He flung his arms wide. "You still don't see it, do you, your Majesty? They had that message ready! They never expected my men to thwart their kidnap attempt. The message had already been sent, even as I was taking your son to a place of safety. And once they saw that you would invade Andaryon and that I would be unable to contact you to let you know your son was safe, they didn't have to change their plans. You were already beyond our help.

"But when she realized you were going to defeat the Andaryan forces, that Sullyan woman had her minions steal Eadan from me, so I would be prevented from returning him to you. They wanted to claim the glory for themselves."

The Baron leaned on the railing and spread his hands in a gesture of earnest supplication. "Why can you not see it? They have been working against you all along. Playing on your sympathies, worming their way into your confidence, gaining your trust, and then, when they thought the time was right, they turned upon you. It was only your great skill on the battlefield that convinced them they had acted too soon. If you do not take this opportunity to banish their kind forever, they will continue to undermine you and work their evil behind your back until they are strong enough to try again. I beg you, your Majesty, listen to me! Listen to the Arch Patrio. He can see through their wiles. The Matria Church has long been concerned for your safety while you insist on treating with such unnatural beings. Take our advice, your Majesty. Follow the holy texts and cast them from your favor."

Elias struck the arm of his chair with his fist. "That's enough, Baron!"

Reen fell silent, realizing he had been on the verge of ranting again. It seemed he found it hard to stay calm when speaking on the subject dearest to his heart. He wiped his mouth, trying to regain control.

Elias's voice was low and cold. "I will hear no more on the subject of your prejudices, Baron Reen." His eyes bored menacingly into Reen's, daring him to argue. The Baron wisely held his peace. "That battle in Andaryon was far from decided when my son was returned to me. It was your ally, Lord Corbyn, who very nearly turned the tide against us and it was he who provided the assassins who were charged with ensuring I never returned alive. But Colonel Sullyan and Captain Elijah, those same Artesans you so blithely accuse of treachery, foiled his attempts by capturing him. They delivered him to me so that we could ascertain the truth of the matter, and I am satisfied that he was your associate and co-conspirator in this affair."

"Then bring him to verify these claims, your Majesty!" urged Reen. "I don't see him here giving evidence to convict me. I know of no Corbyn and I have no demon allies, as I have said before. I would not so demean myself. These are more lies, more false accusations to cover the real culprits of these schemes. I maintain my innocence, your Majesty. You have no proof against me."

Reen folded his arms and glared defiantly at the King. Elias stared back at him in frustration. Taran's heart sank. The Baron was right; as things stood, there was no tangible proof.

Elias glanced at Kinsey and then at General Blaine, looking for advice. Before either of them could speak, the Queen stood in a rustle of silk and faced the court. Elias's expression tightened and his eyes narrowed.

Sofira spoke quietly, firmly. "My Lords and members of this court, I crave your indulgence. We have heard many accusations these past two days, claims and counter-claims, and there has been much anger and recrimination. I should like to redress the balance and bring some semblance of sanity to these proceedings. I ask that you give your attention to His Immanence Lord Neremiah, Arch Patrio of Loxton's Minster and most senior representative of our Matria Church. He stands here as character witness for my Lord Baron and he wishes to say a few words on the Baron's behalf. My Lord Kinsey, will you permit?"

Her question was a mere formality, as everyone knew. No one had the power to forbid her, not even the King. The chamberlain had no choice but to accede to her request as graciously as he could.

"If it please your Majesty. My Lord Arch Patrio, you are most welcome."

Looking resigned, Kinsey sat as Lord Neremiah took the floor. The Queen settled herself, smoothing her gown and wearing a self-satisfied smile. Taran saw the King rest his chin in one hand as he passed the other wearily over his eyes. He was a veteran of Neremiah's sermons and would have no reason to think the churchman would do anything but praise Reen to the skies.

Neremiah stood in the box beside the Queen, his pockmarked face bearing a beneficent smile. He held up the heavy silver symbol representing the Faith of the Wheel and pronounced a blessing on them all. The regular Minster attendees among the court bowed their heads reverently, the Baron among them.

"My friends," he began, his voice smooth and light, his tone patronizing, mildly reproving. "We have witnessed much anger and frustration within these walls. There have been some harsh charges brought, most of which are totally unsubstantiated. I feel it is time we introduced a little calm and order to these proceedings. I urge you all to reflect upon what you have heard in this court.

"In order that you may more clearly understand my Lord Reen's position, his fervor, and the sheer impossibility of his being guilty of any of these allegations, I wish to make you aware of the kind of person he is. There may be some among you"—the sweep of his brown eyes touched briefly on Taran, Jinny, and Denny in particular—"who are not aware of his many good works among our community and for our Matria Church. I am sure that once you hear how avidly he toils for the betterment of our realm and for our spiritual wellbeing, you will realize that not only is it inconceivable for him to have had any dealings with outlanders, but also that he is the most faithful servant our sovereign Lord could ever wish to have."

There was a faint rustling among the members of the court as they realized they were in for a long speech. In his light and monotonous voice, Neremiah extolled the Baron's virtues, cataloguing them efficiently but not swiftly. He revealed in fine detail the many ways in which the Baron had aided and improved the amenities of the city, and told of his invaluable assistance to the Queen. He rambled on at great length concerning Reen's many supporters in his home province of Bordenn, where the young Princess Sofira had found his gentle guidance a source of great strength, and how their own church valued his talents and the conviction of his faith. He found many ways in which to say much the same thing twice over, as if he were deliberately trying to bore his audience into acquitting the Baron.

He then went on to expound his belief that Artesans, and indeed anyone aspiring to powers not enjoyed by the common run of people, were unnatural beings, not espoused by God and not to be trusted. He advised the King at great length on how he should behave toward these unfortunate and deluded misfits, and encouraged him to rid the land of their threat to the authority of the Matria Church once and for all.

He kept one eye on Kinsey and the other on the King, ready to forestall any signs on their part of wanting to interrupt or bring his preaching to an untimely end. Every time they thought he might be approaching some kind of conclusion, he picked up the signals of their relief and began afresh on some obscure aspect of the Baron's character, the Baron's loyalty to Crown and country, or the Matria Church's position regarding outlanders and pagans.

Taran and Ardoch shared many despairing glances during this interminable soliloquy. With the glowing picture Neremiah was painting, the Queen's unshakeable support and the lack of firm evidence against him, there was no way in which the charge of High Treason could be brought to bear upon the Baron. Yet Ardoch also noted Taran's frequent glances toward the double doors of the council chamber and his slightly distracted demeanor.

He hissed into Taran's ear, "What're you waiting for, laddie? Or should I say *who*?"

Taran shook his head and whispered back, "I think it's already too late."

Lord Neremiah finally decided he'd done enough and came to the end of his list of the Baron's impeccable qualities. The court members had long since ceased to conceal their yawns and Elias's blue eyes had glazed over. Taking the moment as it presented itself, Kinsey rose and faced the Arch Patrio before he could resume his speech. But Neremiah was done. He cast a glance at the Baron, who was smiling insufferably within his enclosure, his arms crossed over his chest. The churchman sat down beside the Queen, who bestowed on him a soft-eyed look of admiration.

Kinsey regained control. "My Lord Arch Patrio, we thank you for your testimony on behalf of Baron Reen. Let me assure you that all the points you have raised will be considered in full when the time comes to deliver the verdict of this court." He turned to Elias. "Your Majesty, do you think this might be a suitable time to adjourn? It is well past midday and we have now heard, I believe, from all the scheduled witnesses. I'm sure we would all appreciate some time in which to mull over what has been said."

The sandy-haired monarch nodded resignedly, waving a weary hand. The chamberlain pronounced a full recess, instead of the usual short break, exhorting them all to be back in the council chamber in just over one hour's time.

Elias and Blaine left the chamber together, the General trying to bolster the King's failing spirits. He wasn't having much success. Elias was facing the most humiliating moment of his rule so far, and it would be all too public. Taran wondered whether he should tell them his secret, but then decided against it. He didn't want to raise false hopes. Instead, he crossed the council chamber, a mightily curious Ardoch in tow, and approached Jinella, who was waiting for him. Denny was nowhere to be seen.

Taran was alarmed by Jinny's distress, still in evidence even after so much time had passed. "Was it so bad?" he asked as he sat beside her on the bench. Ardoch stood close by.

"Oh, Taran, it was awful!" Tears started in Jinny's eyes. Taran did the only thing he could; he put his arms around her. She melted against him and laid her head against his neck. He stroked her hair gently until she calmed. With one hand, he raised her tear-streaked face.

"Can you tell me?"

She managed to swallow her tears and tried a smile. The warmth she saw reflected in his eyes gave her courage.

"He took it very badly," she said, her voice low and sad. "At first he was silent, which scared me. And then he was furious, and that scared me even more. I think even the Lieutenant was afraid of him then. But suddenly he went all cold and strange and told us to go away and leave him alone. That was when we were called back and we had to leave him anyway. I don't think the Lieutenant wanted to go. I think he thought the Major might do something … rash. But we had no choice. We came back here."

Taran held Jinny close. He could feel the shaking of her body as she relived the experience. He had gone cold himself at the implication that Denny was worried Robin might harm himself.

"Where did you last see him?"

Jinella told him, her eyes wide and fearful.

"Ardoch, stay with her, will you?" At the Torlander's nod, Taran rose and left the chamber. He had to see that Robin was all right. He had to be sure he hadn't harmed himself.

He ran down the hallways, passing some of the other court members, all of whom turned to regard him curiously. Before he reached the room where Jinny had spoken to Robin, he saw Denny coming toward him. The Lieutenant shook his head.

"He's gone, Taran. I've checked with the guards. He took his horse and rode out right after we left him. He's left the city."

Taran fell into step beside Denny. "Was he all right?"

"He had all his limbs, if that's what you mean. More than that, my men didn't notice. They're not trained to spot potential suicides."

Taran glanced sharply at him. The Lieutenant gave a rueful grimace. "Ah, sorry. I just feel rather bad about this, all right? I left him in a state, something I didn't want to do. I feel responsible for what's happened and I don't know how to put it right. It may be that telling him like this wasn't such a good idea."

Taran sighed. "I couldn't let him leave today without knowing the truth. Too much damage has already been done. But you're right to be concerned. I know how deeply Robin feels things. He'll be devastated by this. I just hope he's strong enough to weather it. I'd go after him, but I can't leave here at the moment. And anyway, I don't think my presence would be of any comfort to him right now."

Denny glanced at Taran as they made their way back to the council chamber. "This must nearly be all over now. No one would convict Reen on the strength of these unproven allegations. Not with Neremiah and the Queen to champion him. Gods, I dread to think what my life will be like once he's acquitted. Not only will he be even more insufferable than ever, but I bet he'll make damn sure my position here is untenable. I think I'll request a transfer before he can accuse me of something serious. Preferably somewhere quiet and obscure."

Taran sympathized. He also wouldn't want to be anywhere near the Baron or the Queen if Reen got off. He felt he had to offer the younger man some hope.

"Perhaps it's not all over yet. A good friend of mine has a saying: 'don't hold the wake before the bloody funeral.' Don't write your transfer request too soon, Denny. The day's not over until the verdict is pronounced."

Denny halted, eyeing him sharply. "What do you know? Come on, man, what's going to happen?"

Taran shook his head. "Just wait and see. Come on, let's get something to eat before they reconvene. Neremiah's preaching has left me ravenous."

✣ ✣ ✣ ✣ ✣

No matter how hard they tried, neither Ardoch nor Denny could get any more out of Taran. They propounded various theories, all of which elicited an enigmatic and unhelpful smile. Jinny, who stayed close by his side, holding his hand for comfort, said nothing. She was content merely to be near him and watched him thoughtfully.

The court reconvened and the room buzzed with speculative

whispers as it filled. Taran, Ardoch, Denny, and Jinella sat together on benches near the General and the King. Blaine wore a resigned expression as his hard blue eyes stared about the room. The Queen, who entered on the Arch Patrio's arm, never even acknowledged Elias's presence. The King's piercing gaze swept once over her stern figure. Taran could imagine only too well how difficult she would make his life once her Baron had been exonerated. He wondered whether thoughts of assassination might not be trickling through Elias's mind.

The Baron, brought in under armed escort, bowed reverently to the Queen and Neremiah. Sofira acknowledged him with a gracious smile and a nod of her head. The Arch Patrio made the Blessing of the Wheel over him. The King was once again ignored. Taran noted the fury rising in Elias's face. Despite their power, he wondered at the wisdom of the Queen and the churchman in so flouting their sovereign's authority. Humiliated Elias may be, but that might only serve to make him more dangerous. He was still High King, after all.

A trumpeter at the rear of the chamber let sound a peal of notes. The court fell silent and all eyes turned to the King. He gestured to Kinsey and the chamberlain rose.

"My Lord Baron," he said, his tone devoid of inflexion, only his eyes showing his distaste, "you have heard all that this court has to present both for and against the charges laid against you, namely those of High Treason. You have had your chance to answer them. Before this court pronounces its verdict, it is customary for the accused to be given the opportunity to speak. This is granted you now if you wish. But I would caution you to remember that the verdict of the court cannot be known until it is spoken. Be aware that what you say could still have a bearing on your future."

Reen nodded curtly. Taran thought there could hardly be any

doubt left in the Baron's mind now as to his full acquittal. Barring a miracle, he must be let off.

He cast another glance at the chamber doors. It was surely too late now. Something must have gone wrong. His stomach knotted in anxiety. What if Robin ...? No, he shouldn't speculate. Whatever was coming, he had to accept it. It was all but over.

Unhindered by the guards, Reen left the iron-railed platform and moved to stand before Kinsey. It was a studied move. He wouldn't speak as an accused man; he would address them as a free servant of the Crown. As he positioned himself, he glanced over at the single door to the side of the chamber, and what he saw there gave rise to a tight smile of satisfaction.

He stood before the royal box and bowed again to the Queen. She smiled and raised a hand in benediction. Reen ignored Elias's thunderous expression and turned to the court.

"My friends, I will not demean your intelligence by going back over what you have heard and witnessed these past two days. I will not reiterate the reasons behind my actions, nor will I again protest my innocence. There cannot be a sane or sensible person within this room who can still be under any misconceptions about the rights or wrongs of the charges brought against me.

"I have been exonerated beyond all doubt from any blame in the events surrounding the abduction of the King's son, and indeed from all allegations of conspiracy or subterfuge against the Crown. Despite these wounding accusations and the humiliations I have been forced to bear, I do not demand retribution. Oh, no. I do not even demand apologies, although I have been wronged beyond belief. I understand why I was so unjustly incarcerated within my own home and denied my basic right of freedom. I do not rage against the humiliating presence of armed guards before my door and around my person. Such things are inevitable, a direct consequence of the atmosphere of suspicion and the glamour of respectability cast by these Artesans. It is this which so clouds the judgment of our sovereign Lord."

A muted gasp sounded at the Baron's audacious words. Taran risked a glance at Elias and wished he hadn't. There was venomous rage within the King's eyes, and Taran wondered how Reen bore the daggers of his glance as they shot with murderous intent toward his unprotected back. But then, Reen's back wasn't unprotected. With Sofira and her pet churchman behind him, how could he fail to display his courage? Still, Taran didn't like to think how Elias might exact his revenge, for the King's expression clearly said he would.

Oblivious, or simply uncaring, Reen carried on. "Friends, with the accusations against me all proven false, we must surely now turn our attentions toward finding the real culprits behind the abduction of the King's son. Kidnap is a very nasty word and a heinous crime wherever perpetrated, but when it involves a Crown Prince it must carry the heaviest of penalties. As does murder, of which these treacherous Artesans are also undeniably guilty."

He spread his arms wide, crying, "And one of the guilty parties is here in this very room! Can we stand to see him go any longer unpunished? Can we suffer him to leave here, liable to escape justice by using those same arcane arts with which he has confounded and ensnared our beloved sovereign? I think not!"

Glancing at the Queen and receiving the slightest of nods, Reen called loudly, "Guards! The Queen's Guards! I command you to seize and hold the treacherous Artesan, Taran Elijah!"

His finger shot out, pointing with righteous, quivering rage at Taran. Shocked, the Adept stared with horror into the Baron's baleful gaze, seeing the terrible triumph in his eye, the mad glitter of his fervor. Taran was completely unable to move, couldn't have run had he wished to. He hadn't foreseen this development. He only vaguely heard the Queen's voice commanding a group of guards, who appeared through the door to the King's left, to advance and take him captive.

Jinny squealed with alarm as they came, her hands flying to her mouth. Denny and Ardoch protested loudly, but as they were unarmed there was little they could do. They were shoved aside with flat blades and unveiled threats. There was shouting and uproar within the court as the four guards surrounded Taran, grasping him painfully by the arms. He dimly thought he heard the General's voice mixed in with the rest. He was dragged roughly from his seat, manhandled to the floor of the chamber and forced to his knees before the Baron, his arms wrenched painfully behind him. He didn't struggle. He only stared in stupefied horror into the malevolent eyes of the Queen and her vindictive Baron, his heart quailing within him.

He only vaguely registered the sudden shocked silence in the chamber, the strange expression that crossed the King's face, and the abrupt intake of breath made by the Baron. But he heard the words that caused the silence. Heard them and absorbed them, deep within his psyche.

For he knew that voice. He knew it well.

Sullyan had come.

Chapter Nineteen

Robin had no idea where he was going as he rode out of Port Loxton's Forest Gate and on into the surrounding woodland. Instinct and habit alone kept him on his horse, and a wary sixth sense kept his hand close to the hilt of his sword. To every other extent, Robin was oblivious to everything but the pain lancing through his soul.

He simply couldn't cope with the enormity of what he'd done. His overburdened mind kept showing him images of first Rienne's and then Bull's distressed and incredulous faces as he constantly rebuffed their efforts to make him see sense. *Why* hadn't he seen sense? Why had he allowed the rumors to take hold of him so? Why had he been so ready to believe such blatant lies? It was almost as if he had become a different person, someone suspicious and jealous. Almost as if some force had heightened those traits within him, made him more vulnerable to them....

He cut off such thoughts. There was no excuse, no one to blame but himself. He didn't deserve Bull and Rienne's friendship. He didn't deserve *anything*.

Well, that was appropriate, because now he didn't have anything. He had forfeited the right to friendship, to forgiveness, even to atonement. He had committed the basest, the most fundamental of mortal sins: he had betrayed not only the love, trust, and commitment of the one person who was dearer to him than life itself, but he had also betrayed himself.

And he had no idea why.

He swayed in the saddle, his muscles turning to water as despair washed over him, draining away what strength he possessed. He still didn't know where he was headed. The one thing clear in his mind was that he certainly couldn't return to the Manor. How could he stand their reproachful eyes? He knew he had broken Bull's heart. He knew the big man held himself responsible, as the one who had first found Robin in Garon's scruffy little garrison and seen the potential within the raw young man.

Potential! That was a laugh, thought Robin bitterly. Whatever potential he might have had, he had now thrown away, and he'd done it all by himself.

Spitting a vicious oath, he kicked the chestnut's flanks. He felt a sudden need for speed, as if he could outrun his aching desolation and his revulsion for his own actions.

He couldn't, of course, although the chestnut tried. Sometime later, Robin pulled the sweating animal to a walk, patting its damp neck in a distracted attempt to apologize for his earlier harsh treatment. He looked about with disinterest, not recognizing his surroundings. Dusk wasn't far off, and he had no idea whether there were lodgings nearby. He hadn't come prepared for a night in the open. Still, it wouldn't be the first time he'd had to improvise a bed. It was summer and the weather had been warm and dry for days. He would survive.

And even if he didn't, it hardly mattered. His life as he had known it was over. There was no point thinking about the future. He had no future. Finally reining the chestnut to a halt by a stand of trees surrounded by grass, he slid to the ground. He unsaddled the horse, removing its bit so it could graze. It wouldn't stray; all runner horses were trained to stay with their riders. And even if it did, it would be no more than he deserved. As it began cropping grass, he slung his pack carelessly to the foot of a tree and cast himself to the ground beside it, shoulders slumping.

He stared ahead, eyes clouded and dark, thoughts bleak and hopeless. Somewhere deep inside great sobs were welling, trying to break through his self-imposed barrier of condemnation. He didn't even deserve the release of tears. It was too much like forgiveness and there was no forgiveness for a crime such as his.

He sat unmoving, his body in stasis but his mind in a riot of guilt, trying desperately to seek a way out. His future at the Manor was gone. So be it. Accepting that, what was left to him? If he had to turn his back on his training and career, what would he do? Become a hired mercenary for a far-off foreign lord? No, that would be more than he could bear. Too much like home. He would be reminded at every turn of what he had so needlessly thrown away. What other trade could he follow? Where could he go to escape, to forget his wicked crime?

There was nowhere he could go where he wouldn't remember happier times. Nowhere on this earth where memories wouldn't sting his soul with loss. No place he could run to where the featherlike touch on his mind wouldn't constantly call to him with seductive and impossible yearnings.

No place but one.

He raised his head, unheeding of the tears that coursed down his cheeks. He stared unseeing over the grass, not hearing the rhythmic champ of the horse's teeth as it grazed, not smelling the familiar scent of leather and horseflesh.

He started to shiver.

Slowly, almost of its own volition, his hand crept to his belt. Numb fingers found the hilt of his dagger. The foot-long, wickedly-sharp blade slid easily from its scabbard. The dying rays of the summer sun flashed redly from the honed steel as it shook in his trembling fingers.

Yes. Here was his answer. Here was the gateway to the one place where he could forget, where love meant nothing, where blame and shame didn't exist. To fade away, to slide into blessed oblivion—yes, that was the answer.

And he could even do it without pain. He could use his metaforce to numb the bite of the knife as it slid through his ribs and into his heart. He could avoid the one excuse that might weaken his resolve before the act was complete, though he deserved the pain. He didn't merit a peaceful death, not with this burden of guilt bearing down on his soul. Maybe the anodyne of pain would help purge his tortured heart.

Quickly, lest he change his mind, he slipped out of his combat jacket and flung it away. He wore only a thin shirt beneath, and he ripped that from his body too, baring his breast to the evening breeze as his soul was bared to the teeth of his guilt. Shaking, he gazed down at the polished steel in his hand, its razor-sharp point glinting in the fading light. He slowly reversed his grip and laid the dagger's tip against his skin, over his pounding heart.

The blade nicked him and he gasped. No, he wouldn't use his powers to dull the pain. In this final act, he wouldn't shrink from what would come. He would face this as he could not face his shame.

His hand tightened on the hilt of the blade, ready to thrust the point home. Before the blurred mist of his sight, he saw the still and bleeding form of his young Apprentice, Tad, lying in the stream just as Bull had seen him. Life leaking out of him, desperate to hang on, to pass on his vital information. Waiting, just barely alive, for the one person he most yearned to see.

Robin's hand trembled. His blood ran freely where the blade had sliced his skin. He went cold. What cruel trick was this, to show him that the only course of action he could possibly take was just one more form of betrayal? He groaned aloud. How could he abandon Tad? The lad had given his all—even to his own life—in order to help a friend. It had only been his love for Robin that had enabled him to cling to existence. If Robin continued now, if he made that one last, tiny thrust, he would be casting Tad's love, his sacrifice, and his blind trust back in the boy's very teeth.

A violent palsy took him in an unbreakable grip. His face stretched in a rictus of pain. So, he was to be denied even this! With a savage snarl, he flung the knife from him. It cut the air with a whine, embedding in the trunk of a tree. It jutted there, quivering.

Gasping and shuddering, his body wracked by uncontrollable sobs, heedless of the blood flowing down his breast, Robin folded to the ground, hugging his arms tight about him. His heart tore as he gave himself over to the fire and the agony of hopeless grief.

✤ ✤ ✤ ✤ ✤

"Baron Reen, I command you to release that man."

Sullyan's clear, ringing voice, well used to command, cut through the torpor that gripped Elias. The King surged to his feet, raging at the guards who had appeared at the Baron's strident call. Who the Void were they? They wore the colors of Bordenn, but Elias didn't know them.

He roared his fury as he strode from his box to the chamber floor. "Reen, I command you to release that man. Stand back, stand away." He turned, snarling, on the Queen. "Madam, what is the meaning of this? *Queen's* Guards? How dare you call men other than the King's sworn forces into this council chamber?"

Sofira glared at the far doors of the chamber, which had been thrown wide, her hard gray eyes wide with fear. The Baron, who had frozen at the earlier authoritative command from behind him, pivoted on his heel and froze again, locked in dismay as he beheld the figure in the doorway. The guards he had summoned milled about, looking uneasily from the Queen to Elias, unsure of whom to obey.

Taran, still held painfully on his knees, allowed himself a tight smile.

Sullyan spoke again, her lilting tones stiff with command. "My Lord Baron, I do not believe this court has yet delivered its verdict. You still stand accused of treason. You have no power and no rights until the verdict has been pronounced. Unless you return immediately to your place, you will be held in breach of his Majesty's court and will be judged guilty by means of contempt.

"Lieutenant Major Denny, summon your men. The Baron has overstepped his authority here."

Denny reacted instinctively and snapped a smart salute. "Yes, ma'am." He gestured to his men, those who had been guarding the Baron, and they came forward, swords drawn, ready to oppose the strangers holding Taran captive. Denny himself, although unarmed, advanced menacingly on Reen.

Taran found himself free of restraint. He brought his aching arms around, rubbing at sore muscles. A strong hand came under his elbow, helping him rise, and he looked up into Blaine's stern face, which now wore a rare, if grim, smile.

"Are you all right?"

Taran nodded, still rubbing his arms. "Only bruised, sir."

Denny and his men had restored order, the strange guards unwilling to resist under the baleful eye of the King. They were summarily disarmed and marched out of the chamber to await questioning at the King's pleasure. The Baron had been hustled back inside the railed platform where he stood stiffly, his face pinched and angry.

Elias coldly eyed his Queen. "I will have your explanation for this outrage, Madam!" Her face turned toward his, her usually stern countenance quailing before his ire. He continued before she could speak. "But that will have to wait. Right now, we have a trial to conduct. You, Madam, will sit and be silent. You, Arch Patrio," he turned in distaste to Lord Neremiah, who was regarding the tableau with confusion, "will return to your rightful place."

Elias stabbed a finger toward a bench at the side of the chamber. Neremiah, with a last glance at the Queen, removed himself from her box and sat where the King had indicated.

Elias stood at the head of the chamber. General Blaine was by his side, with Taran to the General's right. Jinella was watching the Adept with both concern and admiration in her eyes. He gave her a reassuring smile.

The King stared toward the chamber doors, his decisive moment of action now giving way to confusion. On his face was a mixture of relief, incredulity, and shame.

Blaine glanced at Taran. "I suppose this is your doing?"

"I only did as I was asked, sir," Taran replied, his eyes on Sullyan and her companion.

Blaine huffed.

Elias's voice was husky, full of wonder. "They've both come. I thought all was lost, but they've both come." He swung round on Taran. "Did *you* ask them?"

The Adept spread his hands. "I only told her how the trial was proceeding, your Majesty. When she heard how badly things were going, she realized you needed her."

Elias ducked his head, his face reddening. "She came because of me?"

"Yes, your Majesty, and Prince Aeyron is here because she asked him. She came for love of you."

Everyone watched the activity by the doors as two trumpeters stepped forward and let peal a long fanfare of silver notes. As the ringing died away, a herald came forth.

"Your Majesty, my Lords and Ladies, noble members of the court, may I present to you His Imperial Majesty Prince Aeyron of Andaryon, and his sister, Her Royal Highness the Princess Brynne Sullyan."

The Queen made a strangled noise. "Sister?" she spluttered. "*Princess*?" She turned to her husband in fury. "My Lord, what nonsense is this?"

"Silence, Madam!" roared Elias. "You will hold your tongue until I give you leave to speak."

Sofira turned gray at the King's rebuke. She swayed on her feet. All her plans were in disarray. All the Baron's flamboyant promises and assurances had faded to nothing with the shocking appearance of the two who were pacing in stately elegance toward the King.

Taran studied them. Aeyron, tall and regal, was dressed soberly in black velvet trimmed with imperial purple, his long silken mantle flaring behind him. His soft black boots made no sound on the flagged floor. Taran could see how pale he was, and how uncomfortable. It must have taken a deal of gentle persuasion for Sullyan to have gained Aeyron's compliance in this. It was a measure of his regard for her that he was willing to have his terrible ordeal brought into the open merely to aid Elias of Albia. It would cost the Prince much courage and strength to face his tormentor again without flinching.

Sullyan paced serenely beside her adoptive brother, her hand resting lightly on his arm, her pupils large and black as she supported his weakened spirit with her deep well of power. Taran knew her own state was hardly better. The gown she had chosen, a deep forest green with a high waist and a full skirt, concealed her pregnancy from all but those who knew her well. Her mane of tawny hair was unbound, topped by her royal coronet, and a mantle of silk flowed from her shoulders. Her face, too, was paler and thinner than usual, her eyes seeming larger than ever above her prominent cheekbones.

Although she moved with grace and held her head high, Taran could tell that the strain of supporting Aeyron and her own inner weakness was taking a heavy toll. He frowned until he saw the smile that lit her features when she caught sight of him. Instinctively, he reached out to her mind and offered his own strength. She accepted a measure of it, which told him much about her physical state.

The royal pair reached the King and halted. Elias took a hesitant step forward before collecting himself. He came close and took Aeyron's maimed hand in both of his. It was greatly to his credit that he didn't so much as glance at or react to the Prince's injury.

"Majesty," he said, sincerity ringing through his tone, "you are most welcome in my lands."

Prince Aeyron bowed his head in recognition of Elias's greeting. Elias turned to Sullyan, who smiled up at him.

"Highness," he said softly, abashed, "I hardly know what to say to you. My gratitude is boundless. You, also, are most welcome here."

Sullyan gave him her hand, which he raised to his lips in a gentle kiss. His eyes met hers, and Taran wondered at the fleeting pain that crossed her features. It was gone as swiftly as it had come and her smile remained. She murmured something for the King's ears alone before raising her voice for all to hear.

"My Lord, it is our pleasure to be of service."

Elias flushed. "May I offer you refreshment?" he asked to cover his momentary embarrassment.

Sullyan shook her head. "We thank you, my Lord, but if it pleases you, we would like to see this business concluded. My brother the Prince has many duties awaiting his attention at home and would return as soon as he may. If we could continue?" She indicated the Baron with a wave of her hand.

Elias acceded and turned to offer Aeyron a seat beside him in the comfortably appointed box. As the two men ascended the steps,

Sullyan tarried to lay a hand on Taran's arm.

"Did they harm you, my friend?"

He smiled down at her as he bowed his head. "No, Highness. I was shocked, no more." He grinned at her expression as he used her title.

"Were you able to fulfill my request?" she asked, and nodded in relief when he told her Ardoch had indeed done so. Her expression was grimly satisfied as she took Blaine's offered arm, the General escorting her up to the royal box where she seated herself next to Aeyron. Taran returned to his seat beside the swordmaster, who grinned conspiratorially. Jinella clasped his hand.

While the preliminaries of this unlooked-for royal visit were played out, the Baron stood in silence within his railed platform. He cast apprehensive glances at both the Queen and the Arch Patrio. Neremiah returned his look with bewilderment, but the Queen glared back in meaningful rigidity. Reen's eyes narrowed under her stare.

Once the new arrivals were settled comfortably beside the King, Elias stood once more, his voice lighter and stronger than before. "My Lord Kinsey, it appears we are not yet done with the testimony of witnesses in this trial. There are those now in the court who have information that may have a bearing on the charges against the accused."

"Your Majesty, I must protest!" Reen spluttered. "The testimony of outlanders is not admissible in an Albian court."

Elias's face reddened. "Hold your tongue!" he snapped, in no mood to tolerate any more delaying tactics. "It's not unheard of for witnesses to come late to a trial, and despite her new status, the Princess Brynne is still an Albian subject. Hold your peace until invited to speak. Do you understand?"

Elias refused to release the Baron's gaze until he sullenly

mumbled his acceptance. The King nodded once in satisfaction. "Very well. My Lord Kinsey, I believe that her Highness the Princess Brynne has brought someone she wishes us to hear. However"—he threw Reen a hard stare—"since this person is an outlander, from the realm of Andaryon, I will now ask the Attestors to leave the court. Although I personally wish to hear it, the testimony of this outlander will not be considered as evidence in this trial."

The Attestors rose and left the courtroom, Reen visibly relaxing as they went. Taran thought he was wrong to do so, for Sullyan's evidence would be admissible, and totally damning.

Kinsey gestured to Sullyan, who cast her eyes toward the chamber doors. "Captain Dexter, Captain Tyler, would you be so good?"

Taran started as he heard Cal's name and craned his neck to see. Sure enough, there was his dark-skinned Apprentice turning to call to someone outside the chamber. A moment later he marched toward them, leading Dexter and four others of Sullyan's old command who surrounded a black-haired man stalking disdainfully between them with his hands chained behind his back. Taran grinned. Not only had Sullyan persuaded Aeyron to come, but she had also brought the traitor, Lord Corbyn.

Cal gave Taran a knowing wink as he smartly halted the prisoner's escort beside the Baron. Taran grinned back, thinking it was just like Cal not to have told him he was coming. But he couldn't savor the moment for long.

At Corbyn's appearance, Reen's face tightened. The tall and wiry Andaryan lord looked neither left nor right, but stared Elias defiantly in the eye. Cal and Dex instructed their men not to lower their weapons.

Sullyan murmured briefly to Lord Kinsey, who nodded before addressing Reen.

"My Lord Baron. Do you recognize the man standing beside you?"

Reen couldn't stop the involuntary flick of his eyes toward Corbyn's scornful face. He had to swallow before he could answer.

"I d—I do not."

Kinsey frowned and turned to address the Andaryan lord within his ring of steel.

"My Lord Corbyn, do you recognize the man who stands accused in this court? Think carefully before you answer."

Corbyn never flinched, never even blinked. He stared fearlessly at Sullyan, the knowledge of his already sealed fate lending him backbone. He had nothing to lose.

"I've never seen him before in my life. He's an outlander, a barbarian. I wouldn't dirty my hands with such as he."

The Baron's face purpled in outrage and Taran thought he might protest in spite of Corbyn's indignant disclaimer working in his favor. Maybe all was not yet lost.

Kinsey turned back to Sullyan and indicated that she might question the prisoner. She stood, shaking her head sadly. "Ah, my Lord Corbyn, you disappoint me. I had thought perhaps you might appreciate the chance to mitigate your sentence somewhat by showing a willingness to speak the truth at last. But it seems I was wrong. So let us be very sure. On your oath, and in view of what I am able to offer you, I ask you again. Do you know this man? Have you ever had any dealings with him, in person or by proxy? As Lord Kinsey has said, I urge you to think carefully before you answer."

Corbyn did not hesitate. He felt no loyalty toward the Baron and cared not one whit for the Albian's fate, but he was damned if he would do or say anything that might help his captors. He certainly had no faith in Sullyan's promises of leniency. His pale blue eyes were locked on hers as if he held a blade. He never even

259

paused for thought.

"I have never had any dealings with this … man in any shape or form. And you can go to Perdition!"

Cal's sword twitched, but Sullyan gestured to him and he relaxed. On the platform, Taran could see the Baron relax further.

He heard Sullyan's sigh of regret, but before she could respond, there was movement to the rear of the chamber.

"With respect, your Majesties, my Lords, this man does not speak the truth."

Taran's attention, like everyone else's, snapped to the rear of the room, from whence had come the unsteady voice. A young man came forth into the middle of the chamber, his pale slitted eyes proclaiming him of the Andaryan race.

It was Corbyn's son, Kethro.

Sullyan turned to Elias. "My Lord, may I present to you the Lord Kethro of Quarlock. He would speak before this court, if you will permit."

Elias raised his brows. "My Lord Kethro, you are welcome here. Please speak your mind before the court."

Kethro advanced, passing the Baron and his father. Corbyn hissed venomously, "I order you to silence, you ignorant young pup. You don't know what you're doing. These aren't our people. Why should we help them—"

"With respect, Father, you have no authority over me now. *You* disowned *me*, remember? I am now Lord of Quarlock and I will do as I see fit. You spoke for me once, against my will, and bound me to promises I didn't wish to keep. Now, I will speak for myself. I will not betray my lands and my people, and I owe nothing to this scheming Albian Baron."

Kethro turned back to Elias, his pale face composed, his voice stronger now with the courage of his conviction. Corbyn glowered at him with scornful eyes, but wasted no more words on him. The

Baron, however, now looked a little apprehensive.

"Your Majesties, my Lords and Ladies, members of the court, this man, the former Lord Corbyn, has not told you the truth concerning his dealings with the accused. He does indeed know him, and both he and I have had many meetings with him. As an Artesan, I have often been ordered to contact him so that my father and he could discuss some aspect of their agreement together."

There were murmurs of shock and intrigue, but they died as Kinsey asked, "And how did you do that, my Lord Kethro? How did you contact the Baron?"

"Through his captive Artesan, my Lord. The disabled boy, Huw."

Chapter Twenty

The room was in uproar. Both the Queen and the Baron were on their feet, protesting loudly. Even the Arch Patrio risked the King's ire to add his voice. The other members of the court chattered to each other over Kethro's confident statement. Elias, however, was in no mood to tolerate such unruly behavior. He rapped his fist sharply on the arm of his chair, then stood and bellowed for silence.

He glared around the room, his piercing eyes sweeping over them all. "If I hear one more word spoken out of turn," he grated, "I will have this court cleared. Do you understand? One more protest from *you*, Madam," and he jabbed a finger in Sofira's direction, "even so much as a gasp or sniff of disdain, and I will have you removed."

Sofira stiffened as if she would rail against this second public rebuke, but the look in his eye convinced her to keep silent. Elias had never shown her such public disrespect before. Trying not to show her agitation or her injured pride, she sat, smoothed the silk of her gown and stared stonily ahead.

"And you, Reen," said Elias, ignoring the formalities of title, "will also remain silent unless you want to witness the conclusion of these proceedings bound and gagged. Do I make myself clear?"

Reen's face drained of color. Under no illusions regarding whether or not Elias would carry out the threat, the Baron bowed low.

Elias resumed his seat. "I must remind you all that although we have agreed to hear the testimonies of Lord Corbyn and Lord Kethro, what they say is not admissible as evidence in this trial. My Lord Kethro, I apologize for the unruly behavior of my subjects. I believe you were about to tell us of the association of your father with the accused. Would you continue, please? There will be no further interruptions."

Kethro resumed his story, telling of his father's early dealings with the Baron, the reason for them, and his own reluctant part in their plotting. He also described his first meeting with Huw, which brought a frown to the King's brow.

Then the young lord spoke of the proposed hunting trip. Sullyan held fast to Aeyron's hand and murmured softly to him. Her pupils were widely dilated as she supported his flagging strength. Aeyron had turned unhealthily pale and he appeared uncomfortable yet determined. He had come at his sister's request and he wouldn't let her down.

Kethro came to the end of his narrative and turned to stare at his father and the Baron, both of whom studiously ignored him. "So you see, Majesties," he concluded, "these two have been associates for some years, their true alliance commencing after the death of Lord Rykan. This is the sum of my evidence, and on my honor, it is the truth."

Elias stood and spoke warmly. "I thank you, my Lord Kethro, for your invaluable assistance to the Crown of Albia. I can hardly tell you how deeply I appreciate your aid. It can't have been easy for you. We are in your debt."

Kethro bowed respectfully before taking a seat at the side of the chamber. His father gave him not a single glance. Elias turned an enquiring eye on Sullyan, who returned the look.

"My Lord, you must have many questions concerning the testimony of Lord Kethro. Yet before we touch on these matters, I believe it would be best if you heard the full story. Despite the knowledge that what he has to say will have no bearing on the outcome of this trial, my brother, Crown Prince Aeyron, has declared his willingness to recount his experiences at the hands of the accused, which will serve to show what a cruel and basely treacherous nature lies concealed behind that outwardly pious façade."

Elias nodded, gazing with respect and no little pity at Aeyron's strained, pinched features.

Lord Kinsey then addressed Cal and Dexter. "Captains, will you remove the prisoner and see him to a secure holding cell?"

Taran watched with affection as Cal and Dex efficiently hustled the renegade Andaryan lord from the room. Corbyn stared balefully at Sullyan as he went, his eyes promising dire retribution should he ever be in a position to exact it. She ignored him.

When the disturbance of his removal died down, Lord Kinsey turned respectfully to Aeyron. "Your Highness?"

Aeyron seemed to shake himself free of some burdening weight as he tore his gaze from the Baron. Very slowly, the Prince rose from his seat, reluctant to leave the comfort of the woman by his side. Sullyan closed her eyes as she lent him yet more strength. Taran reached out again to offer her his own energy and was amazed to find he was not the only one. He met the enigmatic gaze of General Blaine with surprise. Their gifts were gratefully accepted, but Sullyan didn't open her eyes.

Aeyron faced his tormentor with growing resolve, borne on the back of such loving support. He bowed his head briefly to Elias and began to speak, relating the events of the hunting trip he'd organized for the two young nobles, Kethro and Rand. Kethro hung his head when Aeyron spoke of the ambush, though Aeyron's tone held no censure.

The Prince's gaze remained fixed on the Baron's sweating

face as he dispassionately recounted his ordeal. Reen tried hard not to return that accusing glare, but was somehow unable to tear his eyes away. He seemed fatally fascinated by the soft words as Aeyron recounted his abduction through the Veils and his return to consciousness in a foul and filthy cell.

"There were two men in the cell with me when I woke," he said. "One of them was the leader of the brigands who attacked us. I soon learned to fear his violence. He was cruel and brutal and took obvious enjoyment from my suffering. His name was Izack. The second man was that man there, the accused, Baron Reen."

All eyes swiveled to the Baron. He held Aeyron's gaze, firm and unwavering, safe in the knowledge that the Prince's words held no legal weight.

Aeyron continued with his tale, telling the court how Reen and Izack had taunted him, tortured him, and even forced him to write his own ransom note. There were murmurs of horror when he told them of his maiming. He nearly broke down at that point, but he rallied, aided by Sullyan's continued support. He ended by describing how he'd woken chained in the circle, with Sullyan beside him.

"The rest, I think, you have heard," he said. "I owe my life to Brynne Sullyan, and also to Taran Elijah and Master Ardoch. I also owe the life and sanity of my father to Brynne. For this, as well as other services to our realm, we have taken her unreservedly into our family, for indeed my father's blood runs through her veins.

"This man, Baron Reen, tried to ruin the alliance between the Hierarch of Andaryon and Elias Rovannon of Albia. He abducted and attempted to kill a Prince of the ruling House of Andaryon. He also aided and abetted three renegade lords who were plotting to overthrow the Andaryan throne. This, my Lords, concludes my sworn statement before this court."

Aeyron sat, bowing his head to his hands. Sullyan took him in her arms as the strain of reliving his terrible ordeal finally overwhelmed him. The court remained hushed and respectful while the Prince regained his composure.

Elias's face was pale and drawn. Aeyron's narrative had affected him deeply. He had heard Sullyan's account of the Prince's torment, but the quiet dignity of the man and his courage in coming here to publicly relate it at her behest left Elias humbled and shamed. His expression showed his deep admiration for Aeyron as he stood.

"Majesty, you have our heartfelt thanks for your unstinting aid in this matter. Rest assured that, regardless of the outcome of this trial, we will exact restitution for your sufferings and for the great wrong done to your person and your family. I pledge to you that, somehow, the perpetrator of these unspeakable crimes shall receive his just punishment."

Reen went pale at this threat, but held firm when Elias turned his fury on him. "How do you answer these allegations, Baron Reen? Every accusation put forward in this trial so far has just been upheld by the testimony of a ruling monarch. You have been caught out in your lies and cannot deny it."

Reen drew himself up. "I do deny it, your Majesty! Will *you* deny that this man, this outlander, is also an Artesan? There is a reason why all the accusations we have heard come from the mouths of unnatural beings. This only strengthens my assertion that they have conspired against you, and continue to do so, and we now know that the conspiracy has its origins in the Fifth Realm's highest level. It is even worse than I feared. They are conspiring to take over our realm! Your ill-advised treaty was only another step in their plan to undermine and unman you. Once they have you completely in thrall, they will rule Albia through you. I implore you, your Majesty—I *exhort* you—listen to those who have your safety and the safety of Albia closest to our hearts! Cast out these

Artesans and these demons, cut all ties with them and return Albia to the purity of her Matria Church. Only then will both you and our realm be safe."

Sofira and Neremiah rose to their feet, adding their voices to Reen's rant. Taran glanced in sympathy at Aeyron's trembling form, and then caught the dark fury simmering in Sullyan's eyes. A shiver slid down his spine.

Although Elias roared for silence and glared at Sofira and the Arch Patrio until they subsided once more, Taran thought he looked beaten. He gestured wearily to Kinsey, who gathered himself with an effort and turned to one of the Guardsmen by the door. "Ask the Attestors to return."

The twenty Attestors filed back into the courtroom, looking around with interest, doubtless picking up on the tension in the air. Once they were seated and silent, Kinsey offered Sullyan the chance to bear witness.

Leaving Aeyron with a quick grasp of his shoulder, Sullyan moved forward to confront the Baron, her face set, her eyes glittering. She afforded Kinsey a bow of the head before addressing Reen.

"My Lord Baron. In accordance with Albian court law, the Attestors were not privy to the testimonies of Lord Corbyn, Lord Kethro, and his Majesty Crown Prince Aeyron. I therefore state that I, as a legal denizen of Albia and loyal subject of its High King, Elias Rovannon of Albia, do hereby bear witness that you are guilty of the crimes this trial brings against you. You did indeed plot and scheme with your Andaryan allies to overthrow the Andaryan throne, to cause unrest and foment war between our two realms by the abduction of both realms' heirs, and also to cause the death of his Majesty, Prince Aeyron. I also aver that you did willfully intend the murder of the Artesan boy Huw, for with my own eyes I saw you put a knife in Huw's back, the boy you terrified into doing your will and by whose power you intended to destroy the fabric of our world. From that injury, Huw died.

"It is ironic that when you taunted me that day within the circle, as I lay at your mercy, when you took such delight in telling me I knew the mystery Artesan whom you had in your power, you were nearer the mark than even you knew. For that poor, abused boy was, in fact, my cousin. I did not know it at the time. It was only while chained within the circle, waiting for the destruction of the world, that I finally managed to figure it out. The clues I had been given finally made sense to me, although had I not been so certain of having no birth kin I might have seen it sooner."

Taran could almost see the memories welling within her, and images of what Huw must have endured pained her heart. Her voice took on a hard edge and her face turned to stone.

"My Lord Baron, you used that poor boy shamelessly. You took advantage of his great powers and damaged mind and you used them for your own twisted plans, even while you continued to parade your hatred of those who were gifted by God and by nature in ways you could never hope to understand. How you must have reveled in the hold you had over him! How you must have laughed to see him compelled to your will when the forces he commanded could have snuffed out your life in an instant! My only consolation is that he never knew your ultimate plan and his vital place within it. But he knew your cruelty, my Lord Baron, and he knew Izack's, for that was the way you controlled him. You held the threat of violence over him, knowing how he feared it, and you even allowed Izack to work his evil nature on the boy, just to keep him cowed and fearful. For that alone, I will see you hang.

"But your final abuse of the boy—that vicious thrust of my knife into his heart—was totally unnecessary. Huw could never have accused you, and he would never have harmed you. He had no concept of revenge. There was no need to murder him, to remove my one last link to what birth kin I still had, and for that I will strive to see you suffer the direst penalty this court and my sovereign lord can lay upon you."

Taran had seldom seen her so angry. During this speech her eyes had turned hard as topaz, her face had paled to white, and her lips were bloodless.

It was Elias who broke the ensuing silence.

"Highness, I do not doubt the validity of your testimony. Your account of the death of the boy Huw is corroborated by Captain Elijah. But I do not understand how the Baron discovered the boy's talents, or how he gained the use of them. The lad was constantly about the palace—he played with my children—yet as far as I know, no one else ever suspected what he was. Even you did not. Can you tell us how it came about?"

Sullyan stared at the Baron for some moments before replying. Taran thought she would insist that Reen answer for his actions, but then he realized she was only trying to calm her emotions enough to speak. Uncharacteristically, she had lost some of her iron control and was struggling to regain it.

"My Lord, I had anticipated this question. With that in mind, I have brought here today one who can tell you how the Baron first discovered the talents of my cousin, Huw, so beginning his long and shameful exploitation of the boy. I believe Master Ardoch managed to seek her out."

She turned to Kinsey, who nodded and waved his hand at the swordmaster. Ardoch stood and moved to the door to the left of the King. Elias waited in puzzlement until a young girl, hesitant and nervous, appeared by the swordmaster's side. Queen Sofira gave a hastily-smothered gasp.

The King appeared confused. "But this is Alice. She's one of my daughter's nursemaids. What does she know of this?"

Sullyan sat. "This girl *was* one of your daughter's nursemaids,

269

my Lord. I think you will find she was dismissed from your service some time ago. You will be interested to hear what she has to say on the subject of Huw."

Lord Kinsey smiled at the girl. "Alice, please tell us what you know."

The girl had a soft voice, made all the more inaudible by her nervousness. The court had to strain to hear her tale.

"Sirs, I was walking in the market one day when I heard shouts and angry voices behind me. Before I could turn to see what the trouble was, someone slammed into me and I was flung to the ground. He fell on top of me, kicking and struggling, and we became entangled. I couldn't get free to rise. I was shocked and frightened and started screaming. I thought I was being attacked. Then a man pulled on my arm and helped me up, and when I recovered my breath I saw he was holding by the collar the person who had run into me. It was a strange-looking boy and he wasn't struggling any longer. He just hung limply from the man's fist, looking terrified. Other men ran up and they were all very angry, shouting at the boy, accusing him of stealing, of damaging their trade. I heard someone suggest he should be hanged.

"Then they turned on me, demanding I testify that the boy had attacked me. It all happened so fast and I was still upset and confused. I had bruised my arm quite badly and was in some pain. The men kept demanding I go with them to the constable and swear the boy had deliberately attacked me, but I knew he hadn't. He was running from the angry men and had simply run into me. He looked so frightened, so alone. I knew I couldn't do what the men wanted. But they wouldn't give up, and in the end I had to tell them who I was. I said her Majesty was expecting me back, and so they had to let me go. As I walked away, they dragged the poor, terrified boy off to the constable, still shouting about having him hanged.

"I felt so badly for him that I ran straight to her Majesty and told her what had happened. I begged her to save the boy from hanging. She sent one of the guardsmen to the constable with me, with a note instructing that the boy be turned over to her care. The constable wasn't happy. He told us the boy was dangerous, that he'd been plaguing the traders for months by stealing food and clothing, and that his appearance and wild ways frightened customers away from the market. He said the boy should be locked away so he couldn't do any more damage. But the guardsman had his orders and the constable couldn't go against the Queen's instructions, so he gave the poor boy over to us.

"I nearly cried when I saw him. Someone had given him a beating. He had a black eye and a split lip. He cringed away from us, even when I spoke softly to him. He only had a ragged blanket to cover himself and I made the guardsman buy him a tunic and some breeches on the way back to the castle. He was also very thin, and we got him some meat and an apple. I've never seen anyone gobble food down so fast. He must have been starving."

Alice faltered as her eyes became unfocused, no doubt seeing that poor, pathetic figure once again. Kinsey spoke, bringing her back to her task.

"Tell us how he came to live in the castle, Alice."

The girl took a breath and raised her eyes. "Before, in the marketplace, I hadn't realized what the boy's trouble was, but on the way back to the castle it became obvious he wasn't at all normal. He managed to tell me his name when I asked him, but didn't seem to be able to say much else. What he did say was garbled, and he didn't appear to understand my questions. When her Majesty saw him she was repulsed and told the guardsman to take him away. Princess Seline, who was just a baby then, was having a crying fit that her nursemaid couldn't calm. As the guardsman took Huw's arm to lead him out, he pulled away and went toward the baby. Her Majesty shouted for the guard to stop him, but Huw reached the Princess first. When he put out his hand and touched her cheek, she immediately stopped crying. The nursemaid pushed Huw away, and the little Princess started screaming. It was then that Huw made a funny crooning noise in his throat, and the Princess stopped again.

"After that, the Princess cried every time her Majesty tried to make Huw leave. She was only quiet when Huw was close by, and her Majesty told the guardsman to stay too, to make sure Huw didn't harm the baby. But he never did, and he never harmed Prince Eadan, either, once he was born. Both children seemed to love him, and were always calm and happy when he was with them. He did funny voices for them and made them laugh. Eventually, her Majesty decided he was harmless, and that's how he came to live in the nursery."

When the girl fell silent, Kinsey raised his brows at Sullyan. She nodded gratefully and prompted, "But the royal children were not the only ones entertained by his antics, were they, Alice?"

The girl smiled shyly. "No, ma'am. Huw could do tricks. He was very clever for all he was wrong in the head. He liked to show me. He could make things appear and disappear, and he could make things move along the floor or a table. He never touched them. It was done by blowing, I think, but although you could feel the air moving, you could never catch him doing the blowing. He could make fire without tinder, and I never did find out how he did that. Do you know, ma'am," she said earnestly, her face alight with memory, "he could even make you believe he held a tiny flame on the palm of his hand without it ever burning him. It was such a clever trick. I'd never seen anything like it."

"Did it look like this?" Sullyan held out her own hand, where a tiny teardrop of Fire flickered and swayed in the air above her palm.

"Oh," cried Alice, "you can do it too! Oh, show me, please. Show me how it's done."

Sullyan glanced meaningfully at Elias as she quenched her power. "Maybe later." She glanced to Kinsey for permission before continuing. "That is how the Baron discovered what a rare find his Queen had made. He came upon the boy one day when he was performing his 'tricks' for Alice and the Princess, and realized what Huw was." She turned back to Alice. "What did the Baron do when he saw Huw playing with Fire?"

The girl's face fell. "He seemed shocked and angry, especially when he saw Princess Seline trying to catch the flame. He shouted at the boy and the fire went away. Huw squealed and sort of crumpled into the corner with his hands over his head, refusing to look at the Baron. Then the Baron just stood and stared at Huw, like he was thinking what to do. I didn't like the look on his face. And then he went over and dragged the boy up by his collar and hauled him off. I don't know where they went, but I could hear Huw crying down the corridor.

"After that, Huw was always with the Baron. He said he was keeping an eye on Huw as he didn't trust him not to play with fire again. He never did, though," she added sadly. "He never did any of his tricks for us after that."

Sullyan leaned forward and murmured to Kinsey. He raised his brows and turned back to Alice.

"Thank you, Alice. You have been a great help. Before you go, will you tell us why you left the Queen's service?"

The girl twisted her fingers, unable to meet Kinsey's gaze. "I didn't leave, sir," she murmured. "The Baron told her Majesty I wasn't reliable, that I wasn't doing my duties properly. Her Majesty turned me away."

Sullyan shot Elias a telling look as Kinsey continued. "I see. And were you given any character references or means of finding a new position?"

Tears appeared in the girl's eyes. "No, sir."

The chamberlain's lips pursed in displeasure. "Master Ardoch, would you care to tell the court where you found Alice?"

The Torlander grimaced. "It wasn't hard, my Lord. She'd ended up where all lasses with no character reference and no sponsor end up—in a brothel."

Taran looked with sympathy on the girl. She was so young. Elias obviously felt the same, judging by the grim look he cast the Queen, but he spoke gently enough to Alice.

"My dear, I had no idea you had been treated so thoughtlessly and cast off so callously. I am sorry for it. You are not to return to your former occupation. You will report to my chatelaine, Madam Delinna. I will tell her I wish her to find you a suitable post. You may go now."

Alice flushed with embarrassment and relief. She stammered her thanks and managed an awkward curtsey before fleeing the courtroom.

Sullyan turned to Elias. "There is one thing more I must tell you, my Lord. It was not only Huw that the Baron manipulated to achieve his own ends. Through Huw's unique talents, Reen also managed to affect the actions and reactions of quite a few others, yourself included."

Elias's eyes narrowed. "What do you mean?"

She held his gaze. "You recall the meeting we had on the day of the fair, just before the horse race?"

He nodded. "When I came in, you were talking with Huw in the antechamber. I sent him out." His lips thinned, no doubt remembering how his harsh tone had frightened the youth.

"Indeed, my Lord. It is my belief that he was sent there purposely by the Baron in order to learn my psyche. He seemed determined to take my hand, although at the time I did not suspect why. Am I correct in thinking that you yourself touched him at some point?"

"I did. What's the significance of this?"

"I believe Huw was made to touch every person the Baron intended to manipulate. It is through touch that one Artesan can learn another's pattern of psyche, and I have no doubt that Huw was made to touch Lord Ozella while he was here at the castle, too. Through this link, Huw would be able to subtly influence the actions and emotions of those whose psyches he had learned. But because Huw's own emotions were those of a young child, often wild and unrestrained, the people he influenced would also exhibit less restrained reactions."

Elias stared at her and Taran guessed he was remembering his own recent behavior. The King flushed and dropped his eyes.

Into the silence that followed, Sullyan said, "But even that is not the full story, my Lord."

Elias turned, surprised. "Isn't that enough?"

The smile she returned was tinged with sadness. She sat straight-backed in her seat, one hand resting lightly on the Prince's arm, the other held open on her lap. She gazed at the defiant Baron with unfocused eyes. "There is one person whose psyche was influenced by Huw, but whom Huw never touched. Robin Tamsen never met Huw, yet he was one of the worst affected by the Baron's machinations. He did, however, meet the Baron at the Manor. This got me thinking. Over the past few weeks I have wondered why this man is so vehemently opposed to our kind, and why he went to such lengths to seek out obscure and little-known passages in ancient holy texts which he could twist into a denunciation of the Artesan craft. To my knowledge, our Matria Church has never been inclined to reject those who practice it. It was always the ordinary people, those who saw only the destruction and raiding wrought by the other races, who made their prejudice felt. It was as if the Baron sought some higher authority on which to place the blame for his increasingly desperate efforts to rid the world of those who possess such skills.

"My Lord, ever since I began to suspect that the renegade we searched so hard for after the discovery of Rykan's Staff was, in fact, a sport, a small doubt has nagged at my mind. Although I knew it was highly likely that our enemy was being coerced, one part of the puzzle was missing.

"Do you remember, Elias, the day you came to the Hierarch's Citadel and we talked together of what evidence we could gather, and speculated on how certain things had been achieved?"

Elias frowned. "I do. We were trying to decide how the Baron had communicated with Huw during the attacks on my life. You said you needed to speak with Lord Kethro again, and to look at the archives."

"I did indeed. You see, when Baron Gaslek first found the archive referring to the existence of a lay-Artesan, or sport, it seemed to infer that such a being could read the thoughts of those around him—at least, those he knew well. This was the way I guessed the Baron had conveyed his commands to Huw. But something did not ring true. If Huw was able to read thoughts, then I should have been able to communicate with him, especially once I discovered the imprint of his psyche, which was almost identical to mine. Yet I could not. I never managed to speak to Huw's mind, not even while he lay dying in my arms. This told me beyond doubt that he was ignorant of the process.

"Then I began to wonder whether Lord Kethro had ever been contacted by Huw independently of the Baron's instructions. He told me he had not. All Huw knew was how to work his will on his surroundings."

Elias's frown deepened and he looked bewildered. "Then how was it done, Brynne?"

The members of the court watched her also, fascinated despite their ignorance of Artesan matters. Taran understood more, but even he was unprepared for her next statement.

"The reason the Baron is so vehemently opposed to those with Artesan skills, and the reason he was able to force poor Huw so easily to do his bidding can only be that the Baron has some deeply-buried, long-repressed Artesan powers himself."

Chapter Twenty-One

"*N*O!"

The roar of rage that burst from the Baron's lips echoed around the room. His face went purple with rage, his mouth stretched in a rictus of furious denial. His eyes blazed with a manic fervor and his hands gripped the railing before him with such strength that the bones of his knuckles showed white.

"You evil witch!" he raged, his voice spiraling into a screech. "How dare you insult me so. How dare you suggest I share your blasphemous powers! You lie, pagan girl. You're just trying to justify this sham of a trial. *You're* the one who should be standing here accused—*you're* the traitor in our midst! Admit it, witch. Admit you've ensorcelled the King and you may just save your soul from perdition. You've bewitched them all, you and your demon friends. Get away from here. Go back to your hell where you belong. You profane the ground you walk on!"

He might have said more but for the stirring of the Queen. Glancing coldly at Lord Kinsey for permission to speak, Sofira stood, quelling the Baron's rage. Smoothing her gown with her hands, she spoke to the court, pointedly ignoring Elias. "Enough of this farce! These wild and unsubstantiated claims by outlanders and their Artesan cronies have no place in a sober court of Albian law. My Lords, there is clearly no *proof* whatsoever that Baron Reen is guilty of any of the charges brought against him, least of all the charge of High Treason. If anything, the Baron's counteraccusations carry a worrying amount of weight, with at least one accusation of murder having been admitted by the one accused. This whole sham of a trial has been a waste of time. I move that the charges against the accused be withdrawn, and if any doubt remains as to the Baron's innocence, then, my Lord Kinsey, I suggest that the Attestors be instructed to give their verdict."

Her tone implied there should be no doubt at all. Kinsey glanced at the King, who, realizing he had no choice, indicated Kinsey should continue. He sat with stony face and downcast eyes, his hands gripped tightly in his lap.

Despair washed over Taran. Without Parren to testify that Reen had recruited him as a spy, without the parchment detailing their treacherous arrangement, all the evidence against Reen was circumstantial, hearsay. With the testimony of the Andaryans inadmissible, and the accusations against Reen coming only from Artesans, this trial could have but one outcome.

They had lost.

Kinsey faced the twenty nobles charged with judging Reen. "I now instruct the Attestors to deliver their verdict. My Lords, do you need time to deliberate on what you have heard?"

The Attestors' spokesman shook his head. He stood, bowed, and handed a folded parchment to Lord Kinsey. The chamberlain passed it on to Elias. Taran didn't need to see the King's expression to know what it said.

Elias faced the Baron, his eyes stony, his voice a harsh rasp. "My Lord Baron, the verdict of this court is that the charges against you are unproven. For want of tangible evidence, I hereby declare that the charges against you, charges of murder and also of High Treason against the Crown of Albia, are withdrawn. My Lord Baron, you are free to go."

Looking insufferably smug, Reen left his railed enclosure and swaggered over to where Lord Neremiah sat. The churchman rose to greet him, shaking his hand and patting him on the back. The Queen left her place and moved down to the courtroom floor, going over to Reen to show her approval.

Taran's attention was caught by Prince Aeyron, who sat white-faced and shaking, staring with dread and revulsion at the posturing Baron. Sullyan whispered to him, her comforting murmur barely audible over Reen's self-congratulatory tones. Elias, too, looked sick, and Taran wondered how this outcome would affect the relationship between the King and the Hierarch.

His thoughts were interrupted by the Queen, who moved back to the center of the floor to face Elias. Reen stalked at her right shoulder like he would be there forever.

"My Lord." Sofira's tone brooked no nonsense and Taran felt a shiver ripple through his soul. "You have in this courtroom two self-confessed murderers. Murderers who, it is highly likely, also conspired to do your son, your Majesty's person, and the entire realm of Albia harm. I demand the immediate arrest of the Artesan woman Sullyan and her accomplice, the Artesan Taran Elijah. They must answer for their crimes."

Taran's blood froze and his gaze swung to Sullyan. Guardsmen were moving toward him even as Elias rose from his seat. Taran couldn't see how anyone could save him this time, not even the King. As the Guardsmen closed about him, he stood still, determined to maintain some dignity. Elias, at least, knew he was innocent.

"Your Majesty, my Lord Kinsey, there is still one issue to be determined concerning the fate of Baron Reen."

Sullyan's calm voice cut through Taran's fear. He had no idea what she meant. Neither did Elias, judging by his expression. Sofira glared at her, furious at her interruption.

"Keep silence, Lady! You stand accused of murder and High

Treason and will not speak until your trial."

Sullyan was unfazed by Sofira's hostility. "The charges have not been ratified by his Majesty, your Highness, and until they are, I am a free subject of this realm." Sullyan turned calmly to Elias. "My Lord, there is the matter of Baron Reen's extradition to Andaryon to be determined. I am sure you recall the details of the treaty you signed with the Hierarch—terms that require you to make available for questioning in the Fifth Realm any Albian subject accused of crimes against that realm?"

Elias's brow creased further and he opened his mouth to speak, to refute, Taran was certain, that any such terms had been agreed. Sullyan did not give him the chance, nor did she react to Reen's sharp intake of breath.

"I understand your reluctance to relinquish one of your citizens to the justice system of a foreign realm, but you will allow that the Hierarch has more than fulfilled his part of the agreement by sending Lord Corbyn to testify at this trial. He will be gratified, I know, by your swift reciprocation and aid in the matter of the Andaryan court's desire to question Baron Reen over the abduction and torture of Prince Aeyron."

Sofira surged forward, her face a pinched mask. She was closely followed by a purple-faced Reen. "What nonsense is this?" Sofira's voice sliced the air like a dagger. "There is no such agreement! I have not been informed of any such agreement. My Lord, put a stop to this treacherous woman's meddling. The other realms have no authority over citizens of Albia. Such an agreement would be preposterous! You would never be so stu–"

"Madam!" Elias's roar stilled the entire court. Sofira stood shaking with impotent rage, Reen hovering beside her. Taran was pleased to see the uncertainty that had replaced the Baron's air of smug victory.

Elias glanced at Sullyan, then at Aeyron, who rose slowly to his feet. His trembling had subsided, although his face was still deathly pale. Drawing his dignity about him, the Andaryan Prince faced Elias.

"I add my thanks to the gratitude of my father, your Majesty. He will be pleased to know that our new treaty is already proving a strong and mutual bond."

Aeyron held out his maimed right hand and Elias took it without hesitation.

"You have my assurance, Highness, that I will comply as swiftly as I may with the terms of our treaty. My subject, Baron Reen, shall be made ready at once for the transfer to Andaryon to answer the charges laid against him there."

Reen gave a strangled cry. "No! Your Majesty, you can't do this! I've been cleared … the Attestors' verdict cleared me…." He moved forward, hands spread, eyes wild and desperate. How quickly, thought Taran, could triumph turn to fear.

Elias fixed Reen with a stony stare. "My Lord Baron, these are new charges brought by the Andaryan Hierarchy. You will be transferred at our pleasure and under guard to the realm of Andaryon, where you will be required to answer charges that you conspired with the renegade Rykan to create a weapon intended to aid him in his bid to overthrow the rule of Pharikian, Hierarch of Andaryon. Also, that you did conspire to abduct the Andaryan Heir, Crown Prince Aeyron, and that you did hold the Prince on Albian soil against his will and subject him to torture. Also, that you did conspire with the renegade Corbyn to foment war between our realms. You will be judged under Andaryan law and, if found guilty, will suffer whatever penalty Andaryan law decrees."

The Baron gaped at Elias, his swarthy face drained of blood. He swung round to Sofira, hands extended in plea. She stood frozen, confused by the turn of events. She stared at her countryman but made no move toward him. Her silence and the calculating look that suddenly entered her eye made Reen retreat a step. Blood surged hotly into his face as he realized she would do nothing.

He spun on his heel, one finger shooting out to where Sullyan sat beside Aeyron. "This is all your doing, you evil witch! You've been working my downfall all along! You've used your vile powers to ensnare the King, to work your foul magic, to bring us all to our knees! Well, you might have dazzled Elias, but you don't fool *me*!"

There came a deep rumble, as if thunder were raging outside the courtroom. Its timbre shook the floor, rattled windows. Taran heard gasps of concern. Elias's pronouncement had brought Guardsmen striding forward, but the tremor made them stumble and Reen seized the opportunity. With a roar of feral fury he flew at Sullyan, lips scattering spittle, hands raised and grasping like claws, wild eyes promising death if he should lay hands on her.

The entire court was stunned, both by the tremor and by Reen's alteration. The Baron was transformed into a creature out of nightmare, a ravening dervish whose inhuman strength fought off the first guard to reach him as easily as swatting a fly. He screamed imprecations and obscenities, accusations and threats of death, and still he came for Sullyan.

Appalled, Elias surged forward, but he was far too slow and far too late to reach the demented Baron. Prince Aeyron stood transfixed, his weakened state and his torment at the hands of this raving madman forced all too vividly on him by the dreadful sight that assailed his eyes.

The Queen stared in shock. She had never witnessed anything like this. She had seen her Baron in a religious fervor and had listened to him expound his views to an audience who responded with rapt eagerness, fueling the drive of his passions. She had seen him nearly lose control, had caught him on the verge of ranting more than once. But she had never seen him even remotely like this. She stood astounded, hands clasped to her chest, eyes glued to the raging figure before her.

Jinny was screaming, her hands over her ears. Ardoch instinctively leaped the benches in an effort to reach the Baron, but even his trained and conditioned responses were too slow. In a split second and without conscious thought, desperate to protect Sullyan, Taran acted.

The Baron pulled up, shrieking, only two feet from where Sullyan sat. Her eyes were huge and black, but she had not accessed her powers. She hadn't needed to. With a shrill scream of pain, the Baron snatched back the hands that had been reaching for Sullyan's throat. The acrid stench of scorched flesh pervaded the room. He slumped, keening, at the foot of the crackling, sparking wall of Fire that had suddenly appeared before him.

Only the Artesans present could fully see it, of course. Blaine widened his eyes when he realized it wasn't of Sullyan's forging, and he sought the strained and sweating face of Taran. Smiling grimly, the General sat back down, pulling the startled King with him.

The Baron was sobbing, huddled over his scorched hands, cradling them to his chest in an effort to ease his pain. The shock of being burned by Taran's Fire seemed to have drained all the angry strength from him. The crackle of flames could still plainly be heard in the shocked silence of the courtroom.

Sullyan turned from regarding her enemy to the trembling Prince beside her. Before she released the power she'd called up in preparation to defend herself, she reached out to Aeyron's spirit and lent him another measure of strength. His tremor subsided. Then she glanced at Taran, who was still struggling to maintain the imperfect and weakening Fire wall, more through instinct than conscious thought. The pitiful shape of the Baron was hardly a threat anymore.

Taran slowly released his increasingly tenuous hold on Fire, breathing a sigh of relief as the strain of maintaining his construct eased. He was stunned he'd been able to form the Fire wall at all. As the element dissipated through the substrate, he felt Sullyan's pride and approval wash through him. Despite his new-won confidence, he blushed.

Sullyan managed to catch Denny's eye. "Lieutenant, someone should see to the Baron's hands."

Denny sent one of his men hurrying to fetch a healer. There was a stir to Sullyan's left as Elias recovered enough to speak.

"What the bloody hell just happened, Brynne?"

She faced him. "The Baron and Taran Elijah have amply demonstrated the truth of my earlier statement, my Lord. Not only did the Baron just manipulate the element of Earth, causing that tremor, but he would not have been so completely affected by Captain Elijah's Fire wall if he did not have an Artesan's naturally-heightened affinity with the elements. I was right. The Baron does indeed possess latent Artesan powers."

Reen's groaning was smothered by the Queen's shocked gasp. Even Neremiah's face was ashen as he stared, appalled, at the hunched figure on the floor.

✣ ✣ ✣ ✣ ✣

Elias was about to respond to Sullyan when, with a rustle of silk and a strange look in her eyes, Queen Sofira approached her Lord. The court fell to expectant silence, wondering what other revelations might be vouchsafed this day.

Sullyan watched Sofira carefully. The Queen's face was stark and wan, and her earlier fear had been replaced by a righteous anger. She was trembling where she stood, but she faced her husband with courage. She looked like a woman who knew what she had to do to survive and would do it, whatever the cost to her pride.

Respectfully, she stated, "My Lord, it seems I have been cruelly deceived by this man who called himself my friend and advisor. I wish to declare to you now, on my oath as your wife and your Queen, that I had no knowledge of any latent powers. I was ignorant of his appalling abuse of the boy Huw, who, as you know, I took into my care with the best of intentions. If he did plot with outlanders, then I am wholly innocent of such associations, and I wish to state publicly that had I gleaned any suspicions of such plotting, I would have brought my concerns to you.

"If I am guilty of anything in this sorry affair, it is the ease with which the Baron swayed my judgment over many issues of state. If my opposition to them caused you any harm, my Lord, I will tender my sincerest apologies. I swear and avow that I never deliberately sought to undermine you, or to work against your policies, although I admit I shared the Baron's misgivings over the wisdom of encouraging these Artesans you set so much store in."

Sullyan didn't miss the hard-edged glance the Queen cast her way. Elias sat regarding her with some bemusement. She carried on.

"I have been misguided and misled, my Lord, misinformed and manipulated. I have failed in my duty to you in following the words of the Baron. I will suffer whatever punishment you care to mete out. I will make any recompense you see fit. I also apologize unreservedly to any who have suffered harm because of the actions of my countryman, and I will support whatever sentence is passed upon him.

"I pledge to you, my Lord, with this court as my witness, my undying loyalty both to you as my husband, and to the Crown of Albia. I declare that I am still your faithful wife, servant, and subject."

As she completed her speech, Sofira fell to her knees, clasping her hands to her breast and bowing her head before Elias.

Sullyan narrowed her eyes at this clever public display of humility. She wondered how deeply it had cost the Queen, and what revenge she might later seek.

Elias stared at the unusually humble posture his wife had adopted, clearly considering his options. They were few. He had no firm evidence to link her to any of Reen's alleged crimes, and her public repudiation of her countryman left him no room to maneuver. She had artfully taken the initiative and effectively preempted whatever he might have said against her.

He crossed to the kneeling figure and stretched out a hand to raise her. To his intense embarrassment she clung to his hand, fervently kissing the royal signet of Albia and thanking him fulsomely for his tolerance. Irritated, knowing how false her sentiments were, he bade her rise. She did so, the very picture of the penitent wife, although the dutiful expression sat uncomfortably upon her habitually stern features. Sullyan didn't miss the swift look she exchanged with Neremiah. Her eyes narrowed.

She was right to be wary, for Sofira turned once more to her husband, her voice uncharacteristically soft.

"My Lord, since you have so mercifully exonerated me from any taint which might accrue from the Baron's actions"—Elias started at her presumption of his forgiveness, but she gave him no opportunity to speak—"and since by his own actions he has revealed the truth of at least one of the accusations leveled against him, we must therefore consider that he might also be guilty of the malicious abduction of your son and Heir."

Elias turned to look her in the eye, his brows drawing tight, his expression wary. Sullyan didn't like the turn this was taking. To her surprise, rather than waiting for Elias to respond, Sofira turned to her.

"Highness, I take it you are prepared to swear that the

outlanders of Andaryon had no part in the abduction of Prince Eadan?"

Sullyan traded a glance with Elias before she spoke.

"Madam, his Majesty's allies in Andaryon played no part whatsoever in the abduction of his Highness Prince Eadan. Men in Corbyn's service may well have helped in wresting him initially from his nursemaid, but he was never held by them, nor was he ever taken across the Veils until I myself transported him there to return him to the arms of his father. He was held only in the Baron's mansion."

Sofira nodded and turned back to the highly-suspicious Elias. "It would seem, then, that Baron Reen might indeed be responsible for the taking of our son and holding him in secret, leading us—indeed, encouraging us with that false ransom note—to believe him at peril in the hands of outlanders."

"It looks that way, Madam."

"And you did say, did you not, my Lord, that if you found the Baron guilty of any falsehood, you would judge it enough to convict him?"

Elias hesitated. "I did say that, Madam, but—"

"I believe the court scribe noted it, did he not, Lord Kinsey?"

Kinsey glanced at Elias before bowing his head to the Queen.

Sofira nodded in satisfaction. "Then, my Lord, I can see no other alternative but to convict Baron Reen of the charges brought against him. I see no reason to send him to Andaryon. Let Albia deal with its own. There is only one penalty for those guilty of High Treason, and I therefore demand that he suffer death upon the Wheel."

Elias stared at Sofira and the court gasped in shock. Sullyan's brow furrowed as she tried to fathom Sofira's motive for demanding this most savage and ancient means of execution.

Through all this the Baron had sat hunched upon the floor,

mumbling to himself while the healer bandaged his hands. He seemed totally drained and almost insensible to his surroundings. Yet at the mention of the Wheel he jerked his head up to meet Sofira's hard eyes, his expression ghastly.

"No, no, no, oh no!" he breathed, unable to speak any louder. "I beg you—I *implore* you, Majesties, not that! No, not that! I'll do anything. *Anything*! But please, oh please, don't subject me to that!"

The abject terror in his eyes and the draining of all color from his face told Sullyan how acutely terrified Reen was. His body shook uncontrollably. Great beads of sweat broke out upon his brow and he was suddenly unable to speak. She could actually hear his teeth chatter in horror.

Elias stared at his Queen, his own expression hardly less horrified. "Are you sure, Madam? Do you know of what you speak?"

"Indeed I do," she averred, raising her voice to be heard over Reen's gurgling cries. "It is my right, as a victim of his perfidy, to demand just retribution. We have been wronged, my Lord. This man has plotted against us, he has wormed his way into my trust—even my affections—and has not scrupled to use me against you. For the distress this has caused you, and also for the threat offered to the person of our son, I must insist that you exact the harshest of penalties. I cannot see that you would wish to do any less."

There was silence while Elias struggled with her request. Sofira never released his eyes, not letting him retreat from his duty for one instant. And, in truth, he had no desire to be lenient with Reen. His objection was that *she* urged him to this savagery. Her very vehemence and sudden thirst for revenge struck false. It was hard to believe that Sofira's past affection and unwavering protection of Reen had turned so completely to hatred and enmity. Still, even if the King couldn't cast her off or connect her to Reen's crimes, he could, by the means she proposed, rid them both of the Baron's influence. If he let the traitor live, who knew what tactics he might employ to regain Sofira's trust?

Straightening his back, Elias faced the Attestors. "My Lords, I admit this is irregular, but you have all seen the viciousness displayed by the accused, Baron Reen, and have witnessed his use of powers he both denies and professes to abhor. Is this evidence enough to convict him, bearing in mind his acceptance of my statement that if any falsehood were found, it would demonstrate his guilt? Would any one of you refute my Queen's request?"

None of the Attestors spoke up. No one uttered a sound except for the Baron, whose mumbled litany of "No ... oh no ... oh no," droned weakly on as he stared in horror at his sovereign lord.

Elias then turned to Aeyron. "Highness. Will you and your father, the Hierarch of Andaryon, accept the verdict and sentence of this court as just reparation for the terrible wrongs done to your realm and your person by the accused?"

Aeyron inclined his head. "Your Majesty, we will."

Elias nodded once. "Very well. Baron Hezra Reen, in light of your demonstration of powers you denied and professed to abhor, we find that you have willfully misled this court, throwing into doubt every word that has come from your mouth. Thus, as is permissible under Albian law, we uphold the testimony of those who have spoken against you. We find you guilty of the charge of High Treason."

As the King pronounced his doom, the Baron moaned piteously and clasped his bandaged hands to his chest in an attitude of desperate supplication. He was still on his knees and he raised fearful eyes to the King as Elias moved on to his sentence. The mindless litany of denial went on, and Sullyan almost felt sorry for the man.

Elias stared at the pathetic figure kneeling before him. He had never sentenced anyone for such heinous crimes before, and he had certainly never sentenced anyone to death. After the civil uprising that had followed the assassination of his father, all those responsible had been dealt with on the field of battle, not in cold blood like this. And the death that Sofira had demanded for her countryman, the one Elias now had to hand down, was such a fate as he would not wish on any man. He swallowed.

Sullyan knew that the ultimate penalty for the crime of High Treason was slow and brutal. It stated that the accused be stripped naked and bound to the Wheel symbol of Albia's Matria Church. This huge wooden structure would be constructed in a public place, and the accused was to be paraded upon it for two days for all to see and revile as they would.

Once this period was over, a pyre was built below the Wheel. The accused's hands and feet were then severed from his body and cast into the flames, signifying the end of his usefulness to society and his betrayal of the Crown. Yet he would not be permitted to die from loss of blood until the fire claimed his body. The records stated that an experienced executioner could temper the fire to such a degree that the victim took days to succumb.

It was an excruciating way to die. Though Elias clearly had no desire to see this bloody ritual performed, there was no honorable way out of acceding to his Queen's demand. The Baron's crimes were undeniably of the worst kind, and had he succeeded as he desired, the King would now be dead along with most of the Artesans in his service, and Reen would be the power behind the throne. It was certain that Reen deserved the severest of punishments. But this!

The only way in which the Baron might be spared this brutal death was if someone were to speak for him, someone who had suffered by his actions. Yet who among this court would do such a thing? Who of the people gathered here would not wish to see him suffer the ultimate penalty for his dreadful crimes? There was no one. Elias had no choice and he knew it. Steeling his resolve, he pronounced his verdict.

"Baron Hezra Reen, it is my decree that you should suffer the traitor's death of Execution by the Wheel."

The Baron let out a high, thin scream. Sofira's face showed her satisfaction. Sullyan wondered anew why the Queen was being so bloodthirsty. Why had she turned so completely upon this man who had been her confidante and accomplice for so long?

And then it dawned on her. Of course Sofira wanted him dead! He was the only one who could reveal her involvement in the faked abduction of her son. This public declaration of the death sentence, this forcing of her husband to sanction the worst punishment possible, was her insurance against leniency, against Elias's reluctance for revenge. Should the Baron be sentenced to imprisonment or banishment only, he might still be able to implicate her or convince someone else of her duplicity. He might even try to use his knowledge as a bargaining tool, and that would never do. She could not even rely upon the Andaryans to execute Reen.

No, the Baron had to die here in Albia. Having realized the turn events had taken, having seen there was no going back, no middle ground, Sofira had chosen to sacrifice him. She had decided to step back completely from her involvement with him and allow him to carry the full weight of the terrible things they had done and planned to do. Once the Baron was dead, and the circumstances of that death made public, Sofira would be safe.

Sullyan's heart contracted with fear at the thought. For as long as Sofira held on to her position by Elias's side, the King would never be safe.

The Queen turned to her husband with a grateful yet beseeching look which sat falsely upon her hard features. "My

Lord, we have heard and wholeheartedly concur with your assessment of the evidence brought before us, and we recognize and bow before the justice of your sentence. But I feel it is necessary—vital, in fact—that the Baron be encouraged to admit to himself, to this court, and to his God, his sole responsibility for his crimes. The events we have heard related these past two days have been damaging in the extreme, and there might yet be those who doubt the complete nature of the truth that has been revealed. In view of my lamentable association with this man, I fear a stain might remain upon my character. I would find it impossible to resume my duties by your side with even the merest hint of doubt as to my faithfulness in the minds of our people. Therefore, my husband, I beg a boon of you.

"Before the Baron is taken from here to his prison, I desire that he should publicly declare my innocence of all wrongdoing in these matters."

Sullyan regarded the Queen narrowly as she stood straight-backed and righteous before the King. There was a glitter in Sofira's hard eyes and a fervor in her tone. Lord Neremiah also stood, adding his approval to her plea.

"Your Majesty," he boomed, "our Queen reveals the generosity of her spirit in this request. The free and open admission of his guilt and the exoneration of her Majesty are necessary for the purging of the Baron's soul before he goes to meet his spiritual Lord. Our Queen is most compassionate even in the midst of the betrayal of her trust by this misguided and deceitful man. How can we be any less merciful? I ask that you grant her plea."

Sullyan knew why Sofira had made this request, and it had nothing to do with the fate of the Baron's soul. Albian law stated that should a condemned man confess to his guilt and take sole responsibility for his crime, then no further examination of the facts was permitted. No new evidence, however damning or convincing, could ever be brought to bear against any other suspected party. Sofira wanted to establish her innocence beyond any doubt, and before as many witnesses as possible. She wouldn't risk any of these events coming back to haunt her in the days ahead, and she would thus be free to work in whatever way she chose to further her own ends.

Elias couldn't refuse her. Sullyan could see the warring emotions within him—the mistrust, the doubt, the plain unhappiness of the man—but he was helplessly constrained by his own law. His shoulders sagged as he accepted Sofira's victory, and Sullyan's heart flooded with sympathy and another emotion, one she did not wish to examine too closely. It was the one that had caused her skin to shiver when he'd placed a kiss in the palm of her hand. The one that had enabled her to bear the unjust accusations he had thrown at her. The one that had buoyed her spirit while she'd been awaiting death, chained within the stone circle. She turned from it to regard the figure sitting hunched and pleading on the floor.

Pity surged within her. Reen had been completely unmanned by the horrific, barbaric sentence passed upon him and had soiled himself in his terror. He was gibbering in panic, frothing at the mouth, his words garbled and incoherent.

Elias took a deep breath and signaled to the guards to help Reen rise. They did so with distaste, for the odor of his shame was strong. He hung within their arms, staring dumbly at the King, eyes dull and hopeless. Elias could hardly bear to look at him and spoke in an emotionless tone.

"Baron Hezra Reen, you stand accused and sentenced of the crime of High Treason. Before you are transported from here to await your execution, I require that you freely and publicly declare your sole responsibility for your crimes and accept that you alone deserve to bear the justice of our punishment. Do you so declare?"

The Baron's empty eyes stared around at those assembled. He seemed not to recognize them or even know where he was. A glistening line of spittle ran down his chin. Sofira's avid gaze fixed with dark triumph upon his slack features.

A light rustle of silk caught the court's attention. Prince Aeyron gave a startled gasp as his sister beside him said, softly but clearly:

"Majesty, I claim clemency for this man."

Chapter Twenty-Two

"*WHAT?*"

Sofira's shriek grated on every ear as she spun to glower at Sullyan. The clamor in the chamber increased as the other court members voiced their amazement. Kinsey rapped sharply on the table before him.

"SILENCE!"

The noise died instantly, except for the ragged sounds of the Baron's labored breathing.

Sullyan's eyes hadn't left the King's as she awaited his response. Before the King could gather his wits to respond, the Queen spoke again.

"What is this nonsense? You can't claim clemency now! You have no right. The traitor's been sentenced, his Majesty has spoken."

Sullyan didn't miss Sofira's condescending insult in omitting her title. She bridled, drawing a little on her inner strength to lend her small frame stature and majesty. Sofira's eyes widened, intimidated by the air of power Sullyan suddenly exuded.

"I believe you will find, Madam, that as one of those most affected by the crimes of the accused, I have every right to sue for clemency. Is that not so, my Lord Chamberlain?"

Sullyan didn't even glance at Kinsey, refusing to relinquish her hold on Sofira's gaze. An edge of fear had appeared within the Queen's eyes.

Kinsey didn't let Sullyan down. He had no love for the Queen and no stomach for vengeful brutality. The Execution of the Wheel had not been invoked for many a long year and he didn't wish for it to be so now. He bowed in Sullyan's direction.

"You are correct, Highness. Albian law allows for a plea of mitigation to be entered and considered right up to the moment of execution, provided it comes from a victim of the accused."

Sofira made a sound of disgust. She spun to face Elias. "I trust you will not allow this foolishness, my Lord?" Her tone was imperious, an outright demand.

Elias prized his gaze from Sullyan's calm features to stare in frank dislike at his wife. "Madam," he said bleakly, "I believe I will."

Her face blanched and her breast heaved. Her fists clenched at her sides, her knuckles turning white. Perspiration broke out on her brow. Elias's flat statement had rocked her like a slap to the cheek. She sought furiously for a response.

The King, however, wasn't about to relinquish control now he had it back. He glared at her, daring her to speak. "Madam, I bid you sit."

Sofira opened her mouth. It was a mistake. She had pushed him too far and Elias had finally had enough.

"I said *SIT*!"

She collapsed to her seat, trembling with fear and with fury. There was nothing she could do. Elias dismissed her and turned to Sullyan, visibly reining his emotions.

"Highness, you have entered a plea for clemency. I have heard you. What would you?"

Sullyan gave him a nod. The air of majesty faded from her as she released her power.

"Your Majesty, I crave a moment of speech with the accused."

Elias frowned but nodded his permission, and Sullyan left the box, giving Aeyron's hand a reassuring squeeze as the Prince sought to prevent her, fearful for her safety. The look she sent him quieted his concern.

She stepped toward the Baron, who still hung supported by his guards. Denny closed in protectively, his sword, taken from one of Reen's men, held at the ready. Sullyan waved him back.

"Release him," she instructed the guards. "He will stand unaided."

As they let go of his arms, Reen sagged, but his legs bore him up and he found that he could, indeed, stand. He stared blankly at the woman before him.

"Some privacy, if you please, gentlemen." She cast a hard glance at Denny, who was about to protest. With only a slight hesitation, he and his men withdrew out of earshot. There wasn't a sound in the chamber, all eyes transfixed as Sullyan faced the greatest enemy her kind had known for years.

She pitched her voice for him alone.

"My Lord Baron."

Her formal address ignited a spark of intelligence deep within Reen's hopelessness. Seeing this response, she stepped closer. "Do you fully understand what is happening here?"

A frown creased his brows and his eyes darted feverishly to the King's impassive face. He nodded, licking dry lips.

"Why ..." he tried, his voice husky and shaking, "why would you intervene for me?"

She gave him a small smile. "Why, indeed? Do you not recall, my Lord, what I said to you the night you held my knife to Huw's neck?"

Reen's frown deepened. "You said ... you said you'd plead my case with the King ... if I confessed."

"So I did. And now I am holding to my word."

"But *why*?" He spread his damaged hands, the movement

drawing a wince of pain. "I abhor your kind. I would have killed you. You said earlier you would see me hang. Why this sudden change? Why would you do anything for me?"

"I feel your pain, my Lord," she said gently, noting how his eyes widened. "You have denied your nature all these years. I see how that has damaged you. I could tell you that I pity you for it. I could say I wish to see you healed. I could tell you that I have no desire to watch you die. But that would only be a partial truth and not entirely honest of me."

His eyes were fixed by hers, his face a mask of bewilderment. He simply couldn't understand how she could feel any compassion for him after what he'd done.

She continued, still speaking too softly for anyone else to hear. "You may not believe me, Baron, but despite what I said earlier, I have little desire to witness your death. It is true, you have committed the most grievous of crimes and my heart is sore within me for the torment and abuse you inflicted upon my cousin and adoptive brother. Yet to condone such a death as the Queen has demanded would not alleviate one second of the misery they endured, and would only serve to further her Majesty's ends. I would fight with any power I possessed to ensure that you never again hold any position from which you could endanger those of my craft, or the life and the reign of my sovereign lord. But that aside, it matters very little to me whether you live or die.

"The reason I am willing to plead your case with Elias is very simple. I want something from you."

The Baron narrowed his eyes, a small flare of hope rising in his soul. Sullyan saw it and smiled, but the smile wasn't pleasant.

"Ah, do not mistake me, my Lord, I will not bargain with you. Your life is forfeit, your sentence passed. But it is within my power to release you from the terrible fate that awaits you. You cannot deny the terror you feel."

She glanced meaningfully at his fouled breeches and he flushed with angry embarrassment, his tiny flare of hope dying stillborn. He glared at her, trapped.

"What is it you want?"

Her small smile returned.

"Nothing you should be reluctant to give. Something of small import, but which might even give you a measure of satisfaction, and possibly revenge. You have been most cruelly abandoned, my Lord, most callously thrown on our swords. I merely offer you the opportunity to make your martyrdom meaningful. If that is what you wish."

Reen stared at her. She held his gaze until she saw the tiny flash of comprehension which was the only signal she needed. "Yes, Hezra," she murmured as the slow light dawned in his features. "You hold the power to mitigate your own sentence, do you not? Do this and the death penalty will be revoked, you have my word. Do this and you may retire to some far-off retreat where you may live to serve your God as you will. Do this, Hezra.

"Impeach the Queen."

Sullyan stood back from the Baron, watching him carefully, unsure whether he would comply. If he did, it wouldn't be out of any concern for her or gratitude for her intervention. His decision would hinge upon the depth of his fear and also his true feelings for Sofira. Had he cultivated her merely for the promise of power, or did he really hold her in affection? Sullyan had gambled on the former. Yet even if she were wrong, she'd lost nothing in the attempt. Either he would do as she asked and gain his reward, or he would not.

If he did, she would keep her word and sue for mercy. She would show him how an Artesan forgives. She would beg, at the very least, a cleaner and swifter death than the Wheel. She had no intention of allowing the Queen the satisfaction of bloody revenge for the Baron's failure.

If the Baron refused her, however, and Sofira hung on to her position, at least Elias would now be suspicious of her. Because of Sullyan, he would never again be taken in by the Queen's machinations. That was something to be thankful for.

Sullyan made her careful way back to Aeyron's side. The court remained silent, all eyes on the Baron. The King switched his attention from Reen to Sullyan, but the Artesan woman said nothing.

Elias gave a great sigh as he stood. "Well, my Lord Baron, what have you to say?"

✛ ✛ ✛ ✛ ✛

The Baron glared at Elias, his eyes hot with fear and anger. Now that the shock of his sentencing was over, he couldn't believe how completely the Queen had turned on him. He hadn't expected her to try to save him once Sullyan spoke out, but he had expected her to plead for his life. The fact that she had made no effort to spare him, but rather had demanded awful torture as his just punishment, shocked him to the very core of his being.

Much as it galled and infuriated him to be beholden once again to an Artesan, he knew he could never endure the torture of the Wheel. He would be reduced to a pathetic, gibbering wretch, screaming for mercy that would never be granted, and he'd already had enough of abject public shame. The only way he could escape that dreadful ordeal was to accede to Sullyan's request. Well, if it had to be so, then at least he would have the satisfaction of seeing Sofira lose her damned stiff control. Let *her* see how it felt to grovel in terror. Let *her* feel the hopelessness of imprisonment. She had betrayed him thoroughly; he owed her nothing now.

He turned to face her and smiled. She misinterpreted his look and gave a sigh of relief. Then he opened his mouth and took away her breath.

"Your Majesty, I wish to inform you that your lady wife, the Queen Sofira, has betrayed you. She plotted your downfall. It was she who ordered me to treat with the outlanders. It was she who, in full knowledge, obtained the gold from the treasury reserves with which I paid the demon Lord Rykan for the silver and ceramic to make the Staff. It was she who came up with the plan to assassinate you after the Staff was destroyed, and it was she who ordered me to fake the abduction of your son.

"She is a faithless wife and a false queen, your Majesty. She has lied and schemed behind your back ever since the day you were wed."

✢ ✢ ✢ ✢ ✢

The uproar that followed these words couldn't be quelled. Kinsey shouted until he was hoarse. He rapped upon the table. He even removed one of his shoes and used it as a gavel. Nothing worked.

Denny shouted to his men and they gathered once more about the Baron, in case he should use the confusion to try to escape. He was spent, though. He swayed on his feet, glowering upon the figure of the Queen.

Sofira collapsed in hysterical sobs, loudly denying the truth of his words. One of her maidservants and the Arch Patrio came to attend her. Elias slumped to his seat, his head in his hands. General Blaine stood over him, one hand resting on the King's shoulder while he stared in exasperation at Sullyan. Taran wondered what blistering comment he was directing at her. Sullyan, however, took no notice. Her golden eyes were glazed with fatigue.

Jinny, in the circle of Taran's arms, pelted him with frightened questions, desperate to know what these events portended for her uncle. Taran had no answers.

Order was eventually restored by General Blaine. Well used to making himself heard in the most cacophonous circumstances, he raised the bull roar of his stentorian voice and shocked them all to silence. He then bowed to the chamberlain.

"My Lord Kinsey, it would appear this trial is over. The accused has been found guilty of all charges and sentence has been passed. I suggest you have him removed to a place of safety until such time as his Majesty is free to review his punishment. The court may then be cleared."

Kinsey acknowledged Blaine's orders. He ordered Denny's men to remove the Baron. Reen was led away in chains, casting a mixture of fearful and vengeful glances over his shoulder at Sullyan and Sofira alternately. Once he was gone, Kinsey dismissed the court, thanking them all for their attendance. They went, murmuring in wonder. Kinsey, with a glance over his shoulder at the slumped figure of the King, left also, closing the double doors behind him.

Calm descended on the chamber, the quiet broken only by Sofira's sobs. The General directed her maid and the Arch Patrio to help her from the room. They obeyed without question. Blaine took a moment to speak briefly with Denny, and the young Lieutenant nodded before following the Queen from the courtroom. Taran, Jinny, and Ardoch remained where they were. Taran had no intention of leaving Sullyan right now. He could see she was on the verge of collapse.

She sat in silence beside Aeyron. The Prince was watching the King, who was struggling to come to terms with hearing the death knell sound over his marriage. He had never loved Sofira and knew she hadn't loved him, but he had believed they shared respect. Now he knew differently. He had wed a traitor, a web-spinning spider. He had brought her to his bed and had lain with her, trusting her with the secrets of his realm, with his hopes and his dreams. And like a spider, she had turned on him, all too willing to sacrifice her mate in her bid for power and supremacy. The knowledge of her total perfidy had crushed him.

General Blaine sat by his side, his hand on the King's shoulder, trying to bolster his spirit. Elias was no Artesan, so Blaine was unable to lend him physical strength. His uncomplicated and loyal support was all he had to offer.

✠ ✠ ✠ ✠ ✠

Slowly, aching in body and spirit from the ordeals of the day and her own deep unhappiness, Sullyan rose. Her eyes were dull, her face taut. She took no great satisfaction from the day's events. She felt drained and empty, and she could not bear to see Elias brought so low. His condition was partly her responsibility. She had to do something.

She approached the King, gently but firmly pushing Blaine aside. He gave way to her, coming closer to where Taran and Ardoch sat, Jinny between them. They watched as Sullyan took the grieving King in her arms.

Her gentle touch opened the tight knot of Elias's emotions, as Blaine's companionable male support could not. Sullyan's empathy, her deep and intimate knowledge of what Elias was feeling, was too much for the King to bear in silence. The full realization of how he had made her suffer poured into the wound in Elias's soul and he tried to push her away. She took his face in her hands and refused to be denied.

She was vaguely aware of the others leaving the chamber, unwilling to intrude upon the outpouring of grief that suddenly wracked the King's body.

✠ ✠ ✠ ✠ ✠

It was early evening and they had gathered in Elias's private audience chamber. The mood was somber, the atmosphere heavy.

Elias, partially recovered from his enervating, emotional outburst, sprawled disconsolately in a chair by one of the room's four windows, chin propped on one hand, long legs stretched out before him, eyes staring blindly out into the parkland below. An untouched glass of brandy sat by his elbow.

Sullyan and Aeyron, both pale and strained, sat side by side on the settle, drinking fellan in silence. Taran and Jinny also sat together, she within the circle of his strong arms, each taking comfort in the nearness of the other. Sullyan hadn't missed their intimate attitude.

General Blaine stood straight-backed before the cold grate, his hands clasped behind his back, a hard expression on his angular face. He had been busy in the short time since the conclusion of the trial. He had posted a guard outside the door to the Queen's chamber and his heart was heavy at that necessity. He had checked on the security of the Baron's prison and given strict orders that no one be allowed access, ignoring Reen's pleas to know his fate. Blaine had addressed the garrison briefly and had told them of the day's events. He'd had enough of rumors and didn't intend to allow them to run unchecked through the castle. He issued orders for the next few hours and then went to see Lord Levant, instructing the First Minister to take over the running of the realm until such time as Elias recovered his wits and his strength. Then he returned to the King's side.

Sullyan smiled gratefully when Blaine refilled her empty cup for her. It helped, but she really needed more than fellan if she was to cope with the day's events and her own depleted health. She turned lusterless eyes to the brooding figure by the window and voiced the thought that had troubled her ever since Taran reported to her the day before.

"Elias, why did you not send for me sooner?"

The King didn't move, but she knew he heard her. He took a deep breath and spoke without turning his head.

"I feared I had forfeited the right."

His words were so soft, so full of sorrow, that she closed her eyes in pain.

"I thought we dealt with that on the Citadel Tower," she told him, trying to reach through his lethargic depression with sincerity. He heard the love in her voice and it drew his eyes to hers. The strain that showed in her features was a direct affront to his faithlessness and he couldn't bear it. He bowed his head in shame, his words all but inaudible.

"*You* might have."

She gave a heartfelt sigh, knowing how deeply his wounds ran. It would take much time for him to become whole again, and she could not be with him to help him heal. She had troubles of her own.

She changed the subject, this one being too painful to deal with right now.

"What will you do with the Baron?" she asked, hoping to reawaken Elias's sense of duty. It would be his refuge and his anodyne in the lonely weeks to come.

He raised his head and replied tonelessly. "Were you serious in your plea for mercy?"

She made an effort to smile. "I always mean what I say." She held his eyes, trying to convey her deeper meaning, but he disengaged without acknowledgement.

"I'll speak with Neremiah. I think he was as shocked and horrified by your revelations and the depths of the Baron's treachery as anyone. No doubt we can find some isolated clerics' retreat where we can send Reen. I'll set guards to watch over him. He will never be allowed to threaten again."

She nodded and his moody gaze returned to the window.

"And the Queen?"

She voiced the thought they all dwelled on but none other dared ask. His head came around like a hound scenting danger, his eyes showing his deep pain and anger. She thought he might snap at her, but he'd had enough of mistreating his friends. His anger was now reserved for those who deserved it.

"The marriage will be dissolved. Sofira will remain confined to her private rooms until I decide on her future."

Silence returned. Elias took a healthy swallow of brandy before glancing at Jinny and Taran. The hint of a smile played about his lips as he found a happier subject to occupy his thoughts.

"My Lady," he said, drawing Jinny's gaze, "I must tell you how deeply I appreciate your help in the rescue of my son. The events of the trial and the treachery of your uncle must have affected you deeply. You must be fearful for your future. I want to reassure you on that score. I told you during the trial that I would ensure your security, and I intend to do just that. You have already proved your loyalty to the Crown and to my family. So, as reward for your labors on our behalf, I have decided to settle the title of the Baron's lands and estates on you. He has forfeited everything, and so you will receive all of his wealth as well as the inheritance your father left you. I realize that the running of so large an estate is outside of your experience, but I can provide you with guidance until such time as you feel capable of continuing alone. My Lady, will that content you?"

Jinny went white with shock. Then she flushed with pleasure. She left her place at Taran's side and kneeled before the King.

"Oh, your Majesty, you are too kind! I don't deserve so much. I only did what anyone would have done."

He shook his head. "That's a matter of opinion. But please, less of the formality. I've had enough of that for one day. We'll see about ratifying your position and title over the next few days. Until then, you have my permission to assume the title of Baroness."

Eyes shimmering with tears, she kissed his ring as he held out his hand to raise her. Sullyan saw that pleasurable light dim in her eyes as she glanced across at Taran. Jinny turned back to the King. "Your Majesty, would you excuse me and Captain Elijah for a while? There's something I wish to discuss with him."

Elias shot Taran a speculative look before nodding. "Don't go too far, Captain. I'm not finished with you yet."

Taran frowned but nodded. He glanced enquiringly at Sullyan, who smiled and asked him, "Are you returning to Andaryon with us, my friend, or is it your wish to remain here?"

He cast a glance at Jinny, whose expression was sober, but his reply was firm. "I'm coming back with you after I speak with Jinella."

They left the chamber together, his arm around her shoulders.

Chapter Twenty-Three

General Blaine refilled glasses and cups like a page while Elias regarded Sullyan with concern. She knew her fatigue was plain to see. His brow had darkened at her implication of her imminent departure.

"Will you not reconsider and partake of my hospitality tonight, Brynne? You're both exhausted and you need to rest. Prince Aeyron, I am shamed that my home has been a place of suffering for you. I would welcome the opportunity to redress that. Surely you can delay your departure until morning?"

Sullyan heard the plea in his voice. His offer was genuine, as was his desire to show Aeyron his contrition, but beneath it lay his fear of being left alone with black thoughts which might drag him down into despair. Sullyan had already asked more of Aeyron than he was ready to give, and so she left the reply up to him. As she had guessed, he refused the King's offer.

"I thank you for your thoughtfulness, Elias, but I am eager to return to my own realm. I cannot deny that I feel most uncomfortable here. I accompanied my sister because she persuaded me to come and, in truth, she was right to compel me. I can feel that the healing process has begun, but as yet it is still too raw and fresh.

"Once I am recovered and whole, I should like us to meet again and come to know each other better. Maybe in this way we can avert anything similar from ever happening again. But for now

I must beg your indulgence. I would rather be with my family."

Elias accepted the Prince's refusal with understanding and a heavy heart. Sullyan could sense the uncharacteristic twinge of envy Elias felt. Aeyron had his father, a sister, and a brother-in-law, and now he also had Sullyan. He would have access to all the help and support he needed in order to heal and become strong again. Elias felt completely alone. He may not have endured physical torture, but his heart and spirit had been deeply wounded and he felt lost, abandoned, and bereft. The fact that some of his wounds were self-inflicted only made his isolation and pain more unbearable.

Sullyan's heart was sore, but she had no choice. She simply couldn't stay. As in her relationship with Taran, her emotions and Elias's could all too easily swing toward dangerous ground, and her own defenses were weakened right now. She, too, needed support, and Aeyron, Timar, Marik, and Idrimar were her family now. She would need them very badly in the weeks to come and she wasn't even sure they would be enough. Fighting down a tidal wave of sorrow, she bowed her head, unable to bear the weight of Elias's grief as well as her own.

✢ ✢ ✢ ✢ ✢

Taran and Jinella strolled through the hallways toward the castle's main doors. There was activity outside in the courtyard and Taran could see a carriage being readied. It must be the one that had brought Sullyan and Aeyron from Caer Vellet, he thought. He also caught sight of a familiar face.

"Cal!" He drew Jinny with him as he went to greet his Apprentice. The dark-skinned young man heard him and ran over, embracing Taran warmly.

"That was some Fire wall you called in there!" Cal said. Taran grinned and introduced Jinella. Cal bowed outrageously over her hand, flashing his dark eyes and making her giggle in flustered pleasure.

Taran laughed. "Cal, you stop that at once or I'll tell Rienne."

Cal gave Jinny's hand one last flamboyant kiss, winking at her flushed face. He looked shrewdly into Taran's eyes. "You've moved on, master."

Now it was Taran's turn to flush. "I'm just the same," he said, sending a silent warning to Cal. He didn't want to talk about that just now. "Are you and Dex staying here with the General?"

Cal nodded. "The Colonel collected us from the Manor on her way from Caer Vellet. She wanted her own men to guard Corbyn at the trial, but he's already gone back. Anjer fetched him." He grinned evilly. "I wouldn't be in Corbyn's shoes right now. Anjer was spitting with fury when Kethro told him how his father refused to cooperate. But Dex and I will hang on here with the other lads and go back when the General does, unless he sends us off before that. What about you? What are you going to do now?"

"I'm going back with Sullyan, at least for the time being." Taran glanced at Jinny. "She needs me right now. After that, we'll see. Cal, I should warn you that Robin knows the truth about the rumors. Jinny and Denny told him earlier, and he was very distressed when he left. Denny was so worried about him he was even concerned he might … you know … harm himself. Will you watch out for him?"

Cal blew out his lips. "I'll do my best. Bull's washed his hands of him, did you know? They had a fight. Bull flattened Robin and nearly knocked him unconscious. You should have seen the state of his jaw. Bull's so upset he's taken to the bottle again. He seems to think he's responsible in some way. We've been trying to cheer him up, but you know what he's like. At least with Blaine busy here, Bull will have to stay sober some of the time to help Vassa run the Manor."

Taran nodded sadly. "Just do your best. I haven't a clue how all this will turn out, or what the future holds. Things have changed beyond all expectation since our days in Hyecombe. But whatever happens, you and I are all right, aren't we? You know I'll never abandon you. I care too deeply about you and Rienne. We've been through too much to forget our friendship and I wouldn't want you to think—"

Cal threw his arms about Taran, putting an end to his worry. The rough hug, though it embarrassed them both, cleared the air between them.

Cal grinned. "Of course we're all right. Don't think you can get rid of me that easily. You're still my master. I'm working toward Journeyman now and I'll need your help, so don't you forget it."

Taran gave Cal's shoulder a grateful squeeze. He turned away, leading Jinny toward a quiet corner. He needed to hear what she wanted to say before it was time to leave.

They found an unoccupied space at the side of the courtyard and settled down together on a low stone wall. From where they sat, they had a view of the castle doors and also the Andaryan carriage. A small chestnut was being hitched to it and a groom was leading out a very fine blood-bay stallion with an arched neck and fiery eyes. Taran admired it, guessing it belonged to Prince Aeyron. It wasn't the horse he'd ridden on their progress through the Citadel, but it was certainly a beast fit for a king.

He tore his eyes from the magnificent horse and glanced at Jinella. She sat gathering her thoughts, looking at her hands and twisting her fingers together in her lap. She clearly didn't know how to begin. Eventually, realizing Taran was going to wait until she spoke, she took a breath and leaped straight in.

"Taran, do you like me?"

Her directness caught him off guard and he scrambled to

gather his wits. "You know I do."

"How much?"

He faltered.

"Let me make this easy for you," she said, much to his relief. "I like you very much. Much more than I've ever liked anyone, and certainly more than I expected to. I'll be honest with you. When you and the Colonel rescued Lily and me from the brigands in the forest, I was immediately attracted to you. I told myself that it was only your gallantry and the fact that you took a wound to save me that made me feel something for you. When I asked you to escort me round the fair, it was only to satisfy my curiosity. And it saved me from having to find someone else."

"Thanks very much!" he muttered, but her frank gaze told him she wanted his serious attention. He could see she was trying to be as open as possible.

"When you insisted on singing the praises of another woman all day, I decided you weren't really very nice at all, not even as an escort. No, please let me finish. Once I got over my petty jealousy and thought more rationally, I wondered why I couldn't get you out of my mind. And when I saw you again, that day in the park … well, I can't really describe how I felt. It was like I thought I'd lost something forever only to suddenly get it back. Talking with you and working with you to help rescue the Prince felt good, despite the danger and how scared I was. It felt right. But then the Colonel took Eadan and Aeyron to Andaryon, and you were gone again."

She paused, looking down at her hands. Taran saw the faint flush grow in her cheeks. "I really missed you, Taran," she whispered. "I didn't think I would, but I did. When I knew you were coming back for the trial it almost made up for the fact that it was my own uncle who had betrayed the King and that I'd surely lose everything. That really didn't seem to matter much anymore."

She looked up, her green eyes catching the light. "Am I

making any sense here?"

Taran gazed into the green pools of her eyes. Her pupils were dilated, her cheeks flushed, her breathing quick and shallow. He recognized the signs. "You're saying you have feelings for me."

She gave a laugh and swallowed. "No, silly! I'm saying I think I'm in love with you."

Taran didn't know what to say. His own emotions were mixed up with what had happened at the trial, with the progression of his talents and power, with Sullyan's need and Robin's wounded despair. His heart and soul were too full of feelings, his mind too crammed with thoughts to see clearly what route he should take. He knew he cared for Jinny and he cared what happened to her. But love? He really didn't know.

Not wanting to hurt her, he spoke carefully. "But what of your title? You own lands and property now. You're a lady of substance, a Baroness. You'll have many suitors in the months to come. I'm nothing, Jinny. I'm not even a real captain. I'm only a member of the King's College, and Artesans aren't widely accepted in society. Doesn't that bother you?"

She laughed again. "Oh, Taran! I'm not proposing to you. I'm only telling you how I feel. Who knows what might happen in the future? I know you have a duty and I know how you feel about Sullyan. I know you're not going to leave her side until you feel you've done all you can, whenever that might be. I love you for that, too, for your loyalty and your care.

"I'm not asking you for anything right now, only that you'll think about what I've said and examine your own feelings. I can't see into the future any more than you can, for all your powers. I would just like us to be friends—really *close* friends—and spend some time together to see where it might take us. I would like that very much."

He took her two hands in his with a glad smile. "I think I'd like it too. I don't know when I'll be free, but if you're willing to wait, I can promise you we'll spend some time together and see how we get on. Until that time, if you like, I'll give you something to remember me by, something for *you* to think about."

She gazed up at him as he cupped his hands around her face, looking deeply into her eyes. He felt the delicious shiver that ran up her spine as he bent to kiss her lips.

He savored the moment, taking his time. This was as much an experiment for him as it was intended as a gift for her. He needed to test his own reactions. He'd felt nothing for anyone but Sullyan for the longest time, and the necessity of suppressing those inappropriate feelings had become so second nature that he didn't know if he was still capable of responding to anyone else. He gently brushed Jinny's lips with his, all the while holding her gaze.

She responded, and he felt a stirring deep within as his body told him that this felt right. He slipped his arms around her, pulling her closer. She melted against him and opened to him as he deepened the kiss. Their eyes slowly closed as they gave themselves over to the sweet pleasure of this newfound passion.

✣ ✣ ✣ ✣ ✣

Sullyan remained where she was as General Blaine left the King's chamber to check on the Andaryan carriage and the execution of a request Elias had made of him earlier. Prince Aeyron went with him, taking a genuinely warm leave of the Albian King. They made firm promises to meet again once Aeyron had fully recovered his strength and his courage.

When Sullyan rose to follow Blaine and Aeyron, Elias caught at her hand. She turned, sighing, as he swiftly stepped past her and closed the door, leaning his back to it somewhat breathlessly. She eyed him, suddenly wary. There was a strange light in his eyes.

Seeing her uncertainty, he realized how his actions must look.

He flushed with shame and moved hastily from the door, blinking uncomfortably.

"I'm sorry … I didn't mean … I only wanted a private word."

The wash of relief that went through her irritated her. As if he would ever harm her!

"Then you may have one," she responded.

He raised his head and looked her full in the face, eyes pleading, hands clenching and unclenching in distress. "Have I lost you completely, Brynne? Will you never return to my service?"

Her eyes closed in weary pain. How could she respond without hurting him?

"How can I know, Elias? You ask me questions I find it impossible to answer. I am an Artesan, not a seer. If you want auguries of the future, consult a card-reader or the clerics. Maybe they have answers for you."

He paced before her, voice harsh with pain. "I'm so alone now. I need someone by my side. When I saw how you handled the Baron today, how you controlled … I was right, what I said to you on the Citadel Tower. You would make me a fine queen. You would make a far better job of running the realm than I do, and I was bred for it. Do you really have to go back to Andaryon? Could you not stay here, with me? You don't really belong there, you know. I can give you the same level of care as they can. You would have everything you could possibly wish for. You and your child would want for nothing."

"Nothing, Elias?" Her voice was low, tears filling her eyes. "You know that could never be true. You should not be saying these things to me. You should not be thinking them. You are hurt, you are angry. You need time to think. But you are never alone, however bad it may seem just now. You have many around you who are loyal and faithful. And you will, one day, find another to be a queen to you, one who is free to accept the honor. Only this time, my Lord, marry for love."

He gave a harsh bark. "Love? What chance does a monarch have of marrying for love?"

She refused to be moved by his temper. "Timar managed it. And Aeyron is determined to find a woman who can rule by his side as well as warm his bed."

She took a step closer, drawn by the defeat in his stance, the agony in his eyes. She stretched out a hand. "Ah, you are such an attractive man, my Lord. A powerful man. You will have no trouble finding someone to love you as you deserve. Only choose well."

"I've already found her," he muttered, his words so low she barely heard. He sighed resignedly. "I can't persuade you to stay, then? Not even to help me rebuild my life?"

She had to turn away from the hurt in his voice, in every attitude of his body, wondering why all her choices lately led to pain.

"No, my Lord." She tried for a firm tone, hiding behind the refuge of formality. "My mind is made up. I was born in the Hierarch's Citadel. I wish my child to be born there too. It is the closest he will ever come to his foreparents, and there I can feel close to them also. Would you deny me that?"

Now it was his turn to feel the pang of another's pain. He was being selfish and he knew it. He wasn't proud of it. Sighing deeply, he said, "Of course not, if that is what you need. But let me tell you something *I* need, and then, if I must, I'll let you go. I need to hear you call me 'my friend' instead of 'my Lord.' I need to know we are friends, despite all that has gone before."

She met his gaze. "How can you doubt it, Elias? Of course I am your friend. I hoped you already knew that. My life has been dedicated to your service. I have not revoked my Oath. Even were it not for the Oath, I would still consider you my friend.

"I cannot see into the future, but one thing I do know. This I will pledge to you, not from any sense of duty, but from the love I feel. I will always serve you, my friend, wherever I am. If you have need of me, I will come to you. Whatever I can do for you, I will do. My sword and my powers are yours to command, as they always have been. To the limits of my ability and within the limits of my commitments, my life is yours. It may not be the fullness of what you desire, but it is all I have to give. I give it with pride and with love.

"You are never alone, Elias, my King, my sovereign, my friend."

✢ ✢ ✢ ✢ ✢

General Blaine sighed in relief as he saw them emerge into the early evening sun. Elias's strong arm supported Sullyan as he smiled down at her, his aspect lightened. The General saw her tilt up her head to smile back, the strain of fatigue fading from her face.

Elias looked enquiringly to his General and Blaine nodded, indicating the blood-bay with one hand. The King approved with a nod and Sullyan's smile widened into an impish grin. Blaine moved away, striding over to where Taran still sat with Jinella in his arms.

"Adept-elite Elijah, his Majesty wishes a word, if you please."

Taran started, but Blaine merely waved him forward. The three of them approached the King, who still hadn't relinquished Sullyan's arm. Taran frowned in confusion as Prince Aeyron mounted the small gig, taking the chestnut's reins and holding out a hand to help Sullyan settle in beside him. A groom stood next to the gig, still holding the bridle of the magnificent blood-bay.

Once he'd seen Sullyan settled, the King turned to Taran.

"Captain Elijah, I have already tendered you my thanks for the rescue of my son, but that is poor recompense for the peril you endured and the loyalty you showed to Eadan and to me." He waved away Taran's embryo protest. "No, Captain, reward is due and I intend to see you receive it.

"Adept-elite Elijah, I wish to gift you this steed, one of the finest in my stable. He is of noble lineage and mettlesome temperament. He has a great heart and will bear you well, whether in battle or in pleasure. His name is Bucyrus, and he is eight years old."

The groom handed the magnificent animal's reins to Taran, who accepted them with numb surprise. The beast was fine indeed. Not as stocky as Sullyan's Drum, yet strong and sleek and clean of limb. He had a proud, arched carriage to his neck and a fine-boned head. His dark eyes were large and liquid, his ears small and neat. The blood-red mahogany of his coat gleamed with health and vigor, and his black hooves tapped the cobbles as he felt himself admired. His nose was soft and black, he bore a white star on his brow, and his two front fetlocks were snowy-white.

Taran snapped his mouth shut when he realized it hung open. This was a princely gift indeed. He raised a hand to Bucyrus's nose and the stallion snuffled it gently.

"I ... I don't know what to say, your Majesty."

"Then don't say anything, man, because I'm not finished yet. I'm also granting you the freedom of the city, and a stipend of five hundred pounds in gold per year for life."

"*What?*"

General Blaine could almost feel the shockwaves racing up Taran's spine. Even Jinella gasped. "B–but, your Majesty," stammered Taran, "this is just too much!"

Elias glared at him. "Are you trying to put a price on my gratitude for the life of my son?"

Taran turned pale. "Of course not, your Majesty! I'm sorry, I didn't mean—"

Elias laughed. "Stop apologizing, man. I'm baiting you."

The Adept grinned ruefully. Blaine could tell Taran still thought it was too much, but he couldn't refuse. He went down on one knee, his head bowed.

"You are too generous, your Majesty. I was happy to be of service."

Elias huffed and pulled him upright. "Enough of that." He turned Taran slightly away from the carriage and lowered his voice. "Taran, I hope I can think of you as a friend rather than a subject. We have all been through so much these past few weeks, and I feel the need to be thought of as a man sometimes, rather than merely a king."

Taran's eyes widened at the word "merely," but he held his tongue as Elias continued.

"As a friend, I'll ask you this. Keep an eye on Brynne for me. I care very deeply for her, and I know you do, too. If anything were to happen to her ..." He trailed off, his eyes searching her out before sliding away again, not noticing the calculating look she had assumed at his baiting of Taran earlier. Elias looked back at the Adept. "You know what I'm saying."

Taran nodded. "I do, and I would have done what you're asking anyway. I'm staying with her, at least until her son is born. We've managed to convince Robin ... Major Tamsen ... of our innocence of any wrong-doing, but whether he can overcome his shame and mend his relationship with her, I just don't know. Whatever I can do to help them, I will."

Blaine saw Elias close his eyes in pain. "Just do what you can, my friend. Do what you can."

With a final clasp of the shoulder, Elias released Taran. The Adept bowed, nodded to Blaine, and returned to his new horse. Jinny stood there stroking the beast's sleek neck. Blaine heard the soft words Taran spoke to her.

"I'll be back. I don't know quite when, but you can depend on it. I'll be back."

"I know you will." She reached up to kiss his lips. "And I'll be waiting."

He returned her kiss and released her, swinging up onto Bucyrus's tall back. Waving to Cal, he nudged the stallion forward.

Aeyron chirruped to the little carriage horse as Blaine and Elias approached. It moved away toward the tree-lined avenue through the park leading down to the castle gates. Elias walked beside the carriage, Blaine just behind. As Elias spoke final words of farewell to Aeyron, Blaine noticed a familiar twinkle in Sullyan's golden eyes. What was she up to? Elias noticed it too, when it was directed upon him.

"What?" he demanded.

She replied artlessly, smoothing the silk of her gown. "Why, Elias, I very nearly forgot. I have something to tell you, something that might even please you."

He didn't trust her innocent expression and the General didn't blame him. "What is it?"

She allowed a smile to quirk her lips. "You have a very fine son, my friend. He will grow to be a great Prince, and he will be a credit to you and your House."

Elias frowned in puzzlement. Sullyan took the reins from Aeyron's hands and flicked the little chestnut to a trot, leaving Elias and Blaine behind. As they went, she called to the King over her shoulder.

"As I took your son through the Veils, he showed me his true colors. I just thought you might like to know. My friend, your son will be an Artesan!"

Three voices broke into laughter as the King's outraged, incredulous bellow followed them down the avenue:

"You're a damned scheming witch, Brynne Sullyan, do you know that?"

As Elias stood and watched them go, tears of happiness and of sorrow welling in his eyes, only General Blaine was close enough to hear him whisper:

"And I couldn't even begin to tell you how much I love you."

Chapter Twenty-Four

Three days after the trial ended, Robin arrived back at the Manor. During the journey from Port Loxton, he had constantly reached out with his metaforce to check that Tad's weak and immature psyche was still accessible in the substrate. Shielding strongly at all other times—the last thing he wanted was contact with anyone else—Robin only used his power to assure himself of Tad's survival. He knew full well the boy was mending, albeit slowly, but he still experienced bouts of irrational anxiety when he feared that Tad had died.

He finally arrived as the evening sun slowly dried the ground after a sudden shower of rain. The trees steamed faintly in the humid air, as did Tobias's damp neck. The Major rode listlessly past the sentry at the gates, only barely acknowledging the man's welcome. Wil, the sentry, watched him with a frown.

Robin took Tobias directly to the horse lines and detailed a stable lad to care for him. He usually saw to his horse himself, but tonight he didn't have the strength. He left the animal with a parting slap on the rump and walked unseeing toward the Manor.

He didn't really know what he was doing. Since his aborted attempt to take his own life, he had drifted in a strange limbo world of sights and sounds that meant nothing to him. He had lost all sense of purpose, of belonging, of worth or justification. He'd betrayed everything that had ever meant anything to him. What was left to exist for?

His steps took him automatically to the infirmary door. When he reached it, he halted, confused. Why was he here? He laid his hand against the wooden door and stared at it. It was a few seconds before he remembered why he had come. He pushed the door slowly open and stepped within.

It was always cool in the infirmary, and usually quiet. Tonight it was quieter still, as it was the hour of the evening meal. Most of the healers would be in their own common room, eating or relaxing. Only those attending the desperately sick would be abroad. Robin slouched through the corridors unseen.

He came to the small room where Tad had been placed. The door was ajar and Robin looked through the gap at the small form lying in the bed, swathed in clean bandages. He was fast asleep, lying on his back with his face, so youthful and peaceful, turned toward the door. Robin felt his chest constrict as he stepped inside the room.

The numbness in his wounded soul was receding, and it wasn't pleasant. The knowledge that he had so nearly taken his own life with no thought for the pain this would inflict on others broke sharply through the barrier Robin had built around his heart. In the battered and suffering form of the young boy Robin saw the ruin of his life, the wounding of his love, the betrayal of his life mate as she'd turned her powers upon him. His eyes blurred as tears welled and his legs lost their strength to hold him.

He felt he might swoon. He only just made it to the chair by Tad's side before he collapsed. Shaking and gasping, he took hold of Tad's small, cold hand and clasped it tight. The predominant image in his mind was of Sullyan lying similarly injured and swathed after her incredible defeat of Lord Rykan in single combat, and the same desperate anguish he had felt then strained at his heart now. It was far too late, he knew, to mend what had broken between them, but perhaps he could still do some good by helping Tad. The futility of this thought finally undid him. He bowed his head over Tad's hand and allowed his consciousness to leak away.

✣ ✣ ✣ ✣ ✣

Rienne returned to Tad's room to resume her near-constant vigil, carrying her evening meal on a platter. She was so startled to see the slumped figure in the chair by Tad's bedside that she nearly dropped her meal. It took her a moment to realize who it was.

"Robin!"

When he didn't move or respond, she put down her platter and moved to his side, laying her hand on his shoulder. She could see no signs of injury, but he was very cold and his face was white. In consternation, she felt for his pulse. It was slow and strong. Relieved, she shook his shoulder gently.

"Robin."

Still no response. She turned to the nightstand where stood a large pitcher of water infused with herbs. Taking up a cloth, she soaked and then wrung it and used it to smooth his brow, where beads of sweat stood on his skin. He gave a faint moan and his fingers tightened on Tad's.

"Robin, it's Rienne. Are you ill? What's wrong?"

He raised his head, his eyes unfocused, his lids red. His aspect made her gasp.

"Oh, Robin, we've been so worried about you!"

He pushed himself straighter, running a shaky hand through his hair. "Rienne. Is Tad all right? He won't wake."

She pursed her lips. "I had to dose him with serraflower. He'd got himself into a bit of a state—"

She stopped, but Robin saw what was in her eyes. "Because of me?"

"He's missed you so much. He was worried about you. We all were."

"He had good cause."

His reply was so low Rienne nearly missed it. She drew up another chair and sat, catching up Robin's hand.

"What is it, Rob? Was it the trial?"

Robin frowned, then shook his head despairingly. "The trial? No, not that."

Cal and Taran had been keeping Bull informed via the substrate, and he in turn had told Rienne everything. She thought she knew what plagued Robin. "Was it what Denny told you?" she asked gently.

"What Denny said … what that woman, Jinny, said … I … oh, Rienne!" His voice gave out, his throat too tightly constricted with shame and grief to speak.

She gazed in distress at the tears coursing down his face and took him impulsively into a sympathetic embrace.

That did it.

After what seemed like an age, during which he clung to her like a drowning man, the shuddering and weeping finally eased enough that she could draw back from him. Her empathic senses had overwhelmed her and drawn her fully into his turmoil of self-recrimination. It was the gift and the curse of her talent, and while it made her the best healer the Manor ever had, it also left her vulnerable and drained. She sighed deeply, wiping at her own damp cheeks.

"So now you know the truth," she murmured.

He nodded, eyes still full of pain. "How could I ever have doubted? How could I even have *thought* it? I'm not jealous of Taran, I never have been! I've known all along it was me she loved. Yes, I know she loves others too. She loves Bull, she loves you, she even loves Blaine, for pity's sake! So why should some stupid rumor about Taran set off this … this rampant, unreasoning jealousy? Where did it suddenly come from? Gods, I could have *killed* him, Rienne! I certainly wanted to. I've never felt such anger, such hatred! It was as if it wasn't really me, as if it was some petulant, younger, *uncontrollable* me. I still can't believe …."

He fell silent, shaking his head, staring at his hands in his lap. Rienne sat quietly, sensing the beginning of a cleansing, and hoping—praying—it would be enough to begin a healing. His next words disabused her of this hope.

"I can't stay here. I've gone too far this time. It's too deep, too final. I can never put it right."

Rienne leaned forward, clasped both of his hands, thoroughly frightened. She caught his gaze. "It's not your decision to make! You can't deny others their chance to forgive you. It's not fair. We've all been hurt by this. Don't take away our chance to heal too."

Anguish shimmered in his eyes. "Why does everyone always demand more of me than I can give? Don't my feelings matter at all? I'm the one who caused all this mess and I can't bear it! *I* can't heal. I'm too hurt, too … ruined! My life is just one huge waste and I can't put it right. It'll *never* go back to the way it was, can't you see that?"

Rienne's heart sank, but she refused to crumple before his despair. "I can see it will be a waste if you don't even try. If you don't give it a chance, you'll never know. Oh, Robin, of course things will never be the same. That's how life is. Things change, things happen, and these changes mold us. You should never wish for things to always stay the same. You know now that you have a core of jealousy within you. So deal with it, exorcise it. Cast it out and move on. You'll be the stronger for it. And more than that, you're going to be a father. That's something worth fighting for, isn't it? Well, *isn't* it? Brynne and your son, they're your future. You can't possibly want to throw that away."

He sat with his head in his hands, breathing in deep, shaky breaths. She could tell that her argument had touched him, but he was too raw, his spirit bleeding too freely, to even consider the possibility of healing just yet. And she knew there would have to be yet more pain, more confessions, more shame borne before he was ready. Her mention of his unborn son had only dealt him another blow.

"Everyone knew before I did." He spoke through his hands, his voice low and muffled, infinitely sad. "She couldn't bring herself to tell me. I think she wanted to tell me the day she left. I could see there was something in her eyes. She was desperately hoping I'd come to apologize, to make things right. And then I saw Taran waiting for her and I … well, I just snapped. I don't know what I might have said if he hadn't been there. Maybe we could have begun to put things right. Or maybe I'm just deluding myself. I don't know! I've forfeited the right to happiness. I've thrown the chance away. I don't deserve it, and I don't know what to do."

Rienne's patience snapped. If reason and gentle words couldn't sway him, maybe hard, brutal facts could. She needed to make it impossible for him to back away from his responsibility, no matter how much it might hurt him.

Her tone was sharp as she said, "Let me tell you what you're going to do, Major." He raised his head, her acidity cutting through the mist of his grief. "That young boy there only won his battle for life because of his love for you, and you're going to give him back some of the strength he spent. He has no part in your shame and doesn't deserve to suffer for it. So you're going to tend him until he recovers. I'm detailing you to Tad's care. You'll do everything for him that needs to be done. You'll feed him, wash him, and change his dressings. You'll be solely responsible for him and his wellbeing. You're going to pull him through. I won't hear any arguments, Major. You can check my orders with Colonel Vassa if you like, but from now on, you're excused patrols and training until Tad is able to leave this bed. Do you hear me?"

Robin stared at her, stunned. Her commanding tone and uncompromising attitude cut through his pall of grief and shame, speaking to the soldier in his soul. The healers rarely exercised their right of command, but when they did, they took precedent. Robin couldn't refuse a direct order without being accused of desertion.

"Major!" Rienne snapped, causing him to spring instinctively to attention. "I gave you an order."

"Yes, ma'am." His reply was automatic and he accorded her a salute, which wasn't strictly appropriate. She had surprised him out of his damaging lethargy, and she wasn't about to relinquish control just yet.

"That's better. Now, his dressings need changing. Fresh bandages are over there, with the salve we've been using. He'll probably need cleaning up as well. He's not strong enough to use a bed pot just yet, so there are absorbent cloths around him. I suggest you get on with it while he's sleeping, to save him any pain or embarrassment. If you need me, I'll be in the commons. I want you to call me when he wakes."

She hesitated just long enough to hear his dazed response, then she left the room, walking blindly down the corridor toward the common room. The strength she had expended to drag Robin back from the brink of his personal Void had drained her slender resources, already depleted due to her pregnancy, caring for Tad, and worry over Sullyan. The air of command slipped from her in her exhaustion. She reached the now-empty common room and sank gratefully into a chair, tears of weariness and grief welling into her eyes.

She fully expected Tad to make a miraculous recovery now his hero was back, but Robin's salvation would not be so swift or so easily accomplished. Sighing heavily, she decided she needed a drink. She knew just where to get one.

✤ ✤ ✤ ✤ ✤

The light knock on his door shook Bull from a morose reverie. He straightened in his chair and called, "It's open," turning to face the door. He smiled in genuine welcome as Rienne entered.

Seeing the look in her eyes, he poured her a generous shot of firewater brandy and handed it to her, hooking a chair over with his foot. She accepted the drink and sat, taking a long swallow and closing her eyes.

After a long moment of silence, Bull asked, "How is he?"

Rienne didn't misunderstand him. "On the mend, thank goodness. It'll only be days now, I would guess, before he's able to get up." She raised her eyes. "Have you heard from Cal or Taran today?"

Cal was still in Port Loxton with the General and the rest of the detail that had guarded Corbyn at the trial. Blaine intended to stay with the King for a few more days yet, until Elias sorted himself out. Blaine was using the time to do a complete overhaul of the Loxton garrison, and Cal and Dexter were helping Denny and Valustin drill the men and reorganize the watch system. Cal was having the time of his life, only his concern for Rienne marring his enjoyment. He reported frequently to Bull, building up his control over his metaforce as he did so.

The big man nodded, smiling. "Yes, your young man's in his element. Led a company out into the forest again today, checking for brigands. But word of the General's reforms has got out, and now the forest doesn't seem like such a good place for robbers to lurk. There's not been a single reported incident since Cal and Dex saw off that first band. But they go out daily, just for exercise. Cal's loving it."

It was Rienne's turn to smile, and he knew she was picturing Cal leading his group of men through the forest, his beloved crossbow on his saddle, just itching to find a target. His skill with the weapon, while not quite as superb as Robin's, still outstripped anyone else's. He was justifiably proud of it.

"What about Brynne?" she asked.

"She's fine. Aeyron's keeping her busy, by all accounts. The two of them are trying to reverse the Andaryan opinion as to a woman's ability to reason. Aeyron has her with him in all his meetings and pointedly defers to her suggestions as often as not. Between them, they're scandalizing the nobles."

"Serves them right." Rienne's tone was acerbic, but he could tell her heart wasn't in it. She cared little for Andaryan nobles, except those few she knew personally, of course. She considered them an inbred lot and frequently said if they couldn't see what a valuable resource they had in their women's thoughts and opinions, they deserved to die out. She wasn't being entirely fair—women were hardly more frequently seen in positions of authority in Albia—but the subject of politics and racial prejudices wasn't high on her list of priorities right now. "Is she happy, Bull?"

"Taran doesn't say much on that score." His eyes fell to his half-empty glass. "He steers off the subject if I ask him directly. She's healthy, she's keeping busy, she's being looked after. That's all I get. I'd go and see for myself, but I'm needed here. And Taran as good as told me that she didn't want any of us to interfere. You know what she's like. I think he feels she's had enough to contend with, what with her efforts at the trial and how Elias was afterward. Taran says she needs time to rest, time to think, and that we'd be better leaving her alone."

"Have you told him Robin's back?"

Bull's eyes hardened, his mouth a grim line. The big man wanted nothing more to do with his erstwhile friend; it gave him too much pain. He nodded curtly and Rienne gave a sad sigh.

"Just make sure he knows to call me if she needs me. I promised her I'd be there when her time comes and I don't intend to let her down."

Bull glanced up with a warm smile. "I've told him already. He says he knows. He'd call for you even before Deshan, if there was anything wrong. You know that. And we'd be able to get you there instantly, even without Blaine here. Either Anjer or Pharikian would open the way for you. But she's a few weeks to go yet, before her time comes. Blaine'll be back by then, I hope, and we can both go."

Rienne watched the swirl of amber liquid in her glass, looking sad and frustrated. "Who knows what'll have happened by then?"

Bull pursed his lips at her sorrow, his own heart heavy and joyless. What should have been an incredibly happy time had been irretrievably marred by rumor and suspicion. Why, he reflected sourly, had he ever thought Artesans would be immune to these vices? Surely people so aware of their own emotions should be able to avoid the sort of unthinking prejudices that affected those not so gifted? They had the rare ability to sense the truth in someone's heart, after all. Why, then, had all this dreadful grief been allowed to fester, to take them over?

For the first time in years, Bull felt the inadequacy of his own power. Content for so long with the level he had attained, he found himself fervently wishing he was stronger than Robin. He would have had no compunction about compelling the bloody young idiot to face the error of his judgment! He'd have forced Robin to see the honesty of Sullyan's words, the total lack of deviousness in her, and the vicious falseness of the rumors. Oh, he wanted to knock their heads together sometimes! They were both as stubborn as each other.

A tiny sound caught his ear and he returned to himself. Rienne, unable to contain her sorrow any longer, rose from her chair and crossed to his. He held out his arms to her and she folded herself down next to him, snuggling into his embrace, both of them needing the comfort and security of a trusted friend's warm care.

Chapter Twenty-Five

L ife at the Manor slowly returned to normal. Robin spent as much time as he could tending to Tad. After two weeks of Robin's care, Tad was finally able to leave his bed for the first time since his wounding.

Blaine returned to the Manor after a month in Port Loxton. He'd spent much of his time dealing with the depression that had overtaken the King. Elias had been more deeply affected by Sofira's treachery than Blaine had guessed, and he was surprised by the depth of the King's lethargy. He feared to leave until Elias was more emotionally stable.

He had also dealt with Arch Patrio Neremiah over the subject of Reen's ultimate fate. Blaine left the senior churchman in no doubt as to his tenuous position over his support for Reen during the trial, even going so far as to hint Neremiah might be forced to accompany Reen to his exile. This frightened the man so badly he all but fell over himself to be accommodating.

Reen's fate was agreed. Far to the north of the realm, off the northwest coast of Serna Province, was an island community of reclusive clerics who practiced their own variety of Albia's main Faith. Theirs was a frugal and hard-working lifestyle, and they were a mainly silent order, except during services. The only way onto or off their rocky, wave-battered island was by boat, but the clerics owned no boats themselves. Their needs were supplied by fishermen who visited once a month or so. They had no other human contact, as the Cleric Patrio, the order's leader, considered it detrimental to their spiritual health.

This arrangement would be as secure as Blaine was likely to achieve short of killing the Baron. Even so, he intended to alert the nearest garrison outpost and detail someone to keep an eye on Reen. He wondered grimly how closely Elias would investigate if news should arrive that Reen had met with a fatal accident. Not very, was the General's opinion.

The matter settled, Reen was sent off, still in chains, still pleading for one final meeting with the Arch Patrio under the guise of begging a blessing. It was denied. Blaine let Reen know it wouldn't take much to convince Elias to restore the death penalty and that Reen would do better to reflect on Sullyan's gracious intervention and be thankful for his reprieve. The King was nowhere in sight when Reen's closed carriage rolled out of the castle gates. The four King's Guard who would escort him to his place of banishment were hand-picked and under strict instructions to neither speak to Reen nor release him from his chains until he was handed over to the Cleric Patrio. One of Neremiah's junior clerics traveled with them, to convey the King's orders. Blaine wished them much joy of the long journey.

The arrangements for the Queen were also underway. The Arch Patrio dissolved the marriage. Sofira's betrayal and treachery were reason enough to do so even without Neremiah's fears for his own position. Sofira was forced to sign various papers and agreements rescinding her allowances and rights. Then Elias called local stonemasons to the castle and had them alter the hallways leading to the east wing, where Sofira had her apartments, so she could no longer gain access to the main part of the castle. Her quarters were pleasant and spacious, and she had servants of her own and private kitchens to prepare her meals. A section of the castle gardens was walled off for her use. She was to be, for all intents and purposes, a prisoner in a lavishly gilded cage.

Only two things occurred during the month Blaine stayed in Loxton to give the King's sore heart any ease at all. One was a letter from Beraxia, Ozella's homeland. It was from Ozella's father, mourning the loss of his son and informing the King of the safe return of his daughters. While the news gladdened the King, he was also angered beyond measure over the futility of Ozella's suffering. It seemed the two girls never learned the reason for their abduction, nor the identity of their captors, and although they had been threatened, neither of them was harmed.

The other cause for pleasure was the brief ceremony conducted to confirm Cal Tyler in his new status as captain. Elias had learned of Cal's part in the identification of Corbyn as Reen's ally, and also of his help in capturing the renegade lord. Elias was pleased to reward the young man, and Cal's pride in his single thunderflash captain's insignia knew no bounds.

Blaine had only been back at the Manor for a day when he summoned Robin to his office. It was a private interview and was never spoken of afterward, but the Major emerged two hours later white-faced and trembling, while Blaine wasn't seen for the remainder of the day. When he finally resumed his duties, his eyes were harder than usual and his manner curt and strained. Everyone at the Manor felt like they were walking on eggshells.

Robin resumed command of Sullyan's company the day after his meeting with Blaine, having been released from Tad's care by Rienne. She was too happy at the return of her beloved Cal to notice Robin's wasted appearance. When she came across a tearful Tad a few days later, she wished she'd taken more note of it. She found him sitting in the College holding a piece of topaz which he was turning over and over in his hands. It was only by sheer chance that she came upon him. She regularly checked the College's healer suite, although it hadn't yet been used. She heard

Tad's sniffles as she passed the half-open door and went in to investigate.

His health had progressed so well he was now allowed to go about by himself, provided he didn't indulge in any physical exercise. He had returned to his studies, hoping to improve his mental control and desperate for the day when Robin would confirm him as Apprentice-elite. Entering quietly so as not to disturb his concentration, Rienne soon realized he wasn't working. He was simply crying.

"What is it, Tad? Are you feeling unwell?"

He spun round, his hand clenching on the chunk of topaz, his face flushed with crying. His eyes were full of misery.

"No, Healer Arlen, but I might as well be."

"Whatever is the matter? You're doing so well."

Tad's thin shoulders hunched as he tried not to cry again. "He's gone away."

Rienne's heart skipped a painful beat. "Who has? Robin? Why? Where has he gone?"

She knew it couldn't be a routine patrol that had taken the depressed Major away. Tad wouldn't react like this if he'd simply gone on a normal patrol. It must be something more serious, but Rienne hadn't heard news that would necessitate a company being sent out for any length of time. She sat down beside the unhappy youngster and made him face her. "Tell me."

"He went this morning," confessed Tad, trying to swallow sobs. "He came to tell me, to say goodbye. He was very upset. He's taken leave and gone. He wouldn't say where or for how long. He's just ... gone."

Rienne swore, causing Tad's eyes to widen. It shocked Rienne, too. It had just slipped out. Her expression hardened, but she spoke gently.

"You mustn't be too sad. Robin's been through a lot lately and he's very hurt. Being able to help you recover has meant a lot to him, and he loves you as much as you love him. He won't desert you. He just needs some time to himself. Try not to worry too much. He'll be back, you'll see."

Hoping Robin wouldn't prove her false, Rienne stood, determined to find out what he was playing at. She was surprised at the depth of her anger. Then it hit her: she knew where Robin had gone. Of course! He'd gone to Andaryon, to Sullyan. He knew roughly when the baby was due and must have decided it was time to put things right between them. Feeling lighter and happier than she had for weeks, Rienne went looking for Bull.

He wasn't in his rooms and she made her way to the commons, hoping to find him there. He wasn't there either, but Dexter was, sitting with a group of his friends. He hailed her.

"Rienne, are you looking for Cal?"

"No, Dex, it's Bull I want. Do you know where he is?"

Dexter's usually cheerful face turned somber. "He's with Blaine. I passed the General's door earlier and there were angry voices inside. If you want to speak to Bull, I'd wait a while."

Rienne frowned. Why would Bull and the General exchange angry words? Deciding she wasn't going to let it put her off finding out what was going on, she thanked Dexter and left.

As she approached the General's office, there were indeed raised voices behind the door. She recognized Bull's bass rumble as well as Blaine's hard tones. Hyram, Blaine's valet, stood outside the door. He grimaced as she stopped.

"How long have they been arguing?"

Hyram shrugged. "Ten, fifteen minutes?"

Rienne hesitated. Should she knock or should she wait? Then she caught Bull's irritable voice saying, "What on earth did you let him go for?" and the General snapped, "He's not on a charge and he *is* due the leave. Why should I stop him? What would you have said?"

Decision made, Rienne forestalled what Bull would have said by rapping on the door. She opened it without waiting for the General's call. This was an argument she intended to join.

Both men stared at her, red-faced and angry. They made an effort to calm down when they saw the worry in her eyes.

"Tad's just told me Robin's gone. Please tell me he's gone to Brynne. Tell me he's gone to put things right."

Neither man could hold her gaze. They traded frustrated glances as she stood impatiently, hands on hips. Bull finally said, "We don't know where he's gone."

"What? Why not? What did he say?"

Blaine's shoulders sagged as the anger went out of him. He gave a heavy sigh. "He came to me early this morning. He was in quite a state. He said he couldn't cope anymore and he needed some time to himself. He was due some leave and he asked to take it immediately. I asked him where he was going and he just said, 'somewhere quiet, I need to think.' Then he left."

"You shouldn't have let him go," Bull stated flatly.

Blaine's angular face flushed. "So you keep saying! I want to know just how you think I could have stopped him. I've already told him what I think of him. I've even threatened to dismiss him. What more can I do? Put him in chains and drag him to her? What good would that do? Do you think she'd thank me for it?"

Defeated but still angry, Bull turned away. Rienne was concerned for him. She could see his lips were a little blue. Since the heart seizure he'd suffered, she'd watched over him carefully. Sullyan had done likewise, fearful of losing him before his time. Now he was overexerting himself and his heart wouldn't take much of that.

"Calm down, Bull. This isn't getting us anywhere. The General's right. Robin is his own man and must make his own choices. Brynne won't thank us for interfering. General, do you think we could have some fellan?"

Blaine glanced at her, shamed at his lack of manners. "Of course, my dear. I'm sorry. The past few weeks have been hard on us all. We need to keep a sense of perspective about this, but it's hard. The deeper you care, the harder you feel it."

Rienne blinked, suddenly realizing how little she really knew him. He kept mostly to himself, socializing mainly with Vassa and Sullyan. He was a private and solitary man and she found herself wondering whether he'd ever had a love of his own. She was aware how deeply Blaine cared for Sullyan, but as the man so rarely spoke of or showed his feelings, she wondered if he was aware of them himself. She felt a surge of pity for him. He must often feel isolated in his position.

Hyram served the fellan and withdrew. They sat and savored the hot liquid, its rich aroma diverting them from the irritation in the room.

"You don't think he's gone to Andaryon, then?" Rienne asked.

Bull huffed. "Who knows where the silly sod's gone? And yes, before you ask, I contacted Taran. He's not seen him. He's on the alert, though, in case he shows up. I suppose it's just possible Robin's taken himself off to screw up enough courage to face her."

Rienne's heart sank. She'd been so sure he'd gone to the Citadel. "Where else could he have gone?"

Both men looked at her, worry on their faces. She knew she looked exhausted. She was nearly four months into her own pregnancy and it was showing. Only the day before, she'd felt her baby's first movements. She surprised Cal into sudden tears when she guided his hand to her swelling belly so he could feel them too.

They couldn't be happier, but their happiness only increased Rienne's sorrow in knowing that Sullyan was missing out on all this joy. Her tears were as often for Sullyan's pain as they were for her own glad anticipation of her baby daughter.

Bull sighed. "I don't know, dear heart. The General and I were just discussing whether I should go after him. For myself, I don't want to, but for Sullyan...."

Rienne nodded. "I know. And Brynne doesn't want us to interfere. She wants Robin back of his own accord, not because one of us has forced him. You know, I don't think she'll ever get over using her powers on him. That loss of control affected her more deeply than she knows. It made her realize just how dangerous she could be with all that power to call on. She could snuff out any one of us without even noticing the drain in energy. That's why she's so dead-set against compelling him. She fears it would only compound his resentment or make him fear her. She'd never be able to bear that."

Lost in morose contemplation, they sat in silence, the strong fellan no anodyne to sore and aching hearts.

Chapter Twenty-Six

Midsummer drew near, and the Citadel Plains were baked brown. The forests of fir to the east were still a green line on the horizon, but everywhere else was parched and dry. Frequent thunderstorms swept across the sky from the south, rarely producing enough rain to do more than dampen the surface dust. The central provinces of Andaryon, as they so often did in the summer months, roasted.

Corbyn's execution had been carried out in the courtyard of the garrison cells by a grim-faced and taciturn Anjer. Kethro had not attended. Once it was over and the traitor's pyre no more than ashes and memory, Kethro's position in the nobility and his right to rule the lands of Quarlock were ratified by the Hierarch. Kethro then left the Citadel with Lord Tikhal and Rand to take up his new responsibilities.

Taran slipped easily into the routine of the palace. Sullyan made the best effort she could, but as the weeks went by, it was becoming increasingly more obvious how badly her spirit was suffering. While she was in good health physically, inwardly she sickened daily. Her golden eyes, normally so bright and full of life, were constantly dark and sad. No animation enlivened her face, no grace defined her movements. She was biding time, that was all. Her soul was withering as her heart despaired.

He rarely left her side now. At first, he had attended her only when she requested it, and he'd taken the small suite of rooms opposite hers. After a week or so she'd asked him diffidently whether he'd mind sleeping in her suite, in the small room adjoining her bedchamber. She gave no reason and he asked none, merely moving his gear into the room later that day. From then on, they slept each night with the connecting door ajar.

Taran experienced a strange dichotomy of emotion when Bull contacted him to ask whether Robin had been to the Citadel. His first reaction was a leap of hope. The appearance of her life mate, the chance to put things right, was the one thing Sullyan craved. She had not mentioned Robin's name once since coming to live at the palace. She never even asked whether Taran had seen Robin at the trial, or if he'd spoken to him, but Taran knew he was constantly on her mind.

After the hope came dread. The thought of seeing Robin, of dealing with him face to face, was more than Taran could bear. If Robin had reacted so badly to Jinny's and Denny's confessions, what might he do on seeing Taran? How would he feel? Would he even be able to come here knowing they would meet? It would be uncomfortable in the extreme, especially as Taran had grown so close to Sullyan during her pregnancy. That was Robin's place, not his. One more thing the Major could hold against him.

As much as he knew it was what Sullyan needed and wanted above all else, it would be too much for Taran. The day Robin arrived at the Citadel would be the day Taran left. He didn't tell her of Bull's message. Three days later, all thoughts of it were thrust completely from his mind.

✤ ✤ ✤ ✤ ✤

Sullyan was restless, unable to find ease in any position she chose. She couldn't stand, sit, or lie down for very long without having to move to alleviate some ache or other. She seemed weak, enervated, and uncomfortable. She was irritable and snappish and the hot weather did nothing to help. Taran had become used to tiptoeing around her temper when suddenly, one day, she woke in a completely different mood.

He watched her suspiciously as they broke their fast together. The open windows in the living area allowed the cool morning breeze to blow in from the fragrant gardens. For once, her birdlike appetite seemed to have improved. Taran was glad. He could swear she had actually lost weight recently, rather than gained it. She noticed his gaze and smiled at him, almost normally.

"This will be a fair day, my friend, and I feel the need to get out. Would you drive the carriage for me?"

He was surprised by her request. The past few days she had felt too uncomfortable and ungainly to go anywhere. Looking at her animated expression, he readily acquiesced, hoping this easier mood signaled a change for the better.

Marik and Idrimar requested to come when they heard of the excursion. Taran arranged for the larger carriage to be readied instead of the smaller gig he usually used. By midmorning, under a clear washed sky, they made for the woodlands to the west. Taran kept the Master Physician's words uppermost in his mind as he drove. Deshan had warned the Adept she was very near her time. He advised Taran not to go too far from the Citadel in case events overtook them.

He needn't have worried. The day passed pleasantly, Sullyan taking more pleasure in the simple, refreshing picnic than she had in anything else of late. Her lighter mood persisted despite the onset of a fierce backache her powers were unable to dampen. Taran noticed her massaging her lower belly whenever she thought herself unobserved.

Returning to the Citadel that afternoon, Taran helped Sullyan into her rooms. She disappeared into the bathing pool to soak away her persistent, aching fatigue. Later, she pleaded exhaustion and missed the evening meal. Taran stayed with her. Norkis brought them food, although Taran was the only one who ate. Sullyan's face turned almost green when he offered her some of the fare provided. Worried he had allowed her to overdo things, he helped her to bed, ensuring there was a pitcher full of fresh water within easy reach.

He was woken in the night by the sound of her pacing her room. He rose and went to the door. He could see her in the hazy moonlight, the old green shirt she loved draped over her shoulders as she stood by the open window. Sensing him there, she reassured him, saying only that she was unable to sleep.

Sleep eluded him too, after that. He could still hear her, sometimes pacing, sometimes turning in her bed, unable to rest, unable to find ease. Neither of them slept more that night.

In the first gray light of dawn, he heard her call his name. He was at her door in an instant. Alarmed by the pallor of her face, he came to her side, seeing the large, spreading patch of damp on the sheets below her. Although he had never witnessed it for himself, he'd heard Rienne speak of midwifery often enough to recognize the cause.

"Oh. Your waters have broken. I'd better fetch Deshan."

"No, Taran. I need Rienne."

"Don't worry, I'll fetch Rienne. But first I'm calling Deshan."

She protested, but he sent a call to the physician anyway, grateful when the man responded quickly. He was at the door in minutes, but not before another voice crashed into Taran's mind. The Adept groped blindly for the door to admit Deshan while dealing with General Blaine's urgent message.

Adept Elijah! I've got Rienne here telling me she has to attend Sullyan immediately. What the hell's happening?

With no time to wonder how Rienne knew Sullyan needed her,

Taran told the General the baby was coming.

Can you get down to the Plains? asked Blaine. *I'll be sending Rienne through as soon as you're there.*

Taran broke the link. Deshan was attending to Sullyan, although something was wrong. She seemed unable to afford him access to her metaforce and was on the verge of panic. Taran could hear it in her voice.

He left the room at a run, dashing out of the palace toward the Citadel gates. Barrin was on early duty and Taran reached out to the Journeyman Commander as he ran through the waking town. The Commander had a horse ready and the gates open, and an escort with a carriage accompanied Taran as he rode out to meet Rienne. Blaine sent her through on Taran's word.

"Taran," she snapped as soon as she saw him, "why didn't you call me sooner?"

He eyed her swelling belly. "I didn't know how close she was. I expected her to tell me when she needed you. Are you all right? Are you sure you're up to this?"

Rienne glared at him. "I promised I'd be here and I will. Who's with her?"

Taran answered her many questions as best he could while they made their way to the palace. Rienne was incensed by most of his answers, especially when he told her of Sullyan's listlessness.

When Rienne entered the room, Sullyan calmed, relief radiating from her. Rienne's anger drained away, although she shot Deshan a hard glance before bending to examine Sullyan. Apparently satisfied with what she found, she beckoned Taran over. He'd been watching from the door, glad the healer was there. Now, all would be well.

"What can I do?" he asked.

"Help support her. She needs to move about a bit. She's very tense, and too much tension will only give her more pain to suppress when the contractions start for real. She's got some way to go yet; we're only in the first stages. Talk to her, keep her calm, and let her do whatever seems most comfortable. Get her to drink if you can. I don't want her getting dehydrated."

There was an air of annoyance about her. "Where are you going?" Taran asked as she moved away.

She smiled reassuringly, but her tone was hard. "I'm just going to have a word with Deshan. I won't be long."

✣ ✣ ✣ ✣ ✣

Sullyan gave a soft moan of protest as Rienne turned away. Taran went to her and took her shoulders, murmuring gently. Rienne watched them briefly and then glanced at Deshan. She motioned sharply with her hand and both healers moved outside the room. Once the door was firmly shut, Rienne rounded on the Andaryan physician.

"How could you have let her get into such a state? Haven't you seen how *thin* she is? Hasn't she been eating? Why wasn't I called before this? Why did you let her go so far on her own? I should have been here yesterday, or even the day before!"

Deshan spread his hands. "I was waiting for her to tell me when she needed you. It never occurred to me she wouldn't recognize the onset of labor."

Rienne gaped. "Didn't you tell her what to expect? Didn't you *talk* to her?"

He looked shamefaced. "I thought you had."

"I haven't *been* here! I haven't seen her for weeks. You're the physician here!"

Before he could reply, footsteps heralded the arrival of the Hierarch. Despite her irritation, Rienne gave him a polite curtsey. He greeted her warmly, although his patrician face was lined with worry.

"Has it begun?" he asked.

"We're lucky it's not already over!" snapped Rienne. "I'm surprised at you, Timar, letting her get into such a state."

The most powerful man in all Andaryon didn't take offense at Rienne's tone, knowing she was only concerned for her friend. His eyes showed his sadness.

"It's not been easy, these past few weeks. She's been so very unhappy, Rienne. Perhaps now you're here she'll be able to feel some joy of the event. I certainly hope so."

His obvious concern dampened her irritation. "Then it's just as well I felt her calling for me. Right, I want fresh sheets on that bed right now. I want hot water and cloths. I want food and drink sent in. I want quiet. And I want *you*, Deshan, to be available in case I need you."

The Master Physician blinked and nodded. Pharikian smiled as he turned away, sending a page to see about the fresh sheets and the other items Rienne had demanded. The healer huffed and went back into the room, where Sullyan was beginning to fret.

Over the next couple of hours Rienne did everything she could to reassure Sullyan and tell her what to expect as her labor progressed. Taran stayed by her side, growing ever more concerned as Rienne's presence and sensible, unflappable manner failed to raise Sullyan's spirits. Rienne asked her many questions about the reactions of her body over the past couple of weeks, gradually building up a picture of what Sullyan had experienced. Her efficient and knowledgeable hands explored the position of the babe within Sullyan's belly, and she was satisfied at the stage of the labor. Her earlier anger at Deshan, now hidden beneath her professional calm, had been a disguise and an outlet for her chagrin that she hadn't spent more time with Sullyan before things came to such a pass.

In a rare moment of peace, when Rienne had finally persuaded

Sullyan to lie on her side in the clean bed to rest, she drew Taran aside, a worried frown creasing her brows.

"I don't like this, Taran. Something's not right, and I just can't put my finger on it."

Taran drew a breath. "What can we do?"

Rienne shrugged, her eyes misting. "I don't know. I don't really know what's wrong. I can't find any physical signs to worry over. The baby's lying normally and is in no distress. I wish Brynne weren't quite so thin, but that she is comes as no great surprise. Her muscles are strong, and that should help when the baby begins to come.

"It's her spiritual sickness, I think, that bothers me so. That and her inability to use her metaforce. She has an almost total lack of energy. I've never seen an Artesan give birth and I have no idea if this is normal."

The Adept nodded. Sullyan's contractions, occurring at roughly fifteen-minute intervals, were not yet too severe, but she seemed unable to cope with the pain or to alleviate it in any way by accessing her powers. This inability seemed to frighten and weaken her more each time she tried. Her failure to reach her inner resources caused her to fight against the pain instead of accepting it, and this only made the pain worse. Rienne didn't want to imagine what she would suffer when the contractions began in earnest.

She watched the lonely figure in the bed, eyes dark with worry as Sullyan moaned again with the onset of a fresh contraction. "Taran, sit with her, will you? I'm going to have another word with Deshan."

The Andaryan physician was sitting in the living area when Rienne went through. To her surprise, Aeyron was with him. The Prince looked up sharply as Rienne appeared, his face pale and drawn.

"It's not going well, is it?"

"It's not going badly, so far," she amended, unwilling to tempt fate, "but something's not quite right. Deshan, this business of her not being able to access her metaforce—have you come across anything like it before?"

Deshan looked surprised. "Andaryan women don't have access to their own metaforce," he reminded her gently. "For us, the trait runs only in the male line. I've never attended a birth to an Artesan mother before, let alone a human."

Aeyron glanced at him. "Except Bethyn."

Deshan paled and Rienne stared at him fearfully. "What? What is it?"

Deshan flicked his gaze to Aeyron, obviously wishing the Prince hadn't mentioned Sullyan's mother, who had died birthing her. He spoke slowly. "Bethyn was different. She wasn't a full Artesan, only an empath."

Rienne heard the omission. "So?"

He was unable to meet her gaze. "Bethyn had a very difficult labor. We tried everything we could think of. Morgan exhausted himself trying to give her the strength to cope with her pain." The physician's eyes were unfocused, seeing the scene so long ago. Rienne could almost hear the weakening woman's pitiful cries, see the blood, and feel the helplessness. She couldn't bear to think of Sullyan suffering the same way.

"What is it?" she whispered, her hands clenching. "Deshan, what aren't you telling me?"

He lifted reluctant eyes to hers. "None of Morgan's efforts made any difference. He couldn't help Bethyn. She was unable to make use of the strength he offered, even though they were bonded more closely than I have ever seen two people bond before. Even Bethyn's own empathic powers failed her. She couldn't access them. She exhausted herself trying, and I believe it contributed to her death."

Deshan's eyes filled with pain. Aeyron lowered his face to his hands.

Rienne stared at them, feeling hot fury surge through her veins. "No!" she spat. "I *won't* let that happen to Brynne! She's not going to die. She's not her mother. She's as powerful as the Hierarch, maybe more so. There has to be a way of helping her!"

Deshan had no answers, and Rienne was summoned back to Sullyan's side by her cry of pain as a longer and stronger contraction than any before rippled through her.

Chapter Twenty-Seven

Sullyan just couldn't understand it. Wasn't she one of the most powerful people in the world? Why, then, couldn't she dull a little pain? She'd done it countless times before, and with worse agony than this. So why, now, did it wound her so?

She lay back, gasping and exhausted. How many hours had it been? She had no idea. Too many, she thought. Sweat beaded her ashen face, trickled down her back and between her breasts, and soaked her tangled hair. Tears of frustration and despair welled in her eyes. Her whole body hurt, she felt sick, and she was shivering so hard she couldn't stop. The contractions came harder and faster now, and were longer and much stronger. They left her breathless and drained, but they seemed to achieve nothing. She was so exhausted she could barely hear Rienne trying to aid her breathing, the healer desperate for Sullyan to get some oxygen into her lungs so her burning muscles could make use of it.

Under Rienne's guidance she'd tried various positions once the second stage of labor started. Yet in the end her strength gave out, even with Taran's strong arms to support her. She'd had no choice but to let them lay her in the bed, knees wide, supported at her back by as many pillows as they could find.

The healer tried frantically to get her to focus on something other than the pain, but by now Sullyan couldn't hear her. Neither could she feel Taran's hand clasping hers, although at times she'd gripped it so hard he would have cried out if he hadn't been able to use his own metaforce to deal with the pain.

She'd never expected birth to feel like this. When she was younger, long before she met Robin, she had often wondered what it would be like to bear a child. She'd seen countless births—admittedly mostly sheep, cattle, and horses—enough to know the mechanics of it. She'd heard women in her village on the Downs giving birth and been old enough to understand the pain and the blood. Yet her own experience had taken her by surprise. She simply hadn't expected it to be so *hard*.

It wasn't really the labor, of course. It wasn't the completely natural process her body was going through without any volition of hers. She recognized the primal urge in the new life within her that struggled and demanded to be born. And she wanted to help it forth. She so desperately wanted to help her son gain his birthright, his right to the life she and Robin had created.

She just couldn't.

She knew she was dying. Her spirit, her Fire, had withered and gone out, snuffed by despair, smothered by shame, extinguished by recrimination and the waste of a true love thrown away. For the second time in her life, she'd been abandoned in her greatest need. She had no spark left to give her son, no life of her own to pass on to him. She could hear her own heart faltering, the faint, fluttering beat causing sudden panic in the healer who knelt by her belly, urging her to try, to breathe, to *live*.

She vaguely heard a man's voice crying in her ear, words she couldn't make out. They weren't important anymore. There came a stinging slap to her face, but she didn't feel it. The grief, the pain, and the anguish, whether hers or of these others who surrounded her, were nothing to her now. Even the urgent motion of her womb was ceasing, with no reaction from the infant mind within, also given up on life.

She breathed a final, pain-free sigh. Her eyes closed on the world and she drifted away, all sounds fading save a faint, rhythmic susurration, like an exhalation of the softest breeze through fresh spring leaves. The sound cradled her aching spirit as it waned.

✤ ✤ ✤ ✤ ✤

"Oh, gods, Taran, we're losing her. Deshan, quickly! Taran, *do* something! I can't believe this is happening. It's not fair. I *won't* let her go. Brynne. *Brynne!*"

Rienne struggled upright and leaned toward the white, sweat-slicked face of her dearest friend. With all her strength she slapped the pale cheek, desperately willing a reaction, a spark of life in those closing eyes, something, *anything*.

But there was nothing. Taran cried out as Rienne brought back her hand, grabbing her wrist to prevent the second blow. There was no point. Deshan burst into the room, staring in horror at the scene: another woman on the same bed, the pools of blood and the exhausted, ashen-faced man watching him from dull and hopeless eyes, a lifeless hand clasped in his.

Deshan shook his head in furious denial, clearing the nightmare image. Taran stared at him, sensing the man's inner strength. This wasn't Bethyn before him, bleeding to death. There was no excess blood here, no defeated Morgan already sinking into suicidal despair. This was Brynne Sullyan, young, healthy, a powerful Artesan. Deshan was damned if he'd let history come full circle!

He pushed the distraught Rienne away, thrusting her roughly into Taran's arms. He sent out a call for Pharikian and knelt on the bed beside Sullyan's limp form to take her bloodless face between his hands. With no preliminaries, he cast his awareness into her, driving through the intricacies of her convoluted psyche, boosting, supporting, surrounding. Taran reached out and felt Deshan snatch at his offered energy. There was an inrush of incredible power; Pharikian had arrived. Asking no leave and needing none, Deshan grasped the energies offered him and cast a web of power around Sullyan's fading life force. He was only just in time. Straining every nerve and fiber of his body, every synapse in his brain screaming in protest, he halted her drift toward oblivion and shut off the entrance to the Void.

Shivering, gasping, he pulled back.

Rienne was sobbing. Taran felt no better. Pharikian collapsed to the edge of the bed and Aeyron came forward to support him. They all stared at the Master Physician as his eyes cleared.

"There's not much time." His voice was rough with fear and strain. "They'll only last so long within the web. Once it deteriorates, she'll slip through, and the babe with her."

Pharikian shook his head weakly. "I can't believe this is happening again." He could hardly bear to look at the limp form on the bed, belly still large with the promise of life. A promise that, once again, was proving false.

Rienne pushed away from Taran's arms. "What can we do? You've only delayed the inevitable. What good will it do to hang on to her? If she's so weak, so unable to cope, how are we going to help her?"

Deshan stared almost feverishly at Rienne, the light of chance in his eyes.

"You know how!" he said urgently. "There's only one thing she wants—only one person who can call her back now."

"Robin!" breathed Rienne. "But we don't know where he is."

"Then *find* him!" Deshan's fury spilled over. "Scour the land if you have to, but *find* him!"

Rienne turned to Taran, gripping his arms. "What?" he said, startled out of his grief. Then he realized what she was asking.

"No, Rienne. He wouldn't listen to me even if I could find him. I'm the last person he wants to see."

He thought she might slap him. "You *have* to, Taran! Do you want to see her die? It's up to you. You're the only one she's got! If you don't go and find him, then she's finished, and her baby with her. Could you stand that on your conscience? Could you live with yourself if you don't try?"

They all gasped at Rienne's cruel words. She was being unfair, but it had to be him. She couldn't go and Deshan and Pharikian were needed here.

His face flushed in anger. They were all looking at him. "Go *on*," yelled Rienne. "You're wasting time!" She shoved him hard in the chest.

Anger burned in his breast as he once more ran like fury through the palace and out into the late afternoon, making for the stables. As he ran, he called for Anjer. The Lord General caught the desperate urgency in Taran's tone and the overlying futile rage that accompanied it. He had Bucyrus standing saddled and ready as Taran pelted up to the horse lines.

Taran blurted out what had happened and saw the huge man's face turn white with shock. "Where will you look?" he asked.

"I have no idea," spat Taran, still furious with Rienne for forcing this responsibility on him. He tried to calm his mind enough to call Bull.

When the big man answered, fear coloring his mental tone as he caught the echo of Taran's anguish, he immediately offered to help.

I just need to know if you've any idea where Robin might have gone.

Bull didn't hesitate. *The only place I can think of is his home village in Garon. If he's thinking at all, he's probably gone there. If he's not thinking, then he could be wandering anywhere and you'll never find him.*

Taran swore. *Where's this village?*

The big man showed him and Taran passed it on to Anjer. As Adept-elite, Taran didn't yet possess the strength or control to direct the opening of a trans-Veil tunnel, so he had to rely on the Master-ranked Anjer to do it for him. Without his help, Taran could waste hours—even days—riding to his destination. And they didn't *have* hours, let alone days.

Bull wanted to go with him, but Taran couldn't wait. Once Anjer had the location fixed in his mind, Taran took him up behind him on the stallion and Anjer focused his will as the two of them galloped through the town and out the Citadel gates.

Reaching clear ground, Anjer slid from the horse's back. Taran settled his sword by his side and took a firm hold of the stallion's bit. Then he nodded to the Lord General. The huge Andaryan manipulated the gray-shot shimmer of the substrate and Taran set heels to his horse's flanks. He passed out of Andaryon straight into a drenching rainstorm in the far west of Albia, where he'd never been before.

✣ ✣ ✣ ✣ ✣

There was peace and there was warmth. Well, there was an absence of cold, at least. Physical sensations meant less than nothing here. After the agony and the anguish, it was blissful. No pressure, no urgency, no despair. Nothing. No sounds, no scents, no feeling. Drifting … yes, a faint sense of movement, but it was a motion with no meaning; aimless, directionless, endless. And so very peaceful.

The months of heartache, the blame, the despair, and the sickness in her soul had taken a heavy and unbearable toll on her psyche. Heavier than she'd known how to express. Now it was gone, and with it, all strife and the reason for strife. She felt no relief at this cessation of anguish, she merely accepted it was gone.

Relief, along with hope and all the other feelings she once experienced, were washed away and forgotten, having no place in this soft gray limbo where her spirit now drifted.

She wasn't alone. There was another presence with her, or was it just another part of herself? She wasn't sure, but it didn't matter now. Nothing mattered. She had no identity, no sense of who she was or who she had been. Her awareness existed—barely. That, too, would soon be gone. She could feel it fading, waning, and that was right. It was what this place was for, this limbo before the Void. Reabsorption. The reintegration into the substance of the world. Rest and oblivion.

She yearned for rest. With what was left of her awareness, with an echo of the memory of pain and striving, she yearned toward the center of this place where she knew, without knowing how she knew, that she would find what her spirit craved. She wanted to forget all that heartache and suffering. She just wanted it all to be over, to drift like this forever, in this peaceful, silent place.

Her awareness slowly drew closer to that center where life was being absorbed and reborn continually, in the great Circle of Time, the source of existence. It was a place of tremendous energies, ponderous and unstoppable, gyring around a central point. She could feel the turn and pull of primal forces at work here and prepared to give herself up to the ultimate fate of her soul.

Just as she felt she would enter the vortex that held and absorbed everything it touched, she felt a swirl beside her, before her, preventing her from moving closer. What was it, that amorphous swirl? Could there even be a swirl, here at the end of all things? The swirl came again, unwanted, drawing her attention, diverting her from the reabsorption that felt so right, so natural.

And was that a voice? How could there be voices here where sound didn't exist, nor ears to hear? And yet hear it she did. Despite herself, she listened.

A name. It sounded like a name. And that name was familiar. How strange. Why should one simple syllable be familiar?

It came again. This time, she felt as well as heard. Yes, she remembered feeling. It was unpleasant. It *hurt*. She pulled away, yearning for the peace, the endless gray drift. She couldn't quite reach it.

Pretty Brynne.

Why did those words strike sensations within her? Why did they tug at emotions she no longer possessed?

Brynne. Pretty Brynne.

A name came to her, seeming from nowhere. Huw? Yes, she remembered now. That thick voice, those slurred sounds. He had been her cousin. But she had hardly known him. Why did she hear his voice now?

The swirl came again, but this time it was moving away. And the voice never came again, but it left something behind. An image. A feeling of home, of belonging. A faint memory, as if seen through another's eyes. Green-clad mountains, deep, lush valleys. Misty rain, gentle sunshine. Musical, lilting voices. Like her voice, when she'd still had one.

She drifted again, for a length of time that had no meaning. She wasn't thinking, not consciously. Yet the images planted within her by her cousin's echo tugged uncomfortably at parts of her she had thought to cast off. The images were evocative, teasing. They held out vague promises, as if of a life she might have had, or might have yet. She knew they weren't real. Her time was over and she was content it should be so. She drifted toward the center of reabsorption once more.

Another tug, another strange sensation. She halted her imperceptible movement. This presence was unlike the first. There was no swirl, no voice, yet she could discern something. It had a name, she knew, she just didn't remember what it was. Once, it had meant much to her. Now, here, it was nothing.

Yet if that were true, why did she linger?

Music.

If she could have smiled, she would have. She knew that music. She'd known it since before she was born. She'd heard it in the protection of her mother's womb, heard it and learned it and loved it. She'd sung it herself many times.

Words formed within the music, sung by a virtuoso, a Master of the art—a voice she loved so well.

Love? Yes, she remembered even that. A painful wrench twisted at the heart she no longer had, a wrench of loss and longing.

The singer came closer and she felt again the swirl. These, then, were *identities*; beings within this place of no substance, this melting-pot of spirit, of creation. And she recognized the spirit drifting beside her.

Fiann.

She felt the caress of a mind, and it was the answering voice of the bard. She felt his melodic response, his acknowledgement of her naming. She felt gratitude for a service lovingly rendered, the final service she had performed for him. And with her acceptance of his gratitude came the knowledge, once again, of her own *self*. She felt a gentle, companionable thrill as if of fingers resting on the skin she no longer inhabited. She smiled.

As the essence of the Sinnian bard drifted away and out of her ken, more memories returned.

✤ ✤ ✤ ✤ ✤

Within moments, Taran was drenched to the skin. He'd left a sweltering summer climate and was dressed only in a light cotton shirt and breeches. He carried no cloak. He was fortunate to be wearing soft boots instead of the thin house shoes they normally wore within the palace. The torrential downpour soaked him through, causing him to shiver. He cursed under his breath. This was a fool's errand, he was bound to fail, and he would probably catch pneumonia into the bargain. He guided Bucyrus morosely toward the cluster of village roofs he could just make out half a mile away down the rain-soaked road.

It was early evening and the rainstorm had driven the villagers into their homes. Taran rode down the empty street, reaching within himself for the familiar pattern of Robin's psyche in the scant hope the Major was here. Then he realized that not only was Robin likely to be shielding, but that if Taran announced his presence, Robin would surely avoid him before he got to tell him why he had come. Fighting down his sense of urgency, Taran slid to the ground before the first house he came to and pounded on the door.

He heard an irascible voice before the door was jerked open. The aging farmer standing in the hallway eyed Taran with dislike and suspicion, taking in his sodden and inappropriate clothing and the dejected but clearly valuable stallion at his back.

"What d'you want? We don't take in strangers."

Taran answered the farmer's suspicion with terseness. "I'm looking for Robin Tamsen. It's very urgent. Do you know if he's here?"

"Maybe I do and maybe I don't. Why should I tell you?"

"Because his wife and child could *die* if you don't! Is that reason enough for you?"

The farmer stared at him, undecided. The villagers were rightly suspicious of strangers who didn't have the sense to dress for the weather and who came demanding information it wasn't their business to know.

"Try the smith," he said curtly, slamming the door in Taran's face. Biting back a curse, the Adept swung into his mount's soaked saddle, heartily wishing the stallion would dump something appropriate onto the farmer's doorstep. Bucyrus didn't oblige.

Taran urged him down the street. The village wasn't large or wealthy. Much of the thatch needed repair and some of the cottages looked empty. Only a few showed the glow of lamplight, casting a faint cheer into the slanting rain.

Soon, Taran halted his mount at the forge's open doors and dismounted. Thankful to get out of the wet, he led the stallion inside.

The forge was at the rear of the shop, the blaze of fire hard in Taran's eyes after the gloom. A boy sat at the bellows kicking his heels. He glanced up disinterestedly as Taran came forward. Something about the boy caught Taran's attention. He was about fifteen or so, tall, and had dark curly hair. Taran couldn't see the color of his eyes, but he'd take a bet they were dark blue.

The smith, well-built and muscular if not particularly tall, looked up from the ax blade he was grinding to cast a practiced eye over Taran's dripping horse.

"Come for shoes, friend? You'll have to wait a while. At least it's dry in here."

The smith's amiable tone went some way toward alleviating the irritation the farmer had raised in Taran, but he was in no mood for idle conversation.

"Not shoes, master smith, information." He tried not to sound curt. His fright over Sullyan and his distaste for his errand was making him snappy.

The smith's eyes narrowed and he turned an evaluating gaze on Taran. "Oh yes?"

"I'm looking for Robin Tamsen. I'm from the Manor and my business is extremely urgent. Do you know where I can find him?"

The boy at the bellows started when he heard Robin's name and Taran knew his guess was correct. The boy, at least, was a relative.

The smith laid the ax aside and came closer, watching Taran steadily. Not quite threatening, yet not easy, either. "And what would you be wanting our Rob for?"

Taran allowed his need to leak into his voice. "I need to speak to him on a very urgent matter. Please tell me where I can find him."

"He came here to get away from your lot," growled the smith, turning dismissively away. "I don't know what you've done to him, but he's a shadow of what he used to be. Won't talk to any of us, and he won't talk to you, neither. You'd best leave."

Taran had been afraid of this. How could he convince the man of the urgency of his mission?

With the truth, of course.

"I really do need to talk to him. It's about his wife—"

The smith whirled around, a strange light in his eyes. Taran couldn't tell whether it was born of friendship or censure. "Sullyan? What do you know of her?"

Taran trusted to the former. "She's a very close friend of mine. As is ... or was ... Robin. She's in dire need right now. I'll be honest with you, master smith. She's dying. She may already be dead. And her unborn son with her."

The smith's eyes darkened in shock and his ruddy face paled. "Her *son*?" he breathed. "Robin's son?"

"Well, of course Robin's son!" Taran suddenly feared the awful rumors that had so blighted their lives had reached even this remote and insignificant village. "Didn't he tell you?"

The smith rubbed his rough face in confusion. "No. He won't tell us anything. Is that why he's in such a state? Why would fathering a child send him into such black despair?"

"It's a long story, and one we don't have time for right now," said Taran grimly. "And if you don't tell me where I can find him, he might have neither wife nor son anymore!"

The smith blew out a long breath. "All right, all right. He told us not to speak to anyone who might come looking for him, but something about you makes me want to trust you, so I'll tell you and just hope you're not dealing false with me. You'll likely find him up at the chapel. He's been spending a lot of time up there recently. His ma's that worried about him and she's not strong—"

"Are you his father, then? I can see your boy there resembles him." Taran swung up onto Bucyrus, ducking his head away from the ceiling.

"Uncle. That's his cousin, Darra. Robin's father died a year ago. You'll find the old chapel a mile or so up the road. Take the southerly track. It's a bit overgrown, but you'll find it right enough. If he's not there he'll be off by himself somewhere, and I can't help you more."

Taran thanked the man as he urged Bucyrus out of the forge and sent him down the sodden road in the lessening rain. The true gloom of evening was beginning to fall and the countryside around the village was growing indistinct. Taran prayed he would find Robin at the chapel. He didn't want to waste precious time in a fruitless search of the dusky fields and woods. He pushed Bucyrus into a gallop.

Chapter Twenty-Eight

The bard's gentle music echoed through her half-conscious soul long after the spirit of her old friend had left her. Its undemanding strains brought her to remember pleasure and laughter, companionship and loyalty. She tried to push them away, but the more she tried to deny them, the more insistently they demanded to be acknowledged. She didn't want to remember; she wanted to lie here, in this haven of peace and serenity, cradled in the rebirth and absorption of life, not thinking, not feeling, not *hurting*.

They wouldn't go away, those insistent memories. Once revived, her awareness of who she was couldn't be denied. Once reawakened, she couldn't send her soul back to sleep.

Discontented, she drifted, unable to regain a state of oneness with the substance of the world. Another shimmering began beside her, another disturbance of her peace. She felt a familiar touch on her mind, one she had never thought to feel again, and more memories came flooding into her psyche.

These memories weren't pleasant. They were filled with grief for a life cut short, and sorrow for a strong and loyal friendship denied the fulfillment of its course. Yet behind the pain was a sensation of pride in achievement, of satisfaction, of the peace that comes from atonement and the gratification of succeeding where others could not. And then she recognized the spirit that exuded these seemingly contradictory emanations.

Torman Vanyr?

She felt amazement, and a sudden rush of diffident love, as if this particular spirit hadn't expected to be remembered.

Ah, Torman, my friend! How could I ever forget?

The pain vanished, the regret and sorrow washed away. She shouldn't have been able to weep, but she did. The warmth radiating from Torman Vanyr's steadfast spirit cut through the numbness that had crept into her being and gently but irresistibly nudged her farther away from the sucking Void that had been her goal. She began to plead.

Let me go, Torman! You do not know what you ask. I cannot return—it is too hard....

He wouldn't desist. As she had cradled his dying body until he slipped beyond the world, so he surrounded her now, unrelenting until she yielded to his will and drifted silently beside him, companionable and unresisting. Soon, and before she was ready, she felt him depart.

This was like the first loss. She saw again his poor, ruined face as she'd held him, heedless of the blood, tears falling from her eyes, her heart contracting in sorrow. Yet now she felt anger. Why could she not be left alone? Why must she constantly relive this heartache, this almost unbearable grief? Why must she be hurt all the time? Had she not suffered enough? It wasn't fair. Why couldn't they let her sleep?

Closing her inner eyes on the soft gray of her insubstantial surroundings, she willed herself toward the Void once more.

✣ ✣ ✣ ✣ ✣

Surrounded by majestic beeches and covered in moss, a beautiful little stone chapel nestled in the center of a clearing. From its neglected air it was obvious it was seldom frequented. It was a neat, square building with a thatched porch which had seen better days, and a stout oaken front door which stood slightly ajar. There were no windows at the front, but Taran could see two or three along its sides. The chapel's air of abandonment and the twilit silence of the beech woods lent the place a calm and peaceful feel. Taran could appreciate why someone would choose to come here for solace.

The blood-bay beneath him gave a soft whicker. Taran heard the reply that set Bucyrus's ears twitching. He dismounted and allowed the horse to pull him forward. It led him around the eastern side of the chapel, and there, beneath the scant shelter of a wooden lean-to, Taran saw Torka's familiar white face standing out in the evening gloom. The Adept led his mount over to the chestnut, hoping the two stallions wouldn't take a dislike to each other. He needn't have worried. Torka looked only too happy to have company and Bucyrus had never yet shown any inclination to be hostile. Taran tethered the beast beside the chestnut and patted his damp neck.

He retraced his steps to the doorway of the chapel and peered around the open door. It was dark inside; no candle or lamp lit the damp-smelling interior. As his eyes grew accustomed to the darkness, Taran could see no sign of Robin. The chapel was empty. Puzzled, Taran withdrew.

If not within the chapel, he thought, then where? Robin couldn't be far away, not with Torka tethered there. Cautiously, Taran circled the moss-covered chapel.

At the rear of the building he came upon a crumbling wooden palisade fence. It surrounded an area that once, in times past, had been cleared but was fast being reclaimed by the woods. There had even been a gate at one time, but what was left of it hung askew. He passed it by. The area was large and trees had grown up within it, but there was one section that had clearly been tended, and fairly recently too.

Standing in this section, his back to Taran, head bowed, arms wrapped tightly about his chest, was Robin Tamsen.

Taran soon understood why Robin had chosen to come here. As he came nearer, still undiscovered, he could see a simple wooden grave-marker in the form of a wheel, set upright within the grass. It was gray and weathered with the years. Beside it stood a second marker, this one newer, and Robin stood staring at them both through blank and red-rimmed eyes.

Taran stopped a few paces off. He was still unnoticed and he hesitated. He didn't want to alarm or shock Robin out of his reverie, yet his business was urgent and he couldn't delay. He drew in a breath.

"Robin."

He'd pitched his voice deliberately low but still the younger man gave a cry of shock. He spun to face him. Taran couldn't bite back a gasp of his own for he barely recognized the young Major. Robin had lost weight and his once so-handsome face was hollow and lined. His eyes were bruised and bloodshot, and circled with dark shadows. His clothes hung limply on him and they were none too clean. The words of the smith echoed in Taran's mind and he could well understand why "his ma was that worried." Like Taran, Robin was soaked to the skin, and he shivered as he stared uncomprehendingly at the Adept, although whether from the cold or some other deep emotion, Taran couldn't tell.

"Taran!" The voice rasped harsh and sounded long unused. The tone was downright hostile. "What the hell are you doing here?" Robin's initial shock wore off and his terrible eyes grew hard. "Get out of here. Go away and leave me alone! Can't I even visit my sister's grave in peace? Go on, get out! You have no business here." He made a curt, dismissive gesture with one hand and turned his back.

Taran took another breath, grieving for Robin's pain but unable to spare him. He had no time. "Robin, you have to come with me."

Robin spat a vicious obscenity, the kind of words he never used. Taran ignored it.

"I'm not taking no for an answer, Major. You're needed in Andaryon. Sullyan's in labor and it's not going well. She needs you. She'll die without you—they both will."

He spoke urgently, quickly, and came a step nearer. He could see the tremor of the Major's body clearly and hear his labored, gasping breath. Yet Robin said nothing.

Taran grew angry. "Major! Didn't you hear what I said? She *needs* you! You have to come!"

Robin broke, rounding furiously on Taran. "She doesn't need me! I'm the last person she needs! She has *you*. You go and help her. *I* don't have the right. I wouldn't be any use anyway. What have I ever done except bring her trouble? She's better off without me!"

Taran stared at his frantic expression, at the eyes so wild and strange. His face was white, so white it seemed ghostly in that field of the long-dead. Taran groaned inwardly. He had feared this. Rienne should have come; she'd have been able to reach him, to convince him. He'd have seen her compassion and believed her.

Taran had no compassion to break through Robin's despair. He only had two weapons available to him and he realized he'd have to use them both. Slowly and deliberately, his face grim with determination, he drew his sword.

He saw the shock as Robin's gaze flicked to the length of shining steel. Then his years of training took over and he locked eyes with Taran. The hint of strangeness disappeared behind a calculating gaze as he instinctively reached for his own sword.

Taran had no intention of fighting Robin, not with cold steel, anyway. His action was a feint, a cover, while he prepared his other offensive. For once taking full account of Sullyan's advice and teaching, Taran drew strongly on the Fire of his passions—his anger, his frustration and the desperate urging of his love for the tawny-haired Artesan which was screaming at him to *hurry*! It was all passion, all spirit, and he merged his psyche with it, focusing it into one powerful, unstoppable bolt of metaforce which he hurled at Robin even as the younger man's hand was reaching for his sword.

Shielded though he was, Robin was concentrating on the threat of Taran's steel. This new attack caught him completely off guard. He was unaware of Taran's raised status and even if he had been, he wouldn't have expected this base and treacherous move. Taran's titanic bolt of force smashed through his inadequate defenses and battered his beleaguered brain. It exploded into his mind with raging images, the foremost being the dreadful sight of Sullyan as Taran had last seen her.

This was simply too much for the wounded Major. With a cry, he collapsed to the ground, both hands clamped to his head, an agony of Fire in his mind. Taran dampened his power instantly, shocked and alarmed. He'd never expected to break through so easily or he wouldn't have used such force. He'd realized the only way he could convince Robin of the truth was to make him *see*, to speak to his mind as only an Artesan could, in such a way that he couldn't refute. He'd expected Robin to block him out, which was why he'd employed such underhanded tactics. Yet with Robin's collapse, Taran realized another truth. Like Sullyan, the weeks of despair and spiritual sickness had taken their toll on Robin. Like Sullyan, he was weak as a day-old kitten. He had no strength and no defenses left.

"Oh, good gods!" In an agony of dismay for the damage he'd caused, Taran ran to the stricken young man. He reached out again to Robin's psyche, this time with soothing and calming support. He met with no resistance and poured strength into Robin until the Major dropped his hands, his face streaming tears. Taran forced the younger man to look at him.

"Oh, gods, Robin! I'm so sorry. I didn't mean to … I didn't realize, and I should have done, after Sullyan, but I was so scared you'd not believe me, that you'd refuse to come … Are you all right?"

Damn stupid question!

Taran aided Robin to his feet. The Major appeared confused and bewildered. He was still trembling.

"You're soaking wet," Robin mumbled.

The incongruity of the statement brought a short bark of laughter from Taran's lips. "Well, so are you! That's what you get for standing out in a rainstorm."

They stared at each other for a swift second that felt like it went on forever. Taran saw things in Robin's eyes that the young man needed to say, but now was not the time. For an uncomfortable moment, Taran feared Robin's mind was too overloaded to cope with what he'd seen in Taran's clumsy exchange of images. His next question brought relief flooding into the Adept even while his heart constricted in panic.

"Taran, that image you showed me … was it true?"

"Oh gods, yes! Robin, we have to go. We might be too late, even now. Can you ride?"

Robin nodded and suffered himself to be led toward the horses. It was nearly dark by now, but Torka's white face and Bucyrus's white star stood out like beacons in the failing light. Taran helped Robin up onto his mount and then sprang into his own saddle. For want of something to say—their real purpose and the unresolved issues between them being yet too painful to voice—Robin studied the bay with surprised but appreciative eyes.

"My word, that's a handsome horse, Taran. Where on earth did you get it?"

Taran replied shortly. "He was a gift from the King." He

tossed the startled Robin a glance. "Long story. Look, have you the strength to open a tunnel? If not, Anjer will—"

"Let him." Robin's weary voice, even the line of his body, betrayed his exhaustion. Taran sent out a swift call.

They spurred the horses onto the track. Taran's link with Anjer allowed the Lord General to open the substrate right across their path. The light of it shimmered and died, leaving the moss-covered chapel deserted and silent once more.

✠ ✠ ✠ ✠ ✠

She was determined to succeed this time. She would heed no more spirits, no matter how well-loved they might be, no matter how they called to her. She walled off the vulnerable well of her emotions, hardened the heart she no longer had, set her purpose to her goal and fixed her will upon it.

It seemed she would be successful this time. She could feel the pull of the Void coming closer. Just a little farther. She became aware of movement around her, but steadfastly ignored it. They would not divert her again. She would not succumb to the snare of old love, of friendships past. She would refuse them all.

And so she did, until there came before her one against whom she had no defenses. One whose gentle and undemanding presence had more power to move her than all of those before.

Her resolve crumbled away. The Void lost its clinging attraction and became a place of fear. It appeared as a great whirlpool of life force, leaching, sucking, stealing. Not a safe haven of peace, but a seething maelstrom of confusion. In fear and bewilderment, she looked to this new spirit for guidance, accepting strength and comfort as she herself had given it nearly four years before.

The gentle spirit that had once been Robin's beloved sister, Jessy, led her friend away from danger, away from untimely oblivion. As she followed, Sullyan's psyche slowly became aware that her surroundings were changing.

The soft, featureless gray that was the limbo before the Void was taking on substance. It was indescribable. It had no color, no sounds, no scents—it was just *different*. It was another place, a place where the Void held no sway.

Then, it changed again. She was walking now rather than drifting. And she could see. Before her walked another, one she recognized, although in life she had never seen her walk. The figure she followed was as slender as Sullyan herself, and slightly taller. The long, dark, curling hair was exactly as she remembered it, held back by the colored silk ribbons Robin often brought her. Following, Sullyan recalled time spent brushing that silken mass, taking simple pleasure in the fact that it brought comfort to the stricken young girl. She halted.

Jessy?

There was a momentary hesitation. Jessy made a beckoning gesture, and then she moved on. Suddenly fearful of losing her guide, Sullyan hastened to catch up. She quailed at the thought of being left alone in this strange place.

Abruptly, with no discernable transition, they stood within a room. It was nowhere she had ever been before. It was a plain room, unadorned, with white walls and a white floor. It had an insubstantial air, yet she could feel the floor beneath her feet. When she looked down, she could even see her feet. She raised her head and looked about.

As if summoned by her act of looking, they were all there. She saw Huw, recognizing him by his mismatched eyes, for she would never have known him else. This was Huw as he would have been—should have been if not for the accident of his birth. Tall, slim, no hump upon his back, his two feet hale and whole. His face was fine-featured and handsome, and he smiled at her. With a sudden rush of love, she smiled back.

There was Fiann, revealed as the lord she'd always known him to be; regal, majestic, commanding, yet gentle and unassuming. He held his harp in his arms—the harp she had sent to the Fire with his body—and he fingered the strings, sounding out the music of her soul. She held out a hand to him and he bowed his head in approving silence.

She saw another figure, lithe and loose-limbed, the all-white eyes hard to read as they fixed on hers. The aura of danger that was so much a part of who he had been and which had always emanated from him was still evident, but so was the assurance that it could never be turned on her. His gratitude and his love for her shone forth, bathing her in waves of friendship and trust.

He didn't speak. None of them spoke.

She turned at last to the one who waited patiently beside her, watching her quietly. Jessy's warm blue eyes, lighter in shade than her brother's, sparkled with the life she'd lost too soon, and they smiled her love into the golden eyes that gazed back in wonder. She stood happy and proud, as she'd never been in life, radiating thankfulness, approval and … something else. Anticipation?

Jessy?

We greet you, Brynne Sullyan. We're very pleased you've come back.

Jessy's gentle voice, a treasured memory for so long, broke another barrier within Sullyan. She accepted back her name, and all that went with it. She felt whole again, although until now she hadn't been aware of her fragmentation. She raised tear-filled eyes.

Oh, Jessy!

Two arms came around her and held her tight as she wept out all her despair, all the self-blame, all the regret, the longing, the fear, and the shame. In a cleansing rush it came out, and when it was gone, it left her spent and helpless. She was held all the while, although it was the sense of presence in her heart, now beating again with warm lifeblood, that gave her the most comfort. And she realized, with a start of shock, that they had always been there, those comforting influences, the source of her strength and control.

Then the pressure of the arms eased and the spirit of Robin's sister stepped back.

Come, Sullyan. Time grows short and there is someone yet you must speak with.

The words sounded in her mind—Jessy's smiling lips didn't move. Sullyan felt her hand clasped and she didn't resist the gentle tug. She followed Jessy and, although her surroundings didn't change, they left the others behind, their eyes watchful. She felt no sense of loss as their figures faded. They were always with her.

Then another presence appeared before her. A thrill of recognition and shock ran the full length of her soul. A woman, delicate and slim, like herself. A fine mane of tawny hair, although not as long as her own. A fine-featured, oval face. Beautiful, warm brown eyes. A welcoming smile that said more than words could ever express. The woman stepped two paces forward, her arms held wide.

Sullyan stopped dead. It just couldn't be.

Mother?

She couldn't believe it. Her mother looked just as Sullyan had always imagined her, even before she'd met Pharikian, who showed her the image of her mother from his own memory. Sullyan swallowed a painful lump, tears coming yet again. Could this be real? Surely she must be dreaming? Suddenly, she was afraid.

Oh, Brynne, my dear, dear child! It really is me, you mustn't be afraid. Come closer, touch me. Your heart will know.

Hesitantly, still fearful that this was just some near-death heart's wish, Sullyan stretched out her right hand. She brushed the older woman's fingers. As soon as she made contact, she knew the truth. Bethyn was right. She was an empath, her spirit spoke truly to that of her daughter. Sullyan flung herself with joyful and emotional abandon into the yearned-for embrace of her mother.

They held each other so long. Spirits cannot truly weep, yet Bethyn's face was damp when they finally managed to let each other go. They stood at arm's length, gazing into each other's eyes.

Oh, my dearest child! I have yearned for so long to hold you like this. You cannot know how much it means to me.

But how? Mother, how is this possible?

Bethyn's aura sobered. She stood farther back, still not releasing her daughter's hand, her face serious.

Brynne, my love, you are in grave danger, and your child with you. You have been near to death, so very near. Indeed, if not for the fear and love of your friends, we would have lost you to the Void. You have very strong friends, Brynne! It was Huw's spirit, Huw's great strength that allowed a way to be opened for them to reach you. We have been granted a boon, a brief time of being, to come here to this place and strengthen your spirit, just long enough to give you the will to return where you belong. Our time here is short; even now it is nearly over. It is time for you to go back, Brynne.

Sullyan wailed in dismay, like a lost child. *But I cannot go back! I want to stay here. I have had to endure so much suffering, so much more than I can bear. Can I not stay here with you? Oh, Mother, I have been so alone!*

Bethyn smiled sadly. *My dear child, you have* never *been alone. You have been watched over, steadfastly and lovingly, ever since the day you were born. If you search the depths of your heart, you will find you have always known this.*

Sullyan looked deeply into Bethyn's warm brown eyes, seeing no censure, only pride and love and a fierce desire to protect. That desire, she recognized. *Yes* ...

You have many yet in the world of substance who love you most dearly, Bethyn continued, holding her daughter's gaze, *and one who loves you more dearly than he loves life itself. We want you to know that we approve of your young man, my child. He is worthy of you, and you of him.*

Sullyan's heart shattered. *But I have lost him, Mother! I betrayed his trust and love and our union is broken. We can never go back to the way it was. It is ruined—destroyed—and I cannot bear it ...*

Hush, child, oh, hush, soothed Bethyn, taking her distraught daughter in her arms once again, causing memories of all the times Sullyan had yearned for such comfort to flood into her heart. *Ah, my Brynne, you are wise in the ways of your power—so loyal and true and knowledgeable in the ways of the world. But in the ways of love, you are yet a little girl. Nothing stays the same forever. Didn't you know that? Life is change. People change, things change, and it is wrong of us to desire it to be otherwise. We grow, and as we grow, our love must grow with us. If it does not, then we fall out of love, and it withers and dies. But if it is true love, if it is the love of the soul, then it will weather the change and grow ever stronger. You must not fight it. You must allow it to grow and to change, for then it becomes unbreakable, it becomes the bond between spirits, and such a bond transcends even death.*

I have known such a love twice in my life. It is this love that permits me to stand before you now. I never wanted to leave you. I tried with all the strength of my body not to leave you. But my body was too frail for the task. It could not stand the strain and I was forced to let go. I have never stopped loving you and I never ceased to watch over you. And your father felt the same. Even though his body, too, failed at the final test, his love has never failed. It has surrounded and protected you all your life. I know that you have felt this.

And yet you thought yourself abandoned. This could not be further from the truth. Neither of us abandoned you, although your father has never forgiven himself for failing to find the strength to live for you. He wanted me to tell you that he is proud—oh, so proud!—of what you have become, and he pledges to watch over you always. And now that you have your young man, and your son, we know that at last you will have what you deserve and your life will be fulfilled.

Bethyn's eyes seemed to grow huge, their brown warmth surrounding Sullyan. *But now, it is time for you to go. You don't belong here, Brynne. Your time is not yet over. You are so strong, my beautiful daughter, and you will become stronger still. You have tasks that yet await you in the world of substance, as well as those who love you and depend upon you. But when your time is done, and if you are true, then this I will pledge you. You will return to us here and reunite with us once more. I will yearn and pray for that day. You are the daughter of my heart and you have all my love. Brynne, my beloved child, never forget ...*

As she spoke, Bethyn's image faded, the white room fading too. It was too soon, Sullyan wasn't ready. Wasn't there one more ...?

But there was silence. She was alone. Her heart constricted with sorrow and loss. She had thought ... she had hoped ... and so she called.

Father? Will you not speak to me? Father!

Of all those she had loved and lost, his was the one presence she yearned for now. Her mother had spoken true; she had always known he watched over her. It had given her strength enough to endure some of her greatest trials. The absence of parents had always been a source of pain as well as a source of strength. She'd had to fight from a very early age for what others had as right, and this had taught her to be confident, self-sufficient, and strong. Yet it had also hurt her and caused her much heartache. In order to complete the process her friends had begun, in order to face what she must on her return, she needed this last contact. She called again, a forlorn child crying out from her abandonment.

Please! Oh, Father, please!

And finally, she was answered.

Brynne, my beloved daughter. How can you ever forgive me?

She gasped. She had thought he wouldn't come. With her mind, she reached out and touched a presence insubstantial as mist yet as pervading and enveloping as love itself. She touched a power akin to hers, felt a pattern so like hers, so closely matched that she could have worn it like a glove, could have told out the whorls, the loops, the spirals, and twists of it as she could have told her own.

She sensed reluctance and also a deep well of sorrow. Her father had never forgiven himself for leaving her. She felt her soul fill with compassion.

Father! she cried, and instinctively meshed the intricacies of her psyche with his, this being the only way she could think of to show him how little she blamed him. He tried to resist, but she was the stronger. His shame made him weak—her forgiveness lent her strength. And so she became one with him, as should always have been, and she shared her innermost feelings, her gratitude for her life, her love for him and her mother, and received back from him the same, mixed with his incredible pride in her achievements.

And so it was that her all-encompassing, unconditional forgiveness healed the breach in Morgan's soul, undid the tearing of his spirit, and made him whole. She basked in his love until she knew no more.

Chapter Twenty-Nine

"**G**ood gods, Robin, you look dreadful. Whatever have you done to yourself?"

Rienne's cry of concern caught Robin right in the heart. Taran could see that her instinctive rush to hug him only made matters worse.

"Rienne, I ..." Robin choked on the words, his heart too sore, too full.

Taran stepped forward. "Rienne, give him some space. Let him breathe."

Rienne let him go and stepped back. Her face was pale, full of concern and worry, and Taran suddenly feared the worst. "Oh no," he blurted, "is she—"

"Still holding on." Her voice was hoarse. "The gods alone know how. Her heartbeat's so faint it's almost not there and I can't hear the baby at all. Deshan and Pharikian are still linked to her, but they can't last much longer."

She cast a look at Robin, taking in the pallor of his skin and his terrible weakness. She shook her head in dismay. "And you're no better. Look at you! You're soaked through, the pair of you. And you're filthy," she told Robin. "What use are you like that? I'm not letting you anywhere near her until you've changed. Go on, both of you. Taran, you can lend Robin some clean clothes, can't you? But hurry, poor Deshan's nearly dead on his feet."

Rienne's all-too-familiar bossiness in the area of her expertise, and the fact she could scold them into changing clothes at a time like this, made Robin choke again. To rescue him, Taran took his arm and led him into the small room where he'd been sleeping. He helped him strip off his wet things, seeing as he did so the still-puckered scar on his thigh where Parren's sword had sliced into him, and the other, less serious, scars of that fatal duel.

He didn't comment. Wordlessly, he helped the dazed young man into a clean shirt and breeches, thankful they were much the same size. Once Taran was warm and dry also, he turned to lead Robin back to Rienne. The young Major held back.

"Gods, Taran, what does she expect me to do?"

His voice was low, his tone hopeless, and the tremor of his limbs caused Taran's heart to constrict with pity. He knew what Robin feared. What if there was nothing he *could* do? What if he lost them both? How would he live with the pain? With sudden insight, Taran knew he couldn't. It would be too much.

Trying for strength to encourage the younger man, he said, "Come and try. If it's meant to be, there'll be a way. If not...."

Robin stared from hopeless eyes. Rienne was awaiting them impatiently. She turned without a word and preceded them into Sullyan's chamber. The two men followed.

There had been no change since Taran had left two hours earlier. Pharikian still sat hunched on the bed, his unresponsive face white with strain. Deshan sat by Sullyan's side, one hand on her brow, sweat beading his face, his eyes vacant. Aeyron was at her other side, clasping one cold and lifeless hand. He alone looked up as Robin reluctantly entered the room and stopped dead, the blood draining from his face, shock and horror clearly visible in his eyes.

They should have warned him, thought Taran belatedly. He'd forgotten that the last time Robin had seen Sullyan her pregnancy wasn't visible. Now, here she lay; limp, lifeless, her belly large with his child, both potentially lost to him. Taran could understand and sympathize with the sudden flood of tears that spilled from Robin's eyes.

"Oh, my sweet love."

The words were a hoarse whisper as he moved toward the bed, totally unconscious of anyone else in the room. Aeyron stood and moved aside, releasing the small, cold hand. Robin took his place.

He sat carefully on the bed, placing a trembling hand on the swell of her belly, caressing the soft skin, his eyes full of wonder. Rienne moved to the foot of the bed, watching intently. Robin's other hand came to rest above Sullyan's heart. He sat immobile, staring at nothing, his breathing barely discernable, unaware of them all.

Taran came to Rienne's side and put an arm about her shoulders. His own eyes were wide with awe. He sensed something happening, yet didn't know what it was. Rienne stared at the pair on the bed as if she could see what Taran could not. He saw the slight crease of her dark brows and heard her tiny gasp.

Taran wrenched his gaze back to the bed and saw what had caused Rienne's reaction. The fire opal at Sullyan's throat was pulsing, shooting out sparks of reflected fire from the lamplight in the room.

"Yes!" hissed Rienne, leaning forward. "Look, Taran! She took a breath, I'm sure of it. Yes, there's another! Oh gods, Robin, keep it up, whatever you're doing. She's coming back to us!"

Rienne put her fingers to Sullyan's neck, checking her pulse. Taran didn't need her triumphant smile to tell him what she felt. The sparking fire opal that had once belonged to Sullyan's mother was pulsing strongly with the increased beat of her heart, and color was already returning to the pale face. Rienne turned toward him.

"Taran, this is strange. I don't pretend to understand it, but he's done it just by being here. Deshan was right; his presence was all she needed."

The woman on the bed gave a sudden gasp, then moaned. Deshan jerked awake, his eyes coming to life again as he withdrew his power from Sullyan's mind. Pharikian slumped forward as he was released from his thrall, and his son gathered him into his arms.

Rienne laid a hand on the Master Physician's shoulder. "Deshan? I think you ought to look to the Hierarch. He's badly drained. You can leave us to it now. We'll take care of her. She's in safe hands."

With Taran's help, Deshan rose shakily, still not completely aware. Aeyron guided his father as they followed Deshan from the room. Taran and Rienne turned back to Sullyan.

Rienne watched closely as Sullyan's eyes opened. She stirred painfully. Her gaze turned unerringly to the man beside her, his pale, pinched face looking anxiously into hers. She gave another gasp, half of disbelief, half of pain.

"Robin? Oh, *Robin!*"

The young man gave a soft cry and enfolded his love in his arms. Taran felt his eyes prickling. To distract herself from the emotion, Rienne turned her attention to Sullyan's baby. The final stages of labor had just started when Sullyan's strength had given out, and Rienne was still concerned for the baby's health. Taran watched anxiously, but they needn't have worried. When Rienne checked, all appeared to be as it had been, as if the last two hours of Sullyan's life-and-death struggle had never happened.

Taran heard her mutter, "This is so strange," but they both pushed their thoughts aside as a strong contraction wracked Sullyan's body. She heaved with the pain of it.

"Robin! Rob, listen to me!" snapped Rienne, desperate to catch Robin's attention. "She needs your help now. If you want to see your son safely born, you have to do as I tell you. Can you do that?"

Robin nodded. "Just tell me what to do."

Rienne let out a great sigh of relief and began giving Robin instructions.

Taran moved to the door of the living area where the Andaryans had retreated. Aeyron had laid his father on Taran's bed and the Hierarch was sleeping, thoroughly drained by his efforts. The Master Physician sat by the Prince's side, the Andaryans exchanging concerned glances with Taran as the birth progressed.

They could clearly hear Sullyan's cries of pain and Rienne's calm but firm instructions. It seemed that even with Robin by her side, Sullyan could still not access her metaforce. She had to do all the work by herself, as any other woman would. Yet from somewhere she had found the strength to deal with the pain, and the comfort and support of her life mate enabled her to forget her panic at the failure of her powers and concentrate at last on the wonderful process of bringing new life into the world.

Rienne looked exultant. This might be the strangest birth she'd ever attended, but finally all seemed to be going as it should. Taran could see baby's head, and Rienne supported it with warm cloths. They were nearly there.

"Come on, Brynne," urged Rienne. "Only a few more minutes. His shoulders will come next, so be ready to bear down when I tell you. But gently, remember? Control it. Robin, your son's nearly ready to greet his father!"

Sullyan's body contracted again and she pushed at Rienne's command, striving not to let the urge overtake her. "Short and sharp," cautioned Rienne. "Breathe out, Brynne. That's it, we're nearly there!"

The baby's shoulders came through one by one, and Taran could see his little wrinkled face. Rienne looked rapt. He knew this moment always gave her the greatest sense of joy and wonder—the first moment when a new little soul slithered fresh from the womb to start a new and exciting life of his own. Rienne smiled up at Sullyan and Robin with incredible delight.

"Last one, Brynne. Be ready. Breathe deeply ... that's right. Stay calm and focused. Ready? Now, push!"

With a final cry and a tremendous effort, Sullyan gave birth to the tiny soul she had sheltered and nourished for so long. The baby came forth into Rienne's waiting hands with a rush, and she gathered him in the warmed towels she had placed ready. As his mother lay back with a huge sigh of exhaustion and relief, sweat pouring from her, Rienne gently cleaned the infant's face, concerned until he took a great gasp of air all on his own. Immediately, he began to cry.

Taran felt his eyes prickle with joy as Rienne turned to lay the tiny baby on Sullyan's belly. His blue-tinged skin began to change to a bright scarlet as his lungs drew breath and blood pumped through his body. He squirmed weakly, his cries muted now, and Sullyan reached down with tender fingers to touch her newborn son for the very first time.

Robin had his arm around her shoulders, supporting her, tears streaming silently down his face. He couldn't look away from his infant son. The baby reacted to the gentle touch of his mother's hand and tried to squirm higher on her belly. As Rienne tied off the cord, she glanced impishly at the emotional Robin.

"Isn't that just like a man?" she chuckled. "They always go for the breast first."

Robin stared at her and then back at his son in amazement. "What, already? He's barely born!"

Rienne laughed. "If you'd been through what he just has, you'd be hungry, too. Go on, then, Robin. Give him a hand."

Robin seemed too dazed to do anything, almost fearful of the struggling scrap of life still trying to worm his way higher on his mother's belly. Smiling through her exhaustion, Sullyan spoke softly.

"Go on, Robin, touch him. He will not bite. You do not have what he wants right now."

Robin shot her a glance, startled by her loving tone. Then he smiled shyly and reached a trembling hand to his tiny son. He stroked the baby's cheek and the infant turned his head toward Robin's fingers. The tiny puckered mouth moved. Robin's face was a picture of amazement and awe.

"He is, by the gods—he's hungry!"

His startled exclamation brought more gentle laughter. Rienne nodded to the baby meaningfully and the young man gently helped his son toward the breast, where he finally settled, eyes still tightly shut, little mouth working, tiny fists curled by his face.

Rienne busied herself cleaning up. Sullyan and Robin were so absorbed in watching their son feed that the delivery of the afterbirth took Sullyan quite by surprise.

"Oh!" she gasped, and Rienne grinned at her.

"Nothing like your babe's first suckle to blind you to all else around you," she said happily as she tidied it all away.

✣ ✣ ✣ ✣ ✣

Once Sullyan was clean and settled and Robin given instructions to keep an eye on her, Taran and Rienne went through into the other room. The Andaryans had heard the successful outcome of the labor and there were many more tears of joy and thankfulness. Taran enveloped Rienne in a long hug. They were both too overcome to speak for a while, allowing the joy of the moment to sweep away the awful memories of the past few months. A small movement by the door to the bedchamber caused them to part, looking over in query.

Robin stood in the doorway. He was still shaky, but his earlier aspect of exhaustion and distress was buried for the moment by wonder and awe.

"Taran? She's asking for you. Will you come and greet my son? You've looked after them both so well for so long, it's only right that you be the first to meet him."

Taran stared at the young man. The issue between them still needed resolving, but for now they must put it aside. Taran came forward with genuine pleasure to take Robin's hand and offer his congratulations. Robin didn't follow him into Sullyan's room.

The bedchamber was darker now, lit only by a single lamp. A blanket draped around her shoulders, Sullyan lay nestled within a mound of pillows, her face pale and exhausted, yet serene and joyful. Her eyes glowed like warm embers in the lamplight. The baby was still at her breast, but now he had fallen asleep, his tiny body cradled lovingly in his mother's arms, safe, secure, and warm.

Taran approached quietly, his eyes on Sullyan's welcoming smile. Although it must be past midnight now, all traces of tiredness had slipped from him. He came to her side and took the hand she held out to him, feeling all her gratitude and love through the contact with her warm fingers.

"Taran, my dear, dear friend. I can never thank you enough for what you have done this day. All of it. I am forever in your debt."

She pulled him gently down and he sat, returning her smile. "That's thanks enough for any man," he said softly, nodding at the baby, the infant's snuffling breaths just audible as he slumbered. "But I can't deny you gave us all an awful fright."

"I seem to have made a habit of that lately," she said, acknowledgement of his love and concern shining in her eyes. She saw him smiling at the baby. "Touch him, Taran."

He slowly reached out a hand and caressed the baby's downy cheek. The scarlet of his skin had faded now to a healthy pink, and Taran could hardly believe the velvety softness of it. "Hello, little one," he whispered.

He glanced up at Sullyan, his heart skipping a beat at the depth of love in her golden eyes, directed only at him. He had always thought her beautiful, but she had never, he thought, looked quite so serenely beautiful as she did right now. He ducked his head.

"Do you have a name for him yet?" he asked, realizing he had never asked her before.

"Oh yes," she whispered, glancing back down at the dreaming infant. "He has a name."

But she didn't tell him what it was.

✣ ✣ ✣ ✣ ✣

They all had a quiet word with the new mother and admired the peacefully sleeping baby before Rienne finally shooed them all out. The Hierarch laid a grateful hand on Taran's shoulder as he passed him at the door, murmuring words of praise. Deshan swiftly checked Sullyan's health before he left, giving instructions that he should be called if there was need. Both Taran and Rienne knew it wasn't the services of a physician that were required now to heal what must be healed. Rienne gave Taran a pointed look as she made for the door.

Robin went with them and Taran thought he would say something, but, in the end, Rienne didn't give him the chance.

"You have other concerns now, Robin. I'm within call if you're worried about the baby, but it's Sullyan who needs you most right now. Go to her. And, Robin, keep her off the fellan for a few days, if you can. Goodnight."

She tugged Taran along with her as she left, pulling the door decisively shut behind her. Robin was left within, looking lost and uncertain.

Taran eyed her worriedly as they walked into the suite across the darkened hallway. "Are you sure that was wise? Can they deal with all of that as well as a newborn?"

Rienne replied with finality. "It's now or never. Believe me, this is the best time. They have a very good reason now to mend what was broken between them. Let's just pray they find the strength."

Taran tried to feel hopeful, but his deep love for them both and his awareness of the depleted state they currently suffered from gave him grave doubts. He saw Rienne into the room she usually used and then turned down the lamp in the living area before seeking his old room. He was sitting on the bed, trying to make up his mind to sleep, when a gently questing thought found his wakeful mind.

Taran?

He started, fearful there was something wrong, but there was only exhaustion in Sullyan's mental tone.

There is much that Robin and I must say to each other—much that will be painful to relive. It may take some time. Will you see we are not disturbed? And will you look after Rienne for me and shield her as best you can? This must be done, but it will be very difficult for her as she is too closely bonded to me for her not to feel it. I am too drained to protect her as I should. Will you watch over her for me?

He didn't really understand what she was saying, but he agreed to shield Rienne whenever he was waking. Satisfied with his compliance, Sullyan left him in peace. He finally fell into a deep slumber, worn out by emotion and the incredible events of the day. None of them even realized it was Midsummer Day.

�֍ ✛ ✛ ✛ ✛

For three days there was no sign of them, and no sound from their suite. Taran heeded his instructions and let no one disturb their privacy. He spoke to Aeyron, who had taken over from his father to enable Pharikian to recover from his ordeal, and the tall

Prince stationed Norkis outside the suite to guard their right to peace.

Food was regularly brought and placed outside the door. Once each morning the tray disappeared, to return empty later in the evening. Norkis never said a word about who collected it or who returned it. He was tight-lipped and faithful to his service.

Aeyron spread the news of the birth around the palace, but not yet in the town. People came, hoping for a glimpse of the newborn, but word soon got around that they were to be left alone and the curious kept their distance. Taran knew there'd be a joyful celebration planned once this seclusion was over. He just hoped there'd be every reason for it.

Rienne was his concern and his work during those three intense and emotionally-charged days. He stayed by her side, shielding her from the worst of the pain and the tears. She was so intimately twinned with Sullyan's soul that what the younger woman felt and experienced during that time, Rienne did too.

It was clear from Rienne's reactions that Sullyan and Robin were delving deep into their own distress and hurt, talking out all their despair, reliving each betrayal and every wrong. Taran understood why they were doing it, and so did Rienne. She often smiled up at Taran after a particularly bitter bout of tears, and by this he knew the new parents had overcome yet another obstacle to the healing of their love.

But it was very hard on Rienne, who had her own health and pregnancy to think about. Taran often looked with deep sympathy at the dark circles under Rienne's eyes and rocked her soothingly when the pain became too much.

Taran kept in touch with Bull and Cal when he wasn't too involved in shielding Rienne. Both men were desperate to come to the Citadel, but he held them off. He told them they should wait until the breach between Sullyan and Robin was resolved one way or the other. And late on the third day, he had a graphic indication of what that outcome was to be.

The day had held less of pain and more of acceptance than the previous two. Rienne had only been overtaken by tears twice, although one of those times was a storm of weeping so intense Taran feared as much for her ability to bear it as for what might have caused it. Although she was unable to speak once it passed, Rienne's smiling face assured Taran it had been a good thing, a cleansing thing. He was hopeful.

In the warmth of the early evening, they sat together in Rienne's room, enjoying the cessation of emotional trauma and beginning to hope for an end. Taran had his arm companionably about Rienne's shoulders, not thinking about anything in particular.

She turned to him suddenly, and stared deeply into his eyes.

Before he could stop her, before he even knew what she was doing, she'd taken his mouth with hers. She kissed him urgently, her hands upon his body as his arms tightened about her, pulling her to him. He was overcome by a deep, all-consuming desire that seemed to come from outside himself, and Rienne responded as passionately. They were lost, helpless and drowning in lust.

It was Rienne's unborn child who saved them. The baby took exception to the pressure of Taran's body so close, or maybe the tiny awareness recognized he was not her father. Whatever the reason, the result was the same. She kicked her mother—hard.

"Oh!" Rienne gasped. She pulled back from Taran, hands massaging her belly.

"My gods! Rienne? Are you all right?"

Taran stared at her, aghast. She stared back and he blushed furiously, shocked at their behavior, realizing what must have happened. He stood, thoroughly embarrassed, frantically calling on his recently-learned control to block out the Fire he could feel raging through his body. It was the hardest thing he'd ever done.

When he finally regained control and was able to face her again, he saw she understood. She seemed to feel no shame for her lapse and didn't blame him for his. Her eyes were as dilated as Sullyan's when expending power and he hastily reached out to shield her from the effects of Sullyan's passion.

"No, Taran. Don't."

"But—"

"It's all right. Don't worry about me, I'll be fine. I'm just … oh, good gods!"

She fled into her bedchamber, slamming the door behind her. Taran stared after her, extremely relieved he had persuaded Cal to stay at the Manor. Although if he had been here....

The Adept sighed, trying valiantly to think about nothing. The waves of passion flooding the substrate were just too strong, and he was forced to resort to the bottle of brandy sitting on the table. He reflected wryly that he had much to thank Rienne's unborn child for.

Chapter Thirty

When Robin and Sullyan ended their voluntary seclusion, their closeness and strength in each other and the depth of their reborn love was so obvious that no one ever referred to the rift. Robin was treated like a long-lost son, but as the focus of attention soon shifted to the baby, he was spared any great embarrassment.

The celebrations planned for the welcoming of a new royal babe into the House of Pharikian were huge. Robin was bemused by them. He was only just coming to terms with the idea he was wed to a Princess and that he had acquired a father-by-marriage who was a King. Now he also had to accept he was the father of the Hierarch of Andaryon's first grandchild. It took some doing.

Taran could immediately see the young man had changed. Robin's dreadful experiences had matured him even more. His brush with losing all he held dear had sobered him, all the more so because the loss would have been by his own hand. The hotheaded, impetuous youth he had once been was now replaced by a calmer head and a stronger spirit. Taran thought the change suited him. It was as if he had shed a skin that didn't quite fit and had finally grown into the man he was always meant to be.

His tiny, delicate son gained weight rapidly. He had a dark mop of hair which looked as if it might curl, but in some lights it was possible to see tints of red and gold. His eyes began to settle to a dark blue, like his father's, but there were also flecks of gold deep within.

Robin spent much of his time with his son, trying to get used to the idea of fatherhood. Neither he nor Sullyan had enjoyed the usual length of time to accustom themselves to the thought of a child, and neither had believed such a gift was possible, given her history. Yet here he was, a quiet, calm baby who only seemed to cry or grow fretful when he was hungry, and who loved to be held and handled by as many people as cared to pick him up.

The day before the celebrations, Taran took a break from the endless details of organization and went for a walk through the palace gardens. He strolled among the flower beds and out toward the barracks. Sitting on a low wall in the shade, he pitied the sweating men on the training ground. The sight reminded him of the Manor and brought to mind something Sullyan had said to him earlier in the day. She was concerned for his health after his protracted stay in Andaryon and had told him he couldn't remain here much longer.

He was in two minds about leaving. He missed Cal and Bull and the routine of his life at the Manor, but it would be a wrench to leave Sullyan. He had no idea what her future plans were. And also, he remembered guiltily, there was Jinella.

Taran thought often about the blonde woman, and the promise he had made to her. Here in Andaryon, by Sullyan's side, Jinella held little attraction for him. Yet when he thought more deeply, he realized there was a spark of something at the memory of the kiss they had shared. He owed it to both of them to explore this potential relationship. It wouldn't be what he most desired, but he already knew he could never have that.

Coming out of his thoughts, he registered a presence beside him. He was surprised Robin had been able to approach and sit beside him without alerting him. He raised his brows at the younger man.

Robin smiled pleasantly, a diffident look in his eye. "I wondered when you'd notice me. That was some thought you were thinking."

Taran grinned. "Sorry. I was miles away."

He studied Robin in the afternoon light. The Major had regained some of the weight he'd lost and his face no longer showed the tortured, haunted look it had worn during his weeks of despair. His youthful handsomeness had returned and he seemed contented. Yet Taran, sensitive as only an Artesan could be, saw the shadow lurking behind Robin's eyes and knew the moment he'd been dreading had come. His chest tightened with a reluctance that bordered on fear.

Robin watched the sparring soldiers, aware of Taran's scrutiny. He leaned forward, resting his forearms on his thighs, his hands clasped together. He spoke softly.

"I know you don't want to hear this, but there are things I simply have to say, and so I hope you'll pardon my insistence."

"It's really not necessary. There's no need—"

"Ah, but there is. There's every need. I did you a great wrong, Taran Elijah—a wrong you did nothing to deserve. Oh, I know you've forgiven me, but there are two of us involved here and I have learned a great deal about forgiveness recently."

Robin did indeed have a need to speak of what he had done and what he felt. It was part of the healing process, and Taran couldn't deny him.

"What I've learned is that it's not enough to say you forgive someone. It is necessary to *know* it, deep in your heart. So I ask you to hear me out. When you first came to the Manor—when we first became friends—I sensed very clearly what you felt for Sullyan."

Taran flushed. Sullyan had said the same to him once. He'd never thought he was being so transparent.

His dismay made Robin smile. "It wasn't a failing in you, my friend, believe me. I'd seen it before many times. It's part of the magic surrounding Sullyan. I never minded. I was never jealous. Especially once she and I … became closer. I was secure in the knowledge that what we had was unique and special. So when all those rumors started spreading round the Manor and I reacted the way I did … well, I was as surprised and confused as anyone."

He looked candidly at Taran, seeing his discomfort. The Adept wasn't sure where this was heading.

"I'm still unable to say why I behaved so badly, but I'm not trying to make excuses. Maybe there was a core of jealousy in me after all, I just don't know. I speak truly when I tell you I never suspected it was there. But somehow, and to my great dishonor, I let the rumors eat away at me. I let my fears and insecurities rule me. And you, my friend, took the brunt of it."

He stared off into the distance, his eyes dark with remembered shame. Taran sat silent and uncomfortable, not sure what to say.

"I'm not proud of myself. In the last four years, I've been granted more chances, been given more forgiveness, than any man has a right to, and the fact that it was necessary shames me. The pain and suffering I caused my friends shames me. When I think of what could have happened…."

He swallowed, twisting his hands together.

"You saved me from that, Taran. After all I did to you, it was you who helped me regain what I so nearly lost. I'm humbled before your generous spirit and I can never thank you enough."

Taran flushed with embarrassment, wishing Robin would stop. The young man seemed impervious to the heat of shame, and now he had started, the unburdening of his heart couldn't be halted.

"I know the depth of your love for Sullyan, and I also know she returns it. I know how you have cared for her these past weeks, and I know you never took advantage of her love for you."

Taran stared at him, apprehensive.

"I know you never betrayed me, Taran, and neither did she, although I gave the pair of you ample opportunity and every reason."

Taran swallowed painfully, memories of the night he had lain in her bed holding her nearly naked body in his arms flooding through him. How much had Sullyan told Robin?

Robin went on, unaware of or ignoring Taran's turmoil.

"I know the depth of your commitment and the strength of your spirit. Because of that, I will tell you this. I am very thankful that you love her as deeply as you do. And I will tell you why.

"We live a dangerous life, my friend. In the service of the King, we daily put our lives at risk. Sullyan and I both chose this life and we both chose to continue it once we were wed. And it's not only in a military capacity that we face this peril. Sullyan has already come close to losing her life because of her powers as an Artesan. I myself have come near to being killed more than once, in battle or otherwise, this past year. I live constantly with the knowledge that I might, one day, be lost to her."

Robin paused and turned to regard the man beside him.

"If that were to happen, I take more comfort than I can tell you from the knowledge that there is someone who loves her as I love her, and who would care for her as deeply as I do."

Taran was stunned. He'd never expected anything like this from Robin—this opening of the soul, this frank approval of his love. He was speechless in the face of Robin's humility.

The young Major understood Taran's stunned reaction. Indeed, it seemed he'd expected it. There was a new poise, a new quiet confidence in Robin that Taran had never seen before. In its way, it was as apocryphal as Taran's own discovery of the ability to control and direct his passions. Recent events had clearly left a deep impression on Robin.

He smiled at Taran's confusion.

"I see I've embarrassed you. I'm sorry for that. I think I probably needed to say those words more than you needed to hear them. I beg your pardon. At the risk of embarrassing you further, there's something I want to ask you."

"What?" Taran's voice was husky from the lump in his throat. His cautious tone widened the grin on Robin's handsome face.

"You know that tomorrow will be a feast day in honor of my son. It's traditional at such times to appoint guardians for the babe. Taran, it would please Sullyan and me more than you could ever know if you would agree to be my son's mentor."

Taran stared at Robin. He could hardly think. "Mentor?"

"We would like you to help train him in the use of his metaforce."

Taran's eyes widened. "What on earth are you talking about? He has a Master for a father, another for an uncle, and his mother and grandfather are the two most powerful Artesans in the known world. Yet you're asking *me* to be his mentor? Are you mad?"

Robin chuckled. "I hope not. But I understand your surprise, so let me explain. Taran, you had a unique experience after your father died. You know what it is to struggle for knowledge, to strive and to fail. You know how to value your talents. You know not to take them for granted. I want my son to know this too. I want him to grow up learning that he is privileged, not special, that he has a duty to use his powers wisely and not squander them. You know all these things, and I want you to pass them on to my son. Will you do it? Please?"

How could he refuse? And yet he sat on in silence, unable to speak. Robin watched him, a look of gentle pleading in his eyes.

"Please, Taran."

Sullyan's voice behind him startled Taran. Robin didn't react; he must have known she was there. Taran rounded on her, and the sight of her in the summer sun, slim, serene, and smiling, her sleeping son cradled in her arms, disarmed him completely, as she'd probably known it would.

Witch! he thought. "Have you been standing there all along?"

"No, of course not. I would never do that to you. But will you accede to our request? Will you agree to help train our son?"

As she came toward him and laid the baby in his arms, and he looked down into those newly-woken, trusting blue eyes, he knew he could never refuse.

✣ ✣ ✣ ✣ ✣

A large party came from the Manor to celebrate the feast day in honor of Sullyan's son. General Blaine arrived first, his expression carefully neutral once he had smiled at Sullyan. He returned Robin's respectful salute in silence, and Robin followed Blaine's stiff back with apprehensive eyes. When he heard a boyish shout and turned to see young Tad slither carefully from his horse and come rushing toward him, nothing could have dimmed his joy. The boy hadn't fully recovered from his near-fatal injury, but Hanan knew she had to let him come. He walked off proudly with Robin's arm about his shoulders.

Sullyan, in Bull's embrace, walked behind, with Cal, Taran, and Rienne following. Taran eyed Bull with concern. The big man had joined in the general greeting, but hadn't spoken to Robin. Taran knew the last time they'd met Bull had lashed out in fury and knocked Robin to the ground, breaking his jaw. They hadn't spoken since, and Taran didn't envy Robin his first private meeting with Bull.

The weather was hot and the festivities were held within marquees set up among the palace gardens, fountains and pools and false streams flowing within them to cool the air. Taran estimated there were at least two hundred people in attendance as he wandered through the guests, greeting those he knew. He caught himself wondering how Jinella would enjoy this sort of function, picturing her reaction to Andaryan culture and society. He could just see her strutting in her finery, in her element among all the elaborately dressed and coiffured court ladies.

He caught himself up short. He'd been halfway to imagining her here as his wife. He shook his head, not wanting to examine his reasons for feeling that such an outcome was impossible.

Wearying of the small talk, he joined Rienne and Cal, gratefully accepting a glass of wine from Norkis. The young page had renewed his friendship with Tad and had been regaled with the tale of Parren's blackmail and Tad's near-fatal wounding. It seemed to Taran that the slightly younger page currently held Tad in the same kind of reverent awe Tad felt for Robin.

Thoughts of the Major caused Taran to look round for him. Rienne noticed his preoccupation and, in her disconcerting empathic way, guessed its cause.

"If you're looking for Robin, you won't see him."

"No? Where is he, then?"

"He and Bull went off together about twenty minutes ago."

Taran and Cal exchanged glances. Cal rolled his dark, expressive eyes. "Will they be all right?"

Rienne snorted. "Of course they will. They love each other too much not to be."

"I heard that was some punch Bull threw," remarked Taran, not looking at Rienne. "That doesn't sound much like love to me."

"Then you know less than nothing about—" Rienne saw Taran's grin. "Oh, you!" she grumbled.

At that moment, the two men in question appeared, Bull's arm draped about Robin's shoulders. The Major was pale but smiling and Bull's stern visage dissolved into a vast grin when he saw his friends. Taran breathed a sigh of relief.

Once the heat of the day had passed, the real celebration of new life commenced. Pharikian, in his state robes, his face shining with love and pride, formally greeted his first grandchild. He held the baby up for all to see and proclaimed him a true scion of the House of Pharikian, and welcome in his new family. The guests raised a joyful accolade and the baby behaved perfectly, as befitted a royal Prince, although he did fall asleep almost immediately after.

His guardians were duly appointed, Taran stepping up beside Aeyron to accept their roles as mentors. Taran flushed at the gratitude and love he saw reflected in the eyes of the baby's parents.

The natural conclusion to the ceremony—the baby's Naming—did not take place. Despite her assertion the night her son was born, Sullyan hadn't yet disclosed the baby's name. Taran assumed that Robin knew, but neither of them had given so much as a hint to anyone else. Now, Sullyan ascended the dais and told them the reason for her reticence.

"We have decided that his Naming shall take place after the birth of Princess Idrimar's twins, and also the daughter of my dearest friend, Rienne."

There was a ripple of astonishment and Sullyan smiled.

"It is certain that Rienne's baby girl will be an Artesan, and there is a very good chance that one or even both of Ty Marik's twins will be Artesans too. It seems fitting that all four infant Artesans should be Named together. My son has a special heritage in Andaryon and a unique link to his immediate foreparents here in the palace. It is our wish that the Naming ceremony take place in the stone circle on the tor to the north. That is, if Marik and Idrimar, and Cal and Rienne, will agree."

No arguments were raised.

Later that evening, General Blaine passed a few words with

Taran, letting him know he'd be welcome if he decided to return to the Manor. Taran felt a knot of tension melt away. He hadn't decided on his future, but it was good to know he could resume his former life if he chose. Blaine disappeared soon after, and it was some time before Taran noticed he was missing.

Just as Taran registered the General's absence, Tad came up to him and Rienne, looking for Robin. The boy looked tired, having spent the day in either the Major's company or Norkis's. Rienne glanced sharply at him.

"Sit down, you young idiot. Look at you. You're dead on your feet. Didn't I tell you not to do too much? No, you won't see the Major for a while yet. He's busy."

Taran frowned. "Busy?"

Rienne shot him one of her withering looks. "With the General."

"Ah."

"Brynne's with them too. I imagine she's negotiating her return to the Manor."

That startled Taran and a painful seed of hope grew in his breast. "Has she told you she's going back?"

"Of course not, but it's obvious, isn't it?"

"Is it?"

"Taran, use your wits. Of course it is. Now that she and Robin are back together, she has to return. *He* can't stay here, can he? And she'll not stay without him."

No, the Adept realized, feeling foolish, of course she wouldn't. But....

"Why did you say 'negotiating'? Surely the General would have her back in an instant?"

Rienne stared at him and he colored under her scorn. "But she's not alone now, is she? Have you forgotten the baby? You know, that little scrap of humanity we helped into the world?"

He laughed, holding up his hands in surrender. "All right, Rienne, you win. Just tell me what you think will happen, seeing as I'm so dense today."

She sighed. "I imagine the baby has given General Blaine a few headaches. There are no other wedded couples at the Manor besides Cal and me, and no other young children. At least in Cal's case there's no conflict, as I'm not part of the King's forces. But Sullyan is, and she's also still Robin's commanding officer. If they both have to be in the field at the same time, who looks after the baby? And if the worst should happen and they're both killed...."

It was too awful to contemplate. Despite what Robin had said when asking Taran to mentor his son, Taran hadn't fully considered the implications. He pitied Sullyan when he realized she'd had to consider these problems while still dealing with her other, more personal, concerns.

"So," continued Rienne, "there'll be some changes when she goes home. That's what they'll be working on right now."

When the three returned from their discussions, they all bore signs of a hard and not totally amicable bargaining session. Yet they were cheerful enough, and Taran hoped they'd at least made a start on straightening everything out.

As the evening drew to a close, Taran noticed General Blaine deep in conversation with Timar and Aeyron Pharikian. The subject seemed to be one of great importance, judging by their expressions. Taran nodded his head toward them as he came up beside Sullyan to bid her good night.

"What's going on over there?"

She lifted her eyes from her son and looked over at her father and brother. "Tactical negotiations."

Taran raised his brows.

"Well," she said, "I have to have some kind of ammunition against Elias's possible objections to my return."

Scarcely further enlightened, Taran had to be content as they parted for their own rooms.

Chapter Thirty-One

Two days later, Sullyan announced she was returning to the Manor. Most of the Albians had departed the day after the ceremony, so only Cal, Rienne, Bull, and Taran were left to travel back with Robin and Sullyan.

They bade an emotional farewell to Pharikian, Aeyron, and Idrimar. After all she'd been through, Sullyan could hardly bear to leave them. Aeyron, especially, found the parting hard. He'd become so used to having her by him, both in duty and in leisure, that Taran could see how difficult he would find it to continue alone.

Rienne was startled when Princess Idrimar asked her to return with Sullyan to help deliver her babies. Rienne smiled in genuine pleasure and readily agreed.

Once more dressed in her combat leathers, Sullyan indicated they should leave. Apart from the presence of her baby son, Taran could easily imagine the last three and a half months had never happened. All the trauma, the danger, the anguish, and the pain seemed to have been wiped away now that she stood there in her usual combat gear. He couldn't help but smile, despite the somber mood.

Never one to prolong a painful moment, Sullyan swung up onto Drum, the big stallion eager to be gone after his long sojourn in this foreign realm. He curveted impatiently, but stilled when Robin handed Sullyan their son. They departed, Robin providing their access through the Veils.

There was a surprise awaiting Sullyan as they rode up to the Manor's main doors—or maybe, thought Taran, it wasn't such a surprise. Rienne gave a soft gasp and it was clear that none of the others had expected it. Sullyan slid down Drum's shoulder one-handed, her son in the crook of her arm, her expression carefully neutral.

King Elias stood in silence, staring between the baby, Sullyan, and Robin. The others dismounted and gave him due homage, but he did not acknowledge them.

"Are you well, Brynne?"

"As you see, my Lord, I am well enough."

He reached out a hand and stroked the baby's chubby fist. The tiny fingers immediately grasped the King's hand.

Sullyan smiled. "You see, my Lord? My son already knows his King and whom he serves."

Elias's breath hitched and he ducked his head. Taran could see he still hadn't come to terms with her shocking revelation as she left his castle nearly two months before, never mind this tiny baby.

Elias cleared his throat. "I've been speaking with Mathias. There's no reason why we can't come to some arrangement." He paused, then burst out, "I don't want to lose you, Brynne. I'll do everything I can to help you carry on as before. We'll change the command structure. We'll promote Major Tamsen to colonel—anything, Brynne, *anything*, just so you'll stay. I owe you too much. And I—"

He choked and didn't finish. Just as well, thought Taran, because it would probably have been inappropriate.

Sullyan gazed at him. "There is no need to go that far. Robin and I can work around the command structure. I would never consider taking the field at the same time as him anyway. Leave it to us, my Lord. We will find a way."

Elias held her gaze sadly. "What happened to 'my friend'?"

She sighed. "Elias, you *are* my friend. Never doubt it. But you are also my King—my sovereign lord—and I am oath-bound to your service. There will be times when my mode of address will necessarily be more formal than we might wish. But you will ever be a friend in my heart."

Overcome with emotion, Elias dropped to one knee, caught at her hand—the one bearing his ring—and kissed it gently.

A soft flush came to her cheeks and she suddenly lost all poise. "You must excuse me, my Lord, my son is hungry. I really must feed him."

Elias gazed after her as she fled, her son still slumbering in her arms. The King's face was unreadable, but his eyes were full of meaning.

Taran spent some time away from the Manor at the end of the summer. He sent letters to Jinella on his return from Andaryon, to see if she still wanted to pursue their embryo relationship. Her replies indicated she did, and so he made the journey to Port Loxton and tarried there a month, helping Jinella run her disgraced uncle's large estate and renewing his friendship with Ardoch.

As an experiment it wasn't an unqualified success, but it seemed there was enough to build on. To give them both time to think, Taran returned to the Manor for the winter on the back of the first full gale of autumn, cursing the muddy roads, the long ride, and the ache in his backside. Sullyan, who studied him carefully as he answered her questions, smiled in satisfaction. She said mysteriously, "The journey may be easier next time, my friend. Who knows?"

Taran couldn't tell if she referred to the physical journey to Loxton or his developing relationship with Jinny. As it was unlikely the roads would clear long enough for him to see her again before the spring, it hardly mattered.

Idrimar's time came as the first snow of the season fell. Sullyan and Rienne traveled to Caer Vellett to attend her. Finally, after a labor lasting a day and a half, she produced two healthy baby boys. Rienne and Sullyan left her to the care and love of her father and brother, and retired to sleep around the clock.

As Rienne's time drew near, Taran moved out of the apartment he still shared with her and Cal. No one had wanted to move into Parren's old rooms after his death, so Taran cleared them out. Soon all traces of the bitter young man were erased.

Messages arrived for him from Jinella. Despite the dreadful state of the winter roads, the King's runners stoically maintained their service, proud of their reliability. Taran often thought how convenient it would be for Elias to have his own court Artesan. Once Eadan was old enough and was trained, he'd be able to communicate directly with the Manor, but that could take years and there was no guarantee Eadan's fledgling powers would prove strong enough.

If Taran and Jinny were to take their relationship further—as far as marriage, say—Taran would need a new career. He had his stipend from the King and so was a wealthy man, but he had no intentions of becoming a fat and lazy landowner. The idea of the post of court Artesan would please his sense of duty, but it was far too soon to voice his thoughts and he hadn't yet examined how he'd feel about leaving his friends to go live in Port Loxton. He had much to think about during the bitter weather.

Midwinter Day was marked by a huge gathering of as many of the Manor's inhabitants as could fit into the vast room that had once been the Great Hall. Two huge fires with logs ablaze spat and crackled at opposite ends of the hall, and the long tables groaned with food and drink. All those who could play instruments were pressed into service and the hall rang with music and laughter well into the first day of the new year.

✤ ✤ ✤ ✤ ✤

Six weeks later, Rienne went into labor.

Taran had known his Apprentice for nearly six years. Cal and Rienne had been together for five years. They had all lived in the same house or the same set of rooms for most of that time. If asked, Taran would have said he knew both of his friends very well.

Cal had matured considerably since taking the King's Oath. When Taran first him he was the kind of man who never thought beyond his next meal or his next adventure, the consequences of running wild as a child and then being cared for by Roamerlings. Learning to control his metaforce, even in the limited way Taran had been able to teach him, had made Cal rethink some of his attitudes. Becoming part of Sullyan's company had worked a major transformation in the young man, and his promotion to Captain earlier in the year had brought him to a greater maturity.

So it was with a shock that Taran, called to their apartment at dawn one day by an amused but irritated Sullyan, walked in to find his Apprentice lying on the floor, out cold.

Taran bent over him. "What's the matter with him, is he ill?" It was amazing, thought Taran, how pale someone with Cal's dark skin could appear.

Sullyan snorted. "He just passed out. How many battles has he fought? How many times has he killed? And yet, at the sight of Rienne's waters breaking, he faints like a swooning girl!"

Taran stared at Rienne, who was sitting in some discomfort on the bed, hands to her belly, trying hard not to laugh as a minor contraction took her breath. He shook his head. "What do you want me to do?"

Sullyan waved a hand. "Get him out of my way. He is not to return unless he can behave himself. Rienne needs support and clear heads, not some fainthearted fool who cannot keep his feet. Now, out!"

It got all around the commons, of course. It was too good a story not to spread. And Cal, proudly showing off his baby daughter later that evening, didn't really care. Let them laugh! He was the happiest man alive and he didn't begrudge their amusement.

✤ ✤ ✤ ✤ ✤

Sullyan and Rienne sat on the bed, Rienne leaning sleepily against her friend's shoulder as she waited for Cal to return with the baby. It had been an uncomplicated birth, but she was still exhausted and sore. Now that the process was over, she was able to feel and respond to Sullyan's flow of metaforce, but, like Sullyan before her, the labor had been completely devoid of Artesan help.

"Do you know, Brynne," said Rienne sleepily, "it seems to me that childbirth is a bit like spellsilver."

Sullyan raised her brows, but held her peace and let Rienne carry on.

"I think the process of labor blocks metaphysical function. Only, unlike spellsilver, it blocks the *inward* effects, not the outward. When you were in labor, you were able to access your powers but couldn't use them on yourself. I don't know about you, but during my labor I couldn't feel the link with my baby, either. But it didn't worry me; I was too focused on what my body was doing."

Rienne sat straighter, her eyes going wide. Some of her exhaustion fell away as she found the answer to this riddle, which she and Sullyan had discussed many times.

"Of course, that's the answer! Childbirth is a natural function and it blocks metaphysical powers. Just like an Artesan trying to fight a battle with both metaforce and sword. It's impossible. You can't focus on two things at the same time. Labor must be the same. How could a mother concentrate and focus on her body if half her attention is taken up by her metaforce? You need *all* your strength and willpower to give birth. And if you were to use metaforce to dull the pain, how would you feel the contractions? How would you know when to push, and when to hold back? That's the answer, I'm sure. We have to go through the process naturally. It's as simple as that."

Sullyan had to agree with her. All the facts fit the experience. It was a pity, though. She didn't fancy going through all that again if she was lucky enough to conceive a second child. Yet, as she looked down on her son, she had a sudden premonition that shivered her spine. She would never quicken again. Her body had been damaged by Rykan's abuse; there was no doubt of that. She had been granted a special boon to be able to conceive and carry this precious little bundle of new life, and it would never happen again. And though her eyes blurred with tears at this knowledge, she breathed a silent prayer of thanks for the treasured gift.

✤ ✤ ✤ ✤ ✤

The sun was blinding as the little procession wound toward the tor to the north of the Citadel. It sparkled off the ice crystals and clean white snow which lay thickly on the ground. The horses' breath plumed in the frigid air, causing tiny droplets to freeze on their muzzles. Frost glittered on the fur-trimmed hoods of the riders as their own breath condensed around them.

There were twelve in the party. Of these, eight were experienced Artesans and two more had limited or empathic powers. Three rulers rode at the head of the group. Timar and Aeyron Pharikian flanked King Elias, deep in friendly conversation as they rode. Elias had been invited for courtesy, having no power and no child to be Named.

Behind the three rulers rode Sullyan and Robin, their son nestled in his mother's arms. Behind them came the Duke of Kymer and Cardon, his wife by his side, a twin cradled on each saddlebow. Taran, Cal, and Rienne came next, and behind them rode Mathias Blaine and Bull.

They dismounted just outside the stone circle. Robin took his son and went to stand beside the altar stone in the ring's center. Rienne joined him with her daughter and Idrimar followed with her twins. Marik and Cal took up their place by the western cardinal stone.

The northern cardinal was taken by Taran and Bull. General Blaine and Prince Aeyron stood opposite them. And at the eastern cardinal were Sullyan and Pharikian. Sullyan had stationed Elias behind her, where he gazed in awe at the ancient stones. He wouldn't be able to participate in the ceremony, but his fascination for the Artesan craft was clear for all to see.

When all were positioned, Sullyan nodded at Cal.

The young Apprentice-elite had been practicing with Marik, whose metaphysical powers had never even reached Apprentice level. Cal meshed his psyche with Marik's weaker pattern and called forth the power of Earth.

The young man's touch loosed the Earth's great forces and sent them running sunwise around the ice-encrusted monoliths. They all felt the tremor as it passed through the stones at their backs. Once the force had completed the circle and sealed the stones against leakage, a touch of Cal's controlling power sent the energy surging in waves toward the altar stone. It lapped and broke like sea upon the shore.

There was a gurgling laugh as Robin's little boy stretched out his arms, fists waving in recognition of his heritage. Rienne's baby daughter made a crooning sound and one of Idri's twins began to cry. His response made Sullyan smile, for it confirmed what she had thought and hoped. There was power in Marik's sons.

Sullyan gave Taran his signal and he and Bull linked, forming a minor Powersink to call upon the element of Water. The power pulsing through the stones took on the iridescent shimmer of rainbow refraction from each droplet of water suspended in the flow.

Now the inner ring looked like a shimmering lake. Sullyan nodded to the southern cardinal, where Mathias Blaine and Prince Aeyron had overlaid their patterns. Their mastery over Fire manifested itself as a great crackle and roar which filled their ears. The forces of the circle now glowed with an aurora of Fire, and warmth seeped into their bones. The children responded to the display once again, but Sullyan couldn't look because she needed all her concentration to merge with Timar. The pair of them called upon the tremendous power of Air, harnessing it to a gentle breeze, fanning the Fire and flicking sparkles of Water high into the air where they froze and returned to fall, spitting, into the Fire.

The circle was complete.

Idrimar mounted the altar stone. Her twins were now silent and she handed one to Robin, who cradled him next to his own son. She held her baby high, showing him the full circle, offering him to each cardinal in turn.

"Elemental forces of the world, I show you my son. I pledge he shall be raised in the knowledge of his forebears, in respect for life and in respect for the powers of the world. He shall be raised with love and in pride. This is my son and this is his Name. He shall be called Tynian Pharikian."

Those assembled responded: "All hail, Tynian! Be welcome in this world."

Idrimar exchanged Tynian for his twin. She repeated her

words as she showed her other son the power of the circle and proclaimed his Name.

"He shall be called Mallin Pharikian."

Little Mallin was hailed and his mother left the stone. Rienne took her place, her daughter in her arms. The baby's olive skin stood out against her pale wrappings. She had beautiful, almond-shaped eyes and would be a rare beauty when grown. The healer held her little one up and repeated the ceremony.

"This is my daughter and this shall be her Name. She shall be called Elisse Arlen."

Robin stepped onto the altar stone and shared a brief but intense look with Sullyan. He raised the little boy high above his head and showed him the stones as he spoke the ritual words.

"Elemental forces of the world, I show you my son. I pledge he shall be raised in the knowledge of his forebears, in respect for life and for the powers of the world. He shall be raised with love and in pride. He will be guided in the use of his powers and he shall be watched over and protected all the days of his life.

"In recognition of this protection, I give him his Name. This Name I give in love and respect for his foreparents, whom he never knew. May he bear it with honor and bring honor to it.

"This is my son and his Name shall be Morgan Sullyan."

As the group hailed and greeted little Morgan, Sullyan felt her heart surge with love. She was sure she heard, somewhere in the substrate, two other voices breaching the Void to add their greeting and their blessing.

All hail, Morgan Sullyan! Be welcome in the world.

The End

Glossary

Albian Characters

Ardoch, Master. Elias's legendary swordmaster.

Alice. Former nursemaid at Port Loxton.

Baily. A Major at the Manor under Colonel Vassa.

Bessie. One of Prince Eaden's nurses.

Bethyn Sullyan. Brynne Sullyan's mother, deceased.

Brynne Sullyan. A Colonel at the Manor under General Blaine.

Bull, aka Bulldog, aka Hal Bullen. Colonel Sullyan's friend and aide.

Cal Tyler. Taran's friend, and life mate of Rienne Arlen.

Darra. Robin Tamsen's young cousin.

Delinna, Madam. Chatelaine at Port Loxton.

Dexter. A Captain at the Manor under Captain Tamsen.

Eaden, Prince. Son of King Elias and Queen Sofira.

Elias Rovannon. Albia's High King.

Elisse Arlen. Daughter of Rienne and Cal.

Fiann. A master bard from the realm of Sinnia, deceased.

Fergus. A Kingsman at Port Loxton

Hal Bullen. See 'Bull.'

Hanan. Chief Healer at the Manor.

Hezra Reen. An Albian Baron at Port Loxton.

Huw. A young disabled lad living at Loxton Castle

Izack. Baron Reen's personal Commander.

Jerrim Vassa. A Colonel at the Manor.

Jessy. Deceased sister of Robin Tamsen.

Jinella, Lady. The niece of Baron Reen.

Kinsey, Lord. Chamberlain to High King Elias.

Lerric. Client-king of Bordenn, father of Queen Sofira.

Lily. Lady Jinella's maid

Mathias Blaine. The Manor's senior officer and General-in-Command to High King Elias.

Morgan Sullyan. Son of Brynne Sullyan and Robin Tamsen. Also the name of Brynne's deceased father.

Neremiah, Arch Patrio. Senior churchman at Loxton's Minster.

Owyn Denny. A Lieutenant Major at Port Loxton.

Ozella. A young Lord from Beraxia, sent to study at the Manor.

Parren, Glinn. A Captain at the Manor under Colonel Vassa.

Patrin. One of Baron Reen's men.

Rendan Levant, Lord. First Minister to High King Elias.

Rienne Arlen. A healer and Cal Tyler's life mate.

Robin Tamsen. A Major at the Manor under Colonel Sullyan.

Seline, Princess. Daughter of King Elias and Queen Sofira.

Seth. Baron Reen's manservant.

Sofira. Queen to High King Elias Rovannon.

Solet. The Manor's stablemaster.

Tad Greylin. Former kitchen boy at the Manor, now a cadet.

Taran Elijah. An Artesan who is desperate to learn his craft.

Valustin. A Captain of King's Guard at Port Loxton.

Wil. A corporal at the Manor.

Andaryan Characters

Aeyron Pharikian. The Hierarch of Andaryon's son and Heir.

Anjer, Lord General. Officer in overall command of the Hierarch's forces.

Barrin. A Commander in the Hierarch's forces.

Brianne. Baby daughter of Anjer and Torien.

Corbyn, Lord. One of Lord Tikhal's northern nobles.

Deshan. The Hierarch's Master Healer, also a Master Artesan.

Ephan. General in the Hierarch's forces, overall commander of the Velletian Guard.

Falina, Lady. Widow of General Kryp.

Gaslek. An Andaryan Baron, secretary to the Hierarch.

Hollett, Lady. Ephan's wife.

Idriana. Deceased wife of Timar Pharikian.

Idrimar Pharikian. The Hierarch's daughter.

Jaskin. Sonten's nephew, killed by Taran.

Kethro. Artesan son of Lord Corbyn, a northern noble.

Jaskin. Sonten's nephew, killed by Taran.

Kethro. Artesan son of Lord Corbyn, a northern noble.

Mallin Pharikian, twin of Tynian, son of Marik and Idrimar.

Norkis. Senior page to the Hierarch of Andaryon.

Rand. Artesan son of Lord Tikhal.

Rykan. Deceased Lord of Kymer province, one time aspirant to the Andaryan throne.

Sonten. Deceased general to Duke Rykan. Former Lord of Durkos province.

Tikhal. An Andaryan Lord, also known as the Lord of the North. Pharikian's premier noble.

Timar Pharikian. The Hierarch, Supreme Ruler of Andaryon.

Torien, Lady. The wife of Lord General Anjer.

Torman Vanyr. Deceased commander of the Velletian Guard, the Hierarch's personal Guard.

Ty Marik. Once Count of Cardon province, now Duke of Cardon and Kymer.

Tynian Pharikian. Twin of Mallin, son of Marik and Idrimar.

Realms of the World

First Realm—Endormir

Endormirians are sometimes known as 'Roamerlings' because of their itinerant habits. They are small and slim, dark skinned, with brown or black eyes showing hardly any whites. The Artesan gift runs only through the males, and gifted males always become clan-leaders. As Endormir suffers from severe winter conditions, its people cross the Veils into the other realms for the winter months, where they are well known as traders.

Second Realm—Sinnia

Sinnians are tall and milk-haired, with pale skin. They live in clans and were once nomadic but now live in settlements. All are born able to control their metaforce up to the rank of Adept and are thus considered 'sports'. Their race often produces highly gifted musicians and storytellers.

Third Realm—Relkor

Relkorians are small, fierce and stocky, notorious for raiding the other realms for slaves to work their mines and quarries. Their Artesans, both male and female, invariably become slave-lords.

Fourth Realm—Albia

Albia is the human realm. The Artesan gift runs through both male and female lines, each gender being equal in potential. The craft is currently out of favour due to raiding by both Relkorian and Andaryan Artesans. Albians widely believe that all Artesans use their powers only for gain and control.

Fifth Realm—Andaryon

A warlike race characterised by eyes with slit pupils. They fight constantly amongst themselves, vying for position within the Hierocracy. The Artesan gift passes only through the male line and females play a minor and downtrodden role. Only the most powerful Artesan can become and hold the rank of Hierarch. Their battles for supremacy are governed by strict, ritualistic laws.

Terms

Arch Patrio. The leader of Albia's Matria Church.

Artesan.

A person born with the ability to control metaforce and Master the four primal elements.

Brine rum.

Strong liquor, drunk by pirates on Andaryon's eastern seaboard.

Cardinal stone.

The stones in a stone circle that sit at each of the four compass points.

Cheosian Red. A fine Andaryan red wine from Cheos province.

Codes of Combat.

Strict laws governing any conflict between Andaryan nobles.

Demons.

Derogatory term used in Albia to describe those of the Andaryan race.

Earth ball.

An explosive sphere of Earth element formed by an Artesan for use as a weapon.

Fellan.

A dark, aromatic and bitter beverage brewed from the seeds of the fellan-plant.

Firefield.

A barrier formed from the primal element of Fire, through which only Artesans can pass. Firefields formed by those of inferior Artesan rank can easily be destroyed by those of a higher rank.

Firewater.

Incredibly strong liquor.

Free traders.

Another term for pirate.

Immanence, your. Form of address used when referring to Albia's Arch Patrio.

Kingsman.

Term used to describe members of the High King's fighting forces.

Matria Church.

The Minster in Port Loxton, seat of Albia's primary faith, the Faith of the Wheel.

Metaforce (sometimes also called life force).

The force of existence pertaining to all things, both animate and inanimate.

Perdition.

A state of non-being for the soul – a place where souls with no ultimate destination reside.

Primal elements.

Earth, Water, Fire and Air.

Primal Sacrament.

Andaryan name for the Pact, an agreement brokered between Andaryan nobles. Used to settle wars ending in stalemate, it involves the willing suicide of a powerful Artesan.

Primary Magister.

Chief Justice Minister of Andaryon.

Portway.

Structure formed by an Artesan from a primal element – usually Earth or Water – which gives its creator access through the Veils.

Psyche.

An Artesan's unique and personal pattern through which they can manipulate metaforce and channel the primal elements.

Roamerling.

Slightly derogatory term for the nomads of Endormir.

Sally port.

A small door within a larger fortified barrier, allowing only one person to pass through at a time.

Substrate.

The medium in which the primal elements reside, and in which the world and all things have their being.

Tangwyr.

Monstrous Andaryan raptor trained to hunt men.

The Pact. (See Primal Sacrament).

The Staff.

Mysterious and terrible weapon capable of stealing and storing metaforce. Can only be used by Artesans.

The Veils.

Misty barriers separating the five Realms of the World. Only Artesans have the power to move through the Veils.

The Void.

Dark abyss at the end of life into which all souls pass before reaching their final destination.

The Wheel.

Central principle of Albian faith.

Velletian Guard.

Personal guard of the Hierarch of Andaryon.

Witch.

Derogatory term for an Artesan.

Artesan ranks and their attributes

Level one: Apprentice. Person born with the Artesan gift and the ability to influence the first primal element of Earth. Able to hear other Artesans speaking telepathically but unable to initiate such speech.

Level two: Apprentice-elite. Has some skill in influencing their own metaforce. Has attained mastery over the element of Earth. Able to initiate telepathic speech but only with Artesans already known to them. Able to build substrate structures, identify a person by the pattern of their psyche, and counter metaphysical attack to some degree.

Level three: Journeyman. Has mastery over Earth and is able to influence Water. Able to build portways and travel through the Veils. Has some skill in using metaforce for offense. Also able to initiate psyche-overlay and converse telepathically with any other Artesan. Possesses some self-healing potential.

Level four: Adept. Has mastery over both Earth and Water. Able to build more complex substrate structures such as corridors. Able to influence where such structures emerge. Possesses stronger offensive and defensive capabilities. Able to merge psyche fully with other Artesans. Increased healing abilities.

Level five: Adept-elite. Has mastery over Earth and Water and is able to influence Fire. Possesses great healing powers which can even aid the ungifted (with their permission). Able to initiate powersinks and merges of psyche. Able to construct such structures as Firefields.

Level six: Master. Has mastery over Earth, Water and Fire. Able to control the power of an inferior Artesan against their will. Control over personal metaforce now almost total. Possesses incredible healing powers.

Level seven: Master-elite. Has mastery over Earth, Water and Fire and is able to influence Air, the most capricious primal element. Able to absorb a lesser or even equal-ranked Artesan's power and metaforce provided some link or permission (however tenuous) can be found.

Level eight: Senior Master. Has complete mastery over all four primal elements. Is able to absorb another Artesan's power by force, even sometimes without a link. Possesses a high degree of metaphysical (and usually spiritual) strength.

Level nine: Supreme Master. It has never been fully established whether this rank actually exists. Supreme Masters are supposedly able to influence Spirit - largely regarded as the mythical 'fifth element.' Ancient texts refer only to the possibility; no mention has ever been found of a being attaining Supreme Masterhood.

Sport or lay-Artesan. Freaks of nature, sports are thought to be able to control their own metaforce from birth, to whatever level of strength they inherently possess. As they receive no training their working is often undetectable. They are also believed to be able to 'hear' the thoughts of those around them; gifted or ungifted, and directly, not through the substrate.

C as Peace was born and brought up in the lovely county of Hampshire, in the UK, where she still lives. On leaving school, she trained for two years before qualifying as a teacher of equitation. During this time she also learned to carriage-drive. She spent thirteen years in the British Civil Service before moving to Rome, where she and her husband, Dave, lived for three years. They return whenever thay can.

As well as her love of horses, Cas is mad about dogs; especially Lurchers. She currently owns two rescue Lurchers, Milly and Milo. Cas loves country walks, working in stained glass, growing cacti, and folk singing. She is currently working on writing and recording songs or music for each of her fantasy books. The song associated with *King's Envoy* is "The Wheel Will Turn"; for *King's Champion* it is "The Ballad of Tallimore"; and for *King's Artesan* it is "Morgan's Song (All That We Are)." For *The Challenge* it is "Meadowsweet", for *The Circle* it is "Larksong," and for *Full Circle* it is "Beyond the Veils."

All Cas's book songs can be found at and downloaded (free!) from her website, see below. Also find Cas on www.reverbnation.

Cas's first novel, *King's Envoy*, was awarded a HarperCollins Authonomy Gold Medal in 2008. Her *Artesans of Albia* fantasy series has won the critical acclaim of US fantasy, sci-fi, and non-fiction author Janet Morris. Cas is a member of the British Fantasy Society and had a short story included in their 40th Anniversary commemorative anthology Full Fathom Forty. She's also a contributor to the Janet Morris-edited anthology *HEROIKA 1: Dragon Eaters*.

Cas has written a nonfiction book, *For the Love of Daisy*, which tells the lifestory of her mischievous and beautiful Dalmatian. She is also a freelance editor and proofreader. Details and other information can be found on her website: www.caspeace.com.

Other Books by Cas Peace:
Artesans of Albia Fantasy Series:

Trilogy One: *Artesans of Albia*
Book One: *King's Envoy*
Book Two: *King's Champion*
Book Three: *King's Artesan*

Trilogy Two: *Circle of Conspiracy*
Book One: *The Challenge*
Book Two: *The Circle*
Book Three: *Full Cirlce*

Trilogy Three: *Master of Malice*
Book One: *The Scarecrow* (Winter 2015)
Book Two: *The Vagrant* (Spring 2016)
Book Three: *The Gateway* (Winter 2016)

Anthologies:

Full Fathom Forty:
British Fantasy Society 40th Anniversary Volume.

HEROIKA 1: Dragon Eaters:
edited by Janet E Morris.

Non-Fiction:
For the Love of Daisy

www.ingramcontent.com/pod-product-compliance
Lightning Source LLC
Chambersburg PA
CBHW051512250626
47156CB00001B/64